Collapse at Hidden Verse Three-Three-Two

COLLAPSE AT HIDDEN VERSE
THREE-THREE-TWO

A novel by
BRIAN HOLTZ

Collapse at Hidden Verse Three-Three-Two
© Copyright 2008, Brian Holtz

Cover art by the author, Brian Holtz

Darkside Sally Publishing
To go beyond the book and explore the author's other works go to:
Darksidesally.com

ISBN: 978-0-6152-1132-9

For Becky

CONTENTS

Sector One:
Welcome to the Multiverse

1

   Timothy Rayburn was ripped out of a peaceful dream by his sister's voice from across the hall. She brushed her hair at the bathroom mirror, dancing and singing along with her favorite pop diva. While enthusiasm did have its merits, it would never make up for being tone-deaf. At the end of each stanza, she made an *ooh-uh* noise that resembled a baboon with its foot stuck in a blender. He covered his head with a pillow.

His mother pounded on the bedroom door, complaining about what time it was. She then walked away, mumbling something about pancakes. Startled, he sat straight up rubbing the crust from his eyes. A warm breeze opened the curtain, allowing sunlight onto the sheets. A bird in the tree outside the window chirped as a blow dryer revved to life across the hall. Timothy grumbled and forced himself to his feet, wondering if he could find a pair of clean socks. He took a shower, tidied his hair with a small plastic comb, got dressed in the coolest clothes his mother was willing to purchase and brushed his teeth. He went downstairs. All that remained on the kitchen table was a half-eaten slice of bacon and some burnt toast. He weighed his options for a moment, deciding on the bacon.

His mom spoke. "Maybe if you weren't up all night playing video games you could join us for breakfast." There was no arguing with mother logic, so he stayed quiet, crunching his bacon. He checked the time and then headed for school.

He carried a large backpack over his shoulder. It contained schoolbooks, homework, pencils, a Spiderman comic book and a photograph of his favorite actress, Allie Kincade. To Timothy, all of the items carried in the pack were necessities, except maybe the books.

He could make an excuse about having forgotten his math textbook at home. Mrs. Tomlinson might not appreciate it, but he'd end up sharing with someone else. English and History would be the same. No big deal. Leaving any or all at home one day would not be defined as a tragedy.

On the other hand, Tim finding himself in study hall with no Spiderman comic would be tragic indeed. It would, in his own words, *bum him right out.* Also, his lunch hour wouldn't be the same without Allie. He could spend days gazing into her pale blue eyes.

His dog, Darth Slobbers, followed him to the end of the street and then turned, rocketing after old lady Binkle's cat. Slobs, as Timothy often called him, was a year old Saint Bernard. He had the energy of a pup and the size of a small elephant. He had the appetite of an elephant too, which was obvious. Even after a huge bowl of food he was still eager for some neighborhood cat.
The frequently harassed feline was Doctor Twinkie. The Doc was a four and a half year old calico and extremely overweight. His body was round like a basketball, with a stomach that dragged in the dirt. No one knew what old lady Binkle fed him but his name surely was appropriate. Now a person wouldn't have thought a cat of that shape and size could move with any amount of speed, and normally they would've been correct. But with a raging St. Bernard snapping at his backside, the Doc could throw gravel with the best of them. On *flat* ground that is. Having to jump or climb anything did pose a problem. You see, the Doc was more than twenty-five pounds of feline and gravity had quite a hold on him. If he tried to jump over even the shortest of objects, his belly would get caught and send him tumbling.

Each time the Doc went accidentally acrobatic, Darth Slobbers would be caught by surprise and overshoot his target, having to turn around in a cloud of dust while the cat rolled back onto his fat feet. It was a sight to see, and the sight could be seen on any morning, any day of the week. A person might've thought that all the exercise would've helped Doc loose some of his excessive weight. They would've been wrong.
Maybe he had worms. Maybe he had a gland problem. Maybe he really ate cream-filled desert cakes. Nothing was sure except the

fact that the cat wasn't getting any thinner. He also had clumpy, ratty hair and carried the distinct smell of vomit, which was another story entirely.

2

The particular morning of which we are speaking was a Monday, May third of the year 2004, on Earth, in Hidden Verse Three-Three-Two.

On Moodle Haulla, in Verse Eight-Three, it was All Phokiny day. It celebrated the liberation of mine slaves from the oppression of the Norian droid military.

On Recta 10 in Verse Two-One-Five, it was President Reverend Hoo-Fondu-Be-Flumish IX festival. In the 10th century A.H. (after Hoo I) he led the revolt on the Empirion army. They celebrate each year by watching Scatter Ball in surround-vision telerooms.

It was also Itchv-fil'-cha, on the planet Crichit. They didn't observe the holiday, but every citizen got free passes to their local detoxification center.

It was today that the Pluddicon moisture farmers on Whoole danced in honor of the mythic Ice Pluddam, a monster that devoured the third sun in their system. Hence, the planet dropped four thousand degrees in temperature. It had made life (at two hundred below zero) possible.

Of course on Earth, it was just plain old Monday. It meant back to school for Timothy and his classmates. There were no celebrations going on that Tim was aware of. Summer break and graduation were still four weeks in the future.

So Tim watched his mammoth dog go chasing after Doc Twinkie, as always. He made a left at Elm Street, walked two blocks and then hung a right at Central. It was twelve blocks up the avenue to school and he took his time.

His trek led him past a Diamond Shamrock gas station, a Baskin Robbins ice cream shop, the Quick Stop Texaco and most importantly, Dragon Keepers Game and Comics store. It was there that he spent most of his allowance and summer job money. He loved that place.

In the morning he always stopped to look in the window. The store wasn't open at 7:30 A.M., but he could see comics displayed on the front rack. While other kid's role models were rock stars and actors, his lived within colorful pages and he learned from them monthly. Any time a situation arose where Tim had to make a choice he thought, what would Thor do? Or Spiderman? That kind of thinking had gotten him a black eye and a dislocated jaw once. (Not backing down from a fight with Billy Laramie turned out *not* to be a great decision.) Otherwise, it seemed to work pretty well.

He paused for a moment to gaze at an issue of Batman that was on display. He then turned toward school, wiped his nose with the back of his hand and walked on. After another few steps he realized that he was standing in front of a fast food restaurant, Buddy Burger.

He looked up at the colorful sign as it rotated. The bright blue sky in the background with fluffy white clouds drifting by made the logo look wholesome somehow, more inviting. It looked like a friendly place for a family to eat after attending church or a soccer game.

Tim's eyes scanned down the pole to the roof and across the windows and glass doors. It was too dark to see anything inside. He didn't need to see, he'd been there. He shook his head, grinned and kept going.

Timothy had worked at Buddy Burger the previous summer for two months. He started on fries, but soon moved up to burger flipper, as he called it. His manager had been short bald man named Ronald. The employee turnover rate at the restaurant was high, due in no small part to Ronald, who had the personality of a sack full of disgruntled rats.

His other work experience had come from Blinley's Ice Plant. He managed to stay on the entire summer at that job, but did not re-apply the following year. Bagging ten-pound blocks of ice in a massive freezer was not the ideal way to spend a summer. He could earn minimum wage at any number of places without long underwear, a winter coat, gloves and a wool cap.

He crossed the street, looking over the grounds of Florence High School. Students were gathered outside in groups, talking and laughing. Five girls stopped their conversation as he walked by, scowling in his direction. He saw their sour glares and his

vision shot to the ground. They broke into cruel laughter once he'd passed by, making sure their amusement was loud enough for him to hear. His cheeks flushed with anger and embarrassment, but he didn't dare confront them. He imagined turning and saying something clever that would put them in their place. He imagined the looks on their faces as he really let them have it.
One of these days, he thought, *I'll tell them what I think.*
But not today. Today he kept walking with head down, watching his sneakers tread grass as he approached the east doors.

Nearby, smokers puffed away on their cigarettes, trying to ingest as much nicotine as possible before the bell rang. Jocks flirted with cheerleaders. Cowboys at the Annex steps. Goths by the gym doors. Timothy walked through the self-segregated groups. He didn't belong to any of them and he went around and between to get to the double doors.

Few students noticed when he entered the school. No one approached him at his locker. None acknowledged him when he entered the classroom and found a desk.
He sat in silence, alone, waiting for the bell.

3

First period went the same as it did any other day. Tim sat bored out of his mind, listening to Mr. Marshal talk about United States geography. By the last fifteen minutes of class, he was immersed in a daydream involving a girl he'd seen on a perfume commercial.

Second period was more of the same. He almost drifted to sleep a half hour into Social Studies. He caught himself fading and tried to sit up straighter in his chair.

Third period was the class he hated most of all: Speech. He'd done fine with the written work, but had failed to give two assigned speeches in front of the class. His grade was suffering because of a fear of public speaking.

A third speech was due to begin today and his grade was also due, to drop even lower.
"Who wants to go first?" Mrs. Hershey asked the subdued classroom.

She looked over a silent gathering of nervous tension. All eyes and hands remained down as she leaned against a large desk. The teacher grinned and crossed her arms.

"Come on, guys," she coaxed, "It's not like we're asking you to get naked up here or anything."

A few of the students laughed. Most didn't.

Tim stayed quiet. He knew that standing up at the front of the class and giving a three-minute speech was very much like getting naked, at least for him. Just the idea of all those eyes on him made him feel sick to his stomach. His hands were cold and sweaty. His face went pale imagining what people might think.

Please don't call on me. Please.

"Anyone?" Mrs. Hershey repeated.

Not me. Not me. Not me.

"Mr. Rayburn," she said.

Oh, god.

Tim felt like he might faint.

"How about it? Would you like to go first?"

No, no, no.

"Timothy?"

"Yes?" he said in a weak voice.

"The sooner you begin the sooner it's over," she said with a smile. Tim opened his notebook, in search of his paper. There it was, just inside the front cover. He'd spent three hours writing it the previous night and it had turned out quite nice. It was topical and thoroughly researched. The writing was top notch. His note cards were in order. It would seem that he was ready to go, except for the fact that he wasn't.

His legs were weak and locked down to the floor. The whole room spun. He was sure he would get sick if he stood, or worse, pass out. He slapped the notebook closed as Mrs. Hershey walked over.

"Tim, let's go. We've got a lot of these to do today."

"Um--"

"Is there a problem?" she asked with a stern pinch in her voice.

"No," he said, "I didn't do the assignment. I'm not ready."

Beads of sweat rolled down his pallid face. He kept a firm hand over the notebook containing the speech. It could've gotten him an A if he'd given it. Instead, he got a zero.

"See me after class, Tim. Tina, you're up."

A short blonde girl made her way to the podium and gave a six-minute presentation. The minimum time was three minutes. After four, Tim thought she was just showing off. After five, he was sure she was personally mocking him. At almost six he was ready to kill her with his bare hands. She was perky and smiley and informative. He hated her with all that was in him. When she finished she even asked if there were any questions. There were none.

Thank god, Tim thought.

She trotted to her seat. She smiled looking around the room until she made eye contact with Tim. When she saw him staring, she frowned. It was obvious that she didn't care much for him either. He looked away, not wanting to draw attention to himself.

Her name was Tina McCormick and she was one of the popular kids. Any number of jocks would kick his butt on any day of the week, at her request. And Tina had been known to request.

The previous year Don Newberry got his head dunked in a locker room toilet by the entire football team. He had made the mistake of asking Tina for a date the day before. Anyway, Tim knew better than to mess with an elite, especially since he was just a nobody.

A few more speeches were presented over the course of the next forty-five minutes. They varied in length and quality. Tim didn't pay much attention. He sat distressed and angry with himself, wishing he'd given his. After the bell rang he remained seated and waited for the other students to file out. Mrs. Hershey closed the door.

"Let me see your notebook."

"What? My notebook?"

Her high heels clacked across the tile floor.

"Yes. You heard me."

He offered it to her with clammy hands. She snapped it away and popped open the front cover. Her eyes scanned down the page.

"Can you explain this, please?"

"Explain what?"

She slapped the notebook down on his desk and hovered over him. "This outline looks finished to me. Am I wrong?"

He avoided his teacher's eyes. "No, Mrs. Hershey. You're not wrong."

"Then why didn't you present it?"

"I'm not really good at speeches and--"

"Tim, I know your shy and that's okay. A lot of the others are too. *I* was shy in school, but Timothy," she said pleading, "you've gotta get over it somehow."

"I'm sorry," he said.

"Look, there's an assignment coming up in three weeks. It's another speech. I'm gonna tell the class about it tomorrow."

"Another speech?" He sounded already defeated.

"Yeah. It's an open subject this time. You can talk about anything you want."

"I don't know..."

"Tim, it's a chance to speak about something you care about." Her smile tried to reassure him. "Something you're *passionate* about."

Tim sat with a blank stare, wishing he could think of anything that he cared about that much. There was nothing. Maybe comic books, but he couldn't do a speech about that. He'd be a laughing stock.

"To be honest," she continued, "the way your grades stand now, you'll not only have to give this speech, you'll need to get at least a B+ to pass this course."

"What? Really?" he said with wide eyes.

"Yeah. I'm telling you because I think it's only fair that you know. If you don't give me a great speech in three weeks, you won't graduate."

I won't graduate? Oh god.

"If it helps, just pretend that you're talking to me. Imagine that I'm the only one in the room. Look at me for your eye contact, and remember that I really want to hear what you have to say."

He looked toward the floor again, "Maybe..."

"I know some of the other kids give you a hard time, but listen, for your three minutes they don't exist, okay? It'll just be you and me. You talk. I'll listen. Got it?"

"I'll try," he said.

The teacher walked back to her desk. "Now go find something your passionate about, okay?"

"Thanks, Mrs. Hershey."

Tim gathered his books and went to his next class.

4

He sat down just as the bell rang. His teacher began roll call, going down the list of names alphabetically.

Tim's desk was in the center of the last row. The door was to his right at the back of the classroom. It had a long, thin window running straight up from just above the knob. It was four inches wide, a foot and a half tall and looked out into the second floor corridor. That was the hallway lined with the junior class lockers. Tim stared out the small glass from where he was sitting. He watched a janitor push a dust mop over the smooth green floor. Tim sat in a bored daze, wishing he were outside or at home, anywhere but English class. When his name was called he said "Here" without even realizing he'd done so.

The janitor turned the corner at the far end of the hallway and headed toward the stairs.

A small shadow appeared across from where the custodian had gone. It was a short patch of blackness and seemed to bob back and forth. Tim squinted, leaning toward the door. It looked like the shadow of a dog. Tim figured that it was too small to be anything else.

A tiny, dark figure stepped into the light. It was about three feet tall, maybe less. At first he thought it was a child. He watched as the figure took nervous steps in the middle of the hall. Its gestures were determined as it cocked its head. It seemed to be listening for something.

Tim cleared his throat. As if hearing him from all the way down the corridor, it jumped, startled by the sound.

Tim thought, *Weird. What is that? A midget?*

The stubby figure looked behind him, afraid. It ran bowlegged strides over to the lockers. It jumped, seemed to fall sideways and then ran straight up the wall to the ceiling. Tim screamed. He stood with a jolt and backed up, knocking over his desk. A loud

9

bang shook the floor. All eyes in the room found him. Laughter and chatter broke out. He covered his gaping mouth and pointed at the door.

His teacher, Mr. Nelson, said, "Timothy, what is your problem today, young man?"

Tim shook an outstretched index finger.

"The hall. Look down the hall."

Curious students stood as the teacher walked to the back of the classroom.

"Sit down, people. *Sit.* I want butts in seats now."

Everyone sat. Students stretched to see out the door as Mr. Nelson opened it. He saw nothing but an empty hallway. He paused a moment, listening to the click-clack of approaching shoes. Mrs. Barry, the music teacher, walked around the corner by the stairwell. She stopped in her tracks when she saw Mr. Nelson and his students looking at her. Embarrassed, he gave her and innocent wave and then closed the door.

"Mr. Rayburn, do you mean to tell me that you're afraid of Mrs. Barry?"

The classroom roared with laughter.

"No. It was something else."

"What was it?"

"I don't know. A midget, I think."

Again laughter. Mr. Nelson put his hands on his hips.

"A midget?"

"Yeah. I think so. He ran up the wall!"

"I'm not in the mood for any antics today."

"No really, Mr. Nelson. I saw it. I swear to god."

The rigid teacher shook his head. "Pick up your desk."

Tim looked down at the floor. His pencil, notepad and textbook were strewn around the toppled desk. The wrinkled photo of Allie Kincade was at his feet. He snapped it up and stuffed it in his pocket. Nearby classmates whispered at Tim as the teacher made his way back to the front of the room.

"You are such a dork," one girl said.

"What's your retarded problem?" said another.

    Tim reached out for his English textbook and found a size eleven sneaker on top, holding it down securely. He looked up into the angry face of Rodney Shoemaker, the biggest kid in the senior class, and the meanest. He loved bullying smaller kids like Timothy at every opportunity.

"You think you're funny, loser?"

He called people he didn't like loser, which was pretty much everybody.

"No." Tim whispered.

"Well loser, you ain't funny. You're a friggin' moron."

"Excuse me," Tim said tugging on his pinned down book.

"Is there a problem, gentlemen?" Mr. Nelson asked from the front.

"No, sir," Tim answered, staring at Rodney's lead foot.

The teacher frowned, "Turn around Mr. Shoemaker. *Now*."

With an evil smile he kicked the book away, sending it sliding across the floor. He then turned to face the front. Tim gathered his things and sat down.

He looked over at the door, in search of midgets. At first he saw an empty hallway and shadows. He scanned the lockers and dark ceiling. Then he saw the eyes. They glowed bright yellow, peering out from the upside down head hanging from the neck connected to the upside down body. The little man was sitting on the hallway ceiling, getting comfortable. His small torso was in shadow. His face was a velvet black silhouette, except for the bright yellow eyes. They were tiny flashlights, beams of illumination that lit up his feet. He looked up, smiled and waved with a stubby, fat hand. It was a friendly gesture, carried out with the very best of intentions.

Tim stumbled back once again, sending his desk and books flying. His shrill scream pierced every ear in the classroom. Mr. Nelson was startled, as was everyone else.

Tim cried, "There it is again! Look!"

The teacher pounded a fist on his desk. "I will not have this ridiculous outburst in my classroom! Get out, Timothy Rayburn! Leave this instant!"

"But Mr. Nelson--"

"No. You go tell the principal about it. I don't want to hear any more."

"But--"

"*Go*."

Tim approached the door with stuttering feet, looking into the dark hallway. The figure on the ceiling was out of sight. He struggled to swallow as he creaked the door open.

He turned, "There really was a--"

"Get out," Mr. Nelson commanded, pointing at the door.

Tim cautiously slipped out of the classroom. The latch clicked behind him and he was pinned with fear, his back against the door. He paused, listened and heard a chittering, like the laughter of a squirrel. It was coming from above him. Looking up, he saw a flash of yellow light. Teenaged legs dashed for the stairs. He glanced back and saw the figure drop to the floor and gallop on all fours, racing after him. The high-pitched laughing continued.

Tim hit the stairwell at full speed and slid into the railing. He stomped down the stairs, taking two and three at a time. Lungs heaved for breath as he lept for the ground floor. He turned and sprinted to the office. Twenty feet away, a short silhouette dropped from the ceiling. It hit, tumbled over twice and then popped up to a standing position.

The chittery laugh paused long enough for it to whisper, "Hello Timothy Lee Rayburn." The voice was a helium induced squeak. Tim slid to a stop, his sneakers making a loud chirp against the tile. The little man paused and looked over his shoulder at the office. He whispered "Shhh," holding a chubby hand toward Timothy. The teenager froze as instructed, too afraid to say a word. The man cocked his head and then pushed a red button on a metalic belt. A purple translucent energy shield appeared around the two of them.

A secretary walked into the hall, looked both ways and then shrugged her shoulders. She went back in the doorway. The man smiled at Tim as he clicked the button on his belt again. The purple haziness faded.

Up close, Tim realized that the thing in front of him looked no more human than it moved. Its skin was pale white with a bluish tint. It was bald, its scalp spotty and flaky around the top and back. Its mouth was a strange mix of oversized and abnormally small teeth. The two in the front were square shaped and huge, reminding him of a girl with an extreme overbite that he'd known in eighth grade. Some of the less sympathetic children had taken to calling her 'Bucky'.

The next four teeth on either side of the 'buck' teeth were very small, uneven and close together. The bottom row mimicked the top giving the little man's mouth the visage of a hamster. It was very odd and under different circumstances would have been very comical.

The glowing yellow eyes were piercing beams of light that hurt to look into. Tim blocked the light with his hand, squinting. "What are you?" he forced out.

The inquisitive man cocked his head back and then forth. His chittery laugh continued through the large and small teeth. His smile was friendly, amused and unending.

He looked at Tim's light blocking hand and then said, "Oh. Oh, yes," realizing his own thoughtlessness.

Reaching down, he clicked another toggle switch on his belt and the beams from his eyes shut down with a snap.

"Sorry," he said in a chipmunk voice, "Sorry for that. I mean not to offend."

Tim lowered his hand and took a better look at the small visitor. With the high beams off, the teenager could see the alien eyes. They were all white, with a small black pupil in each. There was no iris, no color at all. To Tim, they looked like vampire eyes. Also, it was the first time he noticed the little man was wearing a gray uniform. It was covered in numerous zippers and had a multi-colored flag over the left breast. A large metal ring encircled his neck and appeared to be a place to attach a helmet.

The little man leaned closer to the earthling. Tim jumped back, shaking.

"Fear me not, Timothy Lee Rayburn of Verse Three-Three-Two. I damage you no."

"What?" Tim said in disbelief, "What did you say to me?"

The tiny astronaut shook his head as if dizzy, stopped and then, "I *will not* damage you. That what meant I, to say at you."

"Huh?"

"That is, the point being, um, I will not cause pain to you…at this time."

Tim found himself more amused than afraid.

"You mean you won't hurt me."

"Yes! That which I say informed your previously ignorant status!"

13

He looked at the man, crinkled his nose and then said, "Whatever, dude."

The man smiled bigger, "In any event, John Wayne."

"What? No, I said *dude*, not duke."

"As in ranch?"

Tim lowered his brow. "Duke Ranch?"

"*Dude* ranch,"

"What?"

"Cowboy."

"I have no clue what you're talkin' about, dude. No clue."

"Cull-ooh," was said with a chipmunk laugh.

"Whatever."

The little man took a step forward. "What-ever. What-*so*-ever. What-when-where-who-why?" He paused and then, "Because!" Laughing broke out again as the delighted man threw his arms in the air.

Fearful eyes targeted the office door. Tim whispered, "Quiet. You're gonna get us in trouble."

"Come," the high-pitched voice said, "Come to another here."

He took off bow-legged, walking down the hall to the double doors. Tim followed. He was still a bit nervous about accompanying an alien dwarf in a space suit, but his current curiosity outweighed his fear.

They slipped by the office undetected and continued to the main entrance. The odd man pushed his way out, hopped down beside the stairs and sat behind a tall hedge. Tim looked around and saw that they were alone. He stepped off the concrete, into the bushes. Excited little hands waved him down.

The midget cleared his throat, shook his head as if dizzy, and then spoke. "Me from Verse Five. I travel over to here from there. I on mission of important. Need you travel to other here with me."

Tim frowned. "What mission?"

The midget cleared his throat again, "Verse machine failing. Universes threaten to shutting off." He rubbed his pale scalp for a moment and then, "Collapsing. Yes. Verses will soon *collapsing*. Need you fix. Come."

Tim looked into the colorless eyes. "You're an alien from like, another planet, right?"

14

"Yes! Alien me! Come I from another here! My here far, far away!"

The teenager squinted, scanning crooked alien teeth. "So, you wanna abduct me or something?"

"Yes!"

The alien celebrated his excitement by swaying back and forth. He chittered like a squirrel, "Abduction for you! Yes! Let's go!"

"Hold it, dude. You can't just take me out of class and kidnap me. Besides, I don't know anything about fixing no universe machine. You'll have to get somebody else."

The man shook his head side to side. "No! You!"

"I'm not going."

"Go you me with!"

"No," Tim said crossing his arms, "I don't even know you... And you're kinda creepy with your Buck Roger suit and them laser beam eyes. Creepy."

"Know me! Yes, know me!" He stood and put a fat hand to his chest. The other he held up to the sky, "I be Tweezor M. Norbinger, um, the great. Um, Captain Space cruiser, um, *Admiral* of armada and um... *King*, yes, King of Verse Five." The little man thought for a moment and then stated, "*And* President of Consolidation Organized Systems." He smiled big, took a bow, saluted, stood at rigid attention and then sat back down laughing.

Tim leaned over, "You're so full of it, dude. That was the biggest pack of lies I've ever heard. King--" he had to laugh and the midget joined him.

"*President.*"

They both laughed so hard Tim thought someone would hear them.

"Admiral!" the spaceman called out as he fell backwards in the dirt chittering away.

The double doors opened and out walked Principal Johnson and another teacher. The AWOL student and alien trespasser froze in silence, ducking down behind the hedge.

"I swear I heard talking out here," the teacher said as he scanned the grounds.

The Principal could see Tim's white T-shirt behind the bush.

"Come out of there now. This instant."

Timothy stood up. They'd been caught. There was nothing they could do now but--

"We no stand for oppression of this sort. Be gone dude people! Be gone!" was the command from the shadowy hedge.

"Who said that?" the principal demanded, "Come out of there right now."

"No way dude. Go fart cheese!" Chittery laughter.

"Both of you are in so much trouble. Timothy Rayburn, you tell whoever that is to get out of there now," the teacher said with a scowl.

Tim looked at his odd friend, "We're busted, okay man? Let's go."

"No can do, buckaroo! Make my day! Asta la vista, baby! We can do eet all night long!"

"What? What did you say?" The principal's cheeks flushed with anger. "Get out now!"

Tim started walking. The midget did not.

"Consume rancid poop, fat man! Blow it out pie hole!"

The teacher had had enough. He stepped down into the weeds and stomped toward the unseen heckler.

"Back off man, I'm a Ghostbuster! Squeal like pig, fat boy!" The amused alien laughed. "I see dead people! Ha, Ha! I see dead people!"

"Who are you, you little creep?" the teacher said just as the alien came into view.

"You can't handle the truth!" He drew a small pistol from his belt and fired. A red beam flashed and the teacher fell in the grass with a limp thud.

Tim yelled, "Dude! Stop!"

The stubby man kicked dirt at the unconscious teacher, "Eat lead, farthead!"

The midget chittered. He looked up and saw the principal was out of sight.

Tim knelt down at the body and felt for a pulse, "Oh man. What did you do?"

"No hurt. Stun."

Tim was relieved to feel blood still pumping through the teacher's neck. "Don't shoot people, man."

"Set phasors on stun, captain. You know, *stun*."

"Yeah, I know stun, man. Just get lost before the police get here. Just go."

"Tim come also. Tim have the right to remain silent! Tim have right to attorney! Come!" he pleaded, pulling on the human's arm. Tim pulled away from the midget. "You're psycho. Get off me, freak."

A stubby finger pressed a green button on the utility belt. Everything went hazy purple again. Tim felt a snapping electric charge dance across his shoulder blades. He went lightheaded and then dizzy. With his equilibrium gone, he fell to his knees holding the sides of his head with shaking hands. He looked up into the spaceman's face. The pudgy mouth was smiling, as always. Beams of blinding yellow light once again shot from the alien eyes. Everything behind the unlikely duo fell away, melting into blackness, then green fog, then bright white.

"What's happening?" Tim yelled, "What are you doing to me?" Tweezor did not answer. He only laughed with an annoyance that would've made Alvin, Simon and Theodore proud. The bright white faded back into green fog and then dissipated. Tim opened his eyes and saw that they were in his bedroom.

"Life quarters of Timothy, correct?" the alien asked.

"How did you-- What just happened?"

"Pack suitcase. Long trip ahead."

"I'm not packing. I'm not going anywhere with you, freak."

"No pack things?"

"No. Go away. Leave me alone," Tim said flopping down on his bed, "I feel sick."

The chipmunk voice laughed, "Travel sick? You barf now?"

"No."

"Ralph?"

"No."

"Toss cookies?"

"No. Go away."

"Blow chunks?"

Tim covered his head with a pillow. Tweezor clicked another switch and began calculation on a small data pad he'd removed from his pocket. It clicked, beeped and made random whizzing sounds.

Pleased with himself, he grinned and said, "All finished. Yes. We go now."

Tim's bedroom rumbled like an earthquake. He was pinned down to his bed. His eyeballs pulled to the back of their sockets. The warm sunlight that had been shining through the window disappeared. It was midnight.

Tim looked around. The midget was gone. Tiny streaks of light caught his attention out the window. He struggled to pull himself up to a sitting position. After a moment he stood, steadying his legs in the quake. He stumbled to the curtains and ripped them open. The sight was unbelievable. Streaming stars flew past at breakneck speed. Twisting galaxies floated in the distance. The sky was pitch black. His bedroom zipped past a huge planet with millions of asteroids orbiting through multi-colored gasses.
My god, we're in space.
Tim screamed.
Somewhere outside his room, down the hall perhaps, he heard chipmunk laughter.
"You little creep!" he said stomping to the door.
With it thrown open he yelled, "Where are you, you crazy midget? I'll kill you!"
"No worries, mate!" he heard above him. It was distant and echoed, like a voice over a speaker.

Looking down the hallway, Tim noticed something strange. The far end was a black void rushing toward him. The darkness raced closer, the hallway got shorter and Tim's screaming became louder. He pinched his eyes shut and felt it whoosh past him, almost knocking him over. He opened his reddened eyes and saw that the bedroom was gone. He was standing in a large room, with metal walls covered in monitors and gauges of every sort. A large panel viewer was mounted on the far wall. The space they flew into was on the screen. The little man sat at a console.
We're on a spaceship.
The alien hummed to himself as he pushed buttons, turned knobs and clicked levers. The tune he hummed was the theme from The Love Boat.
"*Hmm, hmm, hmm,* soon we'll be making another run. *Hmm, hmm, hmm,* promises something for everyone...."

Tim rushed over, "This is kidnapping, freako! Take me back, now!"

The man kept humming and singing, "Set a course for adventure, *hmm, hmm, hmm,* a new romance…"

"Are you listening to me? Take me back!"

The crooning astronaut threw his arms in the air, "And love…won't hurt-anymore…It's an open sea-- and a friendly shore! It's looove! Welcome a-board… It's luu-uh-uv!"

A repeating chime sounded, ending Tweezor's performance. He scowled, looking to the frontal display. A large spaceship popped onto the screen as an incoming transmission came through. The voice was a choppy mix of grunts and barks. The words had an unusual, almost synthesized sound to them. Also, to Timothy it seemed like they talked backwards, like a tape player in reverse. Tweezor responded in what sounded like the same language. It was surprising and creepy hearing those noises come from the space midget. He had no idea what was said, but he guessed by the flow of the words and the pitch that they were being polite to one another.

Tweezor finished the conversation with "Oo-een-ga, yuno. Bok."

Tim looked up at the screen and saw that they approached a giant spaceship. It got bigger and bigger until Tim thought they would crash into it.

The side of the huge ship was all that could be seen in the monitor. Tim saw a space dock doorway slide open and they entered. The little man hummed to himself as he navigated the ship to a landing platform. The large sliding door closed the shuttle inside the larger ship. They set down with a loud metal quake and Tim's heart leapt at the surprise jolt.

A yellow light illuminated the dock.

"Come on," Tweezor said, hopping down from his chair.

He walked to the back of the room and pressed a code into a colorful panel. A door slid out of sight exposing a ramp extending downward, into shadows.

Tim followed the spaceman, demanding that he explain what was happening. The little man said that his captain would explain everything and then continued humming.

Although it was very strange, the tunes did calm Tim's nerves somewhat. He couldn't imagine anyone who was going to kill him humming the theme from Bonanza.

They ascended a staircase to an upper level and entered a bright, large room. What looked like steam shot out from small holes in each wall. The mist washed over them and the spaceman rubbed at his armpits like he was in a shower. Timothy was not amused. The fog dissipated and a pair of double doors slid open.

A gathering of bizzare aliens stood smiling on the other side. There was a pale green-faced male and female in the front of the group with oval, bug-like eyes and impossibly long fingers. Their smiles were wide, exposing small razor-like teeth. There was a brown and black hairy creature, which stood on two muscular legs. No eyes could be seen through the dark hair, only a huge gaping mouth. It was big enough to swallow the human whole. A thick tongue lashed across dark, wet tissue and gigantic molars. Its arms were were hairless and layered with thick strands of muscle. They hung limp at its sides. There were also three tall humanoid creatures that appeared to be connected at the side of the heads with short tubes of cartilage. They stood in an unusual triangle, leaning into the center as they barked backward sounding, synthesized speech at one another. There was another little person that looked very much like his kidnapper and a lanky tall, red-skinned alien. They each had a shiny metal orb floating above their heads.

A moment passed while the human tried to make sense of the sight before him. He then fainted, collapsing to the hard, slick floor.

5

Static twisted the airwaves, leaving behind an irratic jumble of voices overlapping one another. The interference was due to idemic emissions from a mining colony on the planet below, Triptic-Six.

"Cruiser Phazon Twelve, you are cleared for space dock separation." The barely audible transmission originated from space dock control, level one-one-eight, Space Station Orbital.

The satellite was a customs facility and military outpost, but also provided shopping, lodging and starship repair for civilian travelers. It was run by the E-Triptics, natives of all six planets in the local system. The nearest planet supplied the entire quadrant with Carbidd/Funkton, an alloy used in starship construction.

The Phazon Twelve, a massive battle cruiser detaching from dock two-one-two, was the most advanced ship in the fleet. It housed a thousand soldiers and a command crew of fifty officers, each with private quarters. It was also home to twenty plasma cannons, five ion cannons, ten Aggressor torpedo bays and enough bio-terror missiles to infect an entire planet. She was a commanding vessel that instilled Admirals' pride and a fleet's envy.

The ship was used primarily as a negotiator for conflicts that were deemed too near industrial or commercial areas. Four years ago, such a conflict occurred between two neighboring planets in the Tarrin-Ep system. Consolidation Command ordered an intervention.

For more than an hour after her arrival, she went ignored by the opposing fleets. The captain then charged the ion and plasma cannons and opened fire on both militaries. Within minutes every fighter was destroyed and all deployment freighters were crippled. Incoming transmissions flooded the frequencies with terms of surrender. Fire subsided and for a moment all was quiet on Tarrin-Ep.

Then, a primary cannon on the planet's surface opened fire in the direction of the Phazon battle cruiser. She retaliated with a single torpedo. Its payload was ten pounds of concentrated antimatter.

Designers had christened the weapon Aggressor Type D. After an impressive demonstration on the surface of Tellis, Admiral Bine dubbed it a 'Population Inhibitor', which seemed more appropriate. The name caught on with local troops. It wasn't long before the entire fleet referred to the Type D as an Inhibitor.

When the Phazon Twelve engaged its Trans-Wavetime engines and exited the system, the captain remained confident in his resolution tactics. The war was over. Terrin-Ep was left with a crater two miles wide and half a mile deep. The mission was documented as a success. The ship and her crew had since engaged in many similar encounters.

After space dock separation, the vessel eased out of hanger two-one-two. Her skin lights came alive, illuminating letters on the upper hull. They read, *Phazon Twelve, Fleetship Battle Cruiser, Consolidation of Organized Systems, AC12A*. Each word and number painted on the silver Carbidd/Funkton outer shell stood more than two stories high. The size of the vessel was disturbing to most cruiser class ships, and respect was given accordingly. She was a demon, waiting to strike from the black seas of space.

The captain of the beast was Carbaugga Fint, a sensible yet uncompromising Deemadozien. At first sign of threat he would strike hard and swift. Few adversaries opposed him after his first attack. It was a rare occurrence when a vessel survived his second.

They cleared the outer doors and were free of Space Station Orbital. Their mission was to escort a supply freighter to the military base at Ebteon. The freighter had not yet exited a lower dock. Phazon Twelve held her position, waiting.

Captain Fint tapped long fingers on the hard arm of his chair. Aggravation pinched at his brow as he glared at the main viewer. There were angled screens port and starboard of the central, and an aft viewer below. A Cube generator sat below the screens, creating a translucent image. It was a six-sided holographic representation of the local sector. A flashing pinpoint of light showed their current position. The planet, the station and various ships entering and exiting the system were displayed in a green radiance. The three-dimensional projection was invaluable for strategic maneuvering in battle.

Communications Officer Nelle spoke to his captain. "The freighter has been cleared for release, sir."

Fint held his eyes on the screen, "Good. Let's get this mission moving. We have to be at Consolidation Headquarters in eight days. If there's even one glitch, we'll be late."

Nelle responded, "Yes sir," although there was nothing he could do to hurry the freighter.

Captain Fint's tapping turned into a loud knocking on the arm of the chair. "Why do we, the most advanced ship in the Consolidation, get stuck with these ridiculous babysitting missions?"

A large flashing dot appeared at the edge of the cube display. The computer warning system sounded a metronome chime across the bridge.

"What is that?" Fint asked, squinting into the hologram.

"Sir, a cruiser class ship has come out of Wavetime at grid four-one-zero-niner."

An image of the intruding vessel appeared on the central screen. Fint studied the ship with a frown flexing his face.

The ship was oblique and smooth, with an imposing wingspan. Along the breadth, weapon bays glowed with crimson intensity. A tower stood like a massive dorsal fin above the dark fuselage. She was a bird of war; of that he was positive.

Captain Fint squeezed tight fists and stiffened his posture. He slid forward in the chair and planted the soles of his shoes on the textured floor. "Send language protocols and open the address channel."

The lieutenant followed orders and the captain's voice was stern. "Unknown vessel, this is the Phazon Twelve Battle Cruiser, a representative of the Consolidation of Organized Systems. Identify yourself and state your business."

The alien ship did not respond. Interference from the nearby mining facility crackled over the dead channel.

Fint tried again, but received only static. He leaned back, rubbing his chin.

Strange. "Did they get the talk-pack?"

The communications officer checked his screen, "Yes sir, language protocol has been uploaded."

They can hear us, so what's the problem? In the starboard monitor, he saw the nearby station with thousands of sparkling lights, shining like a great beacon above the planet. "Take us away from Orbital, ten thousand pex. Also, advise defense command to raise their shields."

The Phazon increased her distance from the space dock. If fire were to be exchanged, the captain didn't want them catching any stray blasts.

An officer at the diagnostic console spoke. "I'm reading an energy spike from the alien vessel."

Fint's eyes seemed to pierce the monitor, "Battle stations."

"Energy source intensifying at the rear engineering core...Unknown configuration... They're powering up something." The captain tried once more. "Unknown ship, this is the captain of the Phazon Twelve. We are authorized to police this sector. You are ordered to stand down. This is your only warning."
Silence.

The alien cruiser dived and accelerated into position. The crew had spent too many hours watching warring militaries to recognize the maneuver as anything but aggressive.

The big ships, the cruiser battle class, like the one coming at them now, had to be dealt with swiftly. The Captain couldn't afford to let them gain too much confidence. The superior vessel needed to make its statement clear. The Phazon Twelve was always the superior vessel.

Fint's orders were abrupt. "Full plasma spread on my command." A bombardment of plasma was good for eliminating shields and letting the opponent know who was boss. There was the risk of damage to energy systems and life support. According to Fint, those were minor side effects when making a powerful first impression.

A female voice sounded from the engineering station. "Plasma cannons charged and ready, Captain."

"Good. Very good. Let's give 'em a reason to speak up."

The opposing ship changed course, bearing down on the Orbital facility.

"Fire," Fint commanded.

From various bays, the Phazon took the offensive. Eight cannons shot concurrently over a span of five seconds. Each was a shimmering yellow pulse, leaving behind a hazy gas trail. They struck one after another until the enemy ship was alive with explosions.

"All direct hits, sir," weapons control announced.

"Enemy shields are down to fifty percent...wait...*what the...* They're rising back to normal... Shields back at one-hundred percent, Captain."

Weapons control announced, "The ship itself took no damage."

Fint's eyes widened. He'd never seen a vessel take so much punishment and still have any shield remaining. The unknown ship didn't return fire, but kept speeding toward the space station. It released a single shot at the center of Orbital's structure. The impact was a lightning energy across the force shield, crackling at the surface. It fizzled for a moment and then detonated, sending violent shockwaves through the station. Orbital's shields vanished in the blaze with generators shooting white-hot sparks into zero gravity.

A desperate voice cried out, "Mayday, mayday! Our shields have failed!"

Fint eyed the station on the screen. Lights flickered on upper platforms while lower docks lost all power and were left smoking in the shadows.

"Double up plasma spread. Fire."

Two pulses from each cannon shot from random locations across the Phazon's forward arsenal. Sixteen explosions raged in the distance. The captain watched over the science officer's shoulder as his adversary's shields dropped to sixty percent, forty, thirty, twenty…twenty-five, thirty-five…

"Charge seeker bays one through six."

"The enemy weapon is powering again, sir."

"Get us between them and the station--and fire torpedo eight."

The Phazon banked and accelerated to protect Orbital. Number eight torpedo soared into the unknown. It was the infamous 'Population Inhibitor.' The anti-matter detonation sent the alien ship quaking with weakened shields.

"Full plasma spread. Fire." Fint commanded.

Snapping orbs of energy struck one after another. Each blast expanded into the next, creating a terrible and unified explosion. The apex of the billowing punishment hid the enemy from sight. When the cloud faded, the cruiser remained. It appeared shining and new, not a scratch on her.

Fint couldn't believe it. He suspected that somewhere inside the enemy vessel there was a Captain laughing at him.

"Enemy weapon still charging, sir."

"The ship is changing course, Captain. She's coming right at us."

"Brace yourselves. I think we got her attention."

The Phazon Twelve stood waiting for the inevitable. The mysterious alien cruiser accelerated, swooping down for the attack.

The captain called out, "Full spectrum-- Give 'em everything we've got. *Fire.*"

Twenty plasma blasts, five seeker missiles and ten Aggressor torpedoes shot at once. The impacts were a display of fire visible from the surface of the nearby planet.

For a moment Fint was sure that Hell had come to claim the enemy. The moment was brief. The raging wall subsided and the ship emerged from the explosions with orange flames swimming over its surface. He watched in amazement as the enemy pushed through the heat, bearing down on them once again.

Impossible. That was enough to destroy an entire fleet.

The two battle cruisers paused, facing one another. The vacuum of space between them was silent, still, dead. Over the frequencies, popping static.

Every man, woman and child inside the station watched out a window or on a monitor. The conflict was re-broadcast to other stations and command centers across the multiverse. The entire population prayed that the most powerful ship of their fleet somehow, would prevail. The silence stretched out to a million planets and beyond.

Captain Fint looked over his crew. They had served him without question or hesitation. Anything he asked, he knew they would do, even if it meant death. That moment many of them spent staring at the unknown ship and wondering why. Why would an unidentified race start a war with them? The Consolidation was not a threat to outlying systems. It only sought to protect its own. They wanted peace in the quadrant, above all else.

The vessel that had refused communications broke the silence between ships. "We are *Meem.*"

It was a guttural, slow growl. Fint gritted sharp teeth, listening. The static voice echoed into the nearby station. Admirals, generals and soldiers alike from locations across the multiverse heard the speech emanating from the ship that was yet to receive damage. The captain said, "We are listening, Meem ship. We demand that you stand down."

A dark, long pause and then, "Demand?"

"Yes," he said, "You will cease this attack."

The alien vessel didn't respond. Fint pinched his eyes shut, searching for words that would convince the enemy to disengage. "We represent a powerful armada. Any actions today would have serious consequences. The entire Consolidation orders you to surrender."

"Your kingdom will fall."

Fint clicked a toggle switch on his panel so his orders wouldn't be broadcast over the airwaves. He whispered to the weapons control officer.

"Load an Inhibitor in every tube. *All of them.*"

He clicked the switch back over as the officer worked at his station. A voice sounded from the diagnostics console.

"Sir, they still have full shield. We only damaged their outer, secondary shield. The entire hull is protected by a negative-charged idemic firewall."

Fint hurried to double-check the findings on his own readout. Idemic radiation was known to disrupt any electrical system. *How do their computers even function?*

"Captain, they're charging up--wait--a different weapon this time."

"Fortify frontal shields."

"Holding at full, Captain."

For thirty seconds an unknown weapon charged. Fint used the time scanning the vessel, trying to find a weakness. He found nothing.

A particle beam shot out from the nose of the Meem ship, washing over the Phazon's shield. A violent quake melted her defenses away.

"Shields down to forty percent!"

"Evasive maneuvers!"

"We've lost main power!"

"Go to secondary!"

Fint turned to the weapons control officer, who was holding onto his chair, trying to remain standing.

"Fire!"

Four torpedoes were away before weapons control went offline, soaring across the blackness between ships. They were shooting stars, full of flames and desperate hopes. As always, the impacts were beautiful and magnificent, blinding the sky.

When the explosions faded with their glory spent, the enemy reappeared, a great technological phoenix, bathed in fire with an immortal life.

For Captain Fint, everything was in slow motion. He was in a waking dream. Time was sluggish and every second an eternity. "Shields failing, sir!" called out a distant voice.

The Phazon was paralyzed. She drifted into shadow, waiting for the fatal blow.

The predator was in no rush to strike. It sat watching its prey, while a new weapon charged within its alien core.

The space between ships was once again still. Captain Fint sat back in his chair on the crippled bridge, illuminated with dim emergency lights. The officers looked at him with helpless eyes, leaning over dead screens. The communications console faded to life, sending static crackling. Everyone looked into the air above, listening. A voice behind the interference hissed.

"We are Meem."

Fint covered his mouth with shuddering fingers. Somewhere behind him an ensign was crying.

The tremor began at the stern, across engineering and the living quarters, decks ten through twenty-eight. At first it was slight, a vibration below the soles of their shoes. It soon increased into a rumble that knocked pictures from shelves and tools from workbenches. The quake traveled through hallways and rooms and decks, getting stronger as it went.

Panic washed over the crew as soldiers rushed for escape pods. There were a hundred in all and each was a dark, lifeless compartment. They were as doomed as the mother ship that held them.

The rumble increased. Walls and floors ripped with an earthquake that had begun to topple workstations and equipment. They felt it on the bridge.

"Can you *feel* us?" the enemy wheezed.

Fint guessed it was some kind of particle beam, but with no operable scanners he would never know for sure. The brutal energy destroyed training rooms and living quarters. The Carbidd/Funkton alloy ripped at seams and twisted loose. Outer skin panels fluttered away like butterflies.

"Hull breaches over decks nine through twenty-one," said a panic filled voice over a fading speaker.

Fint and four of his officers struggled to remain standing on the darkened bridge. They gripped consoles and beams as the room quaked. The captain held onto the command chair with all of his strength, shaking a defiant fist at the enemy.

"We do not surrender! Do you hear me?"

Terminals around him exploded and the chair broke loose from its mount. It struck the captain, breaking both his legs. He fell to the earthquake below, struggling against pounding chaos.

"Can you feel us?" he heard again.

That time it seemed as if the voice had come from inside his head. He strained to steady himself against a shaking surface that was coming apart. Broken glass flew into his face, cutting his skin.

"Can..."

The weapons station was free and flying. It smashed into the opposite wall with flames spitting.

"...you feel..."

Sparks ignited above him. Hot flakes showered down over his back and arms.

"...us?"

The central screen broke away and came at Fint like an axe. The edge chopped his torso in half just as the ceiling detached. Everything froze in the unforgivable vacuum of space. Fint's body shook into tiny ice particles, escaping the destroyed Phazon Twelve.

The entire cruiser was an expanding, twisted gathering of shaking panels and dust. One Trans-Wavetime engine drifted end over end, bumping along dented beams and unrecognizable debris. Thick chunks of pressure glass glistened across a field of starship and humanoid remains. The last of the Phazon framework shook apart. Small explosions lit up across the dense forest of wreckage.

Thousands watched from the Space Station as a Meem Warbird turned from the fragmented expansion of metal. Thousands gasped as they realized the ship was now facing them.

6

Timothy woke with a pounding headache. He jerked alive and sat up. Looking down, he realized that he was on a soft cushion surface. It was a bed or…an exam table.

Oh god. Their gonna anal probe me.

He jumped off the table in a panic. The nurse was a bright red skinned, three-eyed humanoid with tentacles for arms and legs. She yelled something he couldn't understand. He screamed back at her in horror. Tweezor appeared from behind.

"Calm Timothy. No worry so much."

"What is that thing? Get it away from me!"

"It not it. It her. Her name Neeba."

The nurse stopped yelling and rushed to the doorway. She watched the human with intensity, as one tentacle hovered over the alarm button.

Tim looked at a large electron microscope that sat in the corner. "You're not jamming that thing in me! No way!"

Tweezor was confused, "Huh?"

"My butt is an *exit only*, buddy. Stay back."

"I know not what speak you of." He paused and then, "No worry so much. Be happy."

The little man grinned. A pale green alien walked in speaking what sounded like garbled Japanese.

The human backed away, "Tell him he's not gonna dissect me. You tell him."

The nurse used a long tentacle to jam a small plastic device in Tim's ear.

He threw up his fists. "AAH! Get off me, weirdo!"

He noticed something odd. The alien language continued to sound in his left ear, but he could've sworn it was English he heard in his right. The gibberish confusion made his head spin.

With a pop, a plastic device was placed in his other ear. The alien language dissapeared and Tim understood their words.

"--calm down, please. We'll explain everything," the pale-green alien said.

"What is she doin' to me?" he asked, rubbing his ears.

"Nurse Neeba has inserted a portable talk-pack. It is a translation device so you can understand us."

Tim pointed to the corner. "What's that?"

The alien looked over and then back to the human. He blinked large, oval eyes.

"That is a powerful microscope. It is used for scientific research. We won't be using that today."

Thank God. "So you're not gonna probe me? Um, I mean you *better not* try to probe me because I'm a black belt in…Yoga…or something."

"Don't worry. Our data scans are finished. They were all painless and non-destructive."

"Scans? Oh."

"Now," the alien said with a friendly, yet razor-toothed smile, "I suppose you're wondering why we've acquired you."

"*Acquired* me? Is that what you call kidnapping?" he paused and then, "How about alien abduction? That's more like it."

"Yes, well, in any case we abducted you for a very noble cause, I assure you."

"Yeah right."

Behind them, the little spaceman had started singing. "Nonna-nonna-nonna-nonna, nonna-nonna-nonna-nonna, Batman!"

Tim crinkled his nose, frowning. "What's his spastic deal, anyways?"

The pale alien smiled at the midget. "Mr. Norbinger has always been an enthusiastic one."

He motioned for Tweezor to leave the room. The theme to the Batman television show could still be heard, even after the door slid shut.

The taller alien turned and smiled at Timothy. "I am the Captain of this vessel, the Truthseeker. My name is Gorza Nule." He looked over the human for signs of fear and stress. He saw plenty of both. "Let me begin by saying that we mean you no harm. However, we had to obtain you…*kidnap* you, for a very important reason. We have run out of time."

"Run out of time?" Tim repeated.

"Yes. You see, the universes came to be a very long time ago. Five hundred million years, actually. Or some increment of that, we're not completely sure. The point is, the reason they came to be was this."

31

He touched a button on the wall and a screen lit up with a picture of a strange object. It was a massive sphere with cranks and piston-like arms jutting out from every possible angle. It had huge, twisted gatherings of knotted, multi-colored wires hanging from underneath corroded panels. And thousands of tall towers supporting giant transmission dishes.

"What is that contraption?"

"That *contraption* is the Multiverse Generator. It is what makes all existence possible."

"That robot thing makes something?" Tim looked over the dangling panels and exposed cables, "You mean something other than noise, right?"

"It is not a droid," the captain said, "and yes, it makes something other than noise."

"Yeah, well it looks pretty run down. You want me to change the oil in it or somethin'? Does it need new plugs?"

"No. It is not a vehicle. It is a generator. It creates universes."

Tim's amusement faded. "That thing makes universes? Like there's more than one or something?"

"Yes. There are over five thousand verses."

Tim's eyes got wide, "You've got to be screwin' with me."

"No," the alien said with a razor-toothed grin, "I do not screw."

From behind the door they heard a muffled, "Screw! Ha ha!"

Captain Nule rolled his yellow eyes and then continued. He described the generator in great detail and explained the urgency of their mission.

Tim stayed quiet, listening to Captain Nule. He was in awe of the Multiverse dilemma. He was amazed by his surroundings and the alien that spoke to him. His head swam. His heart pounded.

His bladder ached; he needed a bathroom bad.

Sector Two:
Timeshift Tunnel

1

The generator was commonly known as the Multiverse 5000. As the legend goes, the original three (the first known beings in the Multiverse) designed it to generate five thousand connected universes, providing planets and solar systems for an infinite number of species.

Once initiated, it would need to be reset every five hundred million years by transporting one being from each verse to the generator. And not just any being. Only one individual in a generation contained the proper DNA coding. They became known as the sequence carriers.

The undertaking was nearly impossible until DNA scanners were invented. The detection devices made the daunting task of finding the correct humanoid very easy. They could then triangulate the sequence carrier's location from any point in the universe.

Resetting the generator was meant to bring all life forms together in the partnership of a common goal. A friendship of five thousand verses full of advanced species, standing together, unified in their great purpose. That was the idea anyway.

What the three didn't understand or yet know was that humanoids had a propensity to be violent, jealous and just plain mean. When the systems realized that a being from each verse was needed they set out to reset the machine, no matter the cost. Prisoners were taken from neighboring dimensions, or sometimes more convenient, a decapitation was performed and only the head taken. Battles broke out, wars began and multiversal hatred abounded. Needless to say, resetting the machine caused more chaos and death than anything else.

So a few of the more civilized systems got together to sort out the mess and create some order within the species. Their new government was named the Consolidation of Organized Systems.

Many planets joined the Consolidation in hopes of peace. Many planets also, did not.

Fast-forward one thousand years. The last of the species were delivered to the machine and the DNA input. At last they thought the dimensions would stabilize. But something was wrong. The machine wouldn't reset.

Panic spread across the verses like a plague. The Consolidation nearly crumbled as they tried to resolve the problem. Leading scientists from countless systems worked day and night in efforts to solve the enigma of the mysterious machine. After months of research, analysis and brainstorming, one thing became clear. The technology needed to even access the generator was beyond them. Only a ship with the sequence carrier aboard could enter Verse One, the home of the generator. And after each individual's information had been uploaded, even he was denied further access. It seemed that there was no solution.

And then, the machine told them why it could not reset. It said (in a coded message sent in high frequency) that all of the verses had not signed in. But how could that be? All five thousand were present and accounted for. They had made sure of it. The generator went on the say that there were three hundred and thirty two hidden verses that would need to be found.

Each had been created as a kind of accidental shadow of an intended verse. They were nearly exact duplicates of originally created dimensions, although they contained a few minor differences. An extra sun here, one less planet there, but essentially the same. A list was given of the originals that contained wormhole vortexes to their hidden, shadow verses.

By the time they figured out the problem it was almost too late. Some verses became unstable while others threatened to collapse altogether. The Consolidation sent hundreds of scouts to find the hidden verses and retrieve the necessary specimens from each.

2

"I'm sorry, I think I misunderstood you. Can you say that again?"
"I said we have no sinks, no toilets and no showers. We have no restroom facilities of any kind on this vessel."

"What? What's wrong with you people? Where am I supposed to go?"

The captain smiled, "What we do have is this."

Nurse Neeba placed a round device into her captain's hand. He held it up for Tim to see. It was about the size of a softball and was made of smooth metal. It was similar to the orb floating above the heads of everyone Tim had seen so far on the ship. The human noticed that Nule's was a bit smaller and tarnished as he watched it follow the alien's every movement, hovering above his bald skull.

The captain punched a code into a keypad on the side of the unit. Bright lights flashed as it beeped alive. Tim backed away. He wasn't sure he wanted to know what purpose it served. With the final command punched in, it began to whir like a top. It buzzed, beeped and then shot out of Nule's hand. It hovered over Tim, zipping back and forth.

He ducked away, "Aah! Get off me!"

"Do not be afraid. It is performing a few scans to determine your biological needs. It will not harm you." A long tone announced that its analysis was finished.

Tim felt an odd sensation, like a warm tingling in his intestines. The pressure in his bladder was gone in an instant. The aching ceased. He didn't have to urinate anymore and he looked down to be sure he wasn't peeing himself. His jeans were dry and he was relieved, yet confused.

"What just happened? Did something just happen to me?"

"Do you still need to urinate?"

"No."

"Then I'd say something just happened."

The alien paused a moment to take in his guest's reaction. Tim checked his pants for moisture once more and then looked up at Nule in disbelief.

"This," the captain said pointing at the floating device, "is your quantum assistant. It is the only restroom you'll ever need."

"Did that thing just-- Did it just, um…"

"Yes it did."

"That's impossible."

"It uses quantum dimensional technology to remove any unwanted waste from your body. It also cleans you regularly, ridding you of oil, dirt, perspiration and bacteria."

"I can't take a shower? Is there a water shortage in space, or what?"

"We have little use for water here. You'd be amazed at how small our onboard water supply is. Most moisture is recycled from individual to individual."

"That's disgusting, dude," Tim said covering his mouth.

"You'll get accustomed to not drinking or eating. It's really very-"

Tim was horrified. *"You don't eat?"*

It surprised Nule just how shocking the concept was to the earthling. "We do not consume anything by mouth. All fluids and nutrients are placed into your system by the quantum assistant."

Tim sounded desperate, "Not even sometimes?"

"Never. I personally have never masticated."

"Masticated?"

"Chewed."

"Oh, *chewed*. That's what I thought you meant," he said with a flushed face.

"So, do you have any questions?"

"How long will it take to get me to the multi-uni thing?"

"The Multiverse Five Thousand. Three weeks, give or take."

Tim leaned back against the table and rubbed his chin. "And you absolutely have to use human DNA? *My* human DNA?"

"None other. I'm afraid it's you we need."

"Will it hurt?"

"No. You won't feel a thing. I promise."

"You'll get me back home safe? You swear?"

"I swear that I will do my best to return you expeditiously and preferably alive."

Tim thought to himself. *Am I really gonna do this? Do I have a choice?*

The answer was obvious.

They were taking him whether he agreed to go or not. He figured that he'd better get used to the idea.

"Okay, I'll do it."

The door slid open, revealing a celebrating midget. He wagged his hips and waved pudgy hands while he sang.

"Do a little dance…make a little love…get down tonight!"

Nurse Neeba rolled her eyes and walked out of the room.

3

Captain Nule led Timothy down a long, wide corridor to the elevator. Aliens of every imaginable type lined the hallway, trying to catch a glimpse of the earthling. Most were humanoid and wearing military clothing. The uniforms were mustard colored and shiny slick, with various patches and jagged stripes across the shoulders. Each soldier wore a thick, black belt with a holster and silver pistol. The belts had suspender straps over the shoulders, with pockets and dangling equipment. Also, each had a softball sized quantum ball hovering above his head.

They walked past the crowd and into a large elevator.

"Bridge deck," the captain spoke into the air.

The door slid shut and ten seconds later a chime announced their arrival. The lift opened. Captain Nule and his guest stepped onto the command bridge.

An officer called out, "Captain on deck," as they entered.

A tall female looked up from her console. Her skull was hairless and pale green like the Captain's. She had the same oval, yellow eyes. Tim was positive they were from the same planet. They could've passed for siblings.

"We are nearing the Verse Five wormhole, sir."

"Let's see it, Commander."

They didn't talk like siblings. Tim figured they were just the same species. It felt strange thinking of someone he could have a conversation with as a species, like he was classifying a type of fish. Or dog. He wondered how Darth Slobbers would get along without him. He wondered how long it would take for his parents to miss him.

An image appeared on the frontal viewer. The three-dimensional cube display fizzled to life. The wormhole she'd spoken of was a white spiral vortex. To Tim, it looked like entering a tornado from above.

The bridge rumbled when they entered, making the human's heart leap. The screen flashed twice and then went black. Tiny glimmering dots of distant stars faded into view. The white spiral disappeared. Verse Three-Three-Two was behind them now. They had been transported to a central quadrant of Verse Five, the heart of the Consolidation.

"At this speed we will arrive at Ectopa Crin in eight hours." Nule looked over a star chart on the screen in front of him. "Increase twenty percent."

"Yes, sir." Commander Vulpa Nim replied.

Her long, quick fingers typed over a large keyboard.

A synthesized computer voice above said, *Speed increasing.*

A hairy creature standing behind the captain's chair barked out something low and guttural. The translation sounded in Tim's ear in English, but in the same gruff voice. "Plasma in tubes fourteen through twenty-three showing fluctuation."

"Engineering, watch those levels," the captain instructed.

"Yes, sir," responded three voices at once, "Equalizing now."

Tim walked toward the tall creature. It clacked huge molars as it spoke. A crusty green film covered the middle of its tongue.

"Hello," Tim said, "My name is Timothy Rayburn. Looks like I'll be joining you for a little trip."

Where are this thing's eyes?

All he saw was hair and mouth.

"I am Commander Geesh, head of security. I also attend to the weapons console, from time to time."

"Oh," Tim said, "Weapons, huh? Sweet."

The Rectalin didn't know what the human meant by 'sweet' and didn't ask. Tim looked over a control panel of illuminated buttons and flashing screens. It looked extremely complicated.

He wandered over to the next alien, the one that looked like the captain's sister. She was busy working over an even larger network of gauges and controls.

"Hi," he said over her shoulder.

"Hello," she said in a sharp tone. "I am Commander Vulpa Nim. This is the scientific analysis operations center." A pause and then, "I'm currently occupied."

How rude, he thought. "Okay, then. Nice to meet you."

He walked across the bridge, looking over technology he couldn't possibly understand.

Nule put a hand on his shoulder. Tim jumped.

"I didn't mean to startle you."

"That's okay," he said trying to calm down, "I'm just a little freaked out, I guess."

"That," Nule said pointing to a panel at the rear of the room, "is the engineering control area."

Three engineers stood in a triangular formation attached at the heads with a thick appendage that had grown from the top of each one's skull. The one nearest the wall punched in lightning fast codes with all three fingers of his left hand.

The captain continued, "They are EM, EL, and BE, a Crichets being."

"Why are they connected together?"

The Captain watched the fascination in Tim's eyes and smiled.

"You must think of them as one entity, one individual. It requires all three to make a whole."

"So, they're stuck like that?"

"No. They can separate and function independently, but they work the fastest, they *think the fastest,* that way, connected. Their species is some of the most intelligent beings known."

"So, that's why they're engineers," Tim reasoned, "They're super smart."

"Yes. They also make excellent scientists."

Nule then pointed toward Vulpa.

"She is second in command on this vessel. Her and I are from the same planetary system, Deema. We Deemadozians are well rounded in engineering, the sciences and many other useful talents. Most of the population is in the Consolidation army. Twenty years ago I joined as a pilot. Three intergalactic wars later, I found myself sitting in the captain's chair."

"You've been through three wars? Wow."

The captain nodded toward aliens at different stations around the bridge. "He is Geesh. He is Junley Sorpe. He is Pallen Xaxe."

Tim looked over them all with curiosity. He figured that at least six different planets were represented on the bridge alone. He wondered how many more alien species there were on the ship. Probably hundreds.

While people on Earth wondered if they were alone in the vast sea of space, Tim's universe was getting awfully crowded.

4

Captain Nule sat on a small couch behind the weapons control station, holding a box in his lap. He motioned for the earthling to join him.

"This," Nule said with palms down on the cushions, "is where you will sleep."

The human said, "No way. I can't sleep here. I need my own room."

"I'm sorry, but there are no available quarters. This is all we have to offer you."

Tim squinted, "It's too bright in here."

Nule reached into the box, retrieving a pair of dark goggles. He offered them to the human.

"I apologize. Here is a light blocking device for your eyes."

"And noisy. It's gonna be too loud."

"Here are some earplugs."

The captain dropped two small pieces of rubber into Tim's lap and stood up.

Timothy's protest continued, "This is inhumane, man."

"In-what?"

"I need privacy," he said.

"Here is a soft coverlet," Nule said smiling, pulling out a folded green blanket.

"Did you hear what I said? I need privacy."

"I'm sorry. There is none available." The razor-toothed grin pushed bigger, "Here is a nice pillow."

"This is *bull*, and you know it."

"Bull?" Nule held the empty box at his side.

"Forget it, dude," Tim said in frustration, flopping back onto the cushion.

5

With a few hours to waste, Timothy asked the captain if he could have a look around the ship. Nule saw no harm in satisfying the human's curiosity. He was allowed to roam, but was instructed not to touch equipment or bother personnel.

The Truthseeker's corridors were long, narrow and teeming with workers. Many carried clipboard-sized data pads, rushing to assorted destinations. The majority were male and varied in appearance and physique. There were females scattered throughout, but very few. Some species were impossible to differentiate.

Occasional gatherings of soldiers huddled to avoid blocking traffic. They paused conversation as the human walked by, each intent on having a look at the sequence carrier. Whispering ensued behind covered mouths, making Timothy feel self-conscious. He tried to ignore the hushed comments and staring, but it was impossible. He picked up the pace to evade their probing eyes.

The closer he got to engineering and the living quarters, the fewer workers he saw. After taking a right turn into an adjoining hallway, he realized that he was alone. The solitude was nice and he took a deep breath, studying his newfound surroundings. The floor was dull black, like the surface of an inner tube. The walls, pristine white. Every thirty feet an intercom station with illuminated buttons sat on the wall.

Tim heard voices ahead and went to investigate. The large double doors of a military training gymnasium stood open. He stepped inside for a look.

The room was bright and about the size of a basketball court. On the far side stood two soldiers. The taller alien checked a gauge on a large backpack unit the other had strapped around his torso with a thick harness.

"It's showing a good charge," the Sergeant said.

"The sub-system analysis is complete."

Tim walked closer, looking at the metal pack with curiosity. The soldier turned toward the human.

"Hey, You're not supposed to be in here."

Tim stopped, "Come on guys, I just wanna watch. I won't get in the way."

"Fine. But if somebody catches you, we told you to get lost and you were just leaving. Got it?"

"Yep, no problem. Thanks guys."

With a button pressed, the lights on the unit came alive and it roared like a jet engine. Tim took a step back, startled.

"Okay," the Sergeant yelled over the rumble, "You know what to do. You've done this a thousand times in the simulator. Take it up nice and easy, spin around slowly and set back down. Ready?"

With thumbs up and a smile, the trainee lifted off the floor. The engine screamed even louder as he ascended upward. Timothy was awe struck.

That's the coolest thing I've ever seen.

Careful fingers edged joystick controls on the arms of the Jetpack and the hovering soldier rotated in midair. He drifted a bit, corrected with some quick button pressing, adjusted his liquid fuel mixture and then eased downward. Boots made contact with the floor once again and the motor went silent.

"Real nice, Ensign. Remember to keep an eye on those levels and listen to the motor. If your fuel mixture changes, the way she sounds will change. You take care of her, she'll take care of you. Again."

Tim and the Sergeant walked to a bench and sat down while the rocket man lifted off.

"Do you think I could learn how to do that?" Tim asked with excitement.

"No," was the immediate response.

"Why not?"

The alien frowned, "You are not a soldier. You have no military training." He scanned Tim's face with a sneer, "You're not even an advanced species."

"Hey," Tim said is his defense, "I'm...advanced."

He wasn't sure what was meant by the comment but he knew he wasn't stupid. At least he hoped he wasn't.

"What has flying got to do with advanced anyway? It looks like all hand-eye coordination to me."

"There's more to it than that. Much more."

"Like what?"

"Tell me what you know about rocket science."

Tim smiled, "I don't want to design it, I want to fly it."

The alien paused a moment, looked at Tim, and then laughed. "Maybe you're not as stupid as everyone says you are."

"Who says I'm stupid?"

"Everyone. Come back in an hour if you want to learn something. I'll start you then."

Tim stood up. "Everybody thinks I'm stupid?"

"One hour," he said patting the human on the back. "If you're late I'm locking the doors."

6

The Consolidation freighter Gravity slowed out of Wavetime at sector eight-seven. A hundred thousand gigapex above the planet Triptic Four, she rotated starboard, scanning.

"It's not there, Captain. It's...gone."

Captain Gom stared at the monitor in disbelief.

"Run a diagnostic on the scan receptors. There has to be something."

"Sir," an Ensign said, "I'm not getting anything on spectral, either. They can't both be wrong."

A brown skinned female turned away from the communications panel. "I'm getting no response to my transmissions either. It's like they just disappeared."

Gom refused to believe that an entire space station had vanished. "Set in a course for Tripic-Six and engage, Mr. Beeler. Let's take a closer look."

Gravity rotated in a quiet space, her tanks full of liquid Hydroburst fuel. It was a delivery scheduled for a space station that did not exist. The captain felt like the victim of a very bad joke.

"We are coming up on Triptic-Five, sir."

A small orbiting station, number two fifty-seven, drifted silent and dark in the planet's shadow.

"What is that?" Gom asked.

"That is a small, private facility. My readings show that it is powered down to twenty percent. I see only one life form aboard."

At least it's there.

"Open a channel. Maybe they know what happened here."

A female voice stretched out across space, to the small station. It echoed down dark hallways, inside living quarters, over the kitchen, and into the restaurant.

"Satellite two fifty-seven, this is the Consolidation ship Gravity. Do you copy?"

An excited voice responded.

"Yes! I copy! Come get me, quickly! Before it comes back!"

Gom took a deep breath, "Slow down, sir. Before what comes back?"

A pause and then, "This isn't a rescue mission?"

"Rescue? From what?"

Cursing and banging.

"You don't know anything." The words were angry. "Back away from me. You'll draw its attention."

"Draw what's attention?"

"I can't believe this is happening," was whispered, before the channel went dead.

Gom stood up, looking at the shadowed station. "Well, that was interesting."

"No one is answering from the surface. It looks like a communications blackout."

Beeler said, "I don't like this, sir. We should leave now."

"No, Commander," Gom said, "Not just yet."

The front viewer zoomed in on the area Space Station Orbital should've sat. It looked like drifting rock.

"What the-- Is that a mass of asteroids?"

"No sir," Beeler said checking his readings, "It's debris."

Gom adjusted the focus on his screen. He saw bent panels, hoses, and framework. An engine bumped along, end over end. Tall letters read, *Phazon Twelve*. Gom's eyes went wide.

"Ready the Transwave engines. Get us away from here, Mr. Beeler."

The freighter turned away from Tripic-six as a cruiser class battleship faded into view behind it.

"Sir, a cruiser--"

"I see it. Engage Wavetime."

A bright blue path opened in front of Gravity with a thundering boom. She nosed down and then entered. A moment of stretching colors announced the freighter's departure. It disappeared into blackness.

The Meem Warbird scanned for a moment, studying the path. With a deafening crash it re-opened and the cruiser entered in pursuit.

Commander Beeler couldn't believe his eyes. He doubled checked his screen. And then he checked it again.

"Captain, the cruiser has entered the Timepath, behind us."

"That's impossible."

"I know, sir," he said staring into the aft screen.

The Warbird closed the gap in an instant.

"Increase five percent."

"They're on us."

This can't be.

The Warbird struck from behind, ramming them. Out of control, the Gravity spun down a bright blue path. At point five above bluelight, she exploded. What fell out of Wavetime was a faint dusting of burning photons.

7

"Captain Nule has requested your presence in his office," Vulpa said when Tim walked onto the bridge.

"Okay." He responded.

He knocked and waited.

"Enter." Nule said into the microphone at his desk.

The metal door slid out of sight and the human stepped inside.

A big, round object sat in the middle of Nule's desk. It was gloss black with a thick band of yellow around it. It looked like an oversized bowling ball. Nule leaned to see around it from where he was sitting.

Tim smiled, "What is that?"

The helmet was a round metal casing that closed like a suitcase. It was designed to protect a huminoid's head from damage. When closed around the skull and locked, it was horribly dark with only a tiny slit in the front to see through. It was also uncannily heavy, and to Timothy it felt like carrying concrete blocks around on his shoulders. In fact, if he leaned forward or back even slightly, it

45

sent him crashing to the floor. The struggle to get to an upright position again was comical, to everyone but Tim.

The captain returned the smile, "It's a helmet."

"Yeah? Well, you need to return it, cuz it's too big for you."

Nule paused for a second, deciding how to proceed. He looked Timothy over, evaluating the strength in the human's upper body, and then spoke.

"It's not for me. It's for you."

Tim's eyes got wide and he backed up.

"No way, *huh-uh*. You ain't puttin' no bowling ball on my head."

"It's just for when we consider danger levels high. It's for your personal protection, you see."

"No. *N-O. No.*"

Nule clicked open the latches and opened it.

Timothy found out that standing while wearing the helmet was extremely painful. He had to take great care balancing the weight, utilizing muscles in his back and neck that until then had gone unnoticed. He also leaned against walls or beams whenever possible.

Since the balancing act was required, he couldn't see anything that was not directly in front of him and at eye level. Turning his head only gave him a view of the inside of the helmet. Leaning forward to see the floor sent him plummeting toward it.

Tim hated the helmet. To be more realistic, he despised it, loathed it and sought to destroy it.

"See? It's padded on the inside, real cozy."

"No."

"You'll only have to wear it when we're passing through dangerous sectors of space or when we are confronted with potentially violent situation. These are the only times. I promise."

"No."

The helmet was for his protection, sort of. It would be more truthful to say it was for his brain's protection.

They had to be sure that not only his blood, but all of his brain chemicals reached the generator, even if he were killed. The generator was designed to take a blood sample and a random chemical sample. If the two were not a DNA match, it wouldn't accept the reset command. If the chemical asked for wasn't available, their efforts would be futile. It was designed that way to coax the individual universes to unite in a common cause. It was to promote brotherhood among species and planets and to avoid life forms killing each other to reset the machine. What the designers hadn't foreseen was the brain-stealing fiasco they'd set into motion.

Tim's arrival was imperative for the continued existence of the dimensions. So, in the event of his death, the helmet would separate the head from the neck, sealing and preserving it for the remainder of the journey.

Nule did not tell the human about the 'separation' feature. If the human had known that, the captain would've had to force it on a kicking and screaming Timothy every time. He simply told him it was very important and that the helmet was for his protection. Any other details were on a need to know basis and he definitely didn't need to know.

Nule's eyes narrowed, "It's either this or we put you in hyper-sleep the entire trip."

Tim crossed his arms and gritted his teeth.

"How heavy is it?"

"Very."

The captain motioned at the open headgear with outstretched fingers. To Tim, Nule's gesture looked like Vanna White showing the audience a prize that prompted oohs and ahs.

"Try it on," he said with enthusiasm, "You need to get accustomed to it."

Tim bent down face first, apprehensive. He stopped before his neck touched the foam padding.

"Are you sure about this?"

"Go on."

The moment he was in position, the backside of the helmet closed down and a loud *click-click* echoed in Tim's ears

"Hey, wait!" was the muffled yell.

The blackness was thick inside the cranium prison and Tim experienced a full on panic attack.

"Get me out!"

He pulled up and realized that the helmet must've weighed more than a hundred pounds. He was pinned facedown to Nule's desk.

Pushing with his hands and straining to stand made the helmet bobble side to side. It did not come off the desk. It hurt his neck to push against a weight that would not budge. He heard the Captain at a distance, possibly behind him. It was hard to tell.

"Let me help you," Nule shouted as he lifted on the metal globe. Tim found himself in an upright, standing position. Nule's eyes appeared in front of the small bright slit.

"There you go!" was the muffled voice.

Nule gave him smile. He let go and Tim fell backward into the wall.

He struggled to stay upright yelling, "This sucks! Get me out!"

He lost balance and fell into Nule's arms. The captain lifted him up once again.

"Steady now, steady…" he said, letting go with one hand.

His other hand stayed on top, holding Tim from swaying.

"Take it off now."

"No, not yet."

"Take it off!"

"I'm letting go…steady."

With the hand removed, Nule took a step back. Tim was standing, swaying a bit with muscles aching, but standing.

"Have a walk around now. Get used to it. I'll take it off in a hour."

"An hour?" Tim complained.

He stumbled, caught his top-heavy balance just in time, and bobbled out the door onto the bridge.

Officer Geesh looked over with an amused smile. Tim couldn't see him or any of the crew that watched him tilt and sway across the room. Tweezor chittered a high-pitched laugh, nearly falling over backwards.

Tim ran into a beam and stopped. The deafening clang inside the helmet hurt his ears. His skin vibrated.

"Ow!"

A chime announced an incoming communication.

"Captain, the Ectopal ship Redeemer wishes to speak with you."

"On screen, please." The central panel illuminated with a female face.

48

Her voice was even and respectful, "Greetings Captain Nule. I am Commander Sparrim Gale of the vessel Redeemer. We heard you would be passing through our system. On behalf of my people, I would like to welcome you."

Tim wobbled over in an attempt to see the screen. He fell into the captain. Nule caught him and put an arm around his shoulders. He looked back to the monitor, "On behalf of the Consolidation Command and my crew, thank you for your hospitality, Commander."

The Ectopal woman looked at the flailing human with the big round head.

"Are you having trouble with your droid, Captain?"

"Oh no," he answered holding Tim up, "This isn't a droid. This is our precious cargo. An occupant of Verse Three-Three-Two."

"*That's* him? I didn't realize they would be so…off balance."

"Oh no. He is just wearing a protective helmet. It's made of strong, heavy material. You can't be too safe, you know."

Tim caught a glimpse of the face on the screen through the thin opening.

Oh my god.

He couldn't believe his eyes. He would've fallen backward if Nule hadn't been holding him. He strained to pull his head up enough to see her again.

He saw floor.

Floor.

Wall.

Screen.

Ceiling.

Floor.

Screen.

Wall.

Screen.

Screen.

Those eyes.

Wall.

Floor.

Screen.

Those lips.

49

Wall...screen.

My God. It's her.

"I see," she said to Nule, "Well, if we can be of any..."

Wall.

Floor.

Screen.

"...assistance, please..."

Ceiling.

Floor.

Ceiling.

Ouch. That hurt.

"...let us know. We will be glad to help."

"Thank you, Commander. We will."

The transmission ended. Captain Nule turned and let go of Tim. He fell face forward to the floor with a thud.

"Get me out of this thing!"

The captain shook his head in frustration. "Somebody help him out of that, please."

Tweezor unlatched the helmet, laughing. Once Tim was free of his dark confinement he sat up with a sore neck. He rubbed a shoulder with a massaging hand.

"That thing is a nightmare, dude."

He looked up at the screen and then stood. From deep in his pocket, he pulled out the picture. He unfolded it and showed it to the navigation ensign.

"It was her, right?"

The ensign gave him a puzzled look.

Tim tried again, "The Commander chick, you know. The girl that was just on that screen over there?"

The Deemadozian looked at the central screen and then back at the picture of Allie Kincade. He said nothing.

"Come on, man. You had to see her. Right *there*." Tim pointed at the monitor.

"Let me view the photograph, please," Vulpa said.

Tim rushed to her and held the wrinkled picture up.

Vulpa studied it and then said, "Yes. She has an uncanny resemblance to this human. Almost identical."

"Yes!" Tim exclaimed. "I knew it! I only got a glimpse through the helmet, but I thought it looked like her!"

Nule plucked the photo away from Timothy, "That is unusual. Very unusual."

Tweezor rushed over, "Let see! Let see!"

The captain handed the picture down to him.

He looked it over and grinned, "Yup, that her. Hubba hubba!"

8

Inside the lower level of the Consolidation Command Center on Inner Deema, an officer approached Admiral Kellot.

"Sir, a Meem ship has destroyed the freighter Gravity. It was just outside the Triptic system."

Kellot turned to face the young Lieutenant.

"Why would they have been anywhere near that sector?"

"We don't know at this point, sir. Perhaps it was a communications error. What we do know is that they were traveling point five above bluelight when the attack initiated."

The Admiral frowned, "Someone is playing a joke on you, and a bad one at that. That information is ludicrous."

A data pad was lowered onto the desk, in front of the Admiral.

"That's what I thought too, sir. But I've since double and triple checked the findings sent to us. Everything looks accurate."

Kellot looked over the findings on the green illuminated screen.

"We can verify that the Gravity was traveling at Wavetime by the tracker signal received at the observation center at Outer Deema," Kellot said, "But it is impossible to know why the ship was destroyed. It could have been any number of malfunctions."

"Yes, sir. But have a look at the video transmission we acquired from satellite Two-Fifty-Seven, in orbit above Triptic-Five."

A thick finger pressed the touch screen and a video began. A dark image of the Gravity sat against a backdrop of blackness and stars.

A voice, "Back away from me. You'll draw its attention."

Another voice, "Draw what's attention?"

"I can't believe this is happening."

Static.

The freighter hovered motionless in space for thirty seconds.

The Admiral looked up at the Deemadozian as if to say, *I don't have time for this.*

"Please, sir. Keep watching," the officer said.

Kellot's eyes found the screen once again, just as the Gravity turned, scanning. After a few seconds the ship rotated, powering its Wavetime engines. Just then a distorted ship faded into view behind them. It was a Meem Warbird. A time path boomed open with a brilliant blue light. The Gravity disappeared inside and the light faded. The Warbird sat scanning for a second and then the illumination blasted open once again. The Meem ship nosed downward, entering. Admiral Kellot stared into the readings as the small screen faded to the darkness of space.

The coordinate information for both jumps was identical.

Not similar, he thought, *identical.*

The officer took a step back, watching astonishment on the admiral's face develop. His mouth hung agape. His eyes shot up, into the air above them. The ramifications of the new information settled, flooding him with fear.

The enemy had not only the capability to detect a Wavetime path, which was amazing in itself, but they also could mimic the trajectory. They could enter a timepath in pursuit of any ship they wished and destroy it.

A chill went up Kellot's spine.

"Contact Consolidation HQ at Scorrinwall. I need to speak with Admiral Bine immediately."

9

Captain Nule spoke to his human guest.

"Our first stop will be the Grand Hall of Consolidation Congress at Ectopa Crin. The president has been informed that we have you and he's called an emergency meeting."

"Ectopa Crin? That's the name of a planet?"

"Yes. We'll arrive in about two hours."

Ectopa Crin traveled in orbit around the local star, Ectopa. Another smaller star also orbited Ectopa, much farther out. The combination of two suns made life bright and hot on the planet's surface.

It was a diminutive sphere with large oceans, mountainous continents and frequent coastal flooding, due to five large moons and an unpredictable liquid-gas core. Most cities were built as far inland as the population would allow.

The Ectopal people were known for their artistry in architecture, sculpture, and fabrics. Not to say they didn't have advanced sciences. They were a very intelligent race and had made great leaps in starship design in recent years.

The Ectopal city of New Munsil was a mecca of statues and monuments. The elaborate design created a breathtaking skyline. That is why the Consolidation chose it for the site of the Congress Hall. The surrounding views reminded them of the very peace they fought to achieve, as did the building itself.

Every wall had a large painting or tapestry. The windows were lined with colorful drapes. The thresholds were great curving arches and each piece of furniture had been upholstered with intricately designed, hand woven fabrics. There were glass etchings, marble statues and tall columns ascending to the massive ceiling.

The luxurious surroundings were in direct contrast with some of the deadly serious topics discussed. Inter-dimensional laws had been passed, wars had been declared and the fate of entire systems had been determined. The decisions made there often meant life or death to many.

Today's emergency meeting was no exception. They had to find a way to get past Meem occupied space to the Verse One wormhole. So far, none had made it in or out of the sector alive. The Meem fleet was unrelenting with the most deadly weapons the Consolidation had ever seen. There was no known defense against them. There were no weapons that could penetrate the Meem cruiser shields. Huge ion cannons located at a few bases across the system were the only way to hold them off. It was only a matter of time until the Meem managed to destroy the cannons.

So the race was on. The Consolidation cruisers needed an effective attack against the most formidable ships they'd ever faced. The Meem needed only to wait for their ground forces to arrive. They were specialized battalions designed to eliminate problems such as stationary cannons at military strongholds.

Little did the Consolidation know, they had only a few hours to find a solution.

10

Sergeant Orts was splicing a wire under the simulator when Tim walked into the gym. He slid out, checked the readout on a handheld diagnostic screen and then ducked back underneath for some fine-tuning.

Tim walked over and knocked on the side of the simulator. A loud bang echoed from under the machine, followed by a cry of pain.

"Hello? It's me, Tim."

After a moment Orts slid out with a reddened lump on his forehead.

Tim stepped back, "Geeze, I'm sorry. I didn't mean to--"

The alien interrupted, "Never sneak up on me. I have a pistol, you know."

"Sorry."

The Sergeant rubbed his sore head and sat up.

"So, are you sure you want to learn the flight pack? Absolutely sure?"

"Yes," Tim said, "Positively."

The human was in for a long trip. He needed something to occupy his time. The Jetpack was just the thing to keep him busy.

"This is not an amusement ride. It is a vehicle that operates very much like a small shuttle," the alien paused, "It's serious."

"I'll take it seriously. I swear."

"Okay then. Come on."

Tim followed the soldier inside the large machine. The compartment was rounded and dark with a flight pack hanging in the center, suspended from metal tubing and wires. Tim was led into position and strapped in. Orts stepped out of the chamber and closed the door. His voice sounded above Timothy.

"Begin program."

Red lights flashed for a moment, and then faded. The smooth curved walls illuminated into blue sky, soft clouds and rocky ground below. Tim stood at the edge of a cliff, overlooking a deep valley. The sky was bright and clear. He was startled at the seamless realism of the simulation. If he hadn't known better he would've sworn it was genuine.

"Sweet!" Tim shouted.

Orts said over the speaker, "This will be where most of your flight training will take place. Of course, we will also use a non-gravitational space simulation."

"This is awesome dude!"

Orts wasn't positive he liked being called 'dude' but said nothing. The human took a slow look around the simulated sky and valley, inhaled a deep breath of simulated cool mountain air, and smiled. The curved doorway opened and the seargent entered. He then turned and unbuckled Tim's harness with a click.

"Alright," he said, "Let's get to work."

"Hey, where are we going? I thought you were gonna teach me--"

"Teach you? Yes. Here? No."

"But you just said--"

"End program," Orts said to the machine.

The blue sky faded into dark metal. Tim's euphoria faded with it.

"When you are ready," the alien explained, "This is where you will gain experience in flight. This is what will get you ready."

He pulled out a program disk, handing it to the human.

"What is this?"

"It's everything you ever wanted to know about aerodynamics, liquid and solid fuel mixtures, avionics, flight mechanics, nano technology, quantum propulsion, gravitational fields, timeshift theory and spacetime basics. It also contains a simple overview of deep space survival."

When Tim realized his mouth was hanging open, he closed it.

"Are you trying to tell me I have to learn all that before I can fly?"

"Well, yes. But I'll try to explain it in a way that your underdeveloped primate brain can understand."

"Great," Timothy said with thick sarcasm.

"Okay then." He slapped Timothy on the back, "Let's get started."

Sergeant Orts led Tim to the rear of the gymnasium and into a small classroom. Three others sat at desks, reading from small screens in front of them.

"Sit there," Orts pointed.

Tim sat and looked into a screen on the desk. A series of squiggled lines and angled marks sat in horizontal rows. He raised his hand. "Yes, sequence carrier?"

Tim thought for a moment and then, "Um, well the first thing is, I'd rather you call me *Tim*, not sequence carrier. Secondly, uh…" he looked down at the gibberish on his screen, "I can't read this."

"Oh, yes."

Orts walked over and clicked a toggle switch on the front of the desk. A bright green light shot out, scanning the human's brain. Tim pinched his eyes shut to block the piercing illumination. It zipped back and forth through the air in front of his face. Then, with a 'bing' it was finished. The small computer went to black and rebooted with a blue screen. Text flowed over the surface in English. The top line read, *Deep Space Survival and Zero Gravity Basics.*

Timothy let out a sigh and started reading. He read for about an hour. Some of the information was interesting, but most of it bored him to grogginess. His mind drifted, daydreaming about Allie Kincade and looking around the classroom. The others read and took notes on green sheets of paper. He raised his hand. The training officer looked up from his desk.

"Why do you keep doing that?"

"I was raising my hand to ask you something."

"Then ask."

"Can I continue studying this on the bridge?"

"You wish to remove a computer from this classroom?"

"Yeah. I kinda wanted to keep up on what's happening."

"I am not authorized to sign out equipment. You will need permission from the captain for that."

"Oh."

"But, you may come back at the same time tomorrow, if you wish."

"Thanks," Tim said standing up. "I'll see you tomorrow then."

Orts looked back down at his own terminal as the human left the room.

11

When Tim walked onto the bridge, he saw the helmet sitting on the floor next to the couch. He rubbed his neck, thinking about the panic he'd felt while wearing it. He had to find a way to get rid of it. A smile overcame him.

Down the bright corridor went a human rolling a large, round helmet. It was so heavy that it hurt his back to push it along. He was determined to find a way to dispose of the monstrosity. His neck and shoulders still ached from the first time he'd worn it. He couldn't breathe inside it.

The captain just doesn't understand. This thing has to go.

Soldiers gave him odd looks as he made his way behind the huge black globe. None spoke to him until he got to the pressure junction at blue level, thirty-one.

"Halt," a young officer said, "What is that and where are you going with it?"

Tim stood with a crispy lump in his throat.

"This? It's a protective helmet."

It started to roll away until the human stopped it with his foot.

"Where are you going with it?"

"To um…dispose of it. It's damaged."

"What's wrong with it? It looks fine to me."

Tim forced a smile, trying to look nonchalant. He leaned close to the soldier, whispering.

"I don't think there's anything wrong with it. The captain just got the new model and I think he just doesn't want this one anymore. That's what I think, but you didn't hear it from me."

The officer was intrigued, "Nothing wrong with it, huh? What's it for?"

"It's just your standard invincible helmet."

"What do you think one of those goes for on the black market?"

Tim shrugged his shoulders, "I don't know." He rolled it closer to the soldier, "There's only one way to find out."

"You're positive the captain said to dispose of it?"

"Positive," Tim said, smiling.

"What do you want for it?"

"I'm sore from rolling the stinkin' thing. You can have it."

"Really?"

"Really."

The excited officer bent down, picked up the helmet with ease, and then walked away, glancing over his shoulder every few steps.

Sweet, Tim thought. *That was easy.*

12

"Entering Ectopa Crin orbit, Captain."

Tim looked up at the frontal viewer as he walked onto the bridge. He was amazed at the image. The planet was enveloped in a brilliant violet atmosphere. Patches of sparkling cloud cover hung over dark continents. Massive mountain rages cut across the land, creating a complex network of light and shadow. A nearby belt of asteroids drifted lazily in orbit. It was as extraordinary a view as any astronaut had ever beheld.

My God, it's beautiful.

The Captain said, "Commander Nim, Mr. Norbinger, show our guest to the shuttle bay please."

"Yes, sir," Tweezor replied.

"Come with us," Vulpa instructed, leading the way.

They took the elevator down to spacedock level and walked out into a long hallway. The far end opened revealing a bay with several small shuttles. Tweezor walked up the entrance ramp of the nearest. Tim and Vulpa watched from outside the ship as the engines fired and the wing lights came alive. After a few minutes Captain Nule joined them and they boarded the shuttle.

"Sit there," Vulpa told the human.

A long row of seats lined the walls, facing the center isle. Tim sat across from the captain. Vulpa then clicked him into a five-point harness. Tweezor turned, giving him a thumbs up and a grin.

"You ready, cowboy?"

The commander clicked herself into her own seat.

Nule smiled, "Entering the atmosphere may give you a nauseating sensation."

"You will not vomit," Vulpa added, "Your quantum assistant will see to that."

Tim's eyes glanced up to the air above him. The hovering metal balls were there, one for each of them, as always.

"Oh yeah. I almost forgot about my little buddy."

Nule called out over the revving motor.

"Take us out, Mr. Norbinger."

"Yes, sir," responded a high voice.

The entrance ramp locked with a heavy clunk as the shuttle rose off the platform. They hovered for a moment, turned and then sped through the bay doors. Chipmunk laughter echoed inside the compartment as they shot into blackness. Tim clung to his chair, hoping he wouldn't pass out.

"Are you sure he should be flying? I mean, him being insane and all."

"Tweezor is our best pilot. Do not worry."

Tim pinched his eyes shut. "Did I say I was worried? Oh no, I'm not worried."

I'm way beyond that. I'm terrified.

The shuttle banked toward the hazy planet. Without hesitation, the midget slammed the shuttle through the atmosphere. They fell like a shining comet. Tim thought his stomach might come through the top of his head. Captain Nule and Commander Nim sat with closed eyes, as if they might take a peaceful nap. Tweezor howled the chorus to Free Falling by Tom Petty and the Heartbreakers.

Tim screamed all the way down. He was still screaming when the white-hot light out the window turned into violet sky.

"We arrived at a new here," the midget called out as the human opened bloodshot eyes.

The captain looked at their guest with an amused smile. Vulpa lowered her brow with annoyance. Tim realized his mouth was still open and snapped it shut. He felt cold sweat pouring down his face. His quantum assistant went to work and perspiration vanished.

Swirled white clouds looked strange against the amethyst sky, yet the beauty was overwhelming. The shuttle nosed down and the massive city of New Munsil came into view. Tim had never seen such structures. Each building was a unique architectural masterpiece. There were spiral columns and flowing archways, thick walls of stone and mirrored glass. Golden beams and statues ten stories high lined the busy streets. Shuttles, buses and single seat jetpods buzzed through on regular routes across the city. Timothy stared with amazement.

Tweezor held a position above the tallest skyscrapers until the dome of the Congress hall could be seen. He then dived into traffic for a swift approach and landing. They set down on a pad at ground level and the ramp extended onto hot pavement.

Tim realized how bright Ectopa Crin's two suns were when he stepped out onto the parking lot. His eyes stung in the harsh light and had to be shaded with his hands. He turned away from the glare and squinted toward the Congress Hall. It was a gigantic dome, the largest building he'd ever seen. Tall statues of Ectopal leaders stood along the sidewalk and entryway. They'd been chiseled from green marbled stone and each held impressive detail. Large groups of locals made their way down sidewalks, talking and laughing. The Ectopal people had fair complexions and most wore flowing, colorful robes. One individual had a creature on a leash that looked very much like a dog, except that it had six legs. He saw a young couple sitting on a bench holding hands. Tim was surprised how utterly human they all seemed. He missed home.

He looked back toward the shuttle and saw that Tweezor wore a pair of oversized star shaped sunglasses. The little man offered him a pair coated in reflective glitter with red lenses.
"Protect eyes!" he said with a goofy smile.
"No thanks man," Tim said pushing them away, "I'll be fine."

13

They entered the hall of Consolidation Congress. The room was enormous with seating for eighty thousand delegates, if needed. There would be nowhere near that many today. With such a short notice, the current gathering would be under a thousand.

The ceiling was fifty stories high with massive escalators lining the outside walls. Also, glass lifts zipped up and down carrying admirals, captains and diplomats to higher platforms. The main floor was alive with intelligent species from all over the Multiverse. Hundreds of little metal orbs floated above the crowd. Every now and then, two quantum assistants would knock together making a loud clang.

Most attendees were humanoid in shape, but there were some whose evolutions took entirely different paths. Timothy was amazed at the utter diversity of the alien group. It was unfathomable that beings from so many planets would ever meet each other in the first place, let alone have a single government rule over them all.

His eyes scanned the bizarre, yet official looking room. There was a tall throne at the far end, in the center of a marble platform. There was no one seated in it, although a group of dignitaries stood talking all around. No one was seated anywhere. They all stood talking and debating and some even yelled at one another. The noise level reminded him of a football game he'd gone to with his dad. The Broncos beat the Raiders, 21 to 10. Tim bought a bobblehead figurine of the quarterback. It sat on a shelf in his bedroom.

Captain Nule and Vulpa were a few paces ahead in the crowd, shaking hands with ambassadors from Crichits. Tim's eyes found a slug-like, brown creature.

"What is *that*?" he said out loud.

"There are no whats in attendance today. Only whos," a female voice said, as a matter of fact.

She was standing right beside Tim. He looked over. It was her, Sparrim Gale, the Ectopal commander he'd seen on the screen, the one that looked like his favorite actress.

He stared at her with gaping mouth amazement. She looked just like Allie Kincade, except maybe the pale yellow tint to her skin. That, and the fact that her hair was actually thin black tentacles growing from her scalp.

His eyes journeyed down the curve of her hip. She wore a tight leather jumpsuit. It was bright red with black leafy designs down the legs. Tim couldn't pull his eyes away.

"What are you looking at?" the commander asked with annoyance.

"I'm sorry?"

She cleared her throat and frowned at him, "I said--"

"I'm really sorry for staring. You just look like someone from…uh, my planet."

Her frown didn't change. It sounded like a line to her, and a bad one at that.

He dug into his pocket, pulled out the wrinkled picture and unfolded it.

"See? You look just like each other. Don't you think?"

Sparrim squinted, examining the photograph. She looked at Tim.

"She has *fur* on her head."

He ran the palm of his hand over his scalp, "Yeah. We call it hair."

She reached up, touched his hair and then pulled on it.

"Ouch!"

She smiled, "Interesting."

Tim rubbed his sore head and looked down at the photo.

Sparrim said, "She does look very much like me. Who is she?"

"She's an actress, um…on Earth."

"How do you know her? Is she your sister?"

"No."

"Your wife?"

"No, no. I don't know her at all. I've never even met her."

She gave him a puzzled look, "Then why do you carry her picture?"

Tim tried to think of an explanation that she would understand. He couldn't explain the feeling he got from watching her latest film, Spring Break. The image of her in a small bikini still danced in his head.

Wow, that was entertainment.

He couldn't put into words what her smile did to him. It just wasn't possible.

What he decided to say was, "I'm a fan of hers."

"A fan?"

"Yeah. I've seen all her films. You know, a *fan*."

Sparrim crossed her arms and stepped back, "You are infatuated with someone you don't know because she is recorded on film pretending to be others you don't know?"

Tim was embarrassed, "Well, when you put it *that* way-"

"What other way is there?"

"I don't know."

He folded the picture and slid it back into his pocket.

She looked out over the crowd.

"You seem to be very smitten with appearances. Perhaps it would be best if you kept your mouth shut at today's meeting. I'd hate to see you get killed."

She walked away and did not look back. When she caught up with her crewmates from the Redeemer, she smiled and took a seat.

Tim wiped at beads of sweat across his brow.

That couldn't have gone any worse.

He looked around for Vulpa, Tweezor and Nule. They waited for him down front.

Vulpa frowned, "So I see you have met your fantasy's look alike."

Tim shrugged, "Yeah. She thinks I'm a shallow creep."

She paused and then, "Yes. That's accurate."

A loud gong indicated that everyone should take his or her seats. The crowd filed down the central stairs and sat down. A whispery hush hung in the air, and then complete silence.

Tim scanned the stage area. He saw that the large slug creature he'd referred to as a 'what' sat on the throne. The slimy creature clapped a flat piece of round wood on the arm of his chair. It made a heavy rapping that echoed throughout the hall.

"Order," he announced, "Order and silence. Let this gathering of the Consolidation of Organized Systems begin. Captain Nule, bring forth the sequence carrier."

The Captain whispered, "Let's go Timothy. Follow me."

"What? We have to go up there?"

"Yes. Move."

He followed the Deemadozian up the ramp and to the center of the stage. Quiet chatter broke out across the audience. Cold sweat formed on the human's skin. He could feel the crowd studying him, judging him.

"Silence and order. *Now,*" the slug-like president ordered.

The talking ceased.

Sparrim Gale covered her mouth with slim fingers. "It's him? *He's* the carrier?"

The woman sitting beside her said, "Is that fur on his head?"

Up on stage, Tim stood, feeling a brick expand in his stomach. All eyes were on him and the muscles in his legs went elastic. He was desperate not to embarrass himself in front of Sparrim. It was the only thing keeping him standing.

The president spoke again, "The order is, how do we get this being across Meem occupied space to reset the Multiverse Generator?"

A dignitary stood, "We simply Transwave to the sector. There is no other choice."

Yelling broke out.

Another alien stood, "We cannot use Wavetime. The Meem home in on the signal somehow. Three cruiser class ships have been destroyed trying to pass through the system at Wave. We cannot outrun them."

More talking.

"The order is silence!"

Another angered voice, "Entering the system at any speed is suicide!"

A general from Recta, "The Meem armada will destroy all ships using Wave technology. It cannot be an option. We will not allow it."

The president, "The Order agrees. The delivery ship shall not use Transwave engines. Next."

Commander Sparrim Gale, "The Ectopal ships in our fleet have been fitted with experimental ion shielding. Our analysis shows that it could be effective against the Meem weapons."

More yelling and chatter.

A captain trio from Crichets, "The technology you speak of has not been properly tested. We cannot depend on it for this mission."

The president said, "The Order agrees. Experimental technologies are not to be used. Next."

Commander Gale, "We do not ask that you depend solely on the ion shields. We only ask to escort the delivery ship, as a possible protection in the event of attack."

A dignitary complained, "Your people do not even have Wavetime technology. Your science is inferior to many species in attendance here today. You should leave the problem to the *intelligent* races."

A sea of voices filled the chamber.

"Order and silence!"

Tim stepped up, "Uh, can I say something?"

The hall fell silent.

"Okay, uh, the way I see it, you people should be more open minded and less rude. The commander is a member of the Consolidation, same as any of you. She deserves your respect."

As he spoke he felt a tightness develop in his throat. His hands were like ice.

A rumble of alien chatter filled the chamber.

"Silence and order! Now!"

Tim continued, "The experimental shields sound like a good plan to me. I think it could work. And what's wrong with the ship tagging along? Would it really hurt anything?"

The president said, "The order is agreed. Unless a better plan is devised, the Ectopal vessel Redeemer shall escort."

Loud arguments from the entire congress shook the auditorium.

A captain from Robol Prime suggested, "What if our fleet acted as a decoy while the delivery ship crossed the fire zone?"

Another captain, "Yes, that could work. We could Wave in and out of the system. Keep the Meem busy."

"That's suicide!"

"They are too strong!"

"No! Not suicide! Wave in! Wave out!"

Loud discussion and arguing went on for more than an hour. The president's gavel banged throughout as he tried to keep order. After much deliberation, it was decided that the decoy strategy was the only plan with a slim chance of success.

The president said, "Admiral Feen, the order is you shall organize the decoy mission. We have little time. You will minimize causalities."

Feen answered, "Yes, Mister President. Captains to the war chamber."

The slug president said, "I order this meeting adjourned."

Tim watched the attendees exited the hall.

Nule put a hand on his arm, "Go with Commander Vulpa. I must attend the captain's strategy meeting."

They made their way through the crowd of conversing aliens. Sparrim Gale approached them. She had a confused look on her Allie-like face.

"Why did you say that?"

Tim smiled at her, "Everyone should get the same respect."

"Thank you, but I meant about the shielding. You couldn't know anything about our technology."

"Oh right, that. I guess I figured you looked pretty smart, and uh--"

"There you go with those appearances again."

"Yeah, but don't you ever just get a feeling about somebody?"

"Not really, no. But nonetheless, I am giving this to you."

She held out her hand. On her palm sat a holograph projector the size of a quarter. The image that floated above it was a three-dimensional photograph of herself. It had a greenish tint to the projection and was a very nice image of her face, smiling.

"I want you to have this because we have met. I would like you to discard the photo of the female you do not know. You shouldn't have it."

Tim was excited and confused, "Why?"

"Because she did not give it to you. She doesn't know you have it. It is wrong."

Sparrim pushed a small button on the device and the picture disappeared with a snap. She then placed it in Tim's hand.

He closed his fist and said, "Thank you."

"Now empty your pockets," she told him.

"What? Right now?"

"Yes. Now."

He dug deep and pulled out the folded paper. She snapped it out if his hand, turned and walked away.

"Wait. Um, thank you." he said again.

"You already said that."

"Well I know, but I wanted to say goodbye."

"Then why did you not say that?"

"Sorry. Bye."

"Goodbye."

Tweezor pulled him down to eye level. Tim had forgotten the little man was next to him.

"I think she like you, big boy," he said with a grin.

Tim watched Sparrim walk away.

"Really? You think so?"

"Yes. Yes I do," the midget said, puckering his lips.

Tim crinkled his nose, "Gross, dude."

Nule was finished with the Captain's meeting a short while later. He joined Tim, Tweezor and Vulpa who waited at the back of the hall.

The Truthseeker crew walked the long hallways from Consolidation Congress back to the parking lot. Tim's mind stayed with Sparrim Gale. He still couldn't believe she looked so much like Allie Kincade. The resemblance was unbelievable. It was as if they were twins, separated at birth and taken to different solar systems. Of course, they weren't related. They were two completely different species.

He ran his hand over the small hard lump in his blue jean pocket. The holograph projector was still there. He couldn't wait to look at it again. He couldn't wait to see her again. Grinning, he imagined her smiling just for him.

"What are you doing?" Vulpa asked with a grimace.

"What?" he said with red cheeks.

She glared, "You are becoming infatuated with her. I can see it in your face. I do not recommend--"

"What, me? Infatuated? No way. You're imagining things."

"Am I? It looked like you were doing all the imagining."

"I'll admit that I like her, but--"

"Commander Nim is correct, " the captain interrupted, "Our mission is of the utmost importance. You must put everything else out of your mind. Our mission is the only thing that matters."

He was right, obviously. If they failed, everything was lost. All their universes, all their home worlds. Everything. Tim could dream about puppy love later. It was time to focus on the task at hand.

They exchanged no more words on their path to the shuttle. The ride through the atmosphere and back to the Truthseeker was spent in silence also.

When they arrived Captain Nule called a meeting in his chamber. All of the command crew attended, as did Timothy. The journey in which they would embark was gone over in detail. A large map illuminated behind Nule's desk. It showed the entire multi-system sector they would be traveling across.

As Tim listened he began to realize what the crew already knew. Their travel would be hard and treacherous. Without the use of Transwave speed, they'd be fortunate to get to the generator at all.

From their current position on Ectopa Crin, they would travel straight to Scorrinwall Military Base at Ebteon. It would take three days and they would pass through Timeshift Tunnel on the third day, just before reaching the planet. They couldn't afford taking the time to go around the tunnel. Once at Scorrinwall, they would be safe, if only temporarily.

The ion particle cannons located at the military bases were the only weapons that had provided any effectiveness against the Meem onslaught. The invasion fleet had therefore stayed clear of planets with such weapons.

From Ebteon they would pass by the Asteroid Sea and on to Choxide Mote, the fortress at Choxide. It would be an estimated four-day trip from base to base.

From there they would be entering Meem occupied space, passing by the Triptic Vortex and on to the Stinzotaun Axis, at Zotaun. That last leg of the journey was expected to be the most dangerous.

Admiral Feen would lead a decoy mission intended to distract the enemy. Consolidation cruisers from across the fleet would Transwave through the system in an effort to lure the Meem away from the delivery ship. The volunteer decoys were fully aware that it was a suicide mission. They did not expect to return. Axis scouts reported new Meem Warbirds almost hourly.

The Truthseeker would pass by the Consolidation ships and pursuing Warbirds, to the Stinzotaun Axis. The particle cannon would provide cover for them only when they got close to the base.

Beyond that, the entrance to Verse One and the Multiverse Generator sat just past the far side of the planet. That was their destination. There they would enter Tim's DNA information and everything would be fine, hopefully. That's if they made it, if they got that far.

Everyone in the meeting knew that the Meem would likely intercept the ship before it reached Verse One. They had all heard about the terrible demise of the Phazon Twelve. They'd be passing through that sector, the place where the late Captain Fint met his end.

Some officers worried about passing so close by the asteroid sea. Some were very concerned with the Triptic Vortex. One officer voiced his opinions about the Ectopal escort and their inferior culture and technologies. Tim bit his lip.

Captain Nule addressed each question and concern. He told them that failure was not an option. He said they must find a way, at all costs. Everything depended on the crew of the Truthseeker and her mission. As the commanders filed out of Nule's office they seemed solemn in their duties and professional, yet an unvoiced fear went with them.

Vulpa leaned close to her captain, "They are afraid. Afraid of failing. Afraid of dying."

"Yes," he snapped back, "They should be."

His eyes followed the dotted line on the map.

"If we fail it will not be the fault of my officers. I have the utmost faith in them and their loyalty."

Vulpa gave him a serious smile, "Yes sir. They are a good crew. They will follow any order without question or hesitation, as will I."

"Thank you, Vulpa," he said in a whisper.

She turned, walked past Timothy and out the door.

"Was there something you needed?" the captain asked the human.

"What are the odds that we will, you know, be alive after all of this?"

"The odds?" Nule clenched sharp teeth, "I am a battle cruiser captain, not a gambler. I do not operate by percentages. The odds do not concern me."

Tim could tell his question was considered ridiculous. He felt stupid.

"Sorry, I didn't mean to--"

"Do not apologize. Just know that what needs to be done does not rely on luck or random chance. It relies on individuals. And I can assure you that every individual on this vessel will do their duty."

Tim hoped he hadn't offended Nule. He walked out to the bridge and sat down on the couch. Staring into the frontal viewer, he saw distant stars in the eternal midnight of space. He lay back on the cushions, thinking about Earth. He wondered if he'd ever see his distant home again.

14

Three days travel aboard the space ship went slow for Timothy. He spent most of the time studying at the gym and gazing into the holograph of Sparrim Gale. He got to know *Liquid and solid fuel mixtures* as well as Sparrim's friendly smile.

On the third day he could quote entire paragraphs from his Jetpack manual.

Sergeant Orts, satisfied and surprised with the human's advancement, allowed him to move on to a chapter titled *Propulsion Dynamics*.

The human also spent a good deal of time talking to the little space man. Although Tweezor was odd to say the least, Tim decided that he liked him. The high-pitched humming and singing was always good for calming his nerves. Also, the alien was free with information and happy to answer questions. And Tim had lots of questions.

"So," Tim said, "I don't understand this whole hidden verse thing."
Tweezor, "What no understand?"
"I just don't get it."
"When Multiverse Generator turned on, there was excess of power. The extra caused creation of hidden verses…*Shadow* verses."
The short man grinned, watching the human's face. Tim still looked confused.
"You said Earth was a shadow of another planet, right?"
"Yes. The planet Sellic, in Verse Ten-Twenty-Eight. Verse Three-Three-Two is near duplicate of Ten-Twenty-Eight. Very few differences."
"What kind of differences?"
The midget brought up a picture of Sellic on his screen.
"Earth has one moon. Sellic has two. Otherwise, they have same size, same atmosphere, same surrounding planets, same sun. Almost identical."
"An extra moon is a pretty big difference, man."
With a click, the image of the planet disappeared from Tweezor's screen.
"I guess so," he said shrugging his shoulders.

15

Tim sat studying in an otherwise empty classroom. The glow of the computer screen was the only light source, reflecting off his face in a green glow. He'd surprised even himself in the past few days. He was actually beginning to understand *spacetime mechanics and gravitational facts,* another chapter the sergeant had assigned to him.

A click of the overhead light startled him. Turning, he saw Orts standing at the door.

"Why do you study in the dark?" the E-Triptic asked.

"I like it dark. It helps me focus."

The sergeant walked closer.

"You did well on your first test. You are not as ignorant as I was led to believe."

"Thanks, I guess."

"So," Orts said turning to the door, "follow me."

Timothy stood up, "Where?"

Orts didn't answer. He walked into the shadowed gymnasium. Curious, the human followed. They arrived at the Jetpack simulator and the soldier powered it up as Tim watched. Two large motors vibrated up to speed as humming decibels increased. With the door to the rounded compartment open, he motioned for the human to step inside.

Tim asked, "What's going on?"

Abrupt and emotionless, the answer was, "It is time for simulator training."

Tim went tingly with anticipation.

"Awesome," he said ducking through the door.

It was cool and dark inside. He peered at the rounded metal walls as he was harnessed in.

"Power your pack and then punch in the command for quantum retrieval."

Tim followed instructions by turning a toggle switch and then tapping in 1-8-B-6-ENTER on his chest plate keypad. The quantum assistant flashing above zipped down to the top of the pack behind his head and locked into place.

"Verify fuel readings," was the next command.

With the solid fuel gage showing full, a thumbs up was given.

"Okay," Orts said, "begin standard gravity, surface program twenty-five."

The inside of the machine went bright white for a moment and then faded into blue sky and mountains. The soldier shut the door, leaving Timothy alone on top of a tall summit.

"Oh my god," he said looking over the flawless realism.

Cool mountain air chilled his face as he took hold of the Jetpack control arms.

A voice above him, "It's all yours, now. Show me what you've got."

A chime indicated a training session start.

Timothy fell into a deep, jagged chasm. Simulated air whipped upward.

He plummeted into a shadowy canyon screaming, "Whoa!"

He fired the main thrusters and arched into an upward turn, his head pointing at the sky. He spiraled in a starboard rotation, ripping out of the shadows and into warm sunshine.

"Sweet!" he yelled, laughing.

Timothy flew over the canyon for twenty minutes. The sensation of freedom was amazing. He never wanted it to end, but alas, his time expired quickly.

Tim climbed out of the simulator. Sergeant Orts stood waiting in the small gymnasium.

"Nice job, Sequence Carrier. You handled yourself much better than I expected."

"Really?" Tim said, beaming with pride, "You think so?"

"Yes. You need to keep a closer eye on the solid fuel compartment, but nice job. You are a natural...Are you positive you've never piloted a Jetpack before?"

A natural. Sweet.

"Yeah, I'm positive. I've spent a lot of time playing *Radioactive Space Commando* on my Nintendo, though. I even got to the end on the *pound me like a little girl* setting. That's a difficulty level of ten."

Orts stared at the human, not quite knowing how to respond.

"So um... The commando thing is a, uh..."

Tim smiled, "A video game."

"Yes, well...it must've been good experience, this video training you received."

"Game," Tim said, "And yeah. I saved a whole planet of green chicks from the evil Nuclear Splat monster. It was awesome."

"Right," Orts said, wondering what 'pound me like a little girl' meant.

16

Tim sat daydreaming about flying over the shadowy canyon. "Spacedock complete, Captain," Commander Nim announced. Nule approached Timothy.

"Let's go purchase some bugs, my friend."

"Bugs? What do we need bugs for?"

The captain said, "I'll explain on the way."

Tim followed down the corridor as Nule spoke.

"You see, Timothy," he began, "The Multiverse is complex, yet most of its rules are very simple. A force known as spacetime governs our reality and it remains the same almost anywhere you go."

He watched Tim's face to find an indication that he understood. He saw a blank stare and continued anyway.

"Time moves along at a usual pace into the future, making us all a bit older each day."

"Uh huh," the human said to show he was listening.

"Sometimes unseen forces cause spacetime to bend or warp or what have you. For example, gravity is a major cause of bent space and therefore, bent time."

"You can bend time?"

"Absolutely. You can bend it, stretch it, twist it, or push it backwards. You must think of spacetime as a solid that can be touched and manipulated, because basically, that's what it is."

"Okee-dokey," Tim said with a scrunched brow.

"Now when spacetime is bent, lots of odd things can happen. Things can slow down or stop altogether. Things can speed up or shoot forward to any point in the future. Time can run backwards and the past could become the present." He smiled, "That's why we need bugs."

"I don't get it."

"Of course you don't," Nule laughed, "I haven't finished yet."

Nule clicked on a small holograph screen in the palm of his hand. To Tim's disappointment, it was not a picture of Sparrim Gale. It was a representation of a spiral shifting haze, a stretched corkscrew of energy.

"This," the captain said, "is Timeshift Tunnel."

They arrived at the space dock doors at the end of the corridor. With a key code punched in, the doors slid open to reveal the inside of a station the Truthseeker had docked with. Captain Nule led Tim inside, clicking off the holograph.

"Wait," Tim said, "Can I see that again?"

"Sure you can," Nule said as he walked around the corner.

Tim looked up at the awesome sight in front of them.

The entire far wall was glass, from floor to twenty-foot high ceiling. Just beyond that was the giant shifting vortex, a storm cloud of brilliant sparkling yellow. It churned round and round and looked close enough to jump into from where they stood.

"*My god*," the human whispered.

"This is a multi-versal tear in the cosmic fabric, fueled by a black hole at one end and an anti-gravitational wormhole at the other. Beautiful, isn't it?"

Tim couldn't pull his eyes away, "Yeah, beautiful."

"And quite deadly, I assure you. You see, breaks in the dimensions surrounding it bounce the energy inside, creating random shifts in perceptional time."

"Perceptional time?"

"Yes. Time perceived by living things."

"As opposed to what?"

"Think of it this way. If you entered the tunnel unprotected, time might jump forward, but not beyond your lifetime. It couldn't travel beyond your death. It also couldn't go back any further than your birth. Your personal existence would be the boundary it had to operate in. That is why it's called perceptional time."

Tim thought he was beginning to understand. "Okay," he said with a nod.

"Now, if we were to enter with plasma shields raised, the tunnel would be forced to see everyone aboard as one entity. Therefore, its boundary would be the shortest life span in each direction, past and future. It could not take us beyond the youngest individual's birth and it couldn't exceed the nearest death. Do you follow?"

"Sort of," Tim said with a puzzled stare, "Keep going."

"So, that is why we need bugs. And not just any old bugs will do. We need bugs that are self aware."

"Huh?"

"Most insects run on pure instinct. They have no consciousness. But some bugs, like Chinozian Mica-Mites for example, are aware. They know they're alive."

"Which means what?"

"Which means the tunnel will see them as living entities, and since their life span is only about one minute, just long enough to lay one egg and die, the Timeshift for us will be about one minute. Understand now?"

"So after we buy a mite we'll have to enter the tunnel in under a minute, before it dies?"

"Actually, no. We'll be purchasing an entire breeding colony."

Nule walked to a large counter, where a fat, leathery alien was standing.

The salesman leaned forward, "Hello! Welcome to Space Station Fleeting Insect Roundup! How may I help you fellas?"

"We wish to purchase a class M colony of Chinozian Mica-Mites."

"Sure!" the excited salesman exclaimed, "We've got some fine Mites over here."

His hands reached under the counter and then reappeared with a glass container about the shape and size of a mason jar. There were numerous digital readouts around the top and bottom and the inside looked like sticky honeycomb material. The Captain took the jar in hand, checked a few readouts and set it back on the counter.

"Don't try to pawn your trash on me."

The salesman got serious, "Whatever do you mean? This is top quality."

"Do not insult me, sir. I am not some dense trucker from Deldis Pryn. I am the Captain of a Consolidation starship. I expect to be treated as such."

"But--"

Nule leaned in close, "I could pull your license and have this whole station shut down faster than you can say *broken atmosphere conditioner.*"

The leathery skin seemed to pinch together as the salesman's lips pursed.

"Sorry sir," he forced out, "I'm afraid this one's not for sale. The container's damaged." He shrugged fat shoulders and grinned, "I accidentally dropped it in the back room."

He set it aside, pulled out another jar and slid it across the counter. "I think you'll find this one in order. And we're having a sale today. Only fifteen thousand."

Nule frowned, "Your advertisement said ten."

"That's what I meant. Ten. It's all yours for ten."

Nule looked it over with sharp eyes.

When satisfied he said, "I'll give you eight."

"Okay," the nervous salesman forced out, "Whatever you think is fair."

The Captain handed the jar to Timothy and finished the transaction. Tim strained to see movement inside, but couldn't see anything. The dark honeycomb appeared empty and lifeless.

The twenty billion microscopic mites inside the jar couldn't see Timothy either.

17

"Spacedock separation complete," Commander Nim said watching the screen in front of her.

"Take us out two hundred pex, rotate port one-sixty," Nule instructed.

"Yes, sir."

The Truthseeker backed away from space station Fleeting, turning to face the escort ship. Tim watched the front screen as the Redeemer came into view. A small window popped onto the side of the screen. It was a grainy image of Sparrim Gale's face.

"Captain Nule," she said without emotion, "we are sending flight path information to you now."

Nule watched his readout and then, "Thank you Commander Gale. Will you be needing anything from Fleeting?"

"No, Captain. We have an excellent onboard laboratory stocked with insects. If we'd have thought of it, we could've loaned you some Red Mist Bacteria. They have many of the same qualities as Mica-Mites."

"Thank you Commander, but I like to support local economies whenever possible, let them know the Consolidation cares and all that."

"Right. In any event, we'll lead the way into the tunnel and we would suggest a standard Omega flanking, unless you're more comfortable with something else."

"Omega puts us in pretty tight. Any particular reason you want to keep us so close?"

Sparrim cleared her throat, "The close proximity allows minimal drift, in the event of an emergency. Don't you agree?"

"Yes, I do. But, it also creates a higher danger of collision. Let's keep it wide."

Sparrim sounded agitated, "That will do. We'll make the adjustments."

Tim watched the screen as she turned to face the officer behind her. "Re-configure to Omega wide. Tractor beam and sensors."

After a moment the small video window disappeared, leaving the larger image of the Redeemer cruiser alone on the viewer. Tim watched as the camera turned toward the spiraling vortex of brilliant yellow. The tunnel churned round and round with random strobe flashes popping inside its hazy interior. His stomach tightened and his heartbeat increased.

Vulpa Nim's voice sounded behind him, "The Redeemer's scans are complete and she is ready on our mark."

Nule checked his screen, "Navigator, we are at Omega wide, correct?"

"Yes, Captain. We have a green light."

"Well then," Nule said smiling at Timothy, "Call the mark and let's get going."

The human forced a return smile as the quantum assistant above him multi-tasked. It had become a full time job, emptying his bladder, removing sweat from his skin and excess acid from his stomach. He was quite the ball of nerves.

"And...*mark*," Vulpa called out.

With that, the Ectopal escort ship turned and entered the shifting yellow cloud. After a moment the vessel disappeared inside.

Nule put a long fingered hand on Timothy's shoulder. "For the next couple of hours you are going to experience some very odd things. Do not be afraid. It's all perfectly safe."

Tweezor walked onto the bridge just as the Truthseeker entered the outer haze. He smiled up at Timothy and let out a chittery laugh.

"Welcome to Timeshift Tunnel!" he exclaimed, throwing his pudgy arms into the air. Tim glanced up to the frontal viewer and back down at-- Tweezor was gone. Vanished into thin air. Tim jumped. His heart leapt as he almost fell down.

What was—

Tweezor walked onto the bridge just as the Truthseeker entered the outer haze.

What was—

Timothy jumped. His heart leapt as he almost fell down.

"Timothy? You okay dude?"

"--okay dude?"

"--okay dude?"

"You okay-- "

Tweezor walked onto the bridge just as the ship...

Oh god, what's happening to me?

Oh god, oh—

What's happening to me?

Chittery laughter.

"Welcome to Timeshift Tunnel!"

18

The Meem scout ship hovered, monitoring and scanning the cloud. Due to the interference inside, the scans would only be accurate to about fifty pex. Beyond that, the bouncing dimensional rifts were unreadable. Naturally, that's why he was there.

The Meem occupation had expanded to Choxide and was nearing the Asteroid Sea. Soon the entire sector would be under their control. Timeshift Tunnel was the only weak link in fortifying the area. It cut through the sector like a mammoth snake, stretching from the black hole at Piplen Rio all the way to the wormhole at Deldis Pryn. The Meem couldn't have ships traveling about undetected under the Tunnel's spiraling protection. That would not do at all.

A pair of side bay ports on each dark wing slid open. Two by two and five seconds apart, mines shot into the vortex. Internal positioning computers instructed each one to its individual place in the tunnel. Once the scout ship was finished with that area, its job would be complete. Timeshift Tunnel had been loaded with five-gigaton perimeter charges every thousand pex.

Not even the luckiest captain in the fleet could get through without hitting at least one. The churning snake had just acquired a deadly bite.

19

Tweezor's laughter seemed to go on and on. It echoed and stretched, stuttered backward and forward, changed speeds and overlapped in a bizarre chorus. He was like a herd of midgets, a flock of redundant chipmunks, a gaggle of waist-high voices. Then, just when Timothy thought he could take absolutely no more, it really got strange.

Tweezor paused, holding up both hands like stop signs. "Wait, wait. Check this out."
"Wait, wait."
"--this out."
"--this out."
He cleared his throat, which hiccupped twice in the time stream, and then…He broke into a chorus of *Row your boat*.
"Row, row, row your boat, gently down the stream…"
"stream…"
"Row, row,"
"Row"
"Stream"
"Merrily, merrily"
"Row row"
"Stream"
"Merrily-"
"-row-"
"-gently-"
"-your-"

"-stream.."

Timothy was getting a headache.

And then he wasn't.

Headache.

I need to sit-sit-need-n-need t- to- need-sit d-ddddown.

"Merrily,"

"-merrily-"

"-mer-"

"-merri-"

"-d-down-"

"-stream…"

Two hours of this- two hours of th-- hours of this crap? I'll g-g-g- go insane.

-sane

-ane

-go-go.

"Check th-- this ouuuuut…"

"Strea--"

This sucks.

This--

Th--

-this crap?

"Life is but a dream…"

--sucks.

20

Sparrim Gale sat at the navigation center- stood at the weapons contr- sat- navagation center, watching the screen. The lights dimmed as the alarm went--

Silence.

A flashing dot appeared on the perimeter screen.

-screen. An explosion behind them. The Truthseeker had been hit with-

A low chime accompanied the flashing dot.

-some type of small ship?

No. Oh God it's a-

Is that some type of-

-it's a-

She checked the readout on the screen at her station. Static.

"Commanger Gale, I'm reading a faint-"

Is that some type of small ship? No.

The ensign looked up from her console in a panic.

"Commander, I'm reading a faint signal, sixty pex starboard. It is hard to read, but-"

Small ship? No. Oh god.

"Commander, the Truthseeker's been hit!"

god

ship? No.

"-explosion!"

Oh god. It's a bomb.

21

"Truthseeker, do you copy? Change course to-"

"-do you copy?"

"-thermal grid mine."

"We've detected a therm-"

"...copy?"

Static.

Nule looked up at the screen. Nothing. Just the usual energy fluctuations, but any good pilot knew you couldn't trust scans here. Not in Timeshift Tunnel.

"Full stop," Nule commanded, "-stop."

The Truthseeker jarred backward. Timothy fell to the floor.

"-stop."

    Before the navigation officer could respond, the starboard plasma shield washed over the thermal mine, nudging it.

"Do you copy?"

It tumbled end over end for a moment, scanning the nature of the shield. The millisecond it was identified as quadraphasal-condensed plasma, it detonated. The explosion blasted over the ship's hull, sending her into a spin. Tweezor fell on top of Tim.

"Sheilds down to sixteen percent, Captain."

"Shields down to-"

-Tweezor fell-

"Navigation is offline captain."

"We're in a shockwave rotation!"

Nule shouted to the engineers, "Get navigation back!"
EM, EL and BE worked to re-route control to a different station.
"Ten seconds to impact with next thermal," Vulpa announced.
Next thermal? Tim thought.
"The shields-"
"Ten seconds to-"
"-shields-"
"-won't take another hit like the last one."

The container of Mica-Mites slid across Nule's desk. The bottom hit a thick folder, tipping the jar onto its side. It rolled across to a large book, spun and then fell to the hard floor. The impact did not break the glass. It bounced and then shot out the open door, onto the bridge.
"Twenty seconds to thermal detonation."
The Truthseeker quaked and spun toward the mine.

22
"Have you got her?"

23
Even with the lightning speed of the Critchet's brains and hands it would take longer than twenty seconds to re-route. It seemed they were left with only an explosion and destiny, and no time for contemplation.

24
"Have you got her?"
"No, Commander. Not-"

25
Nule watched the aft monitor as they fell at the grid mine. It sat spinning, waiting to fulfill its purpose. To breach the hull of a starship and send it careening into another mine. To kill the beings inside, eliminating the threat to the Meem fleet.

26
"-got her?"
"No, Commander. Not yet."

Sparrim adjusted the frequency detection on her panel. The time shift interference made it almost impossible to lock onto the signal.

And then a lull in the flux began. It was a dead spot between the ships, a calm stillness in the center of the storm. It lasted for seven glorious seconds and seemed to be a gift from the gods. "The time shift stopped, Commander," Reena said with shock on her face.

"Signal lock! Initiate beam!"

With a bright flash of white particles, the Ectopal ship grabbed hold of the Truthseeker with a tractor beam. It's momentum ripped at Sparrim Gale and her crewmates. With a stutter, both ships came to a stop.

27

It bounced and then shot out the open door, onto the bridge.

"Twenty seconds to thermal detonation," Vulpa announced.

The jar of Mica-Mites did a quick spin in front of the doorway. Three feet away Tweezor tripped and fell onto Timothy, who was already on the floor. With a loud crash, the slick surface tipped upward. The human and the alien midget slid feet first across the bridge.

The glass jar containing twenty billion microscopic insects went tumbling right after them.

28

"Get navigation back!"

The space cruiser Truthseeker was in a shockwave rotation, caused by a thermal grid mine explosion. Shields were down to sixteen percent and wouldn't withstand another similar blow. They headed uncontrollably toward the next mine and would reach it in twenty seconds.

The trio of Critchet engineers worked to re-route, although time would run out before they could finish. They were aware of the imminent impact and continued to work regardless. Commander Geesh had finished calculating the impact area and was evacuating that section of the ship.

"Evac all lower green levels and yellow, fourteen through thirty-one! Get to your pressure doors immediately!"

His brown and black fur shook as he spoke into the microphone. Huge molars clacked together as he got excited. A thick tongue slathered about, from cheek to cheek.

Vulpa remained calm and professional, as always, with no surface emotion whatsoever. Even when the ship quaked and tilted, knocking officers to the floor, she simply braced herself upright against the side of her station and continued working.

Gorza Nule held tight to the Captain's chair, oblivious to the human, midget and insect jar sliding and bouncing across his field of vision.

When the tractor beam engaged, the ship tipped the other direction. The jar hit the top of Tim's skull.

"AAHH!" he yelled as he and Tweezor slid past the Captain again. They then slid head first at the weapons station. The Mica-Mite jar had bounced over them and followed again, end over end. Tim pressed the souls of his shoes down and they made a loud squeak. He and the midget stopped just shy of hitting the station supports. The Mites bounced up, spun in the air and came down hard on Tim's crotch. His scream was shrill as he lifted his feet off the floor.

"I got bugs!" Tweezor heroically stated, raising the container into the air.

Tim cupped his hands over the stabbing pain in his crotch as his head hit the wall.

"They've got us in a tractor lock", Vulpa said.

"Thank you Commander Nim," Nule responded trying to calm his shaking hands. He clasped long fingers, looking up at the frontal screen, "Thank you Redeemer."

Geesh noticed power levels rising on his readout.

"Sir, the tractor is causing an overload in the sub-system matrix."

Nule called to the ship that had just saved them, "Loosen your grip, Redeemer. We are showing a system overload."

No response.

Geesh clacked his molars, "Environment systems on all decks are failing! Tell them to let go!"

"Navigation is coming back online."

"Simulated gravity is going offline."

"Redeemer, release the tractor beam now!"

Electricity snapped over Commander Geesh's station.

"Ack!" he yelled, "I'm shutting it off."

With a click the oxygen generators began to wind down and temperature cells cooled. Geesh's fur got lighter and fluffier. Small tools slid off of workstations, floating in midair. Tweezor pushed off the floor and cartwheeled all the way to the ceiling. Tim was amazed, watching the floating little man. He looked over and saw the jar of mites drifting over the center of the room. *Oh no.*

He lunged for it and lifted off uncontrollably.

Captain Nule gripped his chair trying to keep himself in it. Vulpa watched it all trying not to stir herself into the air. The three Critchet engineers, still connected at the heads, hovered above their stations like a humanoid ceiling fan.

"Almost got it…" Tim said as he approached the jar.

"Environmental re-route complete," Geesh said. "Here goes."

With another click gravity reestablished itself. The jar of Mica-Mites that had been drifting at Timothy's outstretched fingers fell. So did everything and everyone else. There were sounds of crashing equipment. There were cries of pain. There was a loud suction pop and then breaking glass.

It wasn't the impact that killed all twenty billion Mica-Mites. It had been the sudden rush of poisonous oxygen.

29

"Signal lock! Initiate beam!"

With a bright flash of glowing particles the Ectopal ship grabbed hold of the Truthseeker with a tractor beam. It's momentum ripped at Sparrim and her crewmates.

With a stutter, both ships came to a stop.

"Keep hold of her, we don't want her drifting on us."

"Yes, Commander"

"Communications are offline, I'm running a diagnostic now."

God, what else could go wrong? Sparrim thought to herself.

She looked down into the static filled three-dimensional cube display. The only strong signals came from the Redeemer and the Truthseeker. The rest was unreadable.

"Narrow the infrared graph."

"We've tried that Commander, the scans are garbled."

Sparrim said, "Run it through the cube this time and let it filter automatically."

The officer was surprised, "We getting something, refining...Oh my god."

Little red dots appeared in the cube display. There were millions of them, one every thousand pex. Each one represented a five-gigaton proximity explosive. Timeshift Tunnel had become a giant minefield.

"Commander, communications are back online."

Muffled static and then, "Release the tractor beam now!"

Sparrim checked her screen.

"Captain Nule, I am reluctant to let you go just yet. I am sending you the information I just received. I think you'll find it disturbing."

A pause.

"There is no response commander...something's happening over there..."

A faint voice was heard.

"Almost got it..." sounded over the airwaves and then another, "Environmental re-route complete. Here goes."

Numerous crashes and shattering glass. And then a new set of voices began. They sounded different than the others. It almost sounded like –

Is that what I think it is?

Sparrim listened.

Laughter.

Oh my god. It is.

"What is it, Commander?"

"Isn't it obvious? It's children."

30

The shattered jar lay in thousands of pieces across the floor. The honeycomb-like residue had come apart also. It was in three large chunks strewn about the glass. All twenty billion Mites lay unseen and deceased over the clutter.

With their tiny guests no longer with them, the crew aboard the Truthseeker would travel in a much larger time stream. The next youngest being on the ship was Timothy. They'd gone from a one-minute to an eighteen-year window to the past. The future window distance was yet unknown. It would be impossible to know just yet when the soonest death would occur.

Timothy Rayburn looked around the noisy bridge with wide eyes. He realized that he had no idea where he was. There was a bright flashing light above him, accompanied by a very loud alarm. He didn't know what it was for, but he did know that he was afraid of it. It was scary and way too loud. The others didn't seem to like it either. Some cried, but not him. He was brave. He was five years-

-six-

-eighteen years-

-three years old.

-old.

There was a weird looking little man next to him on the floor. His wrinkles kept vanishing and reappearing. It was really creepy, but kind of funny too. The glass strewn across the slick surface was shiny.

Sparkly.

Alarm loud.

The noise was big.

Ears hurt.

He wiped at the tears in his eyes. Wiped at--.

What was that?

A voice above him, broken and static.

"Truthseeker, do you copy?"

I copy, thought little Timmy.

The red light above him continued to flash.

"Troofsicker," he said. "Troofsicker coo*pee*," Timmy repeated, staring into the pretty light.

He smiled excitedly, drooling.

31

"Keep hold of her. We don't want her drifting on us."

"Yes, Commander."

Sparrim listened.

"It's children."

"It looks like we overloaded their environmental systems with the tractor," sounded Commander Reena.

Another voice, "System back online, Commander. Gravity and temperature re-established."

Sparrim watched the forward viewer. The Truthseeker sat silent, surrounded by the particle glow of the tractor beam. She wondered what chaos might be ensuing inside.

"Captain Nule, do you copy? This is the Redeemer. What is your status? Can you respond?"

Laughter, chatter and crying. Sparrim sat back in her chair, closed her eyes for a moment trying to gather her thoughts and then...

"Alright, so be it." She stood up, looking over her command crew. "I am declaring this a class five emergency. As Commander of this vessel and authorized escort of the Consolidation ship Truthseeker, I am assuming temporary command of both ships."

She turned to Reena with a serious gaze.

Sparrim cleared her throat and continued, "Commander Reena, as current second of the Redeemer, if you agree, please indicate that you concur."

"I do, Commander Gale," she glanced down to her screen, "In accordance with section five, paragraph eight-two-three, I declare the ships yours."

Gale clenched her teeth and squeezed her hands into fists, "Alright then, lets get us outa here."

Thousands of mines illuminated in the holograph. Each one meant certain destruction for either ship. With the press of a switch the cube magnified, zooming in on their immediate location. Sparrim walked to the cube and squatted down to eye level with the Redeemer.

"We'll need to tunnel our way through. Weapons control, load a torpedo with twenty pounds of liquid Hydroburst for a remote detonation."

"Yes, Commander. Stand by."

Calculations would need to be precise if she wanted to take out four mines at a time. (And with a limited supply of Hydroburst fuel, even four at a time was pushing it.) Everyone on the Ectopal bridge worked to solve the same equation. The commander stood and walked back to her console. She began her own mathematical problem solving.

After a few moments an officer announced over the intercom, "Torpedo remote standing by, Commander."

The computer compared the mathematics at the individual stations and made a few final adjustments. A chime let them know it was finished and Sparrim Gale ordered the fire. It shimmered to its destination with a faint red light. They watched it on the screen, hoping that the ignited fuel would set off the four mines, clearing the way for them to move forward. The explosion was a small pop in the distance. The unspectacular display prompted an expansion of reddish radiation, reaching out to the surrounding perimeter charges. The first detonation illuminated the left side of the screen a moment before the others blew. The four mines set off as planned and the bright yellow-orange fire sent a slight shockwave into the ships.

"All targeted mines detonated, Commander."

Sparrim's satisfaction vanished as the computer picked up movement. An accompanying alarm sounded an automated battle station alert. She stared into the frontal screen. It was distant, but she could see it unmagnified as it picked up speed.

"Identify," she said, keeping her eyes on the screen.

"It's some type of scout vessel...scanning...identified Commander. It's a Meem ship."

"The middle of a mine field isn't my first choice for a battle," Sparrim said.

"Especially when we're towing another ship," the communications officer added. Sparrim clenched her teeth. The small vessel in the distance banked toward them.

"It's coming about!"

As the scout ship swooped into an attack route, Sparrim noticed something odd. A mine moved out of the ship's path until it was clear and then repositioned itself.

What?

"Did you see that? Did anyone else see that?" she asked scanning her screen.

"Yes, Commander. It seems the vessel is transmitting coordinate information to the mine positioning computers."

"Can you translate?"

"It's coded. It will take some time to crack it."

"Get started. Load up two more remote torpedoes."

The responding officer smiled, "Already loaded and standing by."

"Set one into the next grid path and one at incoming ship."

"Enemy systems are locked on. They're opening fire."

The commander braced herself, "Return plasma fire and launch torpedoes."

Two shining yellow pulses of concentrated plasma were away, along with two torpedoes. The Meem's offensive arrived first, blasting over the redeemer's hull shield in three consecutive detonations. The Redeemer was thrown on her side as lightning energy snapped over and across her skin. The command crew quaked and tried to hold steady. Sparrim looked up at her monitor and realized that the tractor beam had failed. They'd let go of the Truthseeker. It was free and drifting.

No.

Sparrim pulled back into her chair, "Re-establish tractor!"

"It's overloaded Commander. I'm attempting to re-boot."

The two yellow pulses impacted the enemy ship, enveloping it in flames. The following torpedo popped its radiation loose and three nearby mines exploded in succession. Some distance away, the second torpedo caused four mines to spend their destruction, clearing the path.

The Truthseeker drifted from its escort. In less than thirty seconds it would come in contact with the next mine. A hull breach was imminent. Even the reinforced Carbidd/Funkton could take only so much abuse.

"System coming back online...."

"Re-establish tractor, now!"

"Almost there..."

"Do you have it?"

"It's close..."

"Impact in ten seconds."

90

"Do you have it?"

Sweat beaded down his brow. His face was red.

"Manual lock on is tricky…"

"Do you – "

Oh God, please.

A loud chime.

"I got her," he gasped, "I got her."

The Truthseeker came to a stop six feet from the mine.

Sparrim's hands trembled, "Shorten the tractor beam by half. Let's pull her in."

The Truthseeker pulled away from the mine and closer to the Redeemer.

"Commander, the enemy ship's navigation thrusters are inoperable. It can't move."

"Can you identify the code yet?"

"Yes, commander. Would you like me to mimic it?" he asked, looking out at the sea of perimeter charges.

Sparrim paused for a moment, eyeing the crippled Meem ship. "Not just yet. Match the frequency and scramble the enemy signal."

He worked at the terminal punching in the command sequence. "Transmitting."

The garbled message overcame the airwaves and the information received by the mine computers was useless. After a few seconds the charges around the scout ship re-set back to default positions. One such charge's position was blocked by the ship. It knocked once on the hull before exploding. The Meem vessel vaporized in the heart of the five-gigaton blast.

A grin pulled at the corners of Sparrim's lips as her tension eased.

"Now," she took in a deep breath and exhaled, "you can mimic the transmission and get us out of this mess."

32

The Ectopal cruiser Redeemer emerged from the spiraling cloud. A particle tractor beam and another cruiser class ship followed it. The trailing vessel, the Truthseeker, had been in tow for more than two hours with no way to control its eighteen year, sixty-five day, and twenty-one hour time slip window.

Timothy Rayburn was exhausted. It was tiring, to say the least, moving about in time as they had. He was currently ten…four…fifteen…three years old and very grumpy.

The ship passed through the outer haze of Timeshift Tunnel and present time snapped back to the moment they entered the tunnel.

The earthling found himself to be eighteen years old again. The midget space man was twenty-eight and Captain Nule was again forty-five.

Timothy stood in the center of the bridge, rubbing his aching neck. Small piles of material lay strewn across the floor, at his feet and over chairs and panels. Tim looked down and knew right away what the wrinkled mounds were. They were clothing. Pants and underwear mostly.

During the time travel they'd been much younger; many of the crew had been babies or at least children. It seemed that their clothes had fallen off. Some shirts remained, like Tim's black t-shirt, but his Levi jeans and Fruit of the Loom briefs? On the floor in one of the many numerous heaps.
Where had that left Timothy?
In the middle of the bridge with quite a draft.

He looked around to be sure he wasn't having a bad dream. It turned out that what he was having was a bad reality and others around the bridge realized they were too. At some point Vulpa had crawled out of her uniform and was completely naked. She let out an uncharacteristic shriek and dived down below her station in search of attire.
Captain Nule ordered, "Situation report," as he reached for his pants. Eighteen years was not far enough into the past to have made him a child, although he had been considerably thinner. Sorpe slid into his chair and pulled under the shadow of the navigation panel. Commander Geesh stood with long brown and black hair, unaffected. He lashed a thick tongue across his molars, chuckling.

Tweezor emerged from a dark corner shaking his head back and forth and then paused behind Commander Vulpa. He grinned.

The frontal screen popped alive with Sparrim Gale's face.

"Captain Nule, we have--"

Timothy stood in the center of the room, naked from the waist down. His face was bright red.

"*Oh my*," she blurted out.

His mouth fell open as he looked down at himself. He swung around, diving for cover.

33

Captain Nule said, "Stand by, Commander Gale."

He clicked a button on his panel and then stepped into the leg of his pants. The view screen went to black. The most embarrassing moment of Tim's life came to a close with the snap of elastic, the sounds of zippers and alien cursing.

"Quickly, please. We're all adults here. Let's act professional," Nule said in Tweezor's direction.

The midget appeared to be in no hurry to find his pants and strolled around the half naked officers with a smile.

Nule frowned. "Mr. Norbinger, what are you doing?"

"Just looking for uniform," he answered casually, as if browsing in a department store.

"Let's pick up the pace," Nule said, buttoning pinstripe trousers.

Tweezor bent down, retrieved a pair of red underwear and then twirled them on his index finger.

"Yes, Captain," he responded just as they shot across the bridge.

"Those are mine!" sounded from behind the communications console.

Tweezor laughed and kept shopping.

Tim's foot got caught in his underwear and he went off balance, falling to the floor. "Ouch!" he called out as his elbow hit the hard surface. Lying on the floor, Tim slid into his briefs.

"Status report," ordered Nule.

"We are clear of Timeshift Tunnel, Captain," responded Commander Geesh, "The Redeemer has us in tractor tow."

"Well, thank goodness for that."

The broken jar of Chinozien Mica-mites lay in sparkling chunks across the tile. Vulpa, newly dressed and sitting at her station, collected herself.

"We are being hailed."

"Open the channel." Nule scanned the room as officers finished getting their uniforms on. "Audio only."

Across the bridge, Tweezor had just found his pants. Laughing, he bent down to retrieve them.

Sparrim's voice sounded, "Truthseeker, what is your situation?"

"We're performing deck scans now but, I believe we have emerged with no casualties."

"The Meem loaded the tunnel with grid mines. We are all fortunate to be alive," Sparrim said, relieved.

"Yes, the explosion," Nule said trying to remember, "Our shields were damaged."

"Correct, sir. I'm sending you a full report now."

Geesh growled, "Navigation is back online. Disengage tractor please."

"Releasing tractor beam," was the response and with a slight jolt the Truthseeker was under its own power once again.

"Give us a moment, Commander Gale, to finish our analysis. I'll contact you shortly."

Nule stared into an illuminated panel and slid into the Captain's chair. A readout of the time stream they'd experienced came up. The window to the past had been about eighteen years, which was expected. The youngest individual on the ship was Timothy, their guest.

He noticed something strange. It seemed the time slip hadn't exceeded seventeen days into the future. Nule sat back with wide eyes and sharp, clenched teeth.

He realized that someone aboard the Truthseeker was going to die in seventeen days time. It was impossible to know who it would be. He only knew when.

Captain Gorza Nule looked over his officers with fearful eyes. As a crewmember of a cruiser class battleship he was aware, as they all were, of the constant dangers that accompanied deep space missions. He'd seen death many times under various circumstances. But this was different.

This time it was sure and could not be avoided. It was the future. Death was coming for someone on the Consolidation ship Truthseeker. And someone could very well mean everyone.

Sector Three:
Scorrinwall Base at Ebteon

1

"We are entering the Ornetho system, Captain," Vulpa announced.

The local sun had twelve orbiting plancts. Ebteon was the largest in the system. A military complex sat in darkness on the far side of the blue sphere.

"Set a course for the base," Nule instructed.

"They are hailing us, sir."

"On screen, Commander."

The head and shoulders of a pale alien appeared on the viewer. His mouth was large, with thick lips and wide, boxy teeth. He had no apparent nose but there were small openings along folded creases down his cheeks. His eyes were glossy opals, narrow and menacing. The breast of his dark uniform was adorned with multi-colored badges and medals.

He smiled and spoke, "Captain Nule, it's good to see you. How long has it been? Two years?"

Nule stood at ease and returned the smile to his old friend.

"Admiral Bine. Yes, at least two. Wonderful to see you, sir."

"I heard you had quite a ride through the tunnel."

"Yes, Admiral," he answered, looking down at his pinstripe trousers, "The mines were quite unexpected."

Bine's face got serious, "Yes, yes. We should have scouted the entire quadrant days ago, but the Meem onslaught has been so terribly devastating."

Nule's words were solemn. "Yes, sir."

"The base at Whoole Sanctum is lost."

The captain's eyes got wide, "What? Whoole Sanctum?"

"Yes, I'm afraid so. There was a meltdown at the main cannon facility," Bine lowered his head, "That's all it took."

"My god."

"Without the protection of the cannon, they were defenseless. It was a massacre."

Nule stood in silence. Sanctum base had been home to twenty thousand military personnel with a surrounding population of sixty million. To Captain Nule even the word massacre seemed to be an understatement.

He clenched his jaw, "There has got to be a way... I mean...the Meem must have a weakness."

Admiral Bine, "Yes. We have our top scientists on it. We can only hope we'll find an answer soon."

Nule cleared his throat, "How far have they gotten?"

Bine's muscles tensed and his brow lowered, "The Meem occupation has spread all the way to the Triptic Vortex and they will soon reach Choxide. Also, enemy scout ships have been spotted close to Inner Deema. Both locations expect attack and are at high alert."

Inner Deema was Gorza Nule's home world. His parents and sister lived there, along with many of his close friends. Commander Vulpa sat at the station beside the captain in shock. Her family lived on Middle Deema and it would likely be a target soon. Tim watched the fear in their faces as they were told that their worlds were threatened. Tweezor tried to swallow and couldn't. He had family and friends on Choxide.

The Truthseeker bridge got as quiet as an uncomfortable pause at a funeral.

"Thank you, Admiral," Nule said in a whisper.

Bine forced a smile, "We'll see you shortly, Gorza," he looked down at his display, "Continue on grid nine. You are cleared for landing on tower platform forty-three blue. Your escort is cleared for forty-four blue."

The screen faded to black and then a series of code ran across the dark surface, indicating grid coordinates. A crimson flight path illuminated through the cube display. The bright line curved around the backside of the planet. It would guide them to the top platform of a tower at the western corner of the base. It was midnight at Scorrinwall.

The Truthseeker followed the flight path instructions and the Redeemer was close behind. The ships descended down into the bluish atmosphere and the viewer screen went brilliant white, then static, then faded to black as it powered down.

"Take your seats, please," Nule said from the captain's chair.

Tim took a step back and sat on the couch, clamping down on a cushion. Tweezor found an empty chair at the com station and climbed into it. Vulpa helped the little man into his harness belt and then looked up into his eyes. Her face turned from seriousness to unexpectedly, a smile. It was a forced smile and her eyes still looked glaring and cold, but it had been accompanied by the kind gesture. Tweezor figured that something he'd said had finally broken the ice with her. She was never nice to him.

He grinned, "Thank you, Commander."

Her face went serious again.

"You required assistance. I helped. That is all."

His grin got bigger.

She scowled at him, "That is all."

He chittered at her, "Yes, I suppose so."

Her face turned red with angered frustration, "Stop staring at me," she said, clicking herself into her own seat.

The midget kept staring and grinning, "Why? Does it make uncomfortable?"

She clenched her sharp teeth together, forcing herself to remain silent. Veins in her temples flared and her face went even redder.

The ship dipped down into the upper layer of the Ebteon atmosphere and a violent rumble overtook them. G-forces pulled at their skin as they vibrated through a harsh pummeling of gasses. Tweezor yelled with a shaking voice to Commander Nim, "Vulpa, my love! Hold me!"

She gripped the arms of her chair tighter and glared at Tweezor across the quaking bridge. He grinned. After a moment the rumble eased and the frontal viewer went back online.

"We have cleared the Ebteon atmosphere, Captain," announced Geesh in a deep vocal bark.

"Thank you, Commander. Proceed to forty-three blue."

"On grid approach, bearing two-four-six."

Descending downward through a dark blue nighttime sky, the Truthseeker's silver skin reflected light from three bright moons. The Redeemer was just behind, her underbelly leading toward the shadowed continent below. A military base faded into view on the illuminated screen. Tim watched as the yellow glow defined itself into individual pinpoints of light. Three tall towers stood in a triangle formation at the outermost points of the base. Each one was just over a mile high from ground level to the ceiling of the highest cruiser dock. The top third of the western scraper was covered in hazy cloud cover. Its red beacon light lit up the fog, blinking on and off. The two ships descended into the cloud at the west tower, setting down side by side with the clunk of rarely used landing gear.

Nule turned to look at his guest, "Well, this is it, Scorrinwall Base. We'll be here long enough to make some repairs and then be off. It shouldn't take but a couple of hours."

Tim gazed with awe into the frontal viewer, "Did we land on one of those towers?"

"Yes. We are sitting at the highest level of blue dock, a mile above the base."

Tweezor, across the room, unbuckled his harness belt and hopped down to the floor.

He sang, "We're on top of the world, lookin' down on creation and the only explanation I can find…"

He swung around to face Vulpa, who tried hard to ignore him.

"…is the love that I've found, ever since you've been around."

She looked up from her panel and said, "You disgust me."

He paid no attention and continued, "Your love has put me up on top of the world!"

Tim walked over to his little crooning friend, kneeling down, "Karen Carpenter you are not."

Tweezor laughed, "Tim no like my song?"

"It needs work, dude. It needs work," he said with a hand on the midget's shoulder.

The spaceman smiled, "Let's go for walk."

He looked over at Captain Nule.

"We goin' outside."

Nule sent a stern glare at them, "Do not leave the platform," he paused for a second and then, "for *any reason*."

"Yes, sir," Tweezor acknowledged with a salute.

98

They left the bridge and headed down the hallway to the freight elevators. Tweezor squeezed by a thick gathering of personnel and into an empty lift. Tim followed him inside and watched as a pass code was punched into a keypad on the wall.

"Space dock level, please," Tweezor said into the air above him. The door slid closed as a slight vibration began, accompanied by a low hum. The doorway slid open again and they stepped out onto a textured platform. An icy blast of air slapped Timothy across the face as he gazed up into wet fog, shivering. The muscles in his back tensed and goose bumps stood up on his arms.

"It's stinkin' cold, man," he exclaimed, squinting into the frigid howl.

Tweezor clapped his hands on his stomach, "It feels great!" He walked to the railing. Stepping up onto the lower rung, he leaned out over the edge and squinted downward. The cloud cover was too thick to see buildings below, but distant lights at the crest of the south tower were bright. They were tiny starbursts, holes in midnight's deep curtain.

"Woo hoo!" he yelled, "This is sweet!"

Tim stepped reluctantly closer to the edge. Looking past the carefree little man, he gazed into the wet mist. A squall of biting wind shoved and the cloud thinned. With another gust the fog parted completely, leaving a clear view of Scorrinwall.

The military city complex, a mile below, was a vast gathering of buildings caught in the web of criss-crossed streets. There were tight rows of fighters and tanks, machines of war, and training fields, arenas to gain experience in spending their destruction. There were tall office buildings and long warehouses, low to the ground. A great wall surrounded the facility, connecting from one tower to the next, cutting a broad triangle into the shadowed ground. Tim imagined the compound to be a fallen dreamcatcher, a Native American talisman created to protect those who slept. They were meant to hang above, holding a keen eye against the nightmares of evil spirits. Even beautiful as it was, shining multicolored flickering lights, it would do little good on the ground. It seemed that those with bad dreams were on their own tonight.

Sitting in the center of the base, a quarter of a mile high itself, was a huge metal dome with a menacing cannon at the summit. The barrel of the beast was a hundred yards across. It was the Eradicator, an ion weapon powerful enough to devastate a cruiser with a single blast. The sheer size of it might've led one to believe that it would be heavy and slow, but looks were quite deceiving. The weapon was capable of liquid smooth motion, quick enough to pummel an entire fleet of swarming ships.

"Is that a …gun?"

"Yeah, buddy. One of most powerful weapons you ever see. It go *BOOM*, baby."

Tim gazed into its deadly shadow.

"Good God, man. What would you need something like that for?"

Tweezor leaned further over the railing.

"You no wanna know, buckaroo."

Tim stepped back "Don't lean out so far, dude. You're freaking me out."

Tweezor laughed, "You worry too much, Timothy."

He balanced himself with his knees against the top rail and let it go with his hands.

Stretching his arms up and out he yelled, "I'm the king of the world!"

Tim took a nervous step forward and then back again, crossing his arms tensely.

"Don't make Titanic jokes man."

Tweezor cocked his head and hopped down off his perch. He pulled the human down to him, curiously. Tim reluctantly kneeled down. The pale midget scanned the human's eyes.

"How you get through life being so gooked in head?"

"What? What do you mean?"

"You gooked. I mean what said I."

"Huh?"

Tweezor shook his head as if dizzy and then, "You worry too much. You afraid of everything. You obsessive and overly uptight. You *gooked*."

Tim couldn't believe what he was hearing. "You, a crazy spaceman midget, are going to psychoanalyze me? You're the one who's gooked. Not me."

The little man put pudgy hands on his hips.

"You zoom on garbage! Things that no matter! You addict of trivial! You overlook important! Screwed up say I! Screwed up!"

"I overlook important things? Like what?"

The short man smiled, "Having good time important. Friends important. Fun important. Enjoy life, dude. You too self involve."

Tim stood up, "I'm *supposed* to be selfish and neurotic. I'm a *teenager*," he said, feeling justified.

Tweezor pleaded, "If you no enjoy youth, what will you enjoy?"

The midget walked away, shaking his head. With caution Tim walked to the rail and leaned over, looking straight down.

I know how to have fun.

He turned and watched the spaceman bow-leggedly make his way under the gloomy ship. Once in darkness, eyeball lights popped alive. Two narrow beams illuminated the yellow dock. He continued to walk away.

Tim looked back out over Scorrinwall Base.

I zoom on garbage? What does that mean?

He backed up rigidly. The muscles in his neck tensed at a rush of wet air. Sparrim's voice startled him.

"Hello, sequence carrier Timothy Rayburn."

He jumped and swung around.

"God! Don't sneak up on me like that!"

"He is correct, you know. You really should learn to not acquire so much stress."

He was embarrassed and shivering.

"So what, you think I should run around acting like a goofball, singing to myself everywhere I go?"

"If that is what it takes to have less stress, then…yes."

"You must be as Looney Tunes as he is."

She smiled, "Perhaps."

He paused, looking at her Allie Kincade smile, studying her Allie Kincade eyes. She was beautiful and he couldn't help but smile back.

"What do *you* do for fun?"

She was surprised at the question and reluctant to answer. Her smile faded as she turned away.

"I don't know."

"Yes you do. Tell me."

"I also sing," she looked nervously down at the ground, "when I'm alone."

"Really?" he said, "You?"

She looked up, "And why not? I have a very nice vocal range."

Tim laughed, "That is so strange. I never imagined aliens singing."

"If we were on my planet, *you'd* be the alien."

He hadn't thought of it that way before.

"Yeah, I guess we're all aliens out here."

"I prefer to think of it this way. We are all different and that makes us all unique. That's why we're all the same."

Tim soaked in her words looking out at a range of jagged snowy mountains reflecting soft moonlight. If he hadn't known better, he would've thought it was a mountain range on Earth. But he did know better as he stood next to an alien who was the spitting image of an actress he'd watched on screen at the movies. Earth and this planet were quite different places indeed. Earth didn't have giant deep space cruisers, plasma shields or ion cannons.

And there were many differences that he was unaware of. Earth didn't have Meem freighter Tankbirds decloaking at secret locations around the largest military base. Earth certainly did not have hover assault teams waiting to strike strategic power grid targets in and around a primary weapon site.

Earth was not about to be devastated by an unknown alien race determined to wipe out the entire population.

2

Captain Nule exited an elevator at the lowest level of the west tower. A soldier was waiting to issue him a Jetpod.

"Welcome, sir. Please sign here and I can assign you some transportation."

"Thank you," Nule said looking over the vehicle.

The soldier paused, "You've operated one of these before, haven't you?"

The captain smiled, "Oh, yes. I can handle a pod just fine."

"Very good, sir. Have a nice day."

The truth was, Nule hadn't operated a Jetpod in over ten years.

But, he thought, *an officer never forgets such things.*

When he hit the accelerator, he was nearly ripped from the seat. He strained to hold on as the pod rocketed down the road toward the Command Center.

These are more powerful than I remember.

3

Admiral Bine stood rigid in the command center. Numerous screens displayed readouts, information and security views from around the base. A familiar voice sounded behind him.

"Requesting permission to enter secure area, Admiral."

Bine smiled and turned to see his friend, "Granted, Captain Nule. You are most welcome here."

The captain's long fingered hand was held out and accepted with a squeeze and a pat.

"How are you, my friend?" Bine asked, "I'm so sorry I had to tell you about Inner Deema."

"Yes," Nule said with sad eyes, "I just sent message to my family…in case anything should happen."

The Admiral turned back to his displays, "These are terrible times, Gorza. War with an unknown enemy… The verse generator failing… I have to tell you, I'm feeling too old for all of this."

"So am I," Nule said, "But the Consolidation is fortunate that we're here. We practically fought the entire Consumption War ourselves."

The Admiral laughed, "We did, didn't we? Those were the days. That was when we knew our enemy. We knew the politics involved and the technology. Now all we have is speculation and guesses…"

"And gut instinct. Don't forget that," Captain Nule said with confidence.

"I'm not so sure anymore, Gorza. The last thing my gut told me was that my quantum assistant was malfunctioning."

The two of them laughed. It was good to laugh and to see his old friend. Nule smiled, remembering the academy and the dreams and arrogance of youth. He had become more reserved with maturity. Of course, twenty years ago at the academy, they'd sworn to take on the entire Shadow fleet themselves. It was as if they were invincible. But two wars and many lost friends later, they both felt much closer to mortal.

An officer at a station to their left double-checked his findings on infrared. His mouth hung open in a disbelieving gape. "Admiral, I'm getting some strange readings at sector five." Bine looked over, "What kind of readings?"

"I'm seeing a growing concentration of idemic charr."

The admiral and Captain exchanged puzzled looks.

"I'm also picking up similar readings at grids two and six," added another.

Bine, "Have they reported any leaks at the cannon facility?"

"No sir. All levels are showing normal across the board."

Captain Nule, "Idemic charr radiation? The main cannon is the only system here with that kind of exhaust, isn't it?"

"Yes," Bine said, walking toward the satellite control station, "It is. Bring up the overhead of sector five. Magnify to ten."

A grainy image popped onto the large display in front of them. It showed the rough terrain just outside the base perimeter. A dark shadow covered the ground close to the high wall. Beyond that sat a mixture of sharp rocks and thick weeds.

"Give me a spectral."

The screen turned to dark green and white colors with a growing cloud of red coming from nowhere. It puffed out, paused a moment and then puffed again.

"That's exhaust," Nule said.

"Yes it is," Bine responded with clenched teeth, "Zoom out to minus six."

The satellite camera seemed to back up, showing them the entire complex. The growing red radiation made a wafting line around the whole perimeter.

"We have cloaked unknowns at our door, gentleman," He looked up at the commanders on the upper tiers, "Light em' up and lock em' down. Battle stations."

A loud buzzer sounded across Scorrinwall Base. Pilots raced to their ships. Soldiers gathered. The generators at the cannon facility went online as operators hurried to their stations.

4

Commander Vulpa Nim lay on her back, under the navigation control panel, looking up into a thick tangle of colored wires.

"Try that," she called to the one above.

"That looks good," he responded, "Can you see the rear board?"

She stretched her neck to see, ignoring pain in her back.

"Yes, I can see it."

She pointed a small flashlight above a twisted group of yellow and blue wire.

She paused a moment and then, "It's blown. I'll need a replacement."

The tall E-Triptic said, "Give me a few minutes."

He walked away slowly, trying to remember where to find a fresh board.

The Crichet engineers, EM, EL, and BE were separated from one another and lifting a heavy motor component onto a robotic cart. They set it down with a *thud* and the cart whizzed away, beeping.

A chime indicated an incoming transmission. The Captain's voice was urgent.

"Commander Nim, I'm on my way. I want the ships ready to fly in ten minutes."

She sat up and spoke into the air, "Sir, we just got the drive apart."

A crackle and then, "Get it back together, *now*. The base is under attack."

The commander scrambled to her feet.

A rush of adrenaline, controlled panic.

"Get the motor together immediately. Call Tweezor and Timothy inside."

She clapped a nearby officer on the shoulder. He was looking down at the control circuit board he'd just retrieved.

"Get that installed quickly, Mr. Sorpe."

The alert buzzer sounded and Vulpa rushed to the platform to help the engineers with their project. Another droid controlled cart sped in with the new power exchanger. It was even bigger and heavier than the last. The Trio strained to lift it up. An explosion below the ship knocked Vulpa and two Crichets to the floor. The Truthseeker quaked and tilted, sliding down the broken dock. The six hundred pound power exchanger fell off the cart with a loud bang and rolled at Vulpa. She gasped, diving away from the engineering platform. Her leg didn't clear the path in time. The weight of the component pinned her foot against the opposite station, breaking two bones and denting the metal cabinet door. She screamed at intense pain. EL and EM rushed to free her as BE called for, "Medical assistance to the bridge."

The second explosion jarred the Truthseeker upward the other direction and with a loud quake it came to a stop.

Commander Geesh appeared behind an engineer. Pushing him aside, he heaved at the exchanger with powerful arms. With it set aside, Vulpa slid back with sharp pain jolting up her leg. She winced at clamping pain.

"Get that installed," she said gritting sharp teeth, "That's an order."

5

Bine clapped his friend on the back.

"Captain Nule, get your ship and the sequence carrier out of here."

Nule turned and ran for the shuttle bay doors. He claimed the nearest jetpod and fired it up. In the distance he heard the first of the explosions. The ground rumbled under his feet just before the vehicle lifted off the platform. He ascended over rushing personnel and the command center.

With the dome cleared, Nule looked out across the military complex. He stared in disbelief. A swarm of Meem fighters increased speed, bearing down on the central compound.

6

A group of ten hover tanks de-cloaked just outside the wall at the west tower. The three in the lead aimed their main guns up the length of the structure and fired concurrently. Three concentrated blasts of ion energy shot up, one after another.

The Truthseeker and Redeemer battle cruisers sat at the top platforms in thick fog. Timothy Rayburn and Sparrim Gale stood quietly at the rail, looking out over the military complex. Technicians in dark uniforms carried new parts for the Wavetime drive and plasma-shielding unit. Tweezor hummed to himself on the other side of the dock.

An abrupt voice over the loud speaker at the freight elevator, "Tweezor Norbinger, you are ordered to re-board the Truthseeker immediately. Sparrim Gale, to your ship immediately."

The buzzer sounded in a loud repeating roar. Gumball lights at the corners of the dock came alive, spinning red beams of light into the cloud cover. Sparrim knew right away they meant an enemy attack.

She shouted urgently to Tim, "Get back to your ship!"

Just as she looked over to the Redeemer, the first ion bursts made contact. The explosion seemed to be right under their feet and the dock rumbled and split apart. A jagged crack sent thick chunks of floor and dust into the air. The Truthseeker slid down the textured and newly angled dock toward the railing and Timothy.

He fell backward onto the rungs, which had bent and were now flat out over the edge of the tower. The impact of his back on the metal rods shot a stabbing ache across his shoulders and ribs. He cried out and looked past his sneakers quickly. The mammoth space cruiser scraped along with sparks flying, the front landing gear coming right at him. Tim threw his head back to look behind. Fog and open air a mile above Ebteon's surface was all he could see. He gripped the torn rail and tried to pull himself up. Pain squeezed tightly around his chest. The ship was coming.

A pale hand seized his arm from below.

"Jump!" she yelled, "I've got you!"

Sparrim hung from the rail underneath with one hand. The other wrenched down on Timothy.

Panic.

Sparks.

Another explosion.

He could've rolled out of the way of the approaching ship. It would've left Sparrim alone in its path. He gritted teeth and stayed where he was.

Screaming.

Sparrim pulling.

He turned, flexing every muscle in his body.

With a loud crash, the space cruiser stopped, the front tip of the landing gear just inches from his shoulder. The center of the broken dock had buckled up into the underbelly of the ship. It had come to rest, momentarily.

Just then, a weld cracked in a rail beside Tim. The pole bent downward under his leg. Sparrim let go of the rung and her entire body weight was then supported by Tim's wrist.

"I'm gonna fall!" she screamed.

No.

He threw himself onto his stomach and grabbed for her arm. With it in hand, he utilized all the strength he had to hold her from falling. He saw the panic in her eyes.

They were watering and pleading.

"Please," she said to him, "Don't let go of me."

A new determination pumped through his veins as he struggled against gravity.

The lower clouds parted, leaving a clear view, all the way down. Seams in the twisted railing popped free underneath Timothy's weight. A loud clang echoed to his left.

"I'm not letting go," he grunted out, "I promise."

At that moment, the railing let go of both of them.

7

Tweezor, sitting at the opposite end of the dock, hummed a happy tune with feet dangling over the edge. He was amazed at the beautiful view. The bluish light of three moons illuminated a distant mountain range. Small shuttles and pods zipped past, leaving glowing jet trails across the black sky.

A loud crackling voice boomed across the frigid air, ordering him and Sparrim back to their ships. The alarm buzzer followed. Spiraling red light.

He looked up at the ships and then under to try to spot the human.

The first explosion ripped the floor in half. The little man was thrown hard into the railing. Flames shot up through a covered duct in the dock floor, rocketing the lid fifty feet into the air. The broken floor tipped downward and the landing gear against the textured dock made an arc of sparks on each side, ten feet high.

The lower rail had created a deafening headache just behind Tweezor's eyes. The pain was intense. A gash in his right arm streamed bright red. He sat stunned, rubbing the ache out of his temples with stubby fingers.

The crumbling dock thrust upward, away from the second detonation as a violent quake twisted the tower in its punishment. Tweezor fell sideways, sliding. He rolled onto his stomach, digging in fingernails. The surface dipped down and then popped up, in a kind of springboard action that threw the little man into the air.

"Whoa!" he yelled, flying.

He came down, bounced, tumbled, and fell into the duct opening. The spitting flames, luckily, had ceased.

8

Nule hit the air brakes, leaned the pod onto its side and skimmed the roof of the command center dome down to ground level. He hit the thruster just in time, before crashing into the dark pavement. His feet touched down and he pushed off hard hitting the accelerator with his thumb.

The single man pods were quick as lightning and it took Nule's entire grip to remain seated. He shot down the shadowy street like a bullet.

The overhead Meem fighters, blasted past the other direction in an elegant, shifting formation. A single ship broke away, circled around the command dome and rocketed after Nule. The pod's sensors picked it up. A small green display informed him it was closing fast.

A concentrated blast of snapping energy shot past, burning the outside of his elbow and exploding into a building ten blocks ahead. He recoiled to the left, nearly losing control of the pod. His arm stung like fire as he managed to center the vehicle.

He knew that if he slowed down the enemy would be on him fast, so he chose not to. He eased as far to the left as he could go, zipping down the sidewalk. Then, with muscles straining, he cranked right. He leaned deep into the turn with a knee scraping the road, leaving behind bloody skin. He ignored the pain and aimed at the corner of the building. Nule cleared the sharp edge of the structure by inches at just over a hundred and twenty miles an hour. He pulled hard to finish the turn. The building across the street was coming up fast. The captain heaved and floored the accelerator. The bottom of the pod scoured paint off the surface and popped windows into shimmering chunks of glass.

Another blast of yellow energy detonated behind him as he pushed off. Nule eased the pod around and straightened out in the middle of the street.

Up and over a parked street cleaner he went. Once cleared, he dived down low. A ball of plasma blew the truck into fiery fragments in an explosion of orange flames.

Nule zipped close by light poles, armored vehicles and past other low flying pods. The Meem fighter ignored them all, staying on his tail.

Nule eased to the right over the sidewalk, preparing to make a wide left turn. He cranked and leaned the vehicle over. An unexpected blast shot past him, the edge of it striking the back of the pod. Nule was thrown sideways. He gunned the accelerator and leaned deep, but the turn was now way too wide. Out of control, he headed toward a building on the next block.
There was no time to think.
At a hundred and sixty-two miles and hour he smashed through a plate glass window. He and the single man shuttle pod went tumbling down a long carpeted hallway. To his advantage, the corridor was tall and wide. His body shot through a small table, a lamp stand and hanging uniforms on a wheeled clothing rack, skimming the east wall. He tumbled in midair and finally came to rest at the far end.

He lay face up. Pale eyes blurred for a few seconds and then cleared. Pain ripped from his collarbone, shoulder and right leg. Looking up in a daze, he saw the pod was stuck in the ceiling above him. He tried to move his leg. It was badly bruised, but not broken. Sitting up, he figured his collarbone and shoulder hurt due to dislocation. He wasn't positive he could push himself off the floor, but looking up he realized he would have to.

For one thing, the pod was ready to fall down on top of him. For another, the Meem fighter had just entered the hallway.

9

Tweezor traveled down a dark, slick tube. His eye lights popped alive as he slid into the shadows. On his stomach, he zipped past large round openings, pathways winding over and down to unknown destinations. He strained to grab hold of an edge or a seam, anything to stop him. But momentum kept his small body moving, a projectile rocketing into mystery.

A distant blast rocked the metal slide, slowing his progress. A nearby explosion tore a long gash in the tube a hundred feet in front of him, sending billowing orange flames inside. He could not slow down. He covered his face with his hands trying to protect himself from the scorching temperature. He sucked in a deep breath, and held it.

10

Timothy, the broken railing and Sparrim fell into the open air above Ebteon.

Panic.

The rushing tower beside them became a blur of metal and glass, faster and faster.

Her watering eyes.

God.

The icy chill was everywhere.

No.

Please.

Tim's world was slow motion. They were a mile above the surface. At that height they would fall for almost forty seconds before...

Tim's parents flashed in front of him. His mother.

Mom.

Those eyes.

His chest hurt.

Falling.

Oh god, falling.

Nothing.

Eyes watering.

Nothing to stop them.

Oh god, we're gonna die.

11

In a burst of adrenaline, Captain Nule rolled out of the way just as the heavy pod came loose. It crashed down over torn carpet in the corridor. His shoulder raged with intense pain as he pulled himself up. He forced his left arm to move in spite of the stiffness.

The Meem fighter, at the other end of the hall had been hovering in place. Once Nule got to his feet, it shot forward. The whining motor was loud and getting louder. Nule pulled the jet pod upright and checked the controls. The levels looked good. With a quick glance back he kicked off and hit the accelerator. He leaned right and headed down a connecting corridor. He got the pod up to full speed, rocketing for a tall window, a hundred feet away.

The fighter's motor screamed from behind. It rounded the corner, paused a moment, and then fired.

12

At the North wall a squadron of twenty Meem fighters picked up speed. They rocketed overhead as cannons blasted at them from the ground. A few Consolidation ships were in the air and had begun to engage the enemy.

Explosions lit up the dark sky above Scorrinwall. A wave of bombers dived down low, covering the buildings beneath in billowing hot flames.

Meem hover tanks devastated everything in their paths, leaving behind craters and fallen structures. Another weapon ambled down the street behind the tanks. Unlike the others, it ran on large tracks. It had a thick U shaped weapon on a short post mounted over the roof. It plodded along in no apparent hurry and had yet to open fire. It, and the deadly machines leading the way, worked toward the facility's primary weapon. The cannon at the heart of Scorrinwall was busy sending powerful ion blasts at highflying groups of Meem fighters.

No Warbirds had yet been detected, although it was likely they were cloaked nearby.

Admiral Bine watched the enemy movement on a large screen. He was in a secure bunker beneath the command dome, as were many of the other commanders.

He spoke into a handheld microphone, "What is the Truthseeker's status? What information do we have about the west tower?"

The response was choppy and barely readable.

"We've lost-- post at-- location, over."

Admiral spoke into the microphone, "The Truthseeker and the west tower are priority one, do you copy? The ship must get away."

Static and silence. Bine watched his screen pan and zoom in on the west tower grid. A growing gathering of enemy tanks pummeled the central and upper platforms. Bine opened a channel to his air squads.

"This is Admiral Bine. Protect the west tower! The sequence carrier must survive!"

Crackling silence and then, "Red Stripe has a copy, Admiral. We are at grid nine-eight. Tower ETA-- twenty seconds."

The Red Stripe was the elite fighter squad of the Consolidation. Each of the Reeomeez Impath fighters had been modified with Stinzotaun type S (Ripper) motors. They were known as the 'Birds of the Axis' and were the fastest, deadliest vehicle the Admiral had at his command.

The Stripe leader led the squad of eight birds across the complex, calling out to the forces on the ground.

"Red Stripe approaching west tower at grid four-one. Clear the floor, gentlemen. We're coming in hot."

The Consolidation troops pulled back to get clear of the coming punishment from above.

"Ready spider charges," Stripe leader instructed, "Config system lock on-- on my mark."

Cylinder weapon bays on the Impath wings rotated two clicks. The squad screamed past the west tower and a storm of hundreds of small metal objects rained over the area like hail. Each one was a golf ball sized sphere with three L shaped appendages. They fell, bounced and came to rest over the ground and tanks. A tiny red light lit up the top of the 'Spiders' and they rolled and stood on their rigid legs. The ones that had come to rest on the Meem vehicles clamped down hard, attaching themselves to the armored surface. The ones on the ground scanned the enemy and then charged, scuttling underneath the hovering tanks.

A platoon Commander called out from two blocks away. "The floor is cleared, Stripe leader. Do your worst."

With that, "Mark," was called out from above.

The remote detonation saturated the area around the base of the west tower in harsh yellow-orange flames. The explosions sent tanks upward into the air, flipping over and spinning, crashing down with sparks flying. A wave of tanks not caught in the blast rotated and opened fire on the squadron. A winding group of seeker missiles blazed into the sky.

"Incoming," a pilot said as he pulled the Impath on its side, banking north.

"Increase to escape velocity," the leader barked, watching an intelligent seeker missile on his readout.

"Stripe five, increase speed!"

Before the pilot could respond, a weapon connected and blew the fighter into shining, fiery shrapnel. Thick, black smoke trailed a remaining chunk of fuselage into the city. The Stripe leader gritted his teeth, looking away.

"Target remaining ground forces and fire at will."

With a missile on his tail the leader dived down, pointing his nose at the ground. He pulled up in time to miss the roof of a Meem tank. The following missile did not react in time. The explosion ripped the vehicle on its top and spun it on the pavement.

The Red Stripe squadron opened fire, releasing an arsenal of the most sophisticated weapons the Consolidation of Organized Systems had.

It wouldn't be enough to save Scorrinwall. The waiting cruisers would be free to de-cloak once the main cannon was destroyed. Even the elite Red Stripe would be no match for the Meem Warbirds.

13

Nule floored the accelerator and lowered his head and shoulders. The pod shot down the corridor at top speed. His grip strained as he smashed through the tall window. A shower of glass filled the air as he rocketed through. Little pieces imbedded into his scalp with blood streaking. The ball of ion energy ignited behind him as he flew into the cool open air. A group of Consolidation Soldiers below scattered and took cover when they saw the blast. Nule shot out through the flames touching down in the alley across the street. His boots scraped in the gravel as he turned to look back.

Three battered Consolidation soldiers were ducked down behind a crashed troop carrier. They worked on a long plasma cannon. It was at least fifteen feet in length and had been recently torn from a vehicle mount.

Nule looked across the road at an overturned Consolidation tank. Sure enough, the secondary cannon had been blown off and the empty mount was still smoking.

Nule yelled to them, "Are you sure you boys know what your doing?"

"Oh, sure," said the shorter soldier, wiping his nose, "We'll get it to work."

The taller and much more intelligent looking one called for a wrench and got no response. The solider holding the necessary tools was hunkered down on his knees, obviously shaken from the closeby explosion. The taller one knocked on his helmet rudely.

"Wake up, Nibs! Give me the stupid wrench!"

The soldier held the silver tool into the air. With it in hand, it was used to tighten a bolt on the cannon.

"Hold it up," he ordered.

The others propped the weapon over the back of the troop carrier. The flames dissipated in the window and the Meem fighter appeared. The ship nosed down, aiming.

Before Nule could warn them, a thick blast of condensed plasma shot from the barrel of the long gun. The cannon recoiled violently and hit the ground, ricocheting over Nule's head. The Meem fighter tipped, spun and fell to the pavement with a huge crash. The three surprised soldiers looked over and back, trying to comprehend what had just happened.

Finally the tall one said, "Well, that does it for that," and walked away.

The one on the ground ducked lower, sniffing and snorting. The taller soldier picked an assault rifle. He checked the battery charge. He looked over at the one on the pod. Nule sat, trying to catch his breath.

"So you're a Captain then?" the soldier asked, noticing the stripes on Nule's sleeve.

"Yes," Nule huffed out, "Do you have access to an armored vehicle? I need to get to the west tower."

"The west tower? You don't want to go there. It's full on, over there."

"What? What have you heard? I have to get to my ship."

"Are you the captain of the sequence carrier's ship?"

"Yes, I am. I'm Captain Nule. What's that situation over there?"

The taller soldier, "There's a whole lotta tanks at sector five. I heard them calling in the Red Stripe."

"Good lord." Nule reached for his transmitter, "Commander Nim, do you copy?"

A tinny voice came back, "Yes sir, where are you?"

He looked up at the street sign, "About forty blocks east of you. Is the ship ready to fly?"

"No, sir. We're putting it together as quickly as possible, but the tower has been under enemy fire. Tweezor and Timothy are still outside. I've sent a team to retrieve them, but there is no word yet."

"Do anything necessary to find Timothy. Do you hear me? *Anything*."

Nule turned to the three soldiers that now stood in front of him. He gave them a stern glare.

"I have to be at the top platform of the west tower in less than ten minutes. And you are going to take me."

The tall soldier looked at Nule's single seat jet pod. A thick cloud of smoke flowed from the motor compartment.

"Well, it looks like we're walking. We'd better get going."

The shorter man nervously laughed, "We'll make it, no problem."

The one trailing behind snorted, sniffed and then said, "The Red Stripe? Really? Wow, I hope we get to meet them."

14

Tweezor zipped down the fiery tube. The searing wall of heat only lasted for a second and he tumbled into a horizontally connected duct. He rolled to a stop and gasped for air.

"Whoa," he squeaked.

Another detonation rocked the tower above him. The sudden air pressure knocked him backwards down the next tube.

"Aaahhh!!" he yelled, echoing into darkness.

The midget's shoulder hit the tube hard as he rounded a corner. The back of his space suit ripped out as he scraped over a rough, corroded section. Finally, he fell into a garbage dumpster on the eighteenth floor.

He'd slid down more then twenty floors of ducts.

A putrid stench fumed the air, making him gag. He'd come to rest on a case of rotten Salloric sticky worms.

"Yucko!" he cried as he scrambled to his feet.

He jumped to reach the edge of the dumpster with a worm stuck to the seat of his space suit. It wagged like a black tail as the little man climbed out. He hopped down, picked the worm off his butt and looked around for a way back to the roof. Tweezor smiled.

"Sweet," he said excitedly, "Oh yeah! This good!"

He lifted a jetpack onto his shoulders and clicked the harness. The power levels looked good. He walked to the open window.

A falling blur whooshed downward, startling him.

"What was that?" he snapped, sticking his head out the open window.

His eyes went painfully wide.

"Oh!" he screamed, powering up the jetpack, "Holy chrome!"

He flipped a switch and the boosters roared. The midget dived out the window into the cold. Nosing downward, he hit the accelerator.

Tweezor figured he only had about twenty seconds before Timothy and Sparrim hit the pavement, give or take.

15

Fighter pilot Ooba Neello slammed the type S Ripper motor to a full stop in mid air just North of the west tower. In hover position he rotated the Impath clockwise, pointing out over the dogfight

117

above Scorrinwall Base. With a Meem fighter in his sights a chime indicated target lock. He let the missile fly and then turned slowly around the corner of the building.

A blur from above zipped down at the Stripe fighter. Tweezor caught Sparrim around the waist and heaved. She landed with a scream and a thud across the windshield of the hovering craft. It dipped down at her weight and Neello corrected.
"Timothy!" she screamed into the air below the wing.

Tweezor blasted straight at the pavement. Tim was falling fast. Eight seconds to impact.

Seven.

The midget gasped and soared.

Six.

Small pudgy arms fully extended.

Five.

Stretching, aching.

Four.

God, please.

Three.

With a wrenching thrust the midget pulled upward at Tim's waist and gunned the boosters. Their decent slowed at twenty feet above the ground and they began to climb.

Tim, in a daze, noticed something burning. The toes of his sneakers dangled under the jet boosters. The white leather turned black and his feet suddenly felt as if they were soaking in lava. He screamed and kicked as his socks started to melt. He yanked them out of the jet trail, flailing like a mad man.

Tweezor flew up to find Sparrim and realized that the pilot had already dropped her off at the roof.

He flew up and over the broken railing, setting the human gently onto the dock. Tim ripped his flaming shoes off revealing stick strands of gooey, white socks. An officer from the Redeemer sprayed him down with an extinguisher. The cool foam felt like heaven over his toes.

He looked up. Sparrim smiled at him with a dirty, beautiful face. Tweezor threw the jetpack off with a crash.
"Tim okay?" he asked with a goofy smile.

The human looked up at him, "Yeah. If she's okay, then I guess I am too."

Sparrim knelt down inspecting his foamy toes.

"You need medical attention."

A loud explosion rocked the tower.

Tweezor yelled, "Let's get outta here!"

They took Tim by the arms and dragged him up the ramp, onto the lift. Sparrim hit a button and the door slid shut. They ascended into the ship.

She called over the transmitter, "Truthseeker, this is Commander Gale. We have Timothy and Commander Norbinger. We'll get them out on the Redeemer."

With that, the Ectopal ship lifted off the broken dock and shot into the sky.

16

"Ectopal ship Redeemer calling Scorrinwall air command. We have the sequence carrier. Repeat--we have the sequence carrier."

"Copy that, Redeemer. The Red Stripe will see you away."

Four Impaths found the cruiser as it ascended into the black sky above the base. They paced it all the way to the atmosphere. The Redeemer shot up into the heat, pushing its way into space. The frontal viewer came back online as bright white faded to black.

"We are clear of the atmosphere, Commander."

"Set a course for the far side of the Asteroid Sea mouth and engage."

Medical personnel attended to Timothy's burns. Tweezor watched as a nurse swabbed sticky grease across burnt human toes.

Tim looked up at Sparrim, "Aren't we gonna wait for the Truthseeker?"

"No. They'll catch up."

She gazed into the aft screen, wondering if Captain Nule was all right. She hoped he would make it back to his ship. The Truthseeker had to get away. If not, it would be up to the Redeemer to get Timothy to the Verse One wormhole. Everyone and everything depended upon their success. She stared out at the tiny pinpoint lights in the distance, feeling very alone.

17

"Captain, come in please," Vulpa called from Tim's couch, on the bridge of the Truthseeker. Her left foot was propped up on a soft pillow as Nurse Neeba examined it with and x-ray sensor probe. Nule, still thirty blocks from the west tower, heard the transmission. He spoke while trying to catch his breath.

"This is…Captain…Nule. I copy…over"

"Timothy is on the Redeemer. Do you copy? The escort ship has him."

Nule's lungs heaved, "Well…thank goodness…for that."

"Gale and Norbinger are with him. I thought you'd want to know."

"Thank you, Vulpa…What is your status?"

"The drive is back together and ready, sir. Orders?"

Nule clicked over a switch on the side of the transmitter. A beacon light chimed on and off.

"Come and get me, Commander. I don't think I can take another step."

His shoulder had been aching for ten blocks. The pain approached unbearable.

"We see your signal, Captain. Rendezvous point?"

The shorter soldier looked up the length of the tall building across the street.

He pointed up and smiled, "Will that do?"

Nule smiled back at him, "Yes. That it will."

He spoke into the transmitter again.

"There is an office building at the corner of the intersection I am now standing. I'll meet you at the roof."

Vulpa pushed off the couch, standing on her good foot. She limped to the Captain's chair, wincing at sharp pain.

"Take us up. Give me a cube visual, please."

The dogfight over Scorrinwall showed up as small multicolored dots in the holograph display. The Commander studied it, looking for a safe path. Geesh clacked his teeth and spat as he spoke.

"Grid two seems like our best route right now."

"I agree. Set a course and take us at five thousand."

The Truthseeker lifted off the crumbled yellow dock. The cruiser shot straight up into the clouds, high above the military base. A squad of Meem fighters spotted the ascending ship and shot after it.

Sorpe spoke from the navigation console, "I'm reading six enemy ships closing fast."

"Raise shields and evasive. Increase to eighty percent."

The Truthseeker banked starboard. As she sped upward the squadron stayed with her, blasting seeker missiles and plasma charges. The quaking of nearby explosions shook the bridge. Vulpa held tight.

"Return fire, Mister Geesh."

From bays across the rear of the ship, three torpedoes and four yellow plasma pulses fired. Two of the Meem ships exploded, washing billowing flames over the nearby fighter's hulls. The four remaining zipped through the scorched sky, bearing down on the cruiser. Four seeker missiles rocketed after the Truthseeker.

The first explosion.

"Shields at fifty-two percent. We're losing pressure in canisters one, two and fifteen."

"Isolate and shut them down."

The second and third explosions.

"Shields down to twenty-one percent."

"Switch to Evade pattern green-A."

The cruiser flipped onto its top, pointing its nose at the city below.

The fourth explosion.

Violent quakes rocked the bridge. Sorpe fell forward. Geesh held tight to his console.

"Overload at canister matrix. Shields failing."

The cruiser spiraled in a sharp dive.

Vulpa held on with clenched teeth, "Empty the charge slots."

A trail of small mines tumbled from the back of the ship. Three of the remaining fighters exploded in the expanding mine field behind the Truthseeker. A solitary fighter accelerated through the flames, dodging charges as it went.

"Get the shield back online!"

Lightning fast engineers worked at their stations. Geesh clacked his teeth, drooling.

"Enemy has missile lock on."

With no shield, all that remained between the crew and the outside air were quarter inch panels of Carbidd/Funkton, insulation and pressure glass.

"Engage boosters!"

The Truthseeker's speed went up another eighteen percent.

"Incoming missile."

Vulpa watched the red dot on the screen approaching.

Closer...

...Closer...

And then...

...it disappeared.

A slight rumble under their feet.

"Missile detonated behind us, Commander."

"What the--"

Static over the airwaves.

"Red Stripe squad at your service, Truthseeker. Your threat has been eliminated."

Vulpa's tension eased.

"Thank you Stripe pilot. Can you escort us to the rendezvous point?"

Neello checked his readout, "Affirmative, Truthseeker. Admirial Bine thought you might need a hand."

Vulpa took in a deep breath as her muscles eased. She leaned back in the cushon. Two more Impaths flew up along side the cruiser with failed shields. They paced the Truthseeker to the pick up point where Captain Nule and three Consolidation soldiers waited.

Relief filled Nule as he watched his ship descend from the sky. He smiled as he turned to the battered soldiers.

"Thank you, boys."

They smiled back.

"Anytime sir," the taller one said.

"Good luck, Captain," said another.

The third soldier sniffed, snorted and looked into the sky, talking to himself.

Nule chuckled watching him, "Keep an eye on that one."

"We will, sir."

The Truthseeker rotated and then set down with a jolt on the rooftop. Three Red Stripe fighters hovered above, monitoring the area. One of them turned, let a burst of energy fly out across the city and then settled back into position. An enemy ship exploded three blocks away.

A loading elevator lowered into the darkness below the belly of the Truthseeker. Two medical technicians appeared from the lift as the lower skin lights clicked alive. They helped Nule inside and the metal door slid shut. With an entry code punched into the keypad, the elevator ascended into the ship.

"We have him, repeat-- we have him."

The Truthseeker lifted off, accelerated to escape velocity and rocketed toward the atmosphere. The medical team helped Captain Nule onto the bridge. He limped as they spoke to him.

"Captain, you should accompany us to med level. We need to--"

"You either attend to me here or not at all," he griped.

Vulpa stood on her good leg.

"Sir, it's good to have you back."

"It's good to be back, Commander. What is our status?"

Geesh answered the captain. His thick hair shook as he spoke.

"The main drive has been fully repaired, sir. Sheilds are currently offline."

Nule looked up from the sharp pain in his shoulder.

"We have no shield at all?"

"No, sir," he clacked his teeth, "Four canisters are being replaced now."

Vulpa interrupted, "The Inopton charge will get us through the atmosphere."

"Yes, but it won't protect us from enemy attack."

Nule winced in pain as the doctor re-set his dislocated shoulder. With a crack it was back in place.

"That should do it, sir," he said with a smile as his captain's eyes watered.

"Must you do that now?" he complained.

"Yes, sir. We must."

The doctor grinned, "I could've given you something for your discomfort, but we'd have needed to do that in med level."

Nule forgot his ache in favor of annoyance, "If you're finished, you may *leave now*."

"Yes, sir," the doctor said pleased with himself as he walked away.

"Remind me to have him transferred."

"Gladly," Vulpa agreed, looking down at the cast on her broken foot.

"Incoming transmission from the Redeemer, Captain."

"Visual, please."

The frontal screen faded to an image of Sparrim Gale. She sounded relieved, yet professional.

"Captain Nule. I am pleased you are safely away, sir."

"Thank you, Sparrim." He had never addressed her by first name before and she was surprised. "You have once again proven your worth on this mission and we are in your debt."

She smiled, "Thank you, Captain."

He saw Tweezor singing in the background. The little man wailed the chorus to *Can you feel the love tonight* by Elton John as he spread his arms and wagged his hips. Timothy plugged his ears, trying to ignore the midget.

Nule laughed, "I hope your guests haven't driven you mad yet."

She looked behind her, "Not *quite* yet."

Nule rubbed his shoulder and got serious.

"What is your position?"

"We are holding at the far side of the Asteroid Sea mouth. We suspect cloaked Meem cruisers in the area, although our scans haven't detected anything."

He leaned forward as the Truthseeker cleared the Ebteon Atmosphere.

"It is a valid suspicion, Commander. Stay where you are and continue scanning."

Nule turned toward the engineering crew, at the rear of the bridge. They were occupied as always, diligent and quick. Their current project was routing paths for new shombine canisters for the multiphasal plasma-shielding unit.

"Full stop," Nule called out.

The Consolidation starship came to a halt in high orbit, above the planet.

"Before we go any further," he continued, "we shall finish repairing the shields."

Far below on the surface, the ion cannon was under attack. If it were destroyed, the waiting Meem fleet would be free to de-cloak and engage the base. The Truthseeker, in its current position, sat in front of the invisible enemy Flagship.

Sector Four:
The Asteroid Sea

1

Meem fighters swarmed the sky above as the hover tanks blasted their way into position. The odd vehicle on tracks ambled along down the street, behind them. Its U shaped weapon rose up on its mount, glowing like a star. Electricity snapped between the magnetized tongs as it hummed louder and louder. It bobbled over large chunks of rubble, passed by a nearby tank and stopped.

The main cannon was a quarter of a mile high, a hundred yards away. White jagged streaks of lightning shot out, cutting across the air from the tongs to the ion cannon. It decimated the surface as it went, tearing and ripping the metal with ease. Desperate voices flooded Consolidation airwaves.
"The east wall at the main cannon facility is under attack!"
"Send reinforcements!"

The Admiral ordered troops and tanks into the sector. The Red Stripe responded also, with Spider charges and seeker missiles, but it was too late. With a final white-hot lightning slice, the lower generators at the ion cannon blew apart. With main power offline, the facility was as useless as an empty building. Ebteon's defense against the Meem battle cruisers was crippled. The enemy fleet could now de-cloak anytime they pleased. The result would be nothing less than horrific.

2

"What is the status of the dome shield?" Admiral Bine growled.
"Holding at one-eighty, sir."
He frowned, "It won't be enough. Get your troops to escape shuttles. Full retreat, rendezvous point blue. Send the codes."
Bine slumped back in his chair, biting at his lip with large teeth.
"Evacuate the Command Center," he said to the commanders, "and get to your ships."

His eyes narrowed as he watched the readout on his screen. The Meem cruisers energy fluctuation came into view just above the atmosphere. Bine saw that a Consolidation ship sat in the enemy path. He checked its identification code.

"Gorza, get out of there."

3

"Incoming message, sir. The ion cannon has been destroyed. A retreat is ordered."

Oh no.

Nule looked up at the frontal screen. He realized that their suspicions had been correct. Ten Meem Warbirds de-cloaked directly in front of them.

4

"Evasive and raise shields! Full accel into Asteroid mouth!"

"Shields are still offline, Captain."

The Truthseeker's nose shot starboard, away from the Meem Flagship and toward the nearby gathering of churning asteroids. A Meem cruiser turned in pursuit. The others seemed content to open fire on the planet.

Geesh clacked his teeth, readying the weapons panel. Vulpa punched in codes at her station with lightning speed.

Nule called out, "Aft mine spread!"

A port underneath the Truthseeker opened and small charges rocketed out, one after another. The closing Warbird hit the trail of mines, setting them off one by one. Fire jolted over the enemy shield, slowing their pursuit. A seeker missile shot up, from the top of the Meem ship. It curved down toward the Consolidation cruiser, leaving a shimmering exhaust trail as it went.

"Incoming missile!"

With no operable shields, Nule called out the only option he could think of.

"Ripper barrel. Ten-twenty."

With a shot of Eltic fluid into the carbine matrix, the Truthseeker's speed doubled in an instant. She banked and dived in a maneuver a Red Stripe Impath would've been proud of. The accompanying quake knocked many to the floor.

"Short plasma release, on my mark," Nule yelled from the slick surface beside the captain's chair.

Vulpa, gripped her station, tapping in the command.

"Mark!"

A small cloud of plasma spread out from the rear of the ship. The chasing seeker missile blazed into the shining mist and detonated.

"We cannot maintain this speed, sir." Vulpa said, watching her screen.

Nule knew she was right. The Eltic fluid would damage the chamber.

"Disengage."

The extreme acceleration fell away from the Truthseeker. The Meem cruiser was once again gaining behind them. With a bright flash, a torpedo was away.

"Incoming!"

Nule couldn't use the same maneuver. The chamber hadn't yet cooled.

What now?

A voice from the engineer station, "Shields back online captain."

Thank goodness.

The torpedo struck. A low rumble and snapping electricity from behind.

"Shields offline, captain."

"Meem ship is charging a primary weapon."

Nule's mind jumped to an image of Carbaugga Fint, the captain of the Phazon Twelve. He pinched his eyes shut, trying to think.

He opened them with a grimace, "Full spectrum, Mr. Geesh-- Fire."

Five torpedoes were away along with six blasts of concentrated plasma. They all arrived, one after another, sending a growing shockwave over the Meem hull. The enemy stuttered to a stop.

"Meem outer shields dropping to forty percent. Inner shields holding at full."

Nule couldn't believe the punishment the Meem ships were built to endure.

"The enemy weapon is almost charged, Captain."

The Redeemer cruiser swooped down into the Truthseeker's path.

"Remain on current heading Captain," Commander Gale instructed over the airwaves.

"We're on a collision course with you, Redeemer," Vulpa snapped.

"*Maintain present course*, please," Sparrim reiterated.

Nule looked over, "Follow her instructions, Commander."

The Redeemer had a plan and he, being fresh out of ideas himself, did not want to foil it. Vulpa forced her long fingers not to change course.

"Five seconds to impact," she complained.

The Meem ship gained on them with a fully charged Particle Vacillator.

"Four."

Geesh drooled and barked. Nule tensed and cringed. The crew braced themselves.

"Three."

Vulpa's tense fingers hovered over her panel, ready to change course, to turn out of the way.

"Two," she continued.

Without warning the Ectopal cruiser shot straight down just in time for the Truthseeker to rocket past overhead.

"Fire," Sparrim commanded.

The entire Redeemer arsenal unloaded on the pursuing Warbird. Plasma charges and torpedoes, seeker missiles and particle beams. The enemy turned and quaked. The bombardment forced it to a halt with a weakened outer shield.

"Meem inner shield down to ninety eight percent."

Nule, "Bring her about. Full spectrum, on my mark."

Over the crackling speaker, "No, captain. Do not engage. Continue into the Asteroid Sea."

"You'll be destroyed," Nule said in a panic, "And *you've* got the sequence carrier."

Sparrim smiled at Tweezor and Timothy.

"We are perfectly safe."

She watched the fire fade away from the Meem hull.

"Head for the mouth. We'll be right behind you."

Nule turned to look over his command crew.

"Stand down and set a vector for the entrance."

The Warbird opened fire on the Redeemer with two seeker missiles that turned and sped at them.

"Initiate frequency code," Sparrim said.

With the Meem positioning code duplicated, the missiles straightened out, flying into the void of space.

Tim grinned, "Cool."

"We haven't got much time. They'll figure out what we're doing soon," she said, "Set a course for the Asteroid Sea entrance and engage."

A particle Vacillator beam shot out from the nose of the Meem vessel. It faded into nothingness before it reached the Ectopal hull. The signal they'd learned from the scout ship in Timeshift Tunnel wouldn't let the Meem attack them, at least for the moment. Tim held a fist high in the air at the front screen. He laughed at the Meem.

"What's the matter dude? You havin' a bad day, or what?"

Tweezor chittered beside the human.

"Or what!" he repeated, laughing.

The Redeemer dived and sped. She was a fiery comet, shooting into the Asteroid Sea entrance.

The entrance was known as the mouth. It was the only way in. The exit was at the other end, a day's journey away. Many vessels had been digested in between.

5

All of the asteroids in the sea were once part of a planet known as Empon Tract. The planet had been a rocky wasteland with a rotating liquid core of a mineral, Zero NTR. The mineral in its unrefined form was highly volatile and emanated a deadly radiation known as Zeron Radiite. If synthesized with other chemicals and refined, the Zero NTR became Plus NTR. What it then gave off was an altered Radiite-like emission called the Zeron Negative Field.

In large doses the field would kill most humanoids very quickly. In small doses it had a pleasurable, hallucinogenic effect that was highly addictive. Users called it 'braining' because the initial sensation was like your head being squeezed. After a moment, the pressure faded and the duration of the high was a feeling of calm submergence, blurred vision and hallucinogenic intoxication.

A refining facility was established and demand for Plus NTR was like nothing anyone had ever seen. Natives of the nearby planet, Ebteon, were especially susceptible to NTR addiction, as were E-Triptics. There were individuals in both races who would do anything for a small vial of the liquid mineral alloy. Wars broke out over Empon Tract and the planet was eventually destroyed.

A bombing run at the main facility detonated the volatile planet core. The ensuing explosion formed the Asteroid Sea. Radiation from the Zero NTR formed around the sea and became an impenetrable barrier containing the churning mass of rock. A natural versal slipstream ran through the center of the mass, creating the only entrance and exit. Once a ship ventured in, it couldn't get out until it reached the other side. It was a day's journey (about twelve hours) in the slipstream. A ship could jump out of the stream, but would be at the mercy of the churning rocks surrounding them. If a ship remained in the slipstream they would be perfectly safe from the surrounding asteroids and would be pulled through the sea, to the exit.

Sparrim looked over from the aft screen, rubbing her eyes. She'd been staring into it for more than an hour.

"Continue monitoring and keep me informed."

Tim watched the view screen in awe. The shadowy masses spiraled and drifted in a kind of orchestrated flow. Distant galaxies spun with remarkable radiance, creating a colorful backdrop.

"It's beautiful," he whispered, smiling.

"Tim still wanna go back home?" the midget asked, nudging him.

The human looked down, "Right now? No. I'm right where I wanna be."

Tweezor chittered, "You comin' along, dude."

Tim sat down on the floor in front of the navigation station. Tweezor sat beside him. They both watched the asteroid dance on the screen.

"You know," Tim said, "not even the astronauts on my planet have seen anything like this. It's... It's just amazing."

The little man got serious, "It a good thing you do, Timothy Rayburn. To save verses."

Tim looked at his alien friend.

"It's the *only* thing I've ever done. It's probably the only thing I'll ever do that means anything."

"What we doin' now means *everything*. If re-set machine, everyone Tim ever meet again will owe their lives. It big."

"Yeah, that's pretty cool I guess, but--"

"But what?"

"I guess I'm just afraid that going home after all of this and living a normal, boring life will seem...pointless."

"Hmmm," the little spaceman thought, "It is pretty big thing to top."

"Yeah."

"Well," Tweezor reasoned, "We probably die anyway."

Tim grinned, "Probably."

"It cool. They build statue of us, or something."

The teenager looked at his skinny arms, "I hope they make me look more muscular."

"I hope make *me* look taller," the little man said, patting his bald head.

Tim burst into laughter and Tweezor joined him. The longer the midget chittered the higher pitched it got. It soon became an erratic percolation of squeaks. Tim's eyes watered and his sides ached before their amusement faded. He leaned back against the station support, trying to contain himself. It was difficult with Tweezor chuckling flat on his back, churning his stubby legs as if he rode an upside-down bike.

"You know, the biggest thing I had to worry about before I left Earth was a speech. It seems so stupid now."

Tweezor tried to catch his breath, "It not stupid. It still important."

"Yeah?"

"Yup. You still give speech," he balled his hand into a fist, "Go for it, dude."

"Maybe I will."

Tim gazed into the churning Asteroid Sea. He put his arm around Tweezor's shoulders.

"Maybe I will give my speech. And just maybe it'll be *awesome*."

"Yeah baby!"

"Okay," Tim said with a smile, "I will."

6

Sparrim Gale walked onto the bridge wearing a long silvery gown. Wavy designs had been embroidered into the fabric around the low neckline. Tim looked over from his trance-like gazing into the view screen. He yawned sleepily and sat up.

"Timothy, would you accompany me to my room, please?"

His face went bright red.

"Your room?" he forced out.

Her smile was kind, yet apprehensive. Her hair, which was actually thousands of tiny dark tentacles, had been tied back from her smooth, pallid face.

"Yes, I have something for you."

The image of Sparrim before him was better than any creased picture or grainy holograph. She was real, alive, and smiling just for him.

"Okay."

You have something for me?

Her gown flowed like shimmering liquid with each step. He followed her across the bridge, entranced by the satin-like material. She turned to look at him, reached back and took his hand. His heart was a thumping cannon.

"Come," she said.

The palm of her hand was smooth, like rose petals.

He awkwardly stepped with bandaged feet, limping a bit. The salve on his burns had made him heal unbelievably fast, but the soreness still lingered.

"Is there pain you are receiving?"

"No. No pain. I'm okay."

"Is it your feet? How is your swelling?"

"My swelling is fine. I'm good."

She led the way down a short corridor and he followed with a spellbound smile. He hoped she hadn't noticed the cold sweat in his palm. His entire body was weak as she opened a door and stepped inside. Her small apartment was dimly lit. There was a closet, a dresser, a nightstand and naturally, a bed.

"Sit here," she said, gently touching his shoulders, backing him up to the bed.

The back of his knees hit the mattress and he stumbled. Without thinking, he grabbed her around the waist for support. Their bodies pulled tight against one another and she let out a faint gasp.

"Sorry," he whispered, forcing himself to let go.

"Sit," she said, pushing down on his shoulders.

His entire body felt like it was ready to burst.

She backed away slowly and turned, kneeling down beside the dresser.

"What I brought you here for was this."

When she rose up from the shadows, she was holding a pair of silver shoes. Tim slid around to get a better look. At that moment the heel of his foot caught the corner of the bed frame, jolting pain up his leg. He winced and let out a yelp as he reached for his foot.

"Oh," she said, "You are in awful pain. Let me help you."

Sparrim pulled his burnt feet up onto the bed and removed the bandages quickly. With his feet exposed she reached for a nearby bottle of medicated cream and squirted out a slick dollop. She set the bottle aside and rubbed the lotion between her hands to warm it up.

She stroked the tops of his feet with lubricated hands. She caressed the bottoms with slick palms. She slid her slim, glistening fingers between his toes.

It was soothing.

Fear suddenly gripped him by the throat. He couldn't breathe. Lurching away, he rolled and fell to the floor.

"I've got to go," he grunted, scrambling to his feet. "Sorry."

She looked up, surprised and confused. Timothy's face went tomato red. He stood frozen, afraid of her reaction.

Sparrim only cocked her head and asked, "What's wrong?"

"Nothing."

She looked at him with confusion. His quantum assistant went to work and he felt cold sweat disappear from his face and arms.

"I have to go to…uh, out to do this…thing."

His slimy feet were cold on the tile floor. He swung around and slipped, nearly falling. She rushed to catch him in her arms. He once again found himself in her embrace.

Their faces were so close. He felt warm breath over his cheeks. She was beautiful and he couldn't help himself. He leaned in to kiss her. Their lips met and she abruptly backed away, confused.
"I'm sorry," he said, "I didn't mean to..."
He rushed for the door.
"But what about--"
"I really...um...gotta go."
She held up the shoes.
"Don't you want these?"
He lunged forward, grabbed them out of her glistening hands and backed up.
"Yeah. They're great. Thanks. Bye."
He thrust himself into the hallway and took off speed walking. He didn't know where he was headed; only that he was getting away from there. He gritted teeth and stomped faster. He felt like he'd taken advantage of her, like he'd violated her trust or...he'd tricked her somehow. But, he couldn't help his attraction to her. He was ashamed. He couldn't get her face out of his mind. She was beautiful and he didn't deserve her or anyone.
I'm such a loser.
Tim looked down at the tag dangling from the left shoe. What it said made him feel even worse.
Thank you for saving me at the tower. I may have been wrong about you.
Your friend, Sparrim.
"No," Tim whispered, "You were right. I'm a shallow creep."
He turned to look back down the corridor. It was empty.

7

Tim walked onto the bridge of the Redeemer wearing his new silver shoes. He noticed that Sparrim had changed her clothes. She was back in an official looking Ectopal military uniform. He was happy she wasn't in the gown. It was too much for him to handle.
He approached her, "I'm sorry about...before."
She looked up from her panel, thinking about his lips pressed against hers.
"I did not understand the gesture," she said.

136

"I shouldn't have done that. I'm sorry."

She smiled, "Thanks for saving me."

Tim turned toward the sleeping midget, across the room.

"Tweezor saved us. I didn't do anything."

"You held me from falling long enough for Mr. Norbinger to get to us. I owe my life to the both of you."

"Well, I don't know…"

"I do. Please let me know if there's anything I can do to repay you."

Tim smiled, "Believe me, you already did."

"Huh?"

"The shoes, I mean," His face went red again, "They're great. The shoes. Real comfortable…the *shoes*."

"Yes, well I had the other ones thrown away. They were badly damaged."

"The *shoes*," he said again.

He then turned and hurried away. He sat down on a seat beside Tweezor as he rustled awake. With heavy eyelids the little man gazed into Sparrim's face. She looked at the human with a faint smile. He began to chitter as he grinned with big, square buckteeth.

"Tim *bad boy*," he laughed.

"What?" the human whispered.

"Tim got girlfriend!"

"Shhh… I do not."

Sparrim stepped closer. Tim smiled at her, covering the midget's mouth.

"Shut up, dude," Tim said.

"Tim the man."

He frowned at Tweezor, "I am *not* the man."

"No good to lie. Me know all."

"Yeah well, keep your *all* to yourself."

"Hey," the little man said looking toward the floor, "nice shoes."

8

"Incoming transmission from Admiral Bine, Captain." Nule sat forward in his chair and cleared his throat.

"Visual, please."

A crackling static image popped onto the main screen. The Admiral looked distressed. He had a short scar across his brow. A line of dried blood led from the wound down to the corner of his left eye.

He spoke, "Captain Nule, thank goodness you are safe. Do you have to sequence carrier?"

"Yes, Admiral. He is aboard the Redeemer, currently."

"Good, very good. Make haste for the exit, and then on to Choxide. And keep your wits about you, Gorza. You've got one of them on your tail."

Nule gritted his sharp teeth, "A cruiser followed us in, did it?"

"Yes," Bine answered, "Our scouts spotted it entering the mouth a few minutes ago."

"Thank you, sir. We'll watch for it."

"You know that you cannot trust your scanners in a versal slipstream. Visual is all you've got."

The captain's eyes narrowed, "Yes. I know."

"The Meem has forced a full evacuation of the Ornetho system. Scorrinwall is lost."

"I'm sorry, Admiral."

"Yes, well…the fleet will rendezvous at Ectopa Crin. I will attempt to contact you when we arrive. " Bine's words went icy cold, "You're on your own, Gorza. I can't get any ships past the blockade. They've got the whole sector locked tight."

"I understand, Admiral."

"When you exit the slipstream, you'll be at the core of the Meem occupation. It's a blackout area, so there's no telling what to expect. We've had no communication with the base at Choxide for hours. We can only hope they are still with us."

"Yes, if there is any problem at the base, we will bypass and head for the Vortex."

Bine tried to smile at Nule.

"It's up to you now, Gorza. Be careful. May fate smile upon you, my friend."

"May fate smile upon us all, Admiral."

With that, the screen faded to black.

9

Sparrim Gale watched the rear view screen with a frown. She knew the scanners wouldn't pick up the Meem Warbird that was chasing them. She knew that monitoring the view screen would be the only way of seeing the enemy. The job had been divided into shifts, with two sets of eyes assigned to each hour.

Ensign Rudell and Officer Kinsup were on current watch. Rudell yawned a stretching gape when Commander Gale turned to look his direction. His eyes had become tired, although they did not leave the screen.

"Stay alert, Ensign. You've got ten minutes before the next shift arrives."

Surprised, he snapped his mouth closed, "Yes, commander."

Sparrim looked over to see Kinsup staring into the monitor without blinking. He had his thick, wrinkled lids pinned open with plastic inserts that snapped onto his helmet. Every few seconds he lubricated his eyeballs with a small pump sprayer.

"*I* am alert, Commander," he announced.

"I can see that, Mr. Kinsup. Nice job, but the extent in which you are going is not necessary."

He smiled, which stretched muscles in his cheeks and forehead. It hurt. He grunted at the sharp scraping under his eyelids.

"No, no… Not a problem, Commander. Once, while hunting for slickle bins on my home world, I did not blink for seventeen days."

Tim looked over at the alien with huge bloodshot eyes.

"My God, man. Why would you do that to yourself? It looks so…uncomfortable."

"Well yes," Kinsup agreed, "It is nearly unbearable after three days or so, but after five days the whole face tends to go numb. Then it's not so bad."

Tim scrunched his face in disgust as he looked closer.

"That can't be good for you."

Tweezor sounded from behind, "You a wild man!"

"Yes, thank you," Kinsup said, "I hold the record for not blinking in a least three systems – probably more."

"Impressive!" Tweezor laughed.

"Weird," Tim whispered, still wrinkling his nose.

"Yes, I-- " Kinsup gasped.

"What, dude?" Tweezor asked.

"I…saw *movement*…behind us."

He tapped the screen in front of him. Sparrim spun around to her own panel. The image was hazy. The versal slipstream distorted everything.

"Are you sure?"

"Yes," he swallowed, turning his neck toward the commander with discomfort, "I'm sure."

Without a moment of hesitation she called out, "Battle stations."

10

"Captain Nule," The gritty voice called out over the intercom transmission, "We've spotted movement behind us. It could be the Warbird."

Nule leaned forward, "Do not engage. They may not have seen us. Increase speed twenty percent."

The Truthseeker and Redeemer cruisers sped faster to avoid a confrontation with the Meem vessel. Sparrim watched the monitor close. At first, all she saw was the spiral white haze of the versal stream. After a moment, a faint reflection caught her eye. And then another…and then, fading into view she saw a wide, imposing wingspan. Bays for numerous deadly weapons glowed in the darkness with red neon intensity.

Sparrim clicked a toggle switch on her control panel, "They're gaining on us, Captain Nule." She gritted her teeth, "They've seen us,"

So be it.

Nule, "Prepare to make a jump out of the stream. On my mark."

Vulpa began calculations at her station and spoke to her captain, "The cruiser class ship was not designed to maneuver an asteroid field. Also, our shields will not withstand more than a few minutes of massive bombardment."

"You are correct," Nule agreed, "Mr. Geesh, man the spine."

Geesh spoke into the intercom, "Spine gunners to your stations! Target incoming asteroids! Protect the hull!"

Gunners ran down long hallways that led from the engineering core to the upper and lower 'spines' of the ship. Each stepped inside an egg shaped gun pod, harnessed in, and powered up the

140

individual reactors. Panel lights popped alive and targeting displays faded into thin crosshairs. With duel control sticks in hand, the plasma guns just outside the rounded compartments came up into position. The gunners were then in control of two bi-barrel scatter cannons. Each of their arms would control an individual cannon. The pods lit up the ceiling and underbelly of the Truthseeker. A hundred soldiers waited at his or her controls. They knew that the ship would soon be outside the protective layer of the versal slipstream. What lie beyond that was the largest gathering of asteroids in known existence.

Unlike the Truthseeker, the Ectopal cruiser Redeemer was not equipped with spine cannons. When she entered the Asteroid Sea her shields and maneuvering abilities would be all that stood between her and a pummeling of rock. Commander Gale scanned the readout of the plasma shield generator. Tweezor had taken over an empty console at the rear of the bridge. His pudgy fingers tapped with smooth precision as he attempted to ready the secondary ion shield armature. It was still an experimental technology, but it had shown much promise in simulations. The worst side effects known to occur in idemic tests were electrical interference and shut downs of vital systems. Until perfected it would be used as a last resort. Even in short bursts it would be dangerous.
Tweezor checked radiation levels and made a few adjustments.

11
"Meem Warbird closing in," announced Commander Vulpa.
Geesh added, "I would approximate distance at two thousand pex."
"Prepare to jump into the field."
Connected Crichits jabbered in the background. Vulpa, professional and determined as ever, readied her panel for manual flight. She would fly the Truthseeker in the Asteroid Sea. With Tweezor aboard the escort ship, she was the best pilot available.
"Remember, avoid the larger masses and let the gunners take care of the smaller ones."
"Yes, Captain," she responded as a semi-circle screen lowered down from the bridge ceiling. It curved around her head, from ear to ear, and provided a view of the space around the ship. Reaching

over her shoulders she pulled a harness into position. With a *click-click* it locked together across her chest and around her waist. The Captain followed his first officer's lead, leaning back and pulling on his own harness. Geesh slathered and barked watching them. He would remain standing at his station, as always, on rigid, muscular legs.

Nule said, "Look sharp." His voice echoed over the main intercom, down hallways and over decks of soldiers.

The Meem cruiser speeding behind them fired a single torpedo. It rocketed at the Redeemer.

"Incoming!"

Sparrim tensed.

Timothy gasped.

Tweezor frowned into his screen.

Captain Nule called for the "Jump" and both Consolidation ships pushed their way out of the slipstream. The Torpedo continued down the versal path, with no target and an unknown destination.

The enemy Warbird paused, gazing into the swirling asteroids, trying to decide if pursuit would be necessary.

12

Vulpa took manual control of the Truthseeker. The ship climbed and spiraled away from a huge rock mass and then turned to narrowly miss another. The spine gunners opened fire on the smaller asteroids with thin bursts of white-hot plasma. The cannon chambers rotated, lighting up the field with thousands of energy pulses and explosions in every direction. The next massive shadow darkened the port side of the cruiser and Vulpa pulled the ship on its side and dived. The huge asteroid followed close behind until she pulled them away from its gravitational path. Dust and debris from destroyed rock masses showered the cruiser shield, sending a constant rumble over the hull.

13

Sparrim had spent the previous few hours watching that asteroid dance from a safe distance. Inside the slipstream it had been beautiful, an orchestrated display of color and shadows. But as they broke through becoming a part of it, the aesthetics stopped.

The inspiration gave way to chaos. They'd forced themselves onto a deadly canvas that did not want them. The result of their intrusion was immediate.

Four large asteroids spiraled toward the ship from four different directions. The Redeemer climbed and banked port.
Then starboard.
Then port.
A sharp dive and then it climbed again.

14

The vibration was felt on the bridge as Commander Vulpa Nim pulled back hard on her control stick. The cruiser climbed and turned. Three fast approaching asteroids competed for her attention from three different directions. With two avoided, she increased speed by twenty percent and pulled the stick hard away from the third. It wasn't soon enough. The rock mass caught the rear fuselage and starboard engine skin. The Truthseeker quaked in the impact and spun sideways as Vulpa attempted to correct the trajectory. Critchet engineers yelled to one another in their synthesized, backward talk. Excitedly, they adjusted levels, trying to remain standing.
"Shield status!" Nule called out over the rumble.
No response.
Mr. Geesh held tight to his station, tapping away at his controls. The green-lit screen in front of him flashed and reflected off his large teeth. He slathered, grunted and barked.
"Shield status!" Nule yelled again, pushing his voice louder, "Is the shield holding?"
Geesh, "Yes, sir. Just barely, but yes."
"We've lost four canisters, Captain. I am re-routing now," Mr. Sorpe said from behind. Nule felt the quake fading and he looked over at his pilot.
"How are we doing, Commander?" he asked her.
Vulpa did not look up. She was too busy working to keep them alive. The cruiser tipped downward into another sharp dive.
"I hate to say this, sir..." she began.
"Say what?"
"I hate to say it...but...I wish Mr. Norbinger were here."

Nule said, "Vulpa, you are an excellent pilot. You're doing fine, just fi--"

Another asteroid struck. It came from below striking the underbelly of the cruiser.

"We're losing six more canisters!"

"Environment systems on all lower decks are failing!"

"Evacuate those decks and lock down the outer skin sections!" Geesh yelled.

Nule looked over the rising stress in his command crew and then up at the main screen.

"The lower shields are down to twenty percent," Sorpe announced.

"Seal off one-one-four!"

Vulpa's eyes widened.

"Brace for impact!"

15

A near full stop jolted Timothy before a sharp increase pulled at him again. He looked over the officers on the bridge. Their work was quick and efficient. An explosion rumbled under their feet.

"Port wing shields dropping, Commander," called out a high-pitched midget voice.

"Reconfigure the matrix. Route to link five."

The Redeemer shot upward with unbelievable force. A new group of asteroids came at them. Tim went pale. He stared into the view screen. He couldn't control his breathing; it was shallow and fast. A machine-gun heartbeat pounded at his body. He was powerless, fighting for air. It was happening too fast.

Can't think.

The ship turned, seemed to drop sideways. His stomach was a wrenching knot. He could taste bile. He tried to swallow. His vision tunneled.

Can't see.

"Pull up!" a distant voice called out, "Try to increase power!"

The sounds faded. The little man's face was what he saw last. It went dark. There was no chipmunk laughter. Not even a smile. A thick black void waited for Tim. He fell into it, gasping.

16

It was clear to Captain Nule.

We cannot survive this.

Another dark mass crashed into the ship. Electricity arced over Vulpa's station. Her view screen exploded into hundreds of tiny chunks of shimmering glass right in front of her. Her face streaked with blood. She screamed.

Sorpe called into the intercom, "Medic to the bridge!"

"Manual control is lost," a Critchet engineer complained. "Shields failing!"

Nule tensed, "Mr. Geesh, get us back into the slipstream. *Now.*" The ship rocked under another impact.

"The upper spine reactors have failed."

Vulpa held long fingered hands over her face.

"My eyes...I can't see..."

The captain tried to remain focused on the task at hand.

Geesh barked, "Starboard shields are lost, sir."

"Just get us into the stream."

A loud knocking rained over the hull as they sped toward the protection of the versal slipstream.

Inside, the Meem Warbird sat with a sniper's patience. Its particle vacillator was charged and ready.

17

"Commander, the Truthseeker's re-entering the slipstream."

"What's their status?"

"Failed starboard shields...manual control failure...environment system failure..."

Sparim interrupted, "Follow them in, Commander. Mr. Norbinger, ready the ion armature."

They followed commands without hesitation.

With a final mass dodged, the ship raced for the filmy vein. The versal stream curved its stretching arc into the distance, like an extended whip. The moving energy in its center traveled toward the exit in glowing silver clouds. The enemy was somewhere within, unseen, and undoubtedly ready for them.

"Ready the weapons array, Mr. Pheene."

"Charged and standing by, Commander."

Sparrim sucked in a deep breath. She glanced at Timothy and realized he'd passed out. His limp body hung loose in the harness.

She turned back to the front screen, tightening her jaw.

18

The Truthseeker blasted through the hazy outer layer of the versal slipstream. With a loud rumble, she pushed her way in.

"Full speed," Nule shouted, "Make ready a Ripper mixture. On my mark."

Geesh watched his screen, searching for the Meem ship. In an instant, he spotted it.

"Meem cruiser directly behind us, Captain…" his tongue slathered, "Gaining on us." Medical personnel rushed onto the bridge and attended to Commander Vulpa's bleeding eyes.

"Mark," Nule said, watching the screen.

In a sudden rush, the cruiser's speed doubled. Doctor Clave held tight to a nearby beam while Vulpa gritted sharp teeth, grasping her damaged control panel. Critchet engineers held onto one another, jabbering.

"Charge the aft aggressor tube."

The Redeemer hit the slipstream, racing into position behind the Truthseeker.

"Fire," Nule ordered.

Commander Geesh, for the first time in his career under Gorza Nule's command, hesitated.

"Sir, the Redeemer has entered the stream behind us."

Nule's fists pounded his chair.

He opened a channel, "Move, Redeemer! The enemy is behind you!"

There was no time to react. The Meem seeker missile was already away.

A bright gas trail followed the weapon, like a striking snake. The impact hit an already weakened shield at the rear of the Redeemer. The explosion tore through one of three primary engines, igniting the fuel core. The ensuing blast destroyed the second and crippled the third. The cruiser ripped into a shockwave rotation. Shields dropped. Environment systems failed. Backup systems failed. Aft sections of the hull were not only breached, they were gone altogether. Thirteen decks of Ectopal workers and soldiers died. Their bodies froze and broke apart.

Sparrim was thrown against the tension of her harness, as were Timothy, Tweezor and the command crew. A standing officer was thrown into a beam, the impact crushing his body. He fell to the hard floor, dying.

Tim was awake. Confused and terrified, he looked to Sparrim. Their eyes connected and she saw the panic in them.

Don't let us fall, they seemed to say.

And then she remembered his words at the tower.

I'm not letting go.

But once again, there was nothing to hold onto. It was just them and a mile of open air.

19

Nule gasped, watching explosions engulf the escort ship. When the orange cloud faded he saw the twisted metal and debris where two main engines should've been. Sparks showered the exposed framework and amputated, flailing lines. Gases spewed and flames leapt across destroyed decks. Chunks of pressure glass shimmered like diamonds in drifting fields. It all rotated in an uncontrollable momentum. The Redeemer was paralyzed and falling.

"Full stop and bring us about. Ready the tractor beam, Mr. Sorpe."

The Meem Warbird sat in silence, waiting to strike.

"Tractor standing by, Captain."

"Lock and initiate beam."

The particle tractor beam heaved at the Redeemer until it came to a stuttering halt.

"Redeemer, do you copy?"

Nule kept a careful eye on the Meem ship.

"If anyone aboard the Redeemer can hear this, please respond."

Silence. The enemy Warbird turned to face the Truthseeker.

"Ready the frontal weapon bays, Mr. Geesh."

He growled, "Charged and standing by, Captain."

20

It was impossible to know if the sequence carrier was still alive and Nule refused to assume anything. He did the only thing he could do. He kept fighting.

The Meem cruiser hovered, as if waiting to see what they would do. It turned with the filmy, versal slipstream wall rushing behind it. It was a great shining backdrop, a translucent tapestry with blurred shadows beyond. Just outside the protective stream the sea continued its deadly, spiral dance. Nule knew they wouldn't survive another trip into the asteroids. Nothing could survive for long inside the churning field.

Nule's vision narrowed at his enemy, "Nothing can survive the asteroids. Not even you."

Mr. Sorpe, "Sir?"

Geesh's teeth clacked in excitement. He knew what his captain was thinking.

"Full chain spectrum, Mr. Geesh, and another after that. Do not let them breathe until I give the word. Fire."

Five Aggressors shot one after another, followed by six pulses of bright plasma. Two winding seeker missiles finalized the wave of attack while Mr. Geesh reloaded the torpedo tubes. Nule sat at the front edge of his chair, watching his offense with intensity. The explosions hit the frontal Meem shield as the next wave fired.

Blast after blast, clouds of expanding fire blinded and faded and blinded again. The enemy quaked backward with each detonation. With ripping pulses of snapping yellow plasma, the Warbird's aft section and port wing thrust though the versal stream and into the Asteroid Sea. A large spiraling mass caught the edge of the wing, pounding the Meem cruiser onto its side. Rock and dust rattled over its failing outer shield. The next wave of inhibitors arrived on target, pummeling the underbelly and starboard wing sections. The billowing orange explosions sent it further into the churning field. Yellow balls of plasma once again followed, as did two snaking seeker missiles. Another large asteroid hit the quaking Meem fuselage, punishing the negative charged, ion shielding.

Nule shouted, "Target the next wave to detonate under the starboard wing."

With a group of torpedoes already away, Geesh made trajectory adjustments for the next set. Through the expanding fire, Commander Sorpe spotted a winding projectile. It traveled through a white-hot blast, at the Truthseeker.
"Incoming!"
The weapon hit the center of the cruiser, crackled for a moment and then ignited its lightning energy over the hull. The plasma shields dropped in the ensuing quake. Three final torpedoes released from the Truthseeker arsenal before the devastation sent weapons control offline.
"The tractor beam has failed," EM stated as the Redeemer drifted away.
"Environment systems are failing," Mr. Sorpe said.
"As is navigation and…" Geesh's screen went dark, "everything else."
Overhead lights across the bridge snapped off and dim emergency lights came on. Nule's readout went dead. The holographic cube went to black. The crew sat in the fading rumble, on the paralyzed bridge of the Truthseeker, watching the main screen as the last three Inhibitors approached the enemy. A second before they arrived, the picture went dead.

Nule sat back into the shadow of the captain's chair. His ship was crippled and blind. There was no advance warning of what happened next, although Captain Nule knew what to expect. He'd spent the entire journey going over it in his mind.

He'd been having nightmares about this very battle, and it seemed that his fears would come true.
Critchet engineers rushed to find solutions.
Commander Geesh growled, trying to find a system, any system, to route power from.
Mr. Sorpe shuffled through circuit boards, frantic.
After what seemed to be an eternity, it began.

At first, it was only a slight vibration under their feet.

21

Random screens flickered back to life across the Redeemer's bridge.

Commander Carboo said, "Environment systems are re-booting now."

Commander Pheene, "I've run scanners and cameras through the secondary matrix...we should get a visual..."

The frontal and aft viewers crackled and hissed. Through garbled static they saw the Truthseeker, powerless and drifting.

Sparrim sat forward, "Can you get a reading on their status?"

Tweezor checked his newly booted readout, "No reading. Versal interference too strong."

Sparrim stood up, "Where is the Meem ship?"

All they could see on the screen was the Truthseeker. The aft view showed an empty shot of the slipstream. Consciousness came back to the human in dull waves. A headache pounded behind his eyes as he tried to comprehend what was happening.

"Pan the camera."

Nothing. It didn't move.

"I *said*-"

"I'm working on it, Commander," Pheene said, tapping calculations into his console. Sparrim's frustration pinched at her nerves.

"Have we got *anything* that works?"

"Yes, Commander," Mr. Norbinger announced with a smile, "Weapon system ready to kick butt."

Tim looked at the midget, "Great. We've got no shields and we're blind as a bat, but we can shoot stuff."

Tweezor shrugged, "It something."

"Panning camera view."

They watched as the screen moved from an image of the Truthseeker to an approaching Meem ship.

"There they are!" Tweezor yelled.

Sparrim's heart leapt.

A thick particle beam shot out from the nose of the enemy. It washed over the Truthseeker's hull while the Redeemer crew watched.

"Lock on and fire the seekers!"

Six winding missiles accelerated into space, curved downward and then hit the ceiling of the Meem Warbird. It shook, quaking down and away from the blasts. The particle beam faded and the Meem ship turned to face the Ectopal cruiser.

Tim fell pale, "Oh man. Maybe that wasn't such a good idea."

Sparrim, "Have we got any shields?"

Tweezor tapped at his station, "Are you kidding?"

Commader Carboo frowned at the midget, "No. Shields are *not operational*."

The midget's lower lip protruded, "That what I meant to say."

"Contact Captain Nule."

Pheene looked up from his panel, "Communications are re-booting now, Commander. It should be just a minute."

Sparrim screamed, "We haven't got a minute!"

22

The vibration had stopped. The main screen faded to a view of the Meem Warbird. Captain Nule was surprised to still be alive.

Geesh clacked large teeth, "Systems are coming back online, sir."

Overhead light illuminated the bridge.

Sorpe, "The enemy is accelerating at the escort ship, Captain."

Nule, "Have we got weapons control yet?"

Hatred for the enemy rumbled in Geesh's reply. "Yes, sir."

"Then fire, Mr. Geesh. *Fire*."

23

Every muscle in Sparrim's body felt like a wrenching clamp as she watched the Meem approach.

"Fire all torpedoes. Ready the seeker missiles."

Ten projectiles shot at once, bearing down on the enemy.

Sparrim was confused, "Are those all torpedoes? We haven't got that many tubes."

Reena Carboo grinned, "Five of them are from the Truthseeker, Commander."

Sparrim's face flushed with astonishment and hope. Her lungs seemed to fill with cooler, fresher air.

"Empty the tubes at them, Commander Carboo. And then do it again."

Nule felt a rush of adrenaline watching ten torpedoes strike. The enemy shuttered backward with a weakened outer shield.

"Hit them again," he said clenching his fists.

Blinding blasts of plasma arrived from both ships.

Seeker missiles exploded.

Furious torpedoes detonated over the Meem's shuddering hull.

"Hit them again," Sparrim said.

"Again," Nule said.

The battle lit up the slipstream, the Asteroid Sea and the entire universe. The Meem Warbird, with weakened ion shielding, was shoved out of the protective stream and into the swarming field of rock. Two Consolidation captains, feeling relieved and somewhat victorious, ceased fire.

24

The Meem Warbird shuddered under a pummeling of small rock. It knocked against the hull like hail. A large asteroid caught the port wing and threw the cruiser into a spin. Engines fired to correct the momentum and the ship raced for the slipstream.

A huge shadow overtook the ship and the mass struck in an instant. The asteroid seemed to be the size of a planet. It hit with a rage that smashed the main section and sent bent wings exploding in two spiraling directions. The massive asteroid forced the flaming fuselage away from the stream. The explosion was a faint rumble in the distance.

Sector Five:
Choxide Mote

1

    Vulpa Nim lay in darkness with bandaged eyes on a table in the med lab. A warm hand touched hers.

She was surprised, "Who is it?"

"Vulpa," Nule whispered, "How do you feel?"

"I am in great pain, but it's nothing I can't handle."

Nurse Neeba checked a chart, flipping though the pages with thick tentacles. She looked

down at the captain's hand on her patient's and then left the room. Nule squeezed tighter.

"That was quite a ride. You did an admirable job."

"I would not say that, Captain. If I'd done my job I would be looking at you right now."

"I disagree, Commander. It was a fine display of piloting. You were in top form."

"Thank you, sir." She adjusted that bandages with her free hand. "How long did the doctor say it would take? It seems like I've been here for hours."

Doctor Clave, who stood behind her, cleared his throat before interrupting.

"I am within hearing range, Commander. Perhaps you would like me to leave so you can complain about me some more?"

Vulpa smiled, "I know you can hear me, Clave. Hurry up with my eyes."

"It is a delicate process. I'm sure the Captain appreciates my hard work, even if you do not."

Nule walked over to the doctor's desk.

"How are you repairing her eyes?"

Clave didn't like to be interrupted and exhaled in frustration.

"I'm not *repairing* her eyes, I'm using her genetic information to grow her new ones." He tapped on a round tank full of murky, brownish fluid, "See?"

Nule squinted to see two lumps of flesh floating in the center of the tank.

He frowned, "Those don't look like eyes."

The doctor huffed.

"It's not finished yet. Perhaps you'd better leave."

The captain went back to the table and the blind patient.

He whispered to her, "If this doesn't work we'll find you a real surgeon on Choxide."

Vulpa laughed, "Thank you, sir."

Doctor Clave said, "I can *hear* you. Haven't you got any tact?" he huffed, "Go give some orders or something. I've got work to do."

Nule smiled at Vulpa, "I'll expect you back at your station soon, Commander."

"Yes, sir," Vulpa said as her captain left the room.

The doctor scowled. "How rude."

2

Tweezor sat at a console, programming an ion bubble simulation. Sparrim watched over his shoulder, wiping tears from her eyes. A third of her crew had died in battle and she was shaken. She tried to focus on Tweezor's project.

"You're saying that a properly modified shield would be able to pass through the Meem firewall?"

"Yes," the little man said, "Finding exact modification frequency is the trick. If I get to work, I'll need some type of small ion generator. Something portable."

Sparrim wanted to find a way to end the Meem threat more than anything. She leaned closer to see the code his small fingers punched in.

"The latest versions of our jetpacks have ion field armatures. Would something like that work?"

Tweezors eyes lit up, "That might do it... if I find correct adjustments for idemic matrix."

She thought about what it would mean to the Consolidation if he were successful.

154

"Keep at it, Mr. Norbinger. I believe you're onto something."

3

"Captain Nule to the bridge. We are approaching the Versal exit," announced Geesh's voice over the speaker.

"I'm on my way," Nule responded.

He quickened pace down the corridor. Stepping into the lift, he rode it up four levels. The doors slid open and Captain Nule crossed the threshold, onto the bridge.

In the aft view screen he saw the damaged Ectopal ship following them. Gasses leaked out severed lines. Sparks sprayed over bent framework. One engine, on the portside of the vessel remained, although it seemed to hang on by only a prayer. Nule was surprised it would fly after the damage it had taken. But there it was, trailing them and under its own power.

Nule sighed.

The Redeemer would need extensive repairs, and he couldn't spare the time. There would be no more escort for the remainder of the journey. The Redeemer's part in the mission was finished.

"Call Commander Gale, please."

The interference received from the surrounding Versal slipstream made the transmission distort and hiss. Sparrim's face was covered in static as it faded onto the main screen. A wide bruise sat swollen across half of her forehead and down one cheek. A small line of blood that began somewhere unseen on her scalp dried against the side of her face.

"Yes, Captain Nule?"

He leaned forward and clasped his long fingered hands, "I am so sorry for the losses you have suffered. Our respect and condolences go out for each member of your crew that died honorably."

Sparrim pinched her eyes closed and hung her head lower for a moment. When her gaze found its way back to Nule, it was glossed with sadness.

"Thank you, sir."

Nule paused, rubbed his chin and then, "I'm afraid we will have to leave you at Choxide. Your ship has sustained too much damage.

I won't risk your remaining crew. I hope you understand my reasoning."

"But, Captain...with a few hours of repairs I'm sure we could continue."

"No, Sparrim. I'm sorry. We cannot afford the time," Nule cleared his throat and smiled, "Believe me when I say that you and your crew have been invaluable to us. We would not have made it this far without you. We owe you our lives...I have not made this decision lightly, you can be sure of that."

Sparrim looked across the bridge at Timothy and Tweezor.

"I understand your reasoning. I wish we could've done more. I would like to have seen this mission to the end."

She wiped a tear away from her eye.

"Thank you, for all you have done."

The screens faded to the darkness of space. She turned to find the human and the midget behind her.

Tim frowned, "This blows. Why can't you fix your ship?"

She put gentle hands on his shoulders. His face flushed.

"The Redeemer has taken too much damage. She can't maneuver. She can't defend herself. It would be suicide to get anywhere near the Meem occupation with this ship. And Nule knows that."

Tweezor looked up from the computer screen and sighed, "She right, dude. Ship jacked up."

Tim turned away, "No! This wasn't supposed to happen! You're our escort. We need you."

"Timothy..." she said walking around to meet his gaze.

He looked up at her and his eyes seemed to say, *I need you.*

"We're a team! Can't you see that?" His voice became pleading, "Don't leave now. Something bad will happen. I just know it."

"Nothing bad will happen. You'll make it to the Generator. Captain Nule will get you there."

"What about you?"

"I..." she grinned, "...will see you on your way back."

"You'll wait for me? Cause I'd like to see you again...before I go back home."

"Of course I'll wait. You'll be a big hero by then...Savior of the universes."

156

A voice sounded from navigation, "The slipstream exit is coming up, Commander."

"Well then," she took in a deep breath, "I guess you'd better get harnessed in."

4

Nule, "Go to standby alert until we've reached the base."

"Standby alert," Geesh stated over the intercom, "All personnel at battle stations."

The cruisers shot out of the Versal slipstream and away from the churning sea of rock surrounding them. The filmy layer faded as sensor systems went back online. The holographic cube display fizzled into view.

"Area scan and hail Choxide."

Officer Xaxe, listened and adjusted signal frequencies.

"It's all blocked by a high powered scramble wave. It looks like a total communications blackout."

"Keep trying and check the emergency frequencies."

Geesh, "I'm picking up a few Meem scout vessels in the next quadrant. I have not detected any ships in the immediate vicinity."

"That doesn't mean they're not there. Be ready for anything."

Geesh's thick fingers hovered over the weapons control panel.

"Yes, sir."

He looked out over the calm space between them and the Choxide system. Everything was eerily silent.

"Scan the base."

Mr. Sorpe said, "Choxide Mote has received no apparent damage. All of their systems are functional, as best I can tell. Also, I am reading approximately two million humanoid life forms at the base and four hundred million or so in surrounding areas. Everything would seem…normal."

Communications officer Xaxe added, "Captain, I've found a coded message on Consolidation emergency channel ML-E22. It's audio only."

Nule, "Let's hear it."

A static female voice garbled for a moment and then, "Attention all ships approaching the following systems: Choxide, Triptic, Rizon, Ornetho, Zotaun, and Deema. Emergency status, M.E. Turn back.

Do not attempt voyage to, or through, any of these systems. Do not attempt use of Wavetime technologies near or through these systems. Afore mentioned areas are Meem occupied and highly dangerous. Emergency status M.E. Turn back…this announcement will repeat…"

Nule knew that 'M.E' stood for Mandatory Evacuation. He'd never known it to be used for so many systems at one time. The Meem fleet must've been larger than any army they'd yet faced. Not even the Consolidation of Organized systems could conquer and maintain such a vast area. A campaign of that size would require hundreds of cruiser class warships on regular patrol routes. Nule looked over a map of multi-system eight-seven, illuminated on the small screen in front of him. A scattered sea of red dots sat across the grid, each representing an uncloaked enemy.

Geesh barked, "I am reading a total of one hundred fifty-eight enemy vessels between our position and the verse one wormhole."

Sorpe was surprised, "That many of them…uncloaked."

"Yes," Nule said, "They have no reason to hide as long as they stay out of range of the bases."

5

Vulpa walked onto the bridge wearing shaded glasses. The lenses were dark with her new eyes hidden behind them. She stopped at navigation control, occupied by Commander Sorpe. Nule looked over from the captain's chair.

"Vulpa," he said, "How do you feel?"

"I am…better."

"Shouldn't you be resting?"

She frowned, "I have had quite enough rest."

The captain smiled, "Did the good doctor release you, or is this an escape?"

"I'll never tell."

She slid into a nearby seat and got to work.

6

General Respit watched the viewer as the Truthseeker and Redeemer cruisers approached Choxide. The military base was at high alert, expecting attack soon.

"Send a scramble code message to the Truthseeker. Ask her what she needs."

"Yes, General."

7

Commander Xaxe, "Security transmission from Choxide Mote. They'd like to know what assistance we need."

Nule looked over, "Give them a list of parts and necessary repairs for the Truthseeker. Also inform them that the Redeemer will be remaining here."

"We have been cleared for platform Green five. Our necessary parts will be waiting for us along with two full engineering crews."

Nule smiled, "They must want to move us out quickly. Very good. Commander Nim, how long will the repairs take?"

She looked up from her station with shaded eyes, "With that much assistance, I'd say one hour for the major systems. The rest we can manage in travel."

The captain spoke to his senior security officer, "Mr. Geesh, keep us informed of any enemy activity."

"Yes, sir."

The damaged Redeemer landed at a private garage, outside the base. Sparrim Gale opened a channel to Captain Nule.

"We have set down about twenty blocks South of your location. General Respit is sending a platoon to escort Tweezor and Timothy to you."

"Thank you Commander Gale, for everything."

"You are quite welcome, sir."

Sparrim turned to her guests and smiled. Tweezor sat at a workstation making adjustments to a simulation program. The computer in front of him flashed WARNING in bold letters before blinking, *simulation unstable, ion failure.*

"Poop!" he yelled, kicking the table, "Not good!"

Timothy leaned over to see the screen, "Do you think you can make it work?"

The midget gritted his buckteeth, "I can make work. Need more time though."

"When you get it right, you will need some packs. So I am sending forty with you," Sparrim said.

"Forty?" he grinned, "Thanks."

"I'll get our scientists on this project, also. I think it could work. I have a good feeling about it."

Tim stood up, "I thought you didn't get feelings about things."

"I lied," she said.

"You *lied?*"

She led them down the corridor to an elevator. The three of them stepped inside and stood in silence as it descended. The human gazed at the Ectopal woman with sad eyes. He thought it might be that last time they'd see each other. He wondered why things had gone so bad. It had seemed like destiny, him finding her. And having to part ways now, well, it just felt wrong.

He wished they could go back to Timeshift Tunnel and rewind to a place where they could stay together. Maybe then he could find the courage to tell her how he really felt.

Maybe...

The elevator stopped at the lower dock with a jolt.

She stepped out, "I guess this is where we say goodbye."

She pointed at a large crate on wheels.

"Those are your Jetpacks. I know you'll get the ion bubble configured. You're on the right track"

The little man chittered, "I do it."

She patted him on his bald head, "Take care of yourself, Mr. Norbinger. And take care of Timothy too."

"All good," he said, walking over to inspect the packs.

She turned to Timothy with a sad smile and gave him a hug. He was surprised at her affection. Her slim body was warm against his. She pulled away slightly. Their faces were close and he felt hot breath on his neck. She turned and kissed him on the cheek. His eyes went wide.

"Goodbye, Timothy Rayburn. Be safe," she whispered.

His mouth hung open for a moment as he desperately searched for the right words to say, the perfect words. None came.

A group of Consolidation soldiers approached.

"Commander Norbinger, I am Sergeant Deen. We will escort you to your ship."

The midget walked around the end of the cart and started pulling it out to the street.

"We go now."

"Bye," Tim said, backing away.

Sparrim watched as they joined the group of soldiers and made their way down the road. When they got to the first intersection, she went back to the elevator. With the pass code punched in, she ascended into the Redeemer.

8

"You have a girlfriend," the little man laughed.

"I *do not*. Stop saying that."

"Who is your woman?" the sergeant asked.

"I don't--"

Tweezor chittered, "Commander Gale."

Deen was impressed, "Nice work, soldier."

Tim frowned, "He's exaggerating. We had a moment, I'll admit, but she's not my girlfriend."

Another soldier spoke up, "Did you kiss her?"

"Yes."

"He save her life and now she shower him with gifts," Tweezor said.

The platoon discussed it amongst themselves.

"It sounds like a girlfriend to me," one said.

Timothy's face went bright red.

Another said, "She's yours, kid."

Tim walked faster, "I don't want to talk about it any more."

9

Tweezor looked down the road with apprehension, "Our travel will lead past my childhood house."

Tim stopped in front of Tweezor and knelt down.

"Your house? Like, where you grew up?"

The little man's constant smile faded a bit.

"Yes," he said, "My family still live there."

"We're stopping to say hello, then."

"No, not good idea," Tweezor said, holding his pudgy hands up like stop signs.

"Why not? It's your family."

"Yes…it my relation…"

161

Tim stood and looked down the street.

"Then we're stopping to see them."

"No, we not."

"Yes, we are."

"No. Not good. We bypass."

"Why? You don't get along with them, or what?"

The short man thought hard.

"Mother and I get along…Brothers and I do not. Father and I do not."

"So you can see your mom for a few minutes, then we'll leave."

Tweezor grinned, "Mother love me much. She good."

"Cool," Tim said, "Which one is it?"

The midget looked down the block and frowned, "Two intersections further."

Side by side they continued, passing by dirty metallic dwellings. Each was a smooth and rounded ten-foot high dome with short, four-foot tall doors.

Tim thought how strange that place was to him, how utterly alien it all seemed. There were no mailboxes, no yards or any visible windows in the houses. There were single man jetpods and small ships parked here and there along the narrow paved road. The neighborhood looked deserted.

"You've got brothers, huh?"

"Yes, lots of brothers."

"It sounds like a big family."

"Yes. Norbinger family big. All big."

"Very big," Tim corrected.

"Yes," Tweezor agreed.

For another block and a half the curious human walked, studying structures that had paved parking areas where he thought grass should be. For that same distance, the midget walked along, cringing at the thought of his father's reaction when he saw them. When they reached the second intersection, Timothy gazed out over the houses on the next block. They looked identical to the previous. Tim realized that he could've easily lost his way in such a place. There were street signs at each corner, but the words were all gibberish to him.

"Which one is it?"

The little man didn't look up, he just pointed a stiff finger down the street, staring at his shoes.

"That one."

The third dome on the left looked just like the second one, and the fourth one, and the one across the street. They were all paneled with sheets of brushed, silver metal. At one time they had all shined in the yellow sunlight, reflecting with an almost chrome radiance. But forty years of violent dust storms left the surfaces covered in small dents and scratches. Dark brown dirt had filled the cracks and dusted the doorways.

Tweezor and Tim crossed a small square of paved yard in the front of the third dwelling on the left. The door stood four feet high and Tim bent down to knock on it. It echoed like hollow steel under his fist.

"You better back up," Tweezor said from six feet behind him.

"Huh?"

As Tim looked back at his short friend, a platform dropped down, creating an eight foot deep, rectangle trench in the ground. Startled, the human leapt for the edge. Hanging on with straining fingers, he saw the floor had stopped moving two feet below the soles of his silver shoes. Tweezor looked down at him inquisitively, cocking his head. The little man stood at the top of a staircase, at the outer end of the unexpected metal furrow.

"Is that as low at it goes, man?"

"Yes," Tweezor answered, descending the stairs.

Tim hopped down, "God, dude. You should tell me when something like that's gonna happen." He took a deep breath, "I 'bout had a heart attack."

"Sorry," Tweezor said, "You should no clunk on door with hand." When they turned to face the doorway Tim saw that it was eight feet tall. The lower half had been below ground level.

A deep voice startled him over a nearby speaker.

"Who's there? What do you want?"

He looked at Tweezor, realized the little man wasn't going to speak up and then decided to take his own initiative.

"Hello?"

"What?"

"Yes. Hello. I'm Timothy Rayburn...of a...of the starship Truthseeker and..."

"Go away. We haven't done anything wrong."

Tim smiled, "No, no its nothing like that. I have Tweezor with me. He's come to see you."

He waited for a response. None came.

"I said--"

"We heard you."

Tim looked at his short friend who smiled and shrugged his shoulders. He turned back toward the closed door.

"So, what do you say? How about letting us in?"

Again, silence.

"I said--"

"We heard you."

The human stepped back puzzled. Tweezor remained quiet.

"So um, how about it?"

They heard muffled arguing. Not over the speaker, but from behind the door. A scream. A loud crash, and then...the tall metal door slid open.

It was dark inside and Tim's eyes took a moment to adjust from the afternoon glare. He looked downward to see Tweezor's small alien brother or father or...belly...large belly...connected to long legs and tall frame.

Seven and a half foot tall frame.

Wide, thick shoulders.

Bowling ball head.

Tim let out a gasp and took quick steps backward. The face looking down at him was pale white, with vampire eyes and huge, square buckteeth. Its chitter was slow and deep, like an ape trying to imitate a chipmunk.

"Good lord," escaped from Tim's mouth. "I'm sorry. I think we got the wrong house. We'll be going."

He stepped back, terrified of the mammoth giant in front of him. It wrinkled its nose, and sniffed at the outside air.

"No," the giant said in a growl, "This is the right house. You've just got the wrong brother."

He glared down at Tweezor with a sneer. Tweezor smiled and waved at his brother.

"Hi, Girz. Good to see you."

"What are you doing here, Tweezor?"

"I came to see mother."

Another very tall alien walked up behind Girz, pushing him aside. He scowled at the two in his doorway.

"Hello father," the little one said.

"Tweezor, why do you waste your time like…*that?*"

"Like what?" Tim blurted

A seven-foot female appeared behind the others.

"Tweez! My baby!" she exclaimed.

She pushed past them and lifted the midget into the air with her thick, powerful arms.

"Mama!" he said, hugging her, "Good to see you!"

Girz huffed and then walked away, shaking his head. The father grumbled, scrunching up his face.

"Don't mind them," she whispered in his ear, "I miss you every day."

"Me too," he chittered.

She set her son down, looking out at the group of soldiers in the street.

Then, she looked at Timothy, who stood quiet at the door.

Her smile was big, shiny and welcoming.

"Who is this?"

"This my friend, mama. This Timothy Rayburn."

"Hi," the human said in a weak voice.

"Hello. Please come in. Any companion of Tweezor's is welcome here."

"Humph," sounded the disapproval from behind.

The giant mother alien turned and slapped her husband hard across the face. He winced, cowering away.

"He is your son," she growled at him.

A bright red mark sat across his cheek, in the shape of her thick hand. Without a word he turned and walked away.

"Yes," she said, "Go back to your teleroom. Perhaps you should stay there for awhile." He kept quiet and continued walking. Girz also, had disappeared.

Tim stayed back, afraid of the mammoth female alien before him.

"No fear mama," Tweezor said with a grin.

"Yes," she said, "I don't strike the undeserving."

Tim tried to smile back as he entered the house.

"Come on!" the midget said taking the human by the hand, "I show you my room!"

Suddenly feeling eight years old, Tim let Tweezor pull him to a dark stairwell.

It led downward into the basement. At the bottom of the staircase was a solitary metal door. The panel beside it glowed green. Tweezor spoke his name into a small microphone. With a quick voice recognition security system release, the little man initiated the retina scan.

Tim said, "God, dude. I used to lock my sister out of my room, but geeze, this is hardcore, man."

"There some sensitive equipment here. I have ten ongoing projects and experiments."

A heavy latch released and the door opened. The little man reached in, clicking on a light. Rows of long tables sat in the darkness of a huge room that looked bigger than the rest of the house. Scientific equipment, papers and small tools cluttered every surface. Wadded up paper, trash and dirty clothes had been strewn across the floor.

Tim laughed, "You're a slob, man."

Tweezor scanned a nearby desk, pushing candy wrappers out of his way.

"I agree. Very messy."

"What are we looking for?"

"Oh, just something that might come handy."

The human found a series of tall tanks in the back of the room. Bubbles drifted upward inside each one's green fluid. One other similarity caught his attention. They all contained a shadowed, limp body, suspended by shiny coils. There were at least six.

"Whoa," he said amazed, "What are they?"

"Got it!" Tweezor chirped, gripping a small handheld quantum tracker. He glanced over at Tim, "Those are genetic experiments."

"Did you clone somebody, man?"

"Yes," he answered. "Me."

"You?" Tim said looking over a body that was seven feet tall and bigger around than the midget's brother, Girz. "This doesn't look like you."

"They variations of me. I deciphered DNA code and made a few adjustments."

"Are they alive?"

"No. Not really. Let us go."

"Wait--" Tim said staring into another tank. The body inside was much shorter than the last.

"We go now," Tweezor pulled at Tim's arm.

"Okay, okay," he said, backing away. "What's that?"

A pudgy hand held up a device the size of a walkie-talkie.

"Quantum tracker." He chittered, "We might need."

"Oh," Tim said looking back at the floating bodies.

Creepy.

Once upstairs, they found Tweezor's mother sitting in the kitchen, at a large table. She had a sharp knife and was preparing some odd-shaped vegetables. She looked up from her cutting board, smiling.

"Was everything where you left it, Tweezy?"

"Yes, Mama."

Tim stepped up, "Mrs. Norbinger, I had something I wanted to tell you."

She motioned for him to sit. "Please."

He sat in a chair beside her.

"Well, I just wanted to say that your son, Tweezor, saved my life."

"Oh?"

"Yes, he saved me. He's a good friend. I know you don't get to see him very often...and so I thought you should know."

A big, wide grin grew across her face. She dropped the knife on the table and hugged the human, chittering in his ear. The hug was unexpected and tight enough to make his ribs ache. He gasped for air.

Tweezor covered his teeth with pudgy fingers, laughing. "Mama like you!"

"Yeah," Tim said, "I think she does."

The little man's smile faded.

"We must go, Mama."

167

She released Timothy and turned back to her son.

"I understand."

They embraced one more time.

They said their goodbyes and then Tweezor led Timothy back to the front door. The giant mother waved at them as they walked to the street.

"We had better get moving, Sir," a soldier said.

"Yeah," the midget answered, still looking at his home, "We go."

10

Mr. Geesh growled at his display screen. He adjusted the scan, narrowing the detection path and intensifying receptor nodes. His large teeth clacked. Backing away from the monitor, he spoke to the captain.

"I've detected thirteen Meem freighters in route to this system. At current speed and vector, they will begin arriving in thirty-eight minutes. I would expect them to be Hover tank delivery vessels." Vulpa added, "A trailing wave of cruiser class warships will be at this location in forty-one minutes."

Nule watched the data scroll across his screen.

"Choxide Mote doesn't have a Stripe squadron. The single-man armored pods will be no match for the Meem hover tanks. The cannon facility will be under attack within minutes of their arrival."

"Yes, captain," Geesh agreed, "And then this entire planet will be swarming with enemy Warbirds."

Nule stared out into temporarily calm space.

"Have Mr. Rayburn and Mr. Norbinger arrived yet?

Vulpa, "They are approaching. We should have them shortly."

"Good," the captain said, "It's time to go."

11

Timothy trudged along behind the midget and the soldiers. His mind swam back and forth between Tweezor's family and Sparrim Gale. He was tired, in his feet and behind his eyes. They'd come so far, experienced so much, an unending sprint it had seemed, and there was still a long way to go.

An unvoiced tension rose all around them. The journey seemed to be building toward something big and Timothy feared, something terrible. He'd seen it in Sparrim's face, heard it in her voice. She'd tried to suppress it, but the fear remained underneath her words. It was the same fear the little man in front of him carried along as he made his way to the ship. It would be the same fear he'd find inside, in the eyes of the crew and the captain. It would live on, unacknowledged and silent, like a scent in the air, until the destination was reached.

The Truthseeker and her crew headed into the unknown depths now. From there on out, a dark anticipation would reach for Timothy from every shadowed corner.

Sector Six:
The Triptic Vortex

1

Vulpa Nim's voice called out to workers at the lower cargo dock.

"Finish loading supplies and prepare for lock down. Departure in eight minutes."

A gritty response sounded back, "We copy, Commander. Bay doors are closing now."

Timothy and Tweezor walked onto the bridge. Geesh turned to face them and smiled with huge teeth. He clapped Timothy across the back, nearly knocking his breath away.

"Welcome," he barked.

The human coughed, gasping, "Thanks. Where's the captain?"

"In his quarters, I believe."

The midget chittered, approaching Vulpa.

"Hey baby. You miss me?"

She turned, opened her mouth, stopped herself from saying something rude and then paused a moment, leaning back.

"Your piloting talents have been noticeably vacant."

"Huh?" he blurted.

"I said that your skills have been missed."

"Oh yeah, baby," he grinned, raising his brow, "I got skills."

Her pale face flexed and snapped down toward a monitor.

"I am busy. You may leave now."

He walked away humming.

Once Vulpa was sure the little man wasn't looking, she allowed herself a smile. Tim caught a glimpse and her expression twisted back into a scowl.

2

Tim pushed the chime button outside the closed door of the captain's office. The tall smooth surface slid open.

Nule said, "Enter please."

The human stepped across the threshold and scanned the room. He saw no one.

"Captain Nule? Are you in here?"

"Yes," a voice sounded from the wardrobe closet at the back of the room, "I am here. It is good to have you onboard once again."

Tim walked closer. Nule appeared from behind a rack of hanging clothing. He was shirtless and buttoning a fresh pair of pinstripe trousers. Tim was surprised to find the captain getting dressed.

"I'm sorry, sir. If you would rather me come back later, I could--"

"Don't worry yourself, Timothy." He smiled, squinting his large oval eyes. "After Timeshift tunnel we should be accustomed to each other's…differences."

Tim grinned, "Yeah, I guess so."

Nule turned away to retrieve a clean dress uniform jacket. Two deep scars sat stretched across his back, surrounded by bubbled, swollen skin. They crossed each other like a distorted X over his spine. Tim could tell the cuts were years old and had healed poorly. Nule turned around and saw the look on Tim's face. The human turned away.

"I'm sorry."

"Don't apologize," the captain said to the human, "you may look." Tim stepped closer studying the blackened skin along the twisted grooves in Nule's flesh. Whatever had caused the damage had been not only sharp, but red hot.

"How did you…I mean…what happened to you?"

The captain sat and motioned for Tim to sit in a chair across from him.

"Every scar has a story, and every story has a lesson to be learned." Nule's voice was even and calm and sad.

"The lesson that ended with these scars began with war."

Tim sat waiting for Nule to continue. After a moment, he did.

"It was fifteen years ago, I had recently been promoted to the rank of captain and was in command of a starship cruiser, the Septor Fin. The end of the Consumption War was nearing and we were busy finalizing treaties in the Kallad Een sector. Negotiations had been rough but we were finally making great progress.

We and our sister ship, the Intep Fin held a position near an opposing fleet of Blank Marauders. The cease-fire was being upheld, but we knew the enemy commanders watched us closely and would attack at any sign of aggression. We sat with shields down, awaiting the ambassador's arrival."

The captain's eyes found the floor. His hands had begun to tremble. Tim's vision remained at eye level, trying not to let on that he noticed Nule's sadness. It lingered in between them, nonetheless.

The scarred soldier continued.

"We received a distress call from a Consolidation ship. They were crippled and in tow, approaching our position. The cruiser towing them was a Marauder Flagship. Our Consolidation brothers were being held for supposed war crimes. They were to be executed for engaging enemies after the cease-fire was initiated.

We knew then they were innocent. My own brother, Gorma, was the Captain and he was a *hero*, not a criminal."

A single tear made its way down Nule's cheek to the corner of his mouth. He could taste it. He continued.

"I requested the ship's release. They refused. I practically begged for its release. I was told to mind my business. By the time the ambassador arrived I was demanding my brother and his crew. I was ready to fight for them…I was ready to *die* for them."

Nule paused to clear his throat. He wiped his cheek with long fingers, and started again.

"The ambassador ordered me to stand down. As a token of good will the prisoner's punishments were to be carried out as their captors saw fit."

A silent pause lingered as Nule decided how to continue. He cleared his throat, balled his hands together and then, finally he spoke.

"The executions took place on the nearby planet's surface."

Another tear rolled. Nule tightened his face to contain any more emotion from escaping. Tim's eyes filled with tears too.

"I followed the ambassador's orders not because I was afraid to die, but because of a sense of duty. I justified my inaction by believing the treaty saved lives."

Nule stared into Tim's eyes.

Tim wiped his face with the back of his hand, "The treaty did save lives, didn't it?"

"What I have told you isn't about treaties or war. It's about right and wrong. It was wrong of me to let them die, especially like that…like criminals."

"If you'd fought them, you'd have been killed by the enemy fleet, wouldn't you?"

"Yes, naturally." Nule clenched his sharp teeth, "But some things are worth dying for."

Tim leaned back and looked at the warrior that sat before him. He could only imagine the pain the captain had known. Nule stood to put on a shirt and jacket.

"We were ordered out of the sector by the ambassador. As we were leaving, my ship was hit with a torpedo. Our shields were still down. The scars that I carry were from my own bridge falling down upon me."

Tim frowned, "Why did they do that?"

"It was punishment, I suppose, for my arrogance."

Tim stood also, "If you had it all to do over again, would you attack them?"

Nule swung around with a piercing grimace that filled Tim with fear.

"I would show them no mercy. I would hit them hard and fast. I would empty my arsenal upon them. And if it wasn't enough, if it were my day to die, then by god, I would take at least one of them with me."

Tim took a step forward and put a hand on Nule's shoulder. "I'm sorry, sir."

Silence was thick between them as the captain fought away more tears. Tim couldn't think of anything more to say, so he turned and left the room.

As the door closed behind the human, Gorza Nule broke down. He remembered his only brother, and he cried.

3

Nule entered the bridge buttoning a fresh jacket. He took his place at the central chair with red, swollen eyes. Timothy sat close behind. He was sorry for bringing up such painful memories for

Gorza. Part of him wished he could take back the entire conversation.

" We have green lights across the board, sir," Geesh said.

Gorza Nule cleared his throat and then called the lift off.

"Fire the mains and rotate one-sixty. Take us up."

The cruiser ascended above the shadowed platform.

Geesh snorted, "Sir, I am reading trace levels of radiation just below the atmosphere…It's Idemic charr."

"Increase to escape velocity, now."

The Truthseeker nosed upward, rocketing into the sky above Choxide.

"I've got three ships de-cloaking dead ahead, at grid three o' five."

"Maintain bearing and speed. Get us past them, Commander."

"Yes, sir."

The cruiser laid over counter-clockwise ripping at the slender gap between two close freighters. Enemy torpedoes were away, but not before the ship hit the atmosphere. A loud rumble overtook the Truthseeker as they pushed into space. The torpedoes detonated behind them in the intense heat.

Geesh snorted, "The distant freighters were a decoy."

"Yes. The planet will be under ground attack in three minutes," Vulpa complained, "not thirty, as we were led to believe."

Xaxe, "Enemy cruisers are uncloaking at grid six-two-five!"

Nule's sharp teeth ground together, "Evasive. Increase five percent and head for the vortex."

"The vortex, sir?"

Two more Meem Warbirds uncloaked and raced at them, bringing the ship count up to six.

"Yes," he said watching the coming fleet in the aft monitor; "We won't survive in open space for long."

"Yes, sir," Xaxe said, "but, the vortex?"

Sorpe's voice was distressed, "You don't mean to go in there, do you?"

"I most certainly do, Mr. Sorpe."

The Triptic Vortex spun in the distance. Its shimmering, silver energy rotated like a galaxy of metallic flakes. Tim held onto his rumbling seat, transfixed by the spiral beauty on the central screen.

He leaned over toward his short friend, who sat next to him on the couch.

"What is that?"

Tweezor frowned and pinched his brow down, wrinkling his nose.

"That," he said with apprehension, "is Triptic Vortex."

Tim looked down into fearful eyes.

"What's wrong, dude?"

Tweezor's face was even more pale than usual, "It be better to take chances against Meem."

"What?" the human asked, "Why? What's in there?"

"Monsters," was the reply, "It full of monsters."

4

"Mr. Norbinger, we need you, please."

The midget hopped down and made his way across the vibrating bridge to an empty station.

Geesh growled, "Pursuit ships are gaining."

Vulpa's voice was urgent, "Incoming missiles, Captain."

"Plasma release."

The Truthseeker quaked as weapons detonated close behind them.

"Ships are still gaining sir. I count two primary weapons fully charged."

Nule, "Prepare Wavetime ignition."

Without hesitation, Critchet Engineers opened the antimatter chamber control board, sliding it down into position.

Sorpe spoke up, "The Meem home in on the Wave signal. They will enter our time path and--"

Nule stopped him, "I'm well aware of the Meem ship capabilities, Mr. Sorpe. We won't be in Wave more than ten seconds."

"Calculations complete," the little man said.

A chime at the engineering platform indicated an antimatter chamber green light.

"Incoming torpedoes!" Vulpa called out.

Nule narrowed his oval eyes, "Initiate Wavetime."

Timothy held tight, fell pale and said a silent prayer.

5

A Meem Warbird raced toward its prey. Two torpedoes released, one after another. They crackled their red snapping energy into the distance, striking at the enemy.

The Truthseeker blurred for the slightest moment, its light streaking in all directions. Then, with a thunderous boom, a time path opened in front of the ship. It was a bright blue tunnel leading to the distant Vortex. The cruiser nosed down and then disappeared.

Two torpedoes continued aimlessly into calm, empty space.

6

The gathering of Meem ships paused for a second, scanning. With a clap of thunder the path reopened. Six Warbirds entered, disappearing into the bright blue crack in space.

7

Timothy opened his eyes and looked around the bridge. Everything was in slow motion. Distant voices echoed back and forth, across the room. At first, he thought he was dreaming. He wasn't. All four monitors glowed bright blue with random white streaks. Tweezor's shrill words bounced around Tim's head. He couldn't make them out. He also heard Captain Nule and Commander Vulpa too. But it was Mr. Geesh's low growl of a voice that got his attention. It wasn't only because the low tone was easier to understand under the current circumstances. It was what he said that grabbed hold of Tim's brain.

A gritty snort and then, "The Meem have entered the path behind us...six ships."

Six ships?

The human gasped.

The captain's voice again. Distant, garbled. Something about "holding position."

Vulpa's voice, urgent.

Tweezor and then Geesh again.

"They're coming along side us!"

A huge ship came into view on the starboard screen. Then two on the port screen. They were beside the Truthseeker. In a Wavetime path, weapons were useless. The Meem were fully aware of that. That's why they were going to ram them.

Sorpe yelled something unrecognizable the bounced around the room for a moment. Tim's heart felt like a rock thumping the backside of his sternum. Frantic, he glanced from one screen to the other.

"Hold!" Nule said and then, "Jump!"

Meem cruisers rolled at them from two sides. The Truthseeker seemed to slam to a stop, losing altitude. It fell for a second and then disappeared from the time path. Tim's body slid forward off the couch. He looked up in a panic and realized they were back in normal space. The slow motion and echoes were gone. The frontal screen filled with silver flakes and dust. It swirled all around them.

"Take us in," Nule said.

Just as the Warbirds exited Wavetime, the Truthseeker faded into the Triptic Vortex.

8

The Triptic Vortex traveled in an orbital ellipse around the local sun, thirty-eight thousand miles out from the planet, Triptic-Six. The Phazon Twelve battle cruiser had seen its demise about two weeks ago, not far from there. It had been in that system that the Meem had first shown themselves, and had remained thick with Warbirds ever since.

The Triptic people had been held prisoner on their own planets for weeks, although the populations had not yet been attacked. It seemed the Meem were attacking planets with military targets, for the time being. The few ships foolhardy enough to make a run for it had been swiftly destroyed.

If a ship ever did escape, there was one thing that would be sure. It would not be heading for the vortex.

It would go anywhere but there.

9

"Spine gunners are standing by, Captain." Commander Geesh said, his words slicing into the silence of the bridge.

A calm returned to the air as the ship made its way into the depths of the Vortex. Silver gleaming flakes drifted across the hull. They hadn't seen anything yet, but they knew they were there. Not the Meem. There was something else.

Hiding.

Waiting.

Formulating a plan of attack.

"Keep scanning," Nule said, "and stay sharp."

Tim watched the crew and saw the fear in their eyes. He could take it no more.

"What's in here?"

Nule frowned at his readout, "Blade Vipers."

Hundreds of tiny, moving pinpoints appeared in the cube display, coming at the ship.

"What?" Tim asked.

"Incoming," Vulpa said, "A wave of over two hundred."

"Ready a suppressing fire at the spine on my mark. Increase speed forty percent on the same mark." Nule glanced back at the human, "You see Timothy, the Vortex is essentially one big Blade Viper hive."

The captain's words were calm and the knot in Tim's stomach loosened a bit.

"What are they?"

"A Blade Viper is a snake-like creature that has two exposed bone shards at its tail that it can flex like a pair of scissors."

The wave got closer.

Tweezor said, "*Very sharp* bone shards."

An observable shiver went up Sorpe's spine, "They even sound like scissors."

Closer.

The Captain continued, "A viper can function on its own and is a formidable adversary. They have a limited intelligence and are motivated by aggressive tendencies."

Tim watched the wave of what looked like thousands of snakes, swimming.

"Mark," Nule called out and the suppressive fire began as the Truthseeker raced.

The vipers swam through the silver cloud in small, tight groups. Each gathering was attached at the front of something that looked like a ball or…

"What is that?" Tim blurted.

"They are drawn by and connected to what is known as the brain, another creature that lives in the Vortex. Each brain is highly intelligent and have been known to control up to a hundred vipers at a time."

Tim squinted, trying to focus on the monitor full of moving creatures.

"They control them?"

"Yes. When connected, they are known as a Brain-Viper mass. In that form they are smart, quick and even more deadly."

Tim was confused, "Even to a ship? With our shields up?"

"Shields do not affect them. They can pass right through."

"How?"

"We don't know exactly. It has something to do with a chemical the Brain secretes, Pharabroxin."

Vulpa narrowed the scan receptors from her station.

"We've got another wave, directly ahead."

Nule "Modify bearing, seven point one, starboard."

The ship banked to miss another massive oncoming hoard. Thousands turned to join the already chasing threat. The aft monitor had become an entire ocean of flowing snakes. Spine fire slowed them down but didn't seem to do any permanent damage.

"Two more waves, coming fast."

The cube display filled with tiny red dots from every direction. Tim swallowed with a lump in his throat, "They're everywhere."

Nule, "We're going to plow through. Barrel maneuver, on my mark. The spine will lead the way."

Commander Geesh sounded into spine pods as the ship rocketed head on toward a wall of deadly creatures.

"Mark," Nule commanded and the ship went into a spin.

"Gunners," Geesh said, "Dig a hole."

Spine fire concentrated forward, into the Viper curtain ahead of the Truthseeker. The constant blast knocked enemies back, creating a kind of 'hole' in the otherwise solid mass. The cruiser shot into the dark bombardment like a rotating corkscrew. A violent rumble overtook the ship. Panic hit Timothy once again as they pushed through. He looked up to the ceiling. He could hear them scraping against the ship's skin, like knives on a tin can.

Most of them impacted the hull and bounced away, but a few weren't thrown clear at all. A few of them hung on. And of those few, one made progress at slicing through an exhaust panel above deck forty-three.

10

The shaking Truthseeker blasted out of the enemy mass with an explosion of squirming snakes. The wave of Brain-viper masses turned in pursuit once again.

"We've got a few hanging on that the gunner fire can't reach," said an excited Commander Sorpe.

Nule leaned forward in his chair, "See if you can shake them, Mr. Norbinger."

Tweezor bucked the ship's nose up and down and then side to side. One after another, screeching enemies fell away.

Geesh barked, "Sir, we have a hull breech at deck forty-three." He paused a moment and then, "One of them is inside."

"Evacuate and seal the deck."

Tim shuddered in fear, "One of those things is on the ship?"

Vulpa, "Energy weapons will have little effect against it, Captain."

Nule turned to Geesh, "Have you still got a metal projectile gun?"

Large molars clacked. "I have a set of two," he stated with pride. "They shoot Cartonian alloy bullets."

"Get them and all the ammunition you've got. Meet me at the corridor junction between forty-two and forty-three." He got serious, "We're going hunting."

11

"Commander Nim, you have the bridge. Head for the far side of the Vortex. Get us as close as you can to the Stinzotaun system before exiting."

Vulpa's words strained, "We will likely face many more waves before reaching the other side."

Nule pulled a padded armor chest plate over his head. He knocked on it, as if for luck. It made a heavy clunk sound under his long fingered fist.

"Continue with the strategy I have shown you. We will deal with the individual threats as they arise."

Vulpa didn't like the Captain's solution, and he knew it. He attempted a smile in her direction. It did little good.

"Sir, I..."

"You'll do fine. Trust yourself as I trust you."

"Yes, captain," she said unconvinced.

Tim's face was desperate, "You and Mr. Geesh, you'll be okay, right?"

Nule smiled at him, "Naturally, Timothy. We'll be fine."

He clipped a final leg armor plate around his thigh and then strapped on a shiny black helmet. He walked to the corridor and turned.

"Stay alert. I'm depending upon you all."

He swung around and disappeared into the shadows. With the Captain gone, the knot in Timothy's stomach came back in full force.

"Two incoming waves!" shouted Commander Sorpe.

Vulpa looked over the remaining crew, "Okay, let's take this the same as before. Inform the Spine that we're going in."

12

A group of ten soldiers stood at the corridor junction pressure door with Commander Geesh. Captain Nule walked up to the group.

Sergeant Kallum spoke, "Captain, we are ready to accompany you inside."

"No, sergeant. That won't be necessary. Your pulse rifles would only serve to anger our guest."

"But sir, we can't let you go in alone."

The captain patted his hairy friend's back. I won't be alone, will I, Mr. Geesh?"

Geesh clacked large teeth and snorted.

Nule walked through the crowd of soldiers to the door.

"You will stand by here. Be ready, sergeant. We may need you…or we may not. We shall see."

Geesh pushed through, "Open the compartment."

A thick metal door slid away, revealing a pressure chamber lift. The two of them stepped inside and the door closed behind. Geesh handed two pistols to his captain. They were big silver weapons with twelve inch barrels and black molded grips.

Geesh gurgled flem in his throat, "They kick like a fully grown Snuder, so hold tight."

Nule accepted the pistols, feeling their weight. They were even heavier than they looked.

"What about you, Commander?"

Geesh held up a short staff with a spin handle on the side and a long, razor at one end. The entire weapon was the length of this forearm and he spun it, creating a blur of black and silver.

"I have completed level eight training on this, the Consah. I am quite good."

"I see," Nule said, backing away from the spinning knife. Could you stop that now?"

With a slap to his other hand, the short staff stopped moving.

"Yes, sir," he said.

Nule pressed a button and the elevator ascended one level, to forty-three.

"Ready?" Nule asked.

"Always ready, sir."

Nule took a deep breath.

We'll be fine, he thought, *just fine.*

The tall door slid open and they stepped into the darkened hallway. Severed, sparking lines dangling from the ceiling provided the only light. It took a moment for the captain's eyes to adjust. He took a step forward, squinting. With a pistol in each hand he listened with ears straining.

He heard snapping electricity above him. He heard hissing air escaping a damaged oxygen line…something else…

Mr. Geesh stood rigid, forcing himself not to snort.

Scraping…getting closer…then, out of a thick black shadow in front of them…

Scissors, opening and closing…

Dozens of them.

13

Gunner fire concentrated forward, into the oncoming mass as the ship rolled. Again, the hull rumbled against the storm. Timothy squeezed a pillow over his head with one hand and held onto the arm of the couch with the other.

Sorpe saw that another enemy was hanging on and attempting to cut into a port wing section.

"Gunner forty, fire at upper port wing. Hull breech in progress!" One line of spine fire turned to meet the threat. With so many enemies ripping past between the barrel cannons and the wing they soon realized there was no way to break through. A static response sounded into the bridge.

"It's not reaching the target, control. The path is too dense."

"Copy that, gunner forty. Keep trying."

14

With two pistols pointed into the darkness Nule said, "Stand ready, Commander! Here it comes!"

Growling, Geesh spun the Consah like a mighty propeller.

The Brain-Viper mass entered the light, hovering in midair. It was more horrifying than Nule had imagined. The Brain was just that, a glistening fibrous lump of fleshy, vein-covered brain. Attached to the back half was a thick mass of wet, squirming vipers. Their skin was transparent with clumpy, yellow fat and slick bone underneath. Most of them were long and thin, but there were a few, five or six, as big around as Nule's upper arm. Deadly sheers opened and closed at the end of each one's slithering tail.

Without further hesitation, Nule aimed into the shadows and squeezed triggers on both pistols.

15

"Hull breech at port wing!"

Vipers poured into a small tear in the panel. Fortunately, the opening wasn't large enough for the brain. Twenty snakes were inside before their host was knocked away by a bombardment of its own kind.

"Evacuate and lock it down!"

"Send a platoon to be sure nothing escapes," Vulpa said, "and contact the captain."

16

It was all Nule could do to hang on when the pistols fired. They raged in his fists like cannons, the sound thundering in his head. He stumbled back with ringing ears. Two shrieking vipers fell to the floor squirming and spewing black blood. The floating Brain lurched at them, hissed and then released its remaining snakes. Eighty Vipers swam though the air with lightning speed as they snapped at their target, Captain Nule, whose arms ached from pistol recoil. Surprised and afraid, he fell away as Mr. Geesh stepped up.

With a snarling growl and in a blur of hair and flashing metal, he took the offensive. Teeth clacked as he spun the Consah around his body like an oriental weapon. He sliced at every slither; he chopped at every strike. By two and threes, vipers fell to the floor severed and gushing fluids. A spray of sticky, dark blood shot into Geesh's mouth. Un-phased, he spat and kept swinging.

17

Twelve soldiers ran down corridor one-eighteen across level ten to the port side pressure junction. The thick metal doors were sealed with twenty Blade Vipers trapped inside. Commander Steep called orders as they approached.

"Danton, plug in. I want a diagnostic, now."

A soldier ran up, threw open a box on the wall and then plugged a thick cord into the local computer information system. He held up a portable readout pad, checking the network. The rest of the soldiers lined the hallway in standard flank positions, with weapons ready.

"Commander, I have a good host. I'm logging on."

Steep, from the center of the formation with pistol drawn, "Give me port, B-level status."

The soldier tapped code into the readout pad, retrieving the requested information. A map illuminated onto his screen. Red, moving dots popped alive, one for each enemy.

"We're on. I'm reading twenty bads. They've taken out overhead and power to three grids. One, four and five."
Steep grinned.
You like it dark, do ya?
"We hold here. Nothing gets past this point."
Danton's eyes went wide, "They're entering an oxygen vent."
"Lock it down, soldier."
"I can't," Danton said, "Vent control was on grid one."
All eyes found the vent on the wall above them. Nine assault rifles and three plasma energy pistols aimed at once.
The soldier looked into the display, "They're coming...wait...all but one...It's at the grid box...what's it doing?"
Steep listened, scowling at the vent. A strike behind the aperture plate made a loud clang.
"They're here."
At that moment, the hallway went pitch black.

18

Geesh hacked away. His hair was wet, matted with the rotten stench of viper fluids. Nule, on his feet once again, fired into the slithering shadows. His back and shoulders ached more with each squeezed trigger. Blast after blast, enemies exploded and fell, shrieking to the growing black pool on the floor.
A voice barely audible underneath the ringing in Nule's ears, called him from the bridge.
"Speak up, Commander! I can't hear you!" the Captain yelled, before firing off two more rounds.
"Sir, we've got another hull breech! Port-"
Nule fired again, filling the corridor with thunder. He'd wanted to hear what Vulpa had to say, although he found himself wanting to kill the viper coming at his face more.
"Contain all threats and we will get to them," he fired again, "as soon as we can...We're a bit busy," another shot, "just now."
Vulpa sat back in the captain's chair, hoping they were all right. She switched to a different frequency, "Commander Steep, do you have a copy? Is the area contained?"
Static, silence.
Apparently, the platoon was busy also.

19

Unexpected darkness shrouded the corridor. A scream. Shots fired, bright pulses of plasma scorching the walls, creating a random strobe effect and adding to the chaos.
Voices and another scream.
"I'm cut," someone said, "It *cut* me…"
The commander's voice, "Headlights, gentlemen!"
A small light illuminated atop his helmet just in time to see four fingers on Private Danton's hand get severed between two slicing blades. A piercing cry echoed in the shadows.
"Team two," said a frantic voice over the intercom, "Send the second team!"
Slithering vipers were everywhere.
Plasma fire continued.
The more they were hit, the angrier they got.

20

"Close and lock corridor one-eighteen and send the second team. The blade vipers have gotten through somehow," Sorpe said.
Xaxe checked his screen, "Oxygen vents! Lock down the oxygen vents!"
Three more waves of enemies swooped down, into the Truthseeker's path.
"Here we go again!" Tweezor shouted.
"Yes," Vulpa said, feeling more helpless then ever, "Here we go."

21

Sergeant Gein listened to incoming orders in his headset. A thick index finger pushed the small speaker tight against his ear as he pinched his eyes shut.
"Team two," the voice said, "You're going in. Retrieve team one and secure the area."
Gein's large red eyes popped open. His words were gritty and abrupt.
"Look alive, girls. We're on."
One soldier at the back of the training room spoke up.

"Sir, I request permission to take my pulse rifle."

Gein got angry, "No! You will do what I tell you and nothing more! Why do you think the Consolidation took the time to train you slags on a hand to hand weapon?" He growled, "For this very situation!"

"But, sir--"

"Hold you tongue or I'll cut it out, private!"

Gein shook his head in disgust.

"Move out, you worms! Move! Move! Move!"

The platoon stormed out of the room, each with a staff or razor weapon.

Every soldier in the Consolidation army was proficient at one of thirty authorized non-energy weapons, although few of them were actually used after academy training.

As Sergeant Gein jogged along behind his men, he hoped they remembered their training camp well. It was about to mean life of death for the whole platoon.

After all, only a fool would use an energy weapon against a Blade Viper.

22

Pulse fire was everywhere. The walls of the tight corridor stood spotted, charred with blackened burns. Danton cowered in the corner with his left hand tightly wrapped and oozing bright red blood. He held his wound under the opposite arm, protecting it and keeping it out of sight. In his right hand he gripped a small knife. It was standard issue with a cutting edge of about five inches. He swiped it in front of him every few seconds, whether he saw an enemy or not.

Steep and two others were the only ones still standing. They refused to give up on their assault rifles and kept blasting as lightning quick vipers darted and swam through the air. One such enemy circled Steep's helmet twice then drove its bone shears deep into the side of the soldier's neck.

He fell to his knees, gagging.

23

With the last of the Vipers squirming in a sticky pile, Captain Nule and Commander Geesh searched for the brain. They stepped through the slick black ooze, examining the shadows. Geesh grunted and stepped into the first room on the right.
A quick pan and then, "Clear."
Nule took the next room on the left. A dresser…a bed…an open closet…a mirror hanging on the opposite wall. Nule saw his own dark reflection…and right beside him…a rushing blur. The huge mass of tissue slammed into him, knocking him down. He hit the tile with a grunt of pain.
"Mr. Geesh, it's here!"
In that instant, a flash of whipping hair and spinning metal rushed in. With a piercing yell and uncanny precision he chopped the brain in half, sending it twitching and squirting yellow clumpy liquid to the floor.
"Ack!" Geesh said, spitting.

24

The Truthseeker broke through the sea of enemies. Three Brain Viper masses hung on, clinging to the hull as the ship raced further into the silvery vortex. Spine gunners targeted them with white-hot blasts.
An explosion of plasma across the underbelly of the cruiser sent an enemy spiraling away. Concentrated fire over the upper nose panels caused a group of deadly bone shears to lose their grip. They fell, screeching into the shimmering void.
Spine gunner Sin Mal, sent shot after shot into the slithering monster that held on to a ledge below his pod chamber. Blades dug in as it climbed higher. Over the duel barrels of the scatter cannon, it continued. Point blank shots sent vipers flailing. Whipping snakes stabbed at the pod pressure glass, just over Mal's head. He used the control arms to push the cannon barrels at the mass. They hissed and went around the slick metal.
Another hit to the pod shield. Then another.
The Brain came into view.
The creature rose up, out of the pod's shadow. It turned, studying the humanoid under glass. Another stab.

Mal backed up, grimacing. From underneath the squirming mass came the biggest, thickest Viper he'd seen yet. Its bone shear was at least two feet long. It drew its massive body back, flexing. After a moment, it came down onto the glass in a deafening strike, cracking the outer surface.

"Oh, god," Mal said scrambling out of his harness, "It's coming through."

25

The second platoon stood huddled in a small junction chamber, at the end of corridor one-eighteen.

"Look alive, you slags. This is your chance for glory," Gein said as the pressure door slid open.

The hallway was dark. Soldiers screamed somewhere in the shadows.

Pulse fire from one weapon.

Banging.

"Get away from me," a voice said, "Get away!"

Gein looked at his men.

"Retrieve survivors and watch each other's back. Move out."

"Team two is here!" someone yelled.

Another voice, "Look out! They're above you!"

Eyes shot upward. Over the shadowed ceiling, a group of vipers had been waiting. They swam down with lightning quickness, into the new group of soldiers.

Surprise.

Yelling.

Fluid, spraying.

And scissors.

Opening and closing.

26

Commander Geesh and Captain Nule ran down the hallway, side by side.

Over the communicator sounded Officer Xaxe's voice, "We've lost contact with the first platoon. The second has just entered the area."

The captain, out of breath, "Pull them out, do you hear me? Pull them all out."

27

With the harness thrown aside, Sin Mal lurched away from his chair. The pod compartment was small. He was startled at another strike to the glass. He hit the nearby wall with his shoulder, rushing around the controls. The crack across the pod shield made a crunching sound, getting longer.

A female digitized voice from above, *Damage sustained at cannon pod nine. The chamber has been sealed.*

"What?" Mal said, frantic.

He pulled at the door latch. It was locked tight.

Another hit to the glass.

His voice was deep and his breathing heavy, "Computer, pod nine gunner override. Open the hatch, *right now*."

Another loud strike. Crunching.

The voice was calm and polite, *Breech is imminent. I cannot comply.*

"Open the door!"

Breech is imminent. I cannot-

He screamed in frustration.

Mal scrambled for the small cabinet to this left. Clicking it open, he saw an environment suit hanging in shadow. Without a moment of hesitation, he began pulling it on. Cracks in the glass spidered in all directions.

Another hit.

He stepped into the padded silver suit, squeezing each foot into an attached boot. It was a tight fit.

Not only could Mal hear cracking, he could hear hissing oxygen too.

He pulled it up to his waist. It was made for a much smaller frame. He'd make it fit. He had to.

He tried not to think about how much time he had before the shield shattered. He tried not to think about how cold the space was outside, or what it would feel like to die in the darkness, alone. He strained at the zipper. It was tight against his thick chest.

"Come on," he said clenching his jaw.

Another impact. He jumped at the sound.

He trembled. His hands, his whole body. Hunched over and cursing, he got the zipper all the way up. The suit was two full sizes too small, maybe more. He could barely move. Mal looked around.

Where's the helmet?

Another loud crash.

He peered into the cabinet. All the way to the back, in shadow he saw it. He reached, straining. As gloved fingers seized the lower rim of the helmet, he heard something split. It was a seam across his back. The environment suit had begun to come apart. There was no way to know how extensive the damage was.

An image of his wife and children flashed through is mind.

He lowered his helmet over his head and clicked down the latch.

He promised them he'd come home.

Another impact.

The pod glass exploded outward. He powered up the suit just as he was sucked out, along with the remaining heat and air. The Brain Viper ignored him, climbing into the ship.

Sin Mal drifted into blackness. With the rate at which oxygen was escaping out the back of his suit, he'd be fortunate if three hours of air would last five minutes.

28

Mr. Geesh spoke into the communicator as he jogged beside the captain.

"Have we lost any of our soldiers at one-eighteen?"

Nule interrupted, "They are all alive, Commander. I do not guarantee their condition, but they will all survive."

Teeth clacked, "Sir, how could you possibly know--"

The answer came back from the bridge, over the airwaves.

"I'm reading vital signs on all the members of both teams. Two are weak. The others are showing high heart rates and other signs of stress but...they are all alive."

The corridor junction was coming up, around the next corner.

They slowed as they neared the closed doorway.

A snort and then, "How, sir?"

Nule said, "I know when the next death for a member of this crew will occur. I wish I didn't, but I do."

The captain had been carrying the information with him like a heavy weight. It felt good to let someone else help him bear it.

They stopped at the closed junction doorway.

"Timeshift Tunnel," Geesh said.

He knew that had to be the source of Nule's unknowable information.

"Yes, my friend. I'm sorry that I told you this way, but please, I would prefer that no one else knew."

A tense, muscular arm raised the razor weapon up as he hit the door release. The pressure compartment was bright and empty. He lowered the Consah as the two of them stepped inside.

"Do not apologize, Captain. I am honored to share your secret. I shall tell no one."

Nule opened the next door.

Darkness, screaming and Blade Vipers.

"Thank you, Mr. Geesh."

Nule's relief was forgotten as he pointed duel pistols into the darkness.

Geesh let out a guttural growl and stomped down the dim hallway.

29

"Breech at gunner pod nine!" Sorpe said, "A brain viper is inside."

Vulpa looked to the aft screen. The sea of enemies trailed behind them, as always.

"It's inside? Where is the gunner?"

Xaxe's heart rate leapt, watching his readout. "Outside. He managed to get into an environment suit but…"

Vulpa, "He's *alive*? Full stop and bring us about."

"The vipers are right behind us, Commander."

"Do it," she snapped, "Now."

30

The Truthseeker slammed to a halt, rotating.

"Ready tractor beam."

The dense wall of snakes raced. Sorpe tapped at his console faster than he'd ever done before.

"I have a lock on, Commander."

The wave of enemies bombarded the ship.

"Engage the beam!"

Bright particles of energy shot into the thick gathering. Spine fire drilled at the squirming wall.

"Have you got him?"

"We have him!"

"Get us out of here, Mr. Norbinger."

A glowing particle tractor beam followed, with its cargo inside the red haze.

Its cargo consisted of one humanoid in a badly damaged space suit and ten slithering guests.

31

Sin Mal was surrounded by a bright, snapping light. It made his body tingle, itching under his skin. It pulled him across a silvery nighttime sky. His head swam with partial thoughts and fickle images. The tractor radiation was safe to most humanoids, although it caused a hallucinogenic effect.

Mal thought, *This is like the time we drank that bottle of Rectalin nectar wine.*

That had been more than twenty years ago, on his home planet, Rizon. That had been a wild night, one he'd never forget. He smiled, remembering seeing his wife, who'd been only his girlfriend at the time, flying above him like an angel. Her wings had been pristine white.

She was with him once again, smiling behind the red haze. Her arms stretched out to him, rippled and then melted away.

"My wife," he said to her, "My love."

Her body broke apart into gentle, drifting ribbons. They danced, as if riding a flesh breeze. Sin Mal knew that they weren't really ribbons.

Not anymore.

Anyway, they moved more like snakes…

32

More than thirty enemies hung tight to the Truthseeker's hull,
digging and scraping. The ship raced with pod fire blasting over its
own skin.
"How's the gunner doing?" Vulpa asked.
"Not so good," Sorpe replied, "He's got ten vipers in with him."
"What?"
"It was the best I could do, Commander."
"He is unarmed and undoubtedly intoxicated from close proximity
radiation. He will not survive for long."
Vulpa's words surprised Xaxe, "Throw him, Commander. Two
thousand pex forward…to grid seven five-five. That sector is
clear."
Xaxe, "Throw him? This isn't scatterball, Commander."
Vulpa frowned, "Sling the tractor and then release."
"I can't just *toss* him to that grid. I wouldn't even know where to
begin calculating that…"
Vulpa screamed, "Use your best guess! Do it now! It's the only
way to save his life!"
None of the command crew had seen Vulpa Nim loose her temper.
It was unnerving.
Hesitation was forgotten and the tractor beam was thrust and
released.
Sin Mal shot into the distance.
The Truthseeker raced to catch up.

33

Mr. Geesh, with a soldier's ankle in one hand and a spinning
consah in the other, rushed down the corridor. Black blood
sprayed as he chopped a racing Viper into halves. Private Danton
was on his back, being dragged and screaming.
He kicked, struggling, "Oh god. Something's got me! Help!"
Geesh growled, "It is I who has you. Stop resisting…if you want
to live."
Captain Nule, with a limping soldier under each arm made his
way to the junction chamber. Out of the shadows he carried them
as they moaned in pain. Once they were under the harsh light and

clear of the pressure door, he dropped them to the floor. Cries of
pain sounded as he swung around to meet a darting viper. With
pistols tight in his fists he sent deafening bullets at the enemy. It
exploded in mid-air, showering Nule and the nearby soldiers with
sticky entrails. He wiped blood away from his eyes with an already
saturated sleeve.
"I am beginning to hate these things," he said in disgust.
He raised the barrels and fired again.

34

Away from the Truthseeker and out of the red haze, Sin Mal
flew. The intoxication fell away from his brain as reality took
hold.
"What's happening?"
In a daze, he traveled into silvery space. He saw snakes flying
beside him. He felt oxygen escaping the suit, across his back.
Forsaken by all but a paralyzing fear, he continued on, helpless.
The glass in front of his face fogged. The temperature dropped.
Air thinned.
Oh, no.
Something was coming for Mal, he could feel it.
Right behind him.
He prayed for a miracle, but expected something much worse.

35
"We have a breech attempt at cannon pod nine. The hatch is
holding for now, but--"
"Eject the pod."
Thick latches opened one by one, underneath the damaged gunner
station. The viper hissed as detaching lines popped away from the
wall. Gases drifted into zero gravity. The reactor powered down.
The Brain knew something was happening but didn't know what.
It turned, scanning the compartment.
A dark chair sat empty in the central position.
Crystallized moisture flaked away from duel control sticks.
Something flashed on the targeting computer screen. It ignored the
message and kept searching. *Danger*, the bold letters on the panel
spelled out, *pod ejection in progress.*

Without another moment of warning, rockets fired and spine pod nine shot up and away from the Truthseeker like a missile.

36

"Two waves of Brain vipers are closing on his position."
"Increase another ten percent and ready the tractor."
The ship accelerated to arrive before the oncoming enemies.

Sin Mal drifted, lightheaded and weak. It was getting cold and air was running out.
"Please," he gasped, "Help me."
The image of his wife faded. He was losing her.
Sergeant Orts called to the bridge from bay one.
"I'm ready, just get me close."
"We copy, Mr. Orts," was the reply in his helmet, "Stand by."
He stood at the open bay doors with a long tether strapped to his back. The other end had been connected to a wench system. He gripped a platform rail in zero gravity. Two dock personnel stood at each of his shoulders. They waited to help retrieve the helpless spine gunner.

Dock one was just below the Truthseeker's nose, at the forward most section of the ship. Tweezor needed only to fly directly at Mal, getting as close as possible. Sergeant Orts and his crew would do the rest.

37

Sergeant Gein stood with Nule and Geesh at the med lab entrance. They were weary and still catching their breath. Across the room the doctor worked on a soldier's deep wound with a laser instrument. Nurse Neeba held private Danton's hand and severed fingers in a dish full of brownish fluid. He was pale and looked as if he might pass out. Commander Steep complained on a stretcher, holding his neck. All the members of both platoons were accounted for.
All intruders had been eliminated.

The captain and his hairy companion headed down the corridor, in the direction of the bridge.

38

"Almost there," Tweezor said.

Timothy watched with wide eyes, holding his breath. Vulpa sat rigid, monitoring the trailing enemy wave.

"Be ready now. We won't have much time."

A tiny dark figure came into view on the screen. Mal hovered, fading in and out of silver haziness.

"There he is!" Tim shouted, pointing.

"Here we go!" Tweezor said, easing the control stick downward.

Sergeant Orts watched as they approached.

"Fifty pex...forty."

"Slow," he called out.

The ship's velocity dropped and Orts let go of the rail. He flew out of the dock with a thick tether trailing behind.

"Hang on, I'm coming."

Mal's body numbed. His eyelids were heavy weights. He knew he was dying.

A surprise impact.

Thick arms around his chest.

Something had come for him.

Groggy and weak, he hoped it wasn't too late. It felt like he was pulled backwards, although it was hard to tell. After a few seconds a light filled his helmet.

"We've got him!" a distant voice said, "Close the bay door!"

A rumble told him there was something underneath. Looking down, he saw the dock floor. It was smooth and white. Simulated gravity re-engaged and he fell to his knees.

I'm not dead, he thought.

Orts plugged Mal's suit into a nearby hose. Cool oxygen flowed into his face.

"Breathe deep, soldier," the sergeant said with a smile, "You're okay now."

With a heavy clunk the door closed and the temperature began to rise.

"Not dead," the gunner said out loud.

Orts recognized the one he'd just saved. He'd recently been signed off on Jetpack. Orts had trained the pilot himself.

"No, Mr. Mal," he said to his student, "I'm afraid that today I'm ordering you to live."

"Yes, sir," he answered, catching his breath.

39

    Captain Nule walked onto the bridge wearing a torn and sticky uniform. It was soaked with reeking black blood. The smell was putrid and soon filled the room. The command crew turned to see the source of the foul stench. It was their captain, with a dented and sparking quantum assistant floating above his bald head.

    Geesh followed him in, fresh and clean, snorting. The assistant floating over him looked shiny and new. Tweezor pinched his nose shut with pudgy fingers.

Tim coughed, "Ugh! My eyes are burning!"

Nule walked to the captain's chair, where commander Nim sat. She got up and backed away, covering her mouth.

"Are you alright, sir?" she asked.

"Yes. Would you be so kind as to assign me a new quantum assistant? Mine's been damaged, I believe."

She wrinkled her nose, "Gladly, sir."

Xaxe turned away from his station.

"Captain, we are approaching the far side of the vortex and should be able to exit before making contact with any more waves."

Geesh took over his usual station, weapons control. He initiated a quick scan.

"A Meem Warbird is just outside the vortex and pacing us. When we exit, they will be waiting."

Nule sat still while a fresh quantum unit initiated its scans of his biological system.

"It is as I expected. Ready the tractor. Widen the beam to twelve hundred."

Chritchet engineers made adjustments to particle distributors. Whatever Nule wanted to grab hold of must've been huge.

    The hovering sphere whirred to life bobbing around his head as the black ooze disappeared and the smell faded.

"Much better," he said enjoying his sudden cleanliness.

Vulpa sat down behind her own controls, "Three minutes until we reach the Vortex border. How would you like the tractor used?"

Nule said, "Grab the thickest, darkest gathering of Brain Viper masses you can find. They'll be leaving with us."

40

"Make ready the Wavetime engines. Set a course for the Stinzotaun Axis."
Timothy watched Vulpa make vector adjustments at her station.
"The base," she said, "is currently at the near side of the planet. It is mid-day."
Lunch time, Tim thought.
It was hard to believe he hadn't eaten or drank anything in weeks.

The Truthseeker, towing a thick gathering of brain vipers, shot out of the silvery cloud. The enemy Warbird approached.
"The Meem ship is accelerating, bearing one-two-zero."
Nule leaned forward, flexing.
"Bank port, point five eight. Center the tractor beam behind us."
The enemy cruiser swooped down at its prey.
"Here they come," Sorpe said.
"Release the beam."

The particle beam disappeared and two thousand Brain Viper masses hit the Meem ship like hail, passing through the ion and plasma shielding as if it were non-existent. Snapping shears scraped over the dark hull. The cruiser slowed its pursuit as the slithering attackers chopped into fuel lines and pried at skin panels.

Tweezor scanned, studying the vipers' chemical effect on the ion molecular structure.
"Interesting," he chittered, typing his findings into a data pad, "Yeah, that might do it."

Captain Nule watched the Meem cruiser as it was engulfed in the squirming army. He was quite pleased with himself.
He smiled, "Open the time path and engage."
With a raging boom, a bright blue tunnel appeared in front of the Truthseeker. She nosed down momentarily, and then entered.

Sector Seven:
The Collapse

1

Mr. Xaxe sat studying a coded message from the multiverse generator. They'd just gotten close enough to pick up the signal. After a few moments of reading the translation, the commander gasped.

Oh, no.

The captain leaned down, hovering over Xaxe and his station. "You have the generator transmission de-coded. Please tell us the proper procedure and what can be expected."

Xaxe's eyes left the screen and looked out, across the bridge. He was apprehensive and perspiring.

"Well sir," he said as Nule backed away, "The Verse one wormhole lies, as you know, just beyond the far side of Zotaun, in close orbit."

"Yes," Nule said to let the commander know he was listening.

Xaxe continued, "Only a ship with the sequence carrier on board may pass through. The doorway will close on any others who attempt entry. Once inside, we should be totally safe from the Meem cruisers."

"Very good."

"The sequence carrier, Timothy, will need to be taken into the generator's core, deep inside the machine. One of our smaller shuttles will be needed for this. There is a landing platform provided, once they arrive at the DNA verification unit."

The human was wide-eyed and listening. He hung on every word and was terrified of what might happen. Xaxe glanced over and locked eyes with Tim.

"Beyond that, the information we have is vague, at best."

"Thank you," Nule said.

He spoke to Vulpa, "Commander Nim, I would like you to pilot the shuttle. Please take our guest to bay six and prepare. You will both need full environment suits."

"Yes, sir," She said backing away from her station.

Tim walked over to Nule, trembling with fear, "Remember, you promised me I'd be okay. You *promised*."

Nule smiled, "Timothy, you will be fine. I guarantee it."

"I just...I don't know, I have a bad feeling about it. That's all."

Two long fingered hands grasped two teen-aged shoulders.

"You will survive this. All of the sequence carriers come out alive. Do not worry."

"Okay," he said in a whisper, "I guess so."

Vulpa approached, "I will be with you the entire time. You will not be harmed."

Geesh clapped the human on the back. His tongue slathered as he smiled with gigantic teeth and black lips. A loud snort and then, "You'll be fine."

Tim looked around for his friend.

"Where's Tweezor?"

"He is busy, I believe," Xaxe said. "He said he would see you after."

"Oh," was the disappointed response.

"Let us go," Vulpa said leading the way into the corridor.

Tim followed, dragging his feet.

Once they were out of sight, Xaxe spoke to Nule again.

"Sir, there is something I didn't say when Timothy was here."

"Go on."

"Well, based on the transmission we're now receiving from the generator, there is something disturbing I must tell you."

"What is it?"

"When the machine is re-set, only the original verses will remain streaming. Any unintended transmissions will be eliminated."

Nule, "What are you saying, Mr. Xaxe?"

His voice fell weak, "All three hundred and thirty-two shadow verses will lose their signal. All hidden verses, including Timothy's, will collapse when the machine is re-set."

2

Tweezor, who had de-coded the Multiverse transmission minutes before Commander Xaxe, was busy in science lab one.

"Come on!" the little man yelled at the quantum accelerator.

A nearby flashing screen read, *unstable*.

He pried a panel off the side of the unit. With a long-necked handheld tool, he turned an adjustment screw, deep behind a twisted mass of colored wire. Flashlight eye beams snapped on, illuminating the inside of the machine. He twisted it another half-turn, watching the screen. With the quantum perimeters successfully narrowed, anxiety clamped at his stomach.

There were still dozens of adjustments that needed to be made before a dimensional space fold could be attempted. He moved on to the next, hoping he wouldn't run out of time.

3

"I'm reading forty Meem Warbirds in this sector alone," Sorpe said.

"Contact the decoy fleet."

Nule gazed into the cube display. Numerous red pinpoints of light closed in on the Truthseeker's timepath.

"We're going to need them."

4

Tim followed Vulpa through the pressure compartment and into bay six. Across the nearest platform they walked, past the control booth. To their left stood tall double doors. She hit the switch and the smooth metal slid open, to reveal a large walk-in closet. Rows of uniforms hung with multicolored patches, each with a consolidation flag over the left breast. Black, shiny boots lined the walls, arranged by sizes and styles. And then, all the way at the back, they saw the environment suits. Vulpa took one down and held it up to the human.

"This should fit you. Try it on."

He unzipped the front and then stepped into the mustard colored legs. Each silver sneaker popped into an attached boot. She held the back of the suit as he slipped his arms in. With it over his shoulders, she yanked the zipper up to his neck. She patted his chest with the palm of her hand.

"Nice fit," she said, "Get a helmet from over there."

She pointed to the shelf behind him.

Tim turned, paused a moment, and then said, "I'm pretty nervous about this."

"Yes," she said stepping into her own suit, "You'll do fine."

He held up a small object in his hand. With his thumb he clicked the top of it. A holographic image fizzled to life above. It was an image of Sparrim Gale's face, smiling. Tim took a deep breath, gazing into her eyes. He hoped he'd see her real face again.

Vulpa spoke with unexpected warmth, "I see what she sees in you, Timothy Rayburn. You do have a certain charisma about you, although it is crude and unrefined."

He smiled, "Oh yeah? You think so?"

"Yes."

"Charisma? Really?"

"Yes. Crude and unrefined…and immature. You are highly immature."

With a snap the holograph disappeared.

"Yeah, yeah. Immature," he said, "Get back to the charisma part."

"Yes, well for a small, pinkish humanoid with odd patches of fur, you are…not completely unattractive."

He grinned big, "Yeah, I'm pretty hot, huh?"

Vulpa frowned, "Hot?"

"Yeah, baby," he said, flexing and posing like a bodybuilder.

She turned away, "You have been in the company of Mr. Norbinger too often."

Tim bent down to see her face as she pulled at a zipper.

"Admit it."

She blushed, "Admit what?"

"Admit that you like him. I know you do."

She scowled, "I do not."

"Yes, you do."

"I don't."

Timothy smiled, "You do."

She grabbed a helmet with a frustrated slap and stomped toward the door.

"We'd better get to the shuttle."

Tim chuckled, "Yeah."

5

"Three Consolidation vessels are nearing the coordinates we've given them. They will cross our time path in two minutes." Nule watched nine Meem cruisers turn in pursuit of the decoy ships.

"We can only pray for their safety," he said checking the timer scroll on his screen.

It read, one hour, thirty-six minutes. That was all the time that remained until a death would occur, according to Timeshift Tunnel. For at least one crewmember, time ran short. Nule thought that perhaps the entire crew would meet their end that day. Or, if something went wrong at the generator, all the verses could collapse. It was a possibility, one of many. There was no way to be sure of anything.

The scroll clicked over to one thirty-five.

Another minute was gone.

Vanished like a faint whisper, a partial thought, an unrealized intention.

Nule thought about the things he wanted to accomplish in his life. His hopes and dreams.

What if this is it?

He stared at the screen, mesmerized by the green glow.

What if this countdown is my own?

He knew that he wasn't supposed to have the information he'd gotten in the tunnel. He'd give it back if he could. But naturally, he could not. It was something he'd have to live with for the rest of his life. And he knew that the rest of his life could very well total only an hour and a half.

6

The Truthseeker raced across sector eleven, toward the planet Zotaun. The Axis military base occupied thirty square miles in a central region of South Allus, the largest continent in the southern hemisphere. Surrounding the base was the massive city of Minna.

205

Home to four hundred million, it was one of the largest known cities in the multiverse.

Meem freighters were also on their way, with bellies full of hover tanks and fighters. The battle for the Axis would begin on the outskirts of Minna, with a deadly ground assault working its way down city streets.

Panic flooded over a population that had nowhere to go. All they could do was wait. The enemy was coming.

And with them, a storm of fire…

7

"We are nearing the Stinzotaun system, Captain."

Nule looked up from deep thought, into the frontal screen.

"A group of Meem freighters have set down on the surface of the planet. Ground Assault vehicles are unloading now."

Squadrons of fighters poured out of the low flying carrier. Swarms of small Meem ships darkened skies above the Axis. The primary cannon came to life sending ripping blasts into the air. One such blast tore into a carrier with billowing flames. Four enemy squadrons exploded before they could leave their platforms.

"Nice shot," Nule said watching his view screen.

"Sir?"

"Head for the wormhole," he said, "Get us inside, Mr. Geesh."

The Truthseeker did not engage the enemy. They couldn't help Zotaun, at least not until they'd reset the generator. The Multiverse 5000 was their first priority.

An image of the Verse One wormhole glowed on the screen in front of him. They'd been through a lot to get there and now, they had arrived.

"At last," Commander Sorpe said with wide eyes.

The doorway to the generator was in sight. Inside lay the reason they'd come so far, risked so much.

Nule smiled, "We've made it."

8

Timothy sat next to Vulpa inside the small shuttle. The harness was tight across his chest as he stretched to get comfortable. Engines fired. The seat vibrated underneath him.

"Open the bay doors," Vulpa said to the operations computer. Gumball lights spun beams of crimson illumination into the dock. Thick locks fell open and the bay doors parted. A shiny translucent shield sat just outside the widening threshold, like a swimming layer of shifting water. Beyond the protective haze, thousands of streaking stars. Timothy's breath went shallow.

Here we go again.

A voice sounded over the airwaves, "Shuttlecraft Holiday, do you have a copy?"

"Yes, control. We copy," Vulpa said.

Holiday? Tim thought, *What kind of name is that?*

The voice again, "We are approaching the Verse One wormhole. Make ready for departure."

"Affirmative, control. We'll be standing by."

Tim wished it were a holiday, like Christmas or Thanksgiving. He'd be at home with a bellyful of turkey and homemade pie. He'd be lying on the couch, staring into a football game, perhaps drifting into a peaceful nap.

God, that sounds good.

He hadn't even a chance to say goodbye to his parents or friends. He'd been missing for three weeks. They'd given up on him ever coming back by now.

He was supposed to give his speech this morning. It looked as though he would miss it. Mrs. Hershey and the rest of his speech class felt like a distant memory as the shuttle's engines roared. The Verse One wormhole came into view on the small screen in front of them. It was a hazy white spiral in an otherwise black void. It was the reason he'd left home in the first place.

Timothy couldn't believe it. They were finally there.

9

War was beginning on the surface of Zotaun, far below the glowing blue atmosphere. The Truthseeker flew past, hoping they wouldn't be noticed by the cloaked fleet. Only one raced to engage her while the others held position, ready to attack the military base.

"Captain, we have an enemy closing, point five-one."

"Fire a ripper burn and roll starboard, two-fifty."

The cruiser spiraled and accelerated. Geesh clacked large teeth, hanging onto his station. Nule clicked a harness together across his waist.

The enemy fired.

"Seeker missile is away."

"Plasma release," was the response.

After a moment an explosion quaked behind the ship.

"Head for the wormhole," Nule said with a dry throat, "and empty charge slot one."

Two proximity charges rolled into space. The enemy turned away, but not soon enough. Outer shields weakened at the vessel stuttered port.

"Take us in," Nule said.

The Truthseeker banked, entering the Verse One wormhole.

10

The bright wormhole faded as the ship slowed. The vacuum of space was a deep red with swirls of glowing orange. The colors stretched out forever, in all directions. Verse One contained no stars, no planets and no galaxies. The space surrounding the Truthseeker was empty, except for one thing. The Multiverse dimensional generator.

"We are on approach, sir."

"Good," Nule said, "Establish a close orbit and inform Commander Nim."

The two of them had been sitting in silence for ten minutes. Vulpa's face was emotionless as she sat thinking about what Timothy had said.

Admit it.

She gritted her teeth. The little man was rude. He was obnoxious. He was insane, and she couldn't stand being in the same room with him. He represented everything that she was not. She would admit nothing. Not to Timothy, or anyone. How could she? She wouldn't even admit it to herself.

Mr. Sorpe's voice sounded over the radio.

"We are nearing the generator. Stand by, shuttlecraft Holiday."

"I copy, Truthseeker. We are go at bay six."

Tim stared through the windshield at crimson space outside the open bay doors. The entire universe looked like a beautiful sunset. Slowly, the machine came into view as the ship turned. It was dark, corroded and the size of a small planet. Thick gatherings of twisted wire sat exposed behind large panels. The entire surface of the sphere was covered in huge transmission dishes. Each powered an individual universe, sometimes two, in the case of the hidden verses. Tim's view of beautiful space disappeared completely, blocked by the mammoth creator of universes. The human's awe paused for a moment, in favor of amusement. He had to laugh. Vulpa frowned in his direction, "What is funny?"

"It's just the that the creator, you know, of everything, is…a machine."

"Yes," she responded, "But the machine did not create itself. The original three designed and built it."

"Yeah?" he said unconvinced. "Well, where are they?"

"No one knows. They are a great mystery."

Tim felt an unexpected anger pump in his veins.

"Why don't they re-set this stupid machine their selves?"

"I don't know."

"Why do we gotta risk *our* lives, running around through vortexes and tunnels and wars and-- why don't they help us in any way?"

"Perhaps they are helping us. Maybe we are unaware of their involvement."

"Yeah, right." Tim said in anger, "Maybe I don't wanna re-set their dumb machine. Maybe I'll just say *screw it*, and go home."

"Then," Vulpa said, "You would have no home to return to. None of us would."

She was right and he knew it. He hadn't come all that way to get mad and leave. He was there to save the universes. His home and the homes of countless others. No matter what he thought of the original three, resetting the generator was the right thing to do. It was the only thing they could do.

"Fine," he said in a huff, "I'm gonna do it. Of course I'm gonna do it."

"That's good," Vulpa said.

"I mean…I was just saying…you know."

"Yes."

"If I was just gonna let the universes collapse I woulda stayed home. I could be watching Baywatch right now, you know."

"I'm sure," she said, wondering watch Baywatch might be.

Sorpe's voice came back over the airwaves.

"We are in position, Holiday. You are cleared for space dock exit."

Vulpa reached down, firing the lower thrusters. The shuttle rumbled, lifting off the platform.

"I copy, Truthseeker. Shuttlecraft Holiday is commencing bay exit procedure."

The captain's voice surprised them.

"Timothy..."

"Yes, captain?"

Nule tried to think of a way to tell the human that his world would be lost.

No words came.

Gorza hoped that it wouldn't destroy Timothy. A recovery from that kind of sacrifice might never happen.

"Captain?" Tim said again.

"Yes...I wanted to say, be safe my friend. We'll see you again soon."

Nule's words came across in a whisper, brimming with a sad emptiness.

"Thank you, Captain," was all Tim could think of to say.

Vulpa knew that something was wrong, as did the human beside her. Neither of them acknowledged it to the other. They sat in anxious silence as they left the Truthseeker, wondering what might cause the captain to sound like that.

Tim decided that he didn't want to know and tried to focus on the generator. It took up his entire frontal vision.

"It's really big," he said as a brick developed in his stomach.

"Yes, it is."

Shuttlecraft Holiday sped toward the machine's single dock opening, directly ahead. They could feel the tingle of energy vibrating over their skin. The power inside the massive machine they headed toward was incomprehensible. The wasted energy surrounding it could've ran fleets of ships, entire cities, planets full of people and technology.

The shuttle's cabin went dark and Vulpa was no longer in control.

"We've lost power."

"What do you mean, we've lost power? We're still moving toward it."

Vulpa reached over, clicking a toggle switch on the front of Tim's environment suit. Cool air fanned into his face.

"Put your helmet on, right now."

"Look," he said pointing at the windshield.

He was right. The ship continued toward the generator. She picked up his helmet and forced it into his chest.

"They must have us in a tractor tow. Now, *put your helmet on*."

He took it from her, "Okay, okay. Don't have a heart attack."

She looked at him, confused.

"I do not understand the comment."

"It means, don't get so excited."

She frowned, "Why would you suggest coronary occlusion?"

"Forget it," he said, "It's earth slang. You wouldn't understand."

"Is it humorous?"

He paused, looking at her. Her lips held a faint smile.

"Yeah. It's kinda funny, I guess."

"Oh?" she said, "Are there any other Earth jokes you'd like to share with me?"

Tim wrinkled his nose, "Why? You're not really the joke type."

"Yes, well…" her face flushed, "Perhaps I might relate better with others…who enjoy humor."

Tim smiled from ear to ear, "You want a joke to tell Tweezor."

"I do not."

"Yes you do. If you'd just admit that you liked him, things would be a lot easier."

The shuttle entered the generator bay, rotated a hundred and eighty degrees, and then set down. The dock was small, with room enough for a solitary shuttle. Its walls were pristine white, the floor a pale gray. There was no control booth, no consoles, no stairwells or platforms. One closed doorway at the rear of the bay was all they could see.

Vulpa unlatched her harness.

Dash lights snapped to life as computer systems re-booted. It seemed that shuttlecraft Holiday had power once again. The entrance ramp lowered at the rear of the ship. A pressure lock released also, and the hatch slid open.

Timothy's eyes widened, "Did you do that?"

"No," she answered, "I did not."

The lump in his throat expanded.

"I didn't think so."

He unlatched his harness and made his way toward the door.

11

Dimensional perimeters unstable, the readout said, *system shutdown immanent.*

"No!" Tweezor yelled, "Not again!"

It was impossible to man five different control stations, run the quantum accelerator and the detection devices all by himself. If he was going to have even the slightest chance at success, he needed help.

A lot of help.

12

Tweezor's voice sounded over the intercom on the bridge.

"Science lab one to bridge. Need help please."

Nule recognized Tweezor, "Aren't' you on duty, Mr. Norbinger? Shouldn't you be at your station?"

Silence dominated the channel for a few seconds and then, "I no do it without help."

Nule was puzzled, "Do what?"

A whisper, "Save Timothy's planet."

Chatter broke out across the bridge.

The captain leaned forward, "Just how do you intend doing that?"

"Quantum space fold, sir."

Nule looked over to Commander Geesh, "Is that *possible?*"

Thick hair shook, "In theory, yes sir."

He looked at the Critchet engineers, "EM?"

The three spoke in unison, "We concur."

Nule got to his feet.

"Mr. Norbinger, tell us what you need."

"Command crew. Need command crew."
"Who?"
"All of you," the midget said, "All come."

13

   The Truthseeker crew filed out the doorway, heading for
science lab one. Mr. Geesh led the way, with EM, EL and BE
close behind him. Next were Mr. Sorpe and Mr. Xaxe. Ensigns
Shelby and Leet were after them.
   Captain Nule was last to leave the bridge. He saw a soldier in
the corridor standing at rigid attention in the presence of so many
commanders.
"Private-" Nule looked down at the name badge, "-Adders, is it?"
"Yes, sir! Captain sir!" the anxious soldier said.
Nule smiled, "Private Adders, you have the bridge."
Adders' face went pale, "*Me,* sir?"
"Yes," Nule said, "And don't touch anything."

14

   Timothy and Vulpa stood at the closed doorway. His hands
trembled. She turned to him, noticing the panic in his face.
"Do not worry."
"I don't know why I'm so scared. I guess I've just got a bad
feeling about this."
She smiled at him from behind rounded glass. It wasn't her usual
forced or partial expression. This time it was kind and warm. It
surprised Timothy and his panting stopped.
"You're smiling."
"I am capable."
"It's nice."
She got serious, "What is?"
"You're smile. You should try it on Tweezor sometime."
She pushed a large round button on the wall and the door slid open.
A corridor was revealed, glowing with a green illumination. A
thick haze hung in the air. It was moisture, wet fog. Timothy
watched it collect on his face shield in little droplets. He stepped
inside.
"Keep going," Vulpa said, "I'm right behind you."

With small steps and shallow breath, Tim continued down the green hallway. Visibility was soon lost in the mist.

The human stopped, "I can't see anything."

A hand was felt over his shoulder.

"Do not stop," she whispered.

He held hands out in front of him, like a blind man without a cane. He took a step forward.

And then another.

His fingers touched something hard and smooth.

Dead end, he thought, *what now?*

Running his hands downward, he felt a button. With it pressed, a doorway slid out of sight. Fog swirled as Timothy stepped up to the entrance. The room was large, round and less hazy. Overhead lights shined down on five new doors. Each held a data screen in the center showing alien text. Vulpa walked up to the first door.

"Do you recognize this language?" she asked.

Tim squinted, "Nope."

She walked to the second door. The text was the same.

"Are you sure?"

Tim tapped an index finger on the fourth door.

"I'm sure."

Vulpa hit the nearest button. All five doors slid open. Behind each sat a long dark corridor.

Tim's frustration showed, "What is this place? Some kind of a maze or something?"

"I don't know," Vulpa said, puzzled. "I don't know."

15

   The command crew entered science lab one looking for a midget. The little man wasn't hard to find.

He yelled "Poop!" at a matter distributor in the center of the room.

"Tweezor," Commander Sorpe said, "What-"

"Ah!" he interrupted, "You are here!"

Captain Nule stepped up, "What do you need, Mr. Norbinger?"

He shook his head as if dizzy and then, "Crichet, there!"

He pointed to a dimensional power module.

"Crichet there!"

He pointed to a transwave path generator.

"Geesh there!"

He pointed to the systems power control center.

"Captain there!"

He pointed to the quantum detection unit.

"You," he said grabbing Ensign Leet's hand, pulling, "You, there!"

He pushed him toward the gravity coil.

"You!" he said to Ensign Shelby, "You at quantum send panel!"

Mr. Xaxe stepped up, "What should I do?"

"You with me and other Critchet on command platform for integrated systems. We go now."

Everyone took their places, wondering if the midget knew what he was doing. Nule closed his oval eyes, hoping so.

"Okay," Tweezor took a deep breath, "We go over it."

Without a moment to lose, he explained the procedure in detail. Each one listened, learning their individual responsibilities. They soon realized they would have to work as a flawless team. The margin for error was very small for the type of process they would attempt.

Take your time, Timothy, Nule thought, *we're going to need it.*

16

"Have you got it yet?" Timothy called out across the room.

"I'm working as fast as I can," Vulpa said, trying to decipher the language with her data pad.

The human stared into a panel that showed an unstable power reading. Random levels rose and dropped as lights flickered.

"This doesn't look good over here."

"I've got it," she said. Vulpa swung around to face him. "It's Telliform. The language of a race of beings from Verse Ten Twenty-Eight."

"Why is that language on the screen?"

She smiled, "Because your verse, Three-Three-Two, is a shadow of that one. Ten Twenty Eight is the original, intended verse."

Tim remembered what Tweezor had told him about hidden verses. An excess of power at the generator created them and they were near duplicates of their original verses.

Vulpa began the Telliform translation as the human walked up behind her.

"I can't believe the only reason I exist is a power surge."

"Yes, well," she said, "At least you do exist."

Vulpa looked down at the translation as it appeared on the data screen.

"It's numbers."

"What numbers?"

A pause and then, "Oh, I see. It's verse numbers. This door is Four thousand and One to Five thousand."

Tim walked away, "So the first door is One to a Thousand?"

"Yes. And we're going by intended verses, so we want the second door, a Thousand and One to Two thousand."

Tim turned back to her, "Because my original verse is Ten Twenty-Eight."

"Yes," she said with a smile, "Let us go."

Tim grinned, "You're getting pretty free with those smiles. You might even get used to it."

She pushed him into the second doorway.

"Move," she ordered.

17

Ensign Leet powered the gravity coil.

The captain ran a quantum scan of Verse Three-Three-Two.

After a few moments of systems testing, Tweezor called out to Mr. Geesh.

"Begin accelerator conversion!"

Long, muscled arms flexed as the Rectalin cranked over the control arm at his station. Quantonium flakes flooded the sealed chamber and a spinning gravity coil glowed with an intense yellow light.

"Levels are within operable limits," a Critchet called out over the hum of machinery.

"Initiate dimensional module," Tweezor said.

"We are showing a spike at the integrated matrix," EL said. "I am compensating now."

Tweezor pointed to BE, "Calculate the Transwave path."

With lightning quick taps at his console he checked the readout on a nearby screen. He looked up with a snap.

"The buffers are all full. I need more computation streamlines."

The midget's heart sank.

"There are no more streamlines," EM said, "Every computer in this lab is at maximum capacity."

Ensign Shelby was confused, "What does that mean?"

"It means," Tweezor said in a weak voice, "we finished."

"How many lines are we short?" Geesh asked.

EL studied his screen, "At least a hundred."

"No," Sorpe said, "Everything was looking so good."

Tweezor flopped into a chair, frustrated.

"I sorry, Timothy."

"Can't we just find some more computer systems to supplement?" Shelby asked.

"From where?" Xaxe said. "All of the lab's systems are being used. There are no more."

"Maybe not in the lab," Nule said from the back of the room.

The group turned to face him.

Phlem gargled, "What are you suggesting, sir?"

"I am suggesting that we use the Truthseeker's computers for the purpose in which they were originally intended. To save lives."

"Sir," Xaxe said, "To get a hundred free streamlines we would need to shutdown the entire ship. *Including the backup systems*."

Nule grinned, "Naturally, Mr. Xaxe. That is what I meant."

"But sir…"

Nule picked up a microphone and spoke into it. His voice echoed down every hallway. It sounded into every room.

"This is Captain Nule announcing a class three emergency. All crewmembers, I want you in environment suits immediately. This is not a drill. You have five minutes to comply. Computer systems and life support on all decks will shut down in five minutes. Every member of the crew is ordered into an environment suit immediately."

"I suppose that means us too," a Crichet said, stepping into a suit.

Nule turned to Tweezor, who once again smiled from ear to ear.

"Sweet!" the little man shouted, rushing for more space suits.

18

The corridor was murky black. Commander Nim led the way, feeling along the walls with outstretched arms as she walked. Timothy gripped the back of her oxygen tank, close behind.

An overhead light snapped on, illuminating a doorway thirty feet in front of them. "What's that?"

"It is another entrance. We are likely getting close."

Vulpa's pace slowed, approaching the end of the metal hall. They saw flashing lights reflecting on the floor and walls. Tim peeked over her shoulder at the chamber. It was tall and long, the far wall covered in video screens. On each screen sat a visual of a planet, or a flashing series of planets. Many of them showed warning alerts and versal fluctuation emergencies. The transmission signals from the generator had begun to distort.

Vulpa turned to her companion, "We need to re-set, now."

Tim took a deep breath and stepped up to the input panel.

"Okay," he said, "Let's do it."

19

"Keep the simulated gravity and lights running in this room only," Nule said from inside his environmental suit. "Shut everything else down, now."

The Consolidation cruiser's systems shut down all at once.

Corridors went black.

Oxygen generators stopped.

Heat cells cooled.

Shields.

Scanners.

Navigation.

Diagnostics.

Life support.

The Truthseeker drifted with no power, against a backdrop of crimson space.

"Route ship computers to your control station, Mr. BE."

The gravity coil glowed once more.

The engineer said, "We are now showing another hundred and twenty streamlines. It should be more than enough."

Yes, Nule thought, *This just might work.*

Tweezor started the quantum detection unit.

"I see the planet!" Nule shouted over the rumble of the vibrating coil, "I'm showing a clear signal!"

"Good!" Tweezor answered, "Open space fold perimeter path!"

With a growing hum, the dimensional fold began. Massive amounts of electricity traveled through the panel below Mr. Geesh. He watched it shining inside, behind the metal seams. The electricity traveled across a series of couplings, up through a thick prong above the control board, across an arched cable as big around as Geesh's forearm, to a prong on the other side. From there, it fed into the quantum exchanger. Geesh adjusted the input, being sure to keep clear of the prongs and cable.

"I have a good destination!" EL said. "Synchronization is beginning...*now*."

Geesh's hair stood on end. Static filled the air around him. It made his muscles twitch.

"It look good!" the midget said, "It...wait..."

The quantum lock on the Earth faded.

"What's happening?" Leet asked.

"We are losing the detection path!"

"Increase quantum power another five percent," EM said.

Everyone looked to Geesh's glowing power console.

"It won't take another five percent," Xaxe said, "It's maxed out now."

"He is correct," Nule said, "The matrix can't handle any more."

Tweezor screamed, "Poop!"

Geesh looked down at the station.

He clacked large molars, "The inside grid will sustain another ten percent. I am sure of it."

"It not inside grid we worry about," Tweezor said, "It that cable in front of you."

"He's right. That kind of power would melt it immediately."

Geesh growled, "If that happens, I will compensate."

"What?" Xaxe exclaimed, "What do you mean, *compensate?*"

"Just do it! There is no other option!"

He was right, of course. It was the only thing they could do. If it fried the cable, they'd damage a few systems, but nothing they couldn't repair.

"We have to try," Geesh barked in frustration.

"Okay. We do it. Gimmie five more percent, Mr. Leet."

He turned the power control upward. The gravity coil's illumination raged like a supernova.

"That's good!" Nule yelled, "The signal's back!"
Electricity snapped in an arc over Geesh's station. The cable burst into flames.
"We're losing it!" EM shouted.
"Turn it down!" Xaxe said.
"*Do not* turn the power down," Geesh said, raising his hands up to the prongs, "No matter what."
"Mr. Geesh, no!"
Thick hands grasped the metal prongs on each side of the panel. The flaming cable fell apart and Mr.Geesh was left in its place, keeping the power flowing.

20

The human peered into the shadows of the dim input panel. Vulpa stood beside him, translating the language on the screen with her data pad. After a few seconds of reading, she pushed a lever forward. A low compartment slid open and a padded chair emerged from inside. It swiveled, offering itself to the sequence carrier.
"What's that?" Tim said, backing up.
"You are to sit."
He frowned, "That's what I was afraid of."
He turned, forcing himself into the seat. It was soft and his tension eased a bit as he leaned back into the cushion.
"At least it's comfortable."
Without warning, heavy metal restraints closed over his wrists, ankles and across his chest. Terrified, Timothy screamed.
Vulpa wrinkled her face, "Do not panic. I'm positive that is supposed to happen." She turned to the screen for further instructions.
The chair, without need of outside assistance, rotated toward the input device. It sprang forward, thrusting the human's face into a round opening in the panel. He screamed again. His voice echoed all around his head, hurting his ears. A small motor whizzed to life above him. To Tim it sounded like a like a dentist's drill.
"Oh god!"
He struggled against the solid restraints.
"What is that?"

Lightheaded and in a cold sweat, he twisted, flexed and stretched. It was no use. The generator had him and was not letting go.

Images flooded into his brain. He saw planets, moons and stars. Galaxies.

Comets.

Universes.

Life.

Sunrises and clouds.

Vast masses of land and water.

Every imaginable world.

All five thousand, three hundred and thirty-two verses at once.

It was unbelievable, beautiful, amazing. He felt the life all around him. He heard every voice. Sensed every thought. Every emotion.

Oh, god.

For a brief moment, Timothy Rayburn of Verse Three-Three-Two was one with all of existence. He cried tears of joy and sorrow. It was incredible.

21

When he'd grabbed hold of the prongs it felt as if he was going to explode. Every muscle in his body seized in an uncontrollable knot as the amperage surged through. He didn't lose consciousness but felt as though he would at any moment. Thick teeth ground together as thunder raged in his head.

"Mr. Geesh!"

Nule yelled, "Shut it down!"

Xaxe said, "We're killing him!"

It took unbelievable will and stamina to do what Geesh did next. Shuddering and straining, he spoke.

"You...are n-not...k-killing me..."

Nule looked down at his panel, "Hurry, Tweezor. Let's finish this."

"Initiate space fold!" the little man said.

In an instant, Earth was pulled into a quantum shift.

"Tracking levels are in flux," EL said, "I'm adjusting them to negative one."

Tweezor's hands typed across multiple input keys.

"Hold there," he said, "How does shift sync look?"
Nule was awe struck, "It looks...perfect."
Tweezor spoke again, "In three...two...one..."
Foam spewed between Geesh's clenched teeth as his body
shuddered. Every nerve screamed with fierce defiance. Every
molocule threatened to explode.

22

Tim saw the creation of the universes, as it happened long ago.
He felt the excess of energy as it poured from the generator. He
saw the creation of the hidden verses. Three hundred and thirty
two cosmic accidents, birthed from and excess of primordial
power. Still sobbing and bewildered from all he'd experienced, he
saw what would happen when the generator re-set.
The transmission signals strengthened, the frequency codes re-
vitalized. The excess of energy was eliminated.
"What?"
The hidden verses collapsed.
"No!"
Tim struggled once again. Verse Three-Three-Two, his home, was
about to collapse. Everything he'd ever known would disappear.
And there was nothing he could do to stop it.

23

"--exchange!"
In a flash of snapping atoms, it happened. The Earth found itself in
a whole new universe. In perfect orbit, it rotated around a sun
identical to the one it was accustomed to. Tweezor checked his
reading. Everything looked good.
"Success!" he yelled and then clicked over the master power
switch.
The gravity coil went dark.
Commander Geesh fell to the floor, twitching.

24

The generator verified Timothy Rayburn's DNA. A random
chemical sample was taken. With all the verses signed in and
accounted for, the machine reset. Vulpa looked at the video

screens around her. The dish signals stabilized and warning lights
went dark.

"Timothy," she said, "you've done it."

She noticed something blinking on a small viewer in the corner
accompanied by a low chime. She walked closer to investigate.
The language on the screen was the same as she'd been translating.
It took only a moment to enter it into the data pad. The words that
came back made her gasp.

Energy excess has been eliminated.

Unintended verses have been erased.

Her vision snapped back toward the human, whose head lowered
out of the machine. The metal restraints released and he fell
forward in a daze.

"Timothy," she said rushing to him

He sobbed, looking up at her, "It's gone."

"I'm so sorry."

25

"Mr. Geesh, speak to me!" Xaxe said, rolling the unconsciousness
Rectalin onto his back.

Nule rushed over, "Power the ship and get the doctor in here now!"

Life support reinitiated across the Truthseeker as did scanners,
navigation and shields.

Communications.

"Doctor Clave to science lab one, immediately! Commander
Geesh has been electrocuted!"

Static and then "On my way."

The foam inside the large mouth bubbled. A thick tongue
slathered.

Coughing.

Growling.

"He's awake!"

Huge molars clacked.

"Get his helmet off!"

Tweezor unlatched the large glass dome and lifted it off. With a
loud exhale, Geesh sprayed the entire hovering group with white
lather.

The captain wiped it away from his face shield, "Mr. Geesh?"

Another cough and then, "Did we do it? Were we successful?"
Tweezor chittered in excitement, "Yeah, buddy! We did it!"
Geesh sat up, sore and coughing.
Nule, sticky with wet mucus, breathed a sigh of relief.

26
   In dark silence, Tim and Vulpa sat aboard the shuttlecraft
Holiday, getting into their harnesses. A transmission from the
Truthseeker sounded.
"Shuttlecraft Holiday, do you copy?"
"We copy, Truthseeker," Vulpa answered.
Tweezor's voice blasted over the speaker.
"Timothy! We did it, dude!"
"Tweez man, I don't feel like talking right now…"
A chipmunk laugh, "But we did it! We save Earth, my friend. It
no destroyed."
The human's mouth fell open. He couldn't breathe.
"But, how?"
Thee connected Critchets spoke in unison, "By using quantum,
multi-dimensional technology, we created a bi-universal space
fold, exchanging your home planet with another, identical planet."
"Huh?"
Nule, "Earth has moved to a new universe. We traded it with
Sellic."
Vulpa said, "Earth is a shadow of Sellic."
"Yeah!" the midget shouted, "That why it work so good!"
The unbelievable news sunk into Tim's mind.
"Isn't Sellic the one with the extra moon?"
"You think they notice?" Tweezor asked.
"But how did you-- I mean-- Are you sure?"
Geesh's guttural voice came over the airwaves, "Timothy, your
people are fine. The planet is fine. It now resides in Verse Ten-
Twenty-Eight."
Without warning Tim hugged Vulpa.
"They're okay!" he said to her, squeezing.
She patted him on the back.
"Thank goodness," she whispered.

Commander Xaxe turned to Tweezor, "Don't you think the population of Sellic might be perturbed?"

The little man threw short arms into the air, "There no population on Sellic. It unlivable due to thermonuclear war."

Dr. Clave looked up from his hairy patient.

"Well, thank the makers for that," he said with heavy sarcasm.

Large jaws snapped and Clave yanked his fingers away.

Geesh growled, "I require no more assistance. Go away."

"Fine," the doctor said in a huff. "How rude."

27

Admiral Bine's face appeared on the central screen.

"Gorza," he said with relief, "Our scientists tell me that the generator has been reset. It that true?"

"Yes, Admiral," the captain stated, "The verses have stabilized."

Bine adjusted himself in his seat, "Very good. Your orders are to remain where you are until the conflict at Zotaun has finished."

Nule gritted sharp teeth, "What do you mean, finished?"

"I mean, until the battle is over and you can get safely away."

"You expect us to hide here while the population of Zotaun is slaughtered?"

Bine leaned forward, "I *expect* you to live to fight another day, Captain. There is nothing you can do to help Zotaun."

Nule shook with anger, "We can *fight the enemy*. That is what *we can do*, Admiral--"

"No, Captain Nule. If you engaged the Meem fleet, you would be destroyed."

"But, Admiral--"

"You will be contacted by Consolidation Command when you are authorized to leave Verse One."

"It is home to three hundred million."

Bine got stern, "You will *follow orders*, Captain. That is all." The screen went black.

Three hundred million.

Nule leaned back into his chair, his hands trembling.

Dear god.

The captain stared into the spiraling verse wormhole, beyond which sat a gathering Meem fleet and the doomed planet of Zotaun.

28

Timothy and Vulpa both smiled when they walked onto the bridge. They found Tweezor sitting at his station, quiet and in deep thought.

"I can't believe you did it, man!" Tim said in enthusiasm, "How did you?"

The midget looked up with sad eyes. It was then that Tim noticed the room was a vacuum of silence. Mr. Geesh stood rubbing sore muscles, staring at the floor. Xaxe and Sorpe sat with heads hung low, their eyes at one another's feet.

And Nule. He sat at the captain's chair in a daze, long fingers pressed against a pale mouth.

"Oh man," Tim said, "Don't tell me somthin' happened to Earth."

"Your planet fine," Tweezor said.

"Then, what's wrong?"

Xaxe spoke, "We've been ordered to stay here."

Sorpe continued, "Yes. And Zotaun will be under attack in twenty minutes. It'll be a massacre."

"Oh no," Timothy said, "We can't just sit here. We have to help them."

The crew didn't respond. Tim rushed to the captain and leaned down to look into his face. Nule was a million miles away.

"Come on!" he pleaded, "Somebody say something!"

Large oval eyes found the human, "Timothy, my instructions were clear."

Anger blazed in Tim's voice, "What are you saying to me?"

"I'm saying, that we shall remain where we are until Consolidation Command tells us otherwise." He locked eyes with Timothy, "We're staying here."

Sector Eight:
The Battle for Zotaun

1

"What do you mean we're staying here?" Timothy asked.

"We've been ordered to stand down until the conflict is finished and we can get safely away."

Tim knew that Nule didn't believe in the words or the reasoning behind them. He was distant, deep inside himself. He was a man who'd been mortally wounded and could do nothing about it. Helplessness overcame his eyes and he slumped into the captain's chair.

"This is wrong!" Tim yelled, "What about all those innocent people? Didn't you tell me the population was three hundred million?"

Tweezor stared at his feet. Vulpa remained silent also, watching the human. Geesh ground his teeth, snarling with frustration.

Tim shook his fists, "We can't just sit here!"

Nule whispered, "I'm sorry, Timothy. I am bound to my orders."

"Your *orders?* There are women and children down there. Mothers…fathers..." Tim's eyes pierced into Nule, "*brothers.*"

Nule looked up as if Timothy had cut him with a knife. He stood with every muscle in his body wrenching.

"Don't you dare say another word, sequence carrier. Hold your tongue."

Tim's body shook in frustration, "No. I won't be quiet. You know I'm right!"

The captain's fists were iron hammers squeezing at fifteen years of self-loathing. Guilt threatened to kill him where he stood, stabbing into his nerves like poison talons. The wounds instantly pooled with a stinging rage. He could no more control his reaction than a man in a fire. He had to fight his way out of the pain before it consumed him. Before it was the only thing that remained.

He struck Timothy hard in the face, sending him reeling to the floor. Tim caught himself with sharp pain shooting across his jawbone.

The command crew stood in disbelief. The reality they had known seemed to suffocate, strangled by a new and terrible world. Each was a rigid statue, watching events with chiseled intentions, unable to act. Intervene. Or even breathe.

Nule realized what he'd done in an instant.

"Timothy…I'm so sorry…I…"

A purple bruise covered the left side of Tim's face. He turned to Nule with more determination than ever.

"Some things are worth fighting for."

"Timothy, I--"

"You taught me that. Can't you see? It's you who taught me that consequences don't matter. Only right and wrong do."

Nule's large eyes filled with tears and he broke down completely. Tim continued, "I'm so sorry about your brother. He didn't deserve to die like that."

"No…he did not…" Gorza said, covering his eyes.

He walked closer and put hands on Nule's arms.

"Those families down there don't deserve to die either."

"Admiral Bine said he wanted us to live to fight another day."

Timothy's conviction radiated, flooding the entire bridge.

"I refuse to take a single breath tomorrow if we don't at least try today."

Tweezor smiled at the captain, "Tomorrow may never come."

Vulpa added, "I agree. There are no guarantees."

Mr. Geesh, "Today is what we have captain. The battle is now."

Nule looked over a command crew that had served him honorably. They smiled, telling him they were willing to risk everything for what was right.

He smiled back at them, "We probably won't survive."

Geesh slathered, clacking his teeth, "Some things are worth dying for, sir."

Nule narrowed eyes at the frontal screen. An image of the Verse one wormhole spiraled, beyond which lie a gathering Meem fleet.

"Some things are, Mr. Geesh. I believe three hundred million innocent souls qualify. Wouldn't you agree, Mr. Norbinger?"

Tweezor's eyes lit up, "Yes I do, Captain. Sweet!"

Nule gave Timothy a hug.

"Thank you, my friend."

The human wiped away moisture from his swollen face. Nule touched the bruise he had caused.

"I'm sorry for that."

Tim grinned bigger, "Don't worry. I can take it."

Tweezor chittered at Tim, playfully punching him in the leg.

"You comin' along, dude. You *definitely* comin' along."

Nule spoke with a new confidence, "Contact Admiral Bine. I need to inform him that we're exiting Verse One."

2

Bine's face appeared on the central viewer.

"Captain Nule, what is it? I'm very busy."

Nule leaned forward, "We're going to fight."

Bine frowned, "You will stand down *as ordered*, Captain."

"No," Nule said, "We won't."

The Admiral saw the serious glare in his friend's face.

"Gorza," he pleaded, "Don't do this. You can't win."

"You should know we cannot hide here while helpless civilians die. We refuse."

"Gorza, your mission--"

"Our mission is *finished*, Admiral. The verses are saved. The generator has been re-set. Now, let me do my job."

"You must see the sequence carrier safely home. Your mission isn't complete until you have."

Nule's face twisted in anger, "The sequence carrier's name is *Timothy Rayburn*. He is an honorable member of this crew. He stands with us."

"Your under a lot of stress, Gorza. You're not thinking clearly."

The captain's fists pounded, "*No*. I am clear. For the first time since Gorma died, the first time in fifteen years, I'm thinking clearly."

Admiral Bine sat back in his chair and took a cleansing breath. His eyes scanned over the Truthseeker crew. He rubbed his chin looking at each one. They stared back at him, hoping for his approval. He shook his head, and grinned.

"Have you got a plan of attack, Captain?"

Tim's smile went wide with relief. Tweezor chittered, pumping his arms in celebration. Vulpa watched Nule stand at attention. His jaw flexed.

"We will hit them hard and swift. We will empty our arsenal upon them. And if it isn't enough, if it is our day to die, then we shall take at least one of them with us."

Bine smiled at his old friend, "So be it, Gorza. I see that I can't stop you. Your mind is made up."

"It is."

"Then, may fate smile upon you, my friend."

"May fate smile upon us all, Admiral."

"Carry on," Bine said.

The screen went black.

3

"How long have we got?" Nule asked Commander Geesh.

"The Meem fleet should be gathered in twenty minutes. I wouldn't expect the main cannon facility to last even that long. We can assume they will begin their cruiser air strike on the base when it has been destroyed. That is, if they use the same tactics they used at Choxide."

Nule thought as he paced the floor, "We have as yet shown them no reason to fear us. They won't change their strategy now."

Vulpa said, "I would agree, Captain."

"So," Nule said, "I'm open to suggestions."

Vulpa cleared her throat, "The only success we've had was in the Asteroid Sea. Perhaps we could organize a joint attack with other consolidation ships to--"

"What?" Sorpe asked, "Push them into some asteroids?"

"No," Geesh said, "There is nothing there. They are in open space."

Vulpa, "We could try to push them into ...each other."

Sorpe, "We don't have the fire power for that. We'd be out of torpedoes in a few minutes. The Meem fleet is too big."

Nule, "I would agree. Any other suggestions?"

Tim looked up from his shoes.

"Didn't you say the Meem ships had two layers of shields?

"Yes," Commander Geesh answered, "An outer plasma shield and an inner ion shield."

Tim stepped up to the hairy alien.

"How far off the hull is the outer shield?"

"Approximately seven feet."

"And the ion shield?"

"Half the distance."

"So, the inner shield sits three and a half feet off the Meem hull. I'd say our problem is getting under the inner shield."

Sorpe snapped, "That's always been our problem. We know that."

"Yeah, well Tweezor has made some adjustments to the Ectopal shield packs that will get us through."

"Yes," the midget continued, "Portable shield pack generator is all you need... theoretically."

He punched a pass code into Vulpa's station. The information flooded her screen.

Nule scanned the data in amazement, "How stable is it?"

"Very," the little man said, "It create negative ion bubble around designated area. It pass right through Meem shield."

Nule smiled, "That's it. We're found our offensive. Excellent job Mr. Norbinger. Excellent."

Tweezor's grin faded.

"There a problem, though."

"What's the problem?"

"The bubble is ion."

"Yes," Tim continued, "And no electrical system can operate inside it."

Sorpe, "So you couldn't use it with a torpedo. The guidance systems would shut down."

Vulpa, "Even simple collision detection is program based."

"I agree," Nule said, "The torpedo would simply knock on the enemy hull and drift away. It wouldn't detonate."

"Right," Tim said, "Not until the ion bubble is shut down and the weapons computer is re-booted."

Sorpe scowled, "How do you suggest we do that?"

Nule was beginning to understand their plan.

"Each torpedo would need to be hand delivered."

"Yes."

Vulpa, "We don't have fighters that small. They wouldn't fit under the Meem shield. And if you disengage the bubble with any part of the ship crossing the sheild..."

"It would be destroyed," Geesh said.

Nule, "Right. You would need to be well underneath when you shut it down."

Tim nodded, "That's why we're gonna use Jetpacks."

"Are you mad?" Xaxe said, "Send a single man with a Jetpack against a Meem Warbird?"

Vulpa sat back in her chair.

"You would need to stay close to the hull, under three feet I'd say, so not to get caught in the ion firewall..."

Nule, "The delivery boys would need some type of magnetic system to attach themselves to the hull."

Geesh, "Yes, and I could program a timer into the torpedoes' computers. They would need only to initiate a countdown and get clear."

Sorpe asked, "Couldn't the pilots just let go of the torpedo and let the ion shield detonate the antimatter?"

"No," Vulpa answered, "The idemic energy is a negative charge. The torpedo would simply burn up, it wouldn't detonate."

Nule, "How many of these units do we have?"

Tweezor grinned, "Forty packs, she give us forty."

"Who?"

Tim felt his pocket for the holograph device, "Sparrim."

Nule slapped the human on the back, "Well, thank goodness for Ms. Gale-- *Again*."

"Yeah," Tim sighed.

Nule said, "Mr. Geesh, Mr. Norbinger and I shall attend to the shielding units and torpedoes. We'll be in engineering bay..." He looked at Tweezor.

"The packs in bay twelve," the little man said.

"...Twelve," Nule repeated, "Vulpa, have the torpedoes brought to us there. And anything else Mr. Geesh needs."

Hair shook as he spoke, "I'll need as many portable routers and data pads as can be found, a spool of number nine wire and an electrical kit."

"And Jetpack pilots, Mr. Sorpe. How many have we got on board?"

"We have only twenty signed off on Jetpack, including Sergeant Orts, naturally."

"Is that all?"

Tim stepped up, "Captain Nule, I can--"

Commander Sorpe interrupted, "We've got some recruits in training that have not yet received their certificates. There may be a few that could be used in a desperate situation."

Nule paused, "An entire planet full of lives hangs in the balance, Commander. I'd say the situation is desperate."

"Yes, sir."

"I want every pilot *and trainee* you've got on the bay twelve platform in five minutes. It's time to accelerate their training."

Captain Nule walked to the screen at the central chair. With a pass code punched in, numbers appeared, showing the Timeshift countdown. They read, 14:36.

Fourteen minutes, he thought, *until*... With another command punched in the screen read, *Delete program procedure. Push ENTER to confirm. Press ESCAPE to cancel.*

A long finger hovered over the touch pad for a moment. He looked into the spiraling wormhole on the frontal viewer and then down at Timothy and Mr. Geesh. Without looking down, he hit the enter button. The scroll stopped, disappeared and the screen flashed, *Countdown has been erased.*

Nule walked away, "Yes, well let's get going."

He paused at the doorway.

"Vulpa, you have the bridge. Charge and make ready all weapons systems. Initiate the defense reactors. Send an encoded message to Consolidation ships within range. Include the battle plan, ion shielding data and request assistance."

Vulpa sat rigid in her seat, hoping for some inspirational words from her captain, but trying not to show it.

"Yes, Captain," she said.

Nule checked the time, "We've got about ten minutes. Let's hustle."

With that, he turned and headed down the corridor. Tweezor and Geesh were right behind him.

Without looking back Nule said, "Mr. Rayburn, come along."
Tim smiled and jogged to catch up.

4

"All Jetpack pilots and trainees to shuttle bay twelve immediately,"
Junley Sorpe ordered over the intercom.
Vulpa Nim's words followed his.
"Pod gunners to the spine. I repeat, pod gunners to the spine. Fire
the reactors and make ready."
She turned to the communications officer.
"Have you sent the message?"
"Yes, Commander. It's playing in a loop on scramble channel
COS-A3. The fleet should pick it up immediately."
        Vulpa worked at her station, analyzing and charging systems.
EM, EL and BE prepared the Truthseeker for combat at the
engineering platform. Nule, Norbinger and Geesh rushed down the
corridor to bay twelve. Timothy followed close behind.
        A repeating alarm chime preceded the Commander's voice over
the intercom.
 "Battle stations."

5

        A gathering of five Consolidation cruisers sat in orbit on the
dark side of the planet Rizon, waiting for further orders. One of
them, the smallest in the group, was an older model vessel. Ten
years old, actually. In starship terms, it was ancient. Most ships of
its age had been decommissioned years ago to make room for the
new wave of advanced battle cruisers. But the captain, not unlike
the ship, was old and the Consolidation hoped to retire the two of
them together before the upcoming fiscal year.
        He, Captain Almon Teeg, had been informed months ago of his
mandatory pension for twenty-five years of loyal service. He also
had refused to fill out or return the necessary paperwork. It was his
opinion that the old bird still had quite a few pex left in her and so
did he, thank you very much.
        Teeg hated sitting, hated waiting and despised being left out or
overlooked. He sat twitching and fidgeting in his chair, grumbling
and complaining under his breath. His ship, the Pluddam Freeze,

had been ordered to hold current position and not to engage enemy ships, as were the other four nearby cruisers.

"Set a course for the Stinzotaun system and hold please. We should be ready if they give the order, you know."

The navigation officer, Commander Sig, was close to his captain's age and had served under him for fifteen years.

"Captain, Consolidation Command has ordered us to remain here. We are not to engage the enemy."

"I know that," Teeg said, "Don't you think I heard them? I heard the order."

"Yes, sir."

"And I'm the Captain of this bird, last time I checked, so set the course in. That's an order."

Sig rolled large, oval eyes, "Yes, sir."

"Situations change you know. They might call any second."

"Yes, sir."

"Incoming message on scramble frequency, sir," announced the communications ensign.

Teeg's eyes lit up, "You see? That's probably them…on screen."

Numbers and letters rolled down the main viewer, accompanied by an urgent female voice.

"--message will repeat… This is the Consolidation cruiser Truthseeker, security code B92468H-K. We are sending strategy information and ion bubble conversion instructions for Ectopal class flight pack, Wingman, models EN42 through EN48… Gentleman, we have developed an offense that we believe will be effective against the Meem ships. We request that all Consolidation cruisers within range of this transmission respond. Time is short and we need your help… This message will repeat…"

Teeg looked over the data scrolling down his screen.

"Mr. Sig, analyze this information and then report, please."

"Yes, sir," he responded and then began tapping at his console.

On the bridge of the Judgment, a nearby Consolidation cruiser, a captain watched over his first officer's shoulder.

"What kind of conversion?"

The commander responded, "It creates a kind of ion based bubble, allowing passage through the Meem negative charged shield."

"Is it stable?"

"Yes, sir. It holds in the simulation."

Another gathering of ships, sat at the far side of Inner Deema. Roma Chakkos, Captain of the Expedition, sat studying the ion bubble data.

"Yes, it looks good in the simulation, but do you think it will really work?"

Science officer Ceel, "Based on the information I have here, yes. But, there are many other dangers to consider."

Another captain, aboard another nearby ship, "I agree that attacking a Meem Warbird is dangerous. It's practically suicide, but if Captain Nule has faith that his plan can be successful, I am apt to believe him."

Captain Teeg, "Have we got any Ectopal packs on board?"

Lieutenant Hill, "We have four, but they're pretty old. None of them are the Wingman model."

Teeg, "Everything on this ship is old, Lieutenant. Don't let that stop you."

"Sir, if there is a way to convert them, we'll find it."

"That's what I like to hear. Initiate Transwave to the Stinzotaun Axis."

"We've been ordered by Command to remain here."

"Yeah? Well, what are they gonna do, force us into early retirement?"

"But, sir--"

"But nothing. Nule is a friend of mine and he needs our help. *Engage.*"

The Pluddam Freeze turned and accelerated away from the other four ships. Transmissions brought the airwaves to life.

"Open the channel."

Voices flooded the speaker, overlapping one another.

"*Gentlemen,*" Teeg interrupted, "*Please.* There's a war on, and I don't plan on missing it."

6

Geesh tightened a wire into place on the front of the Jetpack.

"Try that."

Nule checked the data pad.

"Yes, that's better. Mr. Norbinger, run a system diagnostic. We're moving to the next one."

Tweezor said, "Yes, sir," as he slid over to the pack.

That made six units finished and ready to go. A group of soldiers at the other side of the bay programed weapon computers. The stockpile of torpedoes was at twenty and growing.

Mr. Orts walked onto the platform with thirty-four pilots and trainees. Some of them looked nervous. The others were pale, petrified with fear.

Nule said, "Continue with this, Mr. Geesh. I'll return in a moment."

He stood and approached the soldiers.

He addressed the group, "I realize that when you began training on Jetpack you never thought you'd be attacking an enemy cruiser with one strapped to your back. It's highly unusual, I know."

He paused, looking over the fear in their faces.

"I won't try to convince you that what you are about to do isn't dangerous, because it is. You're all aware of that."

Tim walked over and joined the trainees, bringing the pilot count up to thirty-five. It was thirty-seven if you counted Commander Norbinger and Sergeant Orts.

"It is not danger that should concern you today. It is the task at hand. Only you stand between three hundred million lives and those that threaten them. Today you fight for those that cannot fight for themselves. You fight for future generations. You fight for us all. The warrior cares not about the consequences of his actions, if his actions remain true. You are my warriors today. Your battle is for what is right. For all that is good. For life itself. There can be no higher purpose."

7

High above Zotaun, on the dark side of the planet and out of range of the Axis main cannon, the Meem fleet gathered. Five ships sat waiting while another eleven Warbirds approached.

Far below on the daytime side of Zotaun, war raged. The Meem ground assault pummeled its way through the military base, working toward the primary weapon facility. Waves of hover tanks opened fire on low flying Red Stripe squads that in turn, hit them with spider charges and seeker missiles. Explosions billowed over pavement and buildings. Fire detonated, expanded, faded and then detonated again. The remaining structures stood blackened with smoke and death. Smoldering streets were abandoned, reeking of blood and flaming liquid fuel.

The hover tanks were only minutes away from their objective now. An odd weapon on tracks ambled along, following them. Its upper tong snapped with white-hot lightning.

8

Sergeant Orts lifted the Jetpack up, onto Timothy's back from behind. The thirty-pound rocket hung with its weight pulling at his shoulders. He clicked the harness together across the human's chest and then at his waist. Orts walked around in front of him and yanked at the strap adjustment, tightening it around Tim's ribs.
"Does it have to be so freakin' tight? I can't breathe, dude."
Orts grinned, "Yes it does, *dude*."
Tweezor approached bowlegged, sporting his own pack. The space suit he wore was the one from the first time they met, on Earth.
"Hey cowboy, you ready?"
Tim fumbled with his controls, "I don't know."
"You be fine."
"I'm scared, man."
The midget grinned, "No worry. All good."
Tim looked past the pilots rushing to ready their Jetpacks, at the large bay doors. What lie on the other side was a big, dark universe. Shallow breath shuddered in his chest.
"What if I can't do this?"
"You can."
"Okay, but what if I can't?"
Tweezor swatted Tim on the butt with the palm of a pudgy hand. It stung.
"Ow. Get off me, man."
"Tim do it. No problem."
The human backed away from the little man.
"That's not cool."
"Cool," Tweezor said laughing.

Thirty-five Jetpack pilots stood gathered, checking spacesuit systems and making adjustments. A few had their helmets on, most didn't.

Sergeant Orts, "Everyone get your headsets on now. We need individual radio checks from each of you. They'll be dividing us into eight teams. Listen to the controller for further instructions."

9

Video station controller consoles rolled onto the bridge, pushed by engineering personnel.

Vulpa looked up from her console, "Where are you going with those?"

The engineer stopped in the center of the floor, released a grip lever and the unit's wheels slid up inside, sending it clunking into position. He looked around, evaluating the remaining space.

Vulpa, "*I said*, where are you putting those?"

"Right here, Commander. The captain wants them right here." He looked toward the doorway, "Alright, bring the rest of them in. On the double."

Seven more controller stations wheeled in one after another, and set side by side, three rows deep.

"There isn't any room left to walk in here. Are you positive the Captain said--"

Nule stepped up behind her.

"Yes, Commander. They are doing as I instructed."

Vulpa turned, surprised to hear his voice, "I see, sir."

Personel rolled in eight chairs and set them into position. The control officers filed in. Each sat at a video station, slid a headset over his ears and adjusted the attached microphone. Video screens fizzled to life in front of them. Each view divided into five boxes, one for each Jetpack pilot in the team. Team names popped above the vital statistics of the pilots and each one's helmet camera view. The controller in the first station, "I have a successful system boot. We're ready for communications check. If ready, say so now."

Controller two, "Glimmer control, set."

Three, "Glow team, set."

Four, "Shine ready."

Five, "Go for Flash team."

Six, "Haze control ready."

Seven, "Shadow is a go."

Eight, "Dark team standing by."

The first controller again, "And I'll be running Glare team. Begin team member radio checks and assign call numbers."

All the controllers spoke into their headsets at once, contacting the individual Jetpack pilots.

10

A voice sounded in Tim's ears.

"Norbinger, Tweezor."

"Yes?" the midget responded as the human listened.

"You are Shadow leader, position one."

"I copy," the little man said.

The controller called another name.

"Louson, Delder."

"I copy," a voice said.

"You are Shadow team, position two."

"Yes, sir."

"Telner, Rada."

"Yes, control. I have a copy," a female voice said.

"You are shadow team, position three."

"Thank you, sir."

"Mal, Sin."

A deep voice, "I am here."

"Shadow team, position four. And put your helmet on."

"Alright."

"Rayburn, Timothy."

Tim jumped at the sound of his name.

"Um, yes?"

"You are shadow team, position five."

"Okay. I uh, copy."

Tim clicked his radio off, "Tweezor?"

"Yeah?"

"What does position five mean?"

The midget clicked his microphone off.

"It mean," he whispered, "If someone say *shadow five*, they talkin' to you."

"Oh."

"And *I*," Tweezor said, "Shadow one. I Shadow *leader*. If I say, you do. Got it?"

"Yeah, sure."

"And if control say, you do. Yes?"

"So, everyone is in charge except me?"

"Yes. If anybody say you do, you do."

Tim frowned, "That's not fair. Can't I be in charge of something?"

The midget grabbed a handful of Tim's spacesuit and pulled.

"You in charge of Jack."

"Who's Jack?"

The miget looked around, shrugged his shoulders and then grinned, "I guess he no show up."

The human smiled, "That's clever. Did you make that up all by yourself?"

Tweezor chittered, "No."

11

"Red stripe on approach at grid three-niner-one. Clear the floor." The wave of Meem hover tanks aimed energy cannons into the air, opening fire on the incoming fighters. Five Impaths spiraled and dived low, burning the air twenty feet above the street. They screamed past, unleashing hundreds of spider charges.

One charge bounced, rolled and then rose up onto its spindly legs. It scanned the area and scuttled to its target. It ran into the enemy vehicle's shadow, up the winding metal track and then clamped down tightly onto the armored surface.

The street and parking lot raged with blinding punishment.

The explosion ripped the vehicle in half and blew its tracks into shrapnel. A bent and broken tong flew into the air.

"That may have bought us some time," Stripe leader said.

The remaining upright hover tanks turned and fired on the ion cannon dome.

12

Sergeant Orts checked the panel readout at the shuttle bay doors.

"Team leaders, double check helmets and environment suit readiness."

Tweezor looked around.

"Helmet on, soldier," he ordered, pointing at a trainee.

Orts called out, "I want teams on these lines when I call you." With a stiff arm he motioned to black parallel lines on the floor. He pointed down at the first line, the one closest to the bay doors, "Glare team."

Five pilots made their way through the crowd and then stood shoulder-to-shoulder facing the tall exit.

Taking a step to the side, the sergeant motioned to the next line. "Haze team."

Orts assigned the next row, and the next. Tim hyperventilated by the time the seventh line was called out.

"Shadow team," Orts said.

With an uneven number of pilots, team eight consisted of only the sergeant and another military Jetpack trainer, Lieutenant Gibba Styner.

The pilots stood in tight rows and all Tim could see was dozens of shiny glass helmets. Workers shuffled down the rows of pilots, carrying large black bags with metal attachments on two ends. They clicked a bag into rings on the bottom of the breastplate on each pilot's Jetpack harness. Tim fell forward at the sixty-five pounds of extra weight. He now carried an antimatter Aggressor torpedo.

He couldn't pull his vision away from the doors. He kept seeing Sparrim's face, her pleading eyes as they fell over the railing at Ebteon.

And the falling.

Oh god.

A loud voice sounded above them.

"Clear shuttle bay twelve. Prepare for de-compression."

Styner yelled, "Environment suit green light. Fire 'em up, boys."

The falling.

A mile above the city.

No no no.

Tim was frozen with fear.

Don't let go of me, she said.

The panic.

"No worry," a high-pitched voice said beside him.

Tweezor clicked on Tim's space suit. It whirred to life. Cool oxygen flowed into his face. Tim pinched hit eyes shut, trying to calm down.

A voice above them, "Initiate crane hoist."

From the ceiling, a hydraulic arm lowered above each pilot, clamped around the tops of the Jetpacks and then lifted them off the floor.

"What's happening?" Tim said as his boots left the platform.

"All good. Calm down," Tweezor said.

Cold sweat ran, "Oh, man. I don't think I can do this."

"Stand clear. Bay doors are opening."

Yellow gumball lights at the ceiling illuminated and spun. Thick locks released and the shuttle bay doors parted. A slight rush of air pulled at rows of pilots as the last of the oxygen escaped the sealed bay. The curtain of blackness outside was dotted with a million pinpoints of light. It seemed to stretch out forever. Tim's helmet shield fogged with hot breath.

"I can't do this. *Oh my god.* I can't."

The human squirmed, dangling from a ceiling that had begun to move. The hydraulic arms and the platform above them slid out the open doors, creating a canopy on the side of the ship. The suspended Jetpack pilots hung outside the bay, over black nothingness. Tim couldn't breathe, staring down past his feet.

"Oh *god*. I'm gonna fall. I'm not doing this. Take me back."

Tweezor turned, put a hand on each side of the human's helmet and pulled him close. The helmets knocked together.

"Timothy."

"Tweezor? Man, I can't do it. I'm sorry. I..."

"Timothy, listen at me."

Tim's face was pale as he gasped for air.

"I'm gonna fall. I-"

"Timothy. I your friend. Listen to words I say."

Wide, panic filled eyes found a smiling face behind glass.

"What?"

"Tim can do it."

"No, I can't. I feel like I'm falling."

"Of course you do. So do I."

Surprised, he said, "You do?"

"Yes. Falling is life. And life falling into unknown. You see?"

"Um, not really."

"No one know what come next. Future always below us, out of sight."

"I can't get the tower out of my mind. I feel like I'm gonna die." His hands trembled.

"You been falling from tower whole life. Don't let stop you now."

"I don't know…"

"Life is a ride baby, enjoy it."

Tim's breath calmed. "I don't even know what I'm doing out here."

"Same as us. We here cuz of you. We do what right cuz of you."

A surprising voice sounded in Tim's helmet. It was the pilot to his right, Delder Louson.

"The little guy is right. We're here because of you. I heard what you said to the Captain. Personally, I am proud to fly with you." The other pilots spoke up, agreeing.

Tim looked around, "You guys can hear me?"

Orts patted him on the shoulder, "We're all on the same channel now, Tim."

"Oh," he said embarrassed.

Tone Nibbersit of Glimmer team spoke up, "You taught us about heart today, kid. Don't forget that."

Itchit Slype of Shine team, "I'm dedicating my flight today to my family."

Age Mot of Haze team, "I'm flying for my children."

Sin Mal, Shadow team, "For my wife."

"For my sister."

"My parents."

"My girlfriend."

"For my brother," said a familiar voice from the bridge.

Tim smiled, "Yeah, for all those we care about, wherever they are." His hands still shook, but he had begun to catch his breath.

13

Orts, "Okay soldiers, down to business. We will attack the ships in teams. Stick tight to your leader until he calls the attack run. At that point, spread out and deliver your packages."

Styner continued the instructions.

"Fly straight at the hull creating enough momentum to pass through the ion shielding. At two pex, click over your bubble shield control switch. Make sure your knees touch down first. The electromagnets in your kneepads should hold you to the ship. Disengage the bubble armature. Remove the torpedo and attach it to the hull with the blue lever. Turn the switch to 'armed', hit the countdown button and then back away. Double check the countdown scroll, re-start your bubble armature and then push off, *hard.* Once you're clear of the ship, shut down the bubble, re-boot your Jetpack and environment suit and get back to the Truthseeker."

"Yeah," Sergeant Orts added, "and you'll have to look for her, because she's not going to be sitting in one place waiting for us. She'll be maneuvering."

14

"Sir, we are being hailed by Consolidation command, Axis command, about ten different Consolidation cruisers and by Admiral Bine."

"Shut it off," Nule said, "We cannot enter battle with that ruckus going on."

"Yes, sir."

Nule looked over the controller stations.

"Do we have a go, gentlemen?"

"We have a go, Captain. We are standing by."

"Commander Nim?"

"Ready at navigation, Captain."

"Mr. Geesh?"

Teeth clacked, "Weapon systems charged and ready."

"Let's give them a fight worthy of honor, my friends."

He remembered his brother and smiled.

This is for you, Gorma.

"Set a course for the wormhole, and engage."

The Truthseeker banked into the spiraling wormhole, accelerating.

"Here we go. Look sharp."

Tim sucked in a deep breath and held it. They passed through the bright white haze, entering Verse eight-three. The versal doorway faded and the massive planet Zotaun came into view.

Three Meem Warbirds held a position right in front of the Truthseeker, with their backs turned.

"Oh god," Tim said.

"Engage rockets, Glare team! Go, go, go!"

With that, hydraulic arms released the first row of pilots. They dropped straight down, engaging boosters. In a tight formation they rocketed toward a Meem Warbird that had spun around to face them. The enemy cruiser backed up and nosed down, opening fire with snapping balls of energy.

15

"Team one is away, Captain." Vulpa said.

"Full plasma spread on the central ship-- Fire."

Geesh, "Incoming seeker missiles."

"Evasive."

16

Deafening blasts quaked over Tim's head. He jumped at the sound. He realized that the Truthseeker had begun firing.

"Go, Glimmer team, go!"

The second row fell away as the Truthseeker increased speed. The pilots raced into the distance, their exhaust ports glowing like shooting stars. Tim watched as a blast of plasma from the Meem cruiser shot at them. They broke formation, scattering like flies. One pilot, Tone Nibbersit, didn't get clear in time. His body fell away, end over end, burning.

Tim gasped.

After a moment the torpedo he carried exploded, vaporizing him and the other four pilots. Their weapons detonated also, filling the space between the Truthseeker and the Meem cruiser with billowing fire. Tim's heart and body leapt in shock. His eyes filled with fear.

"Oh no," he said in disbelief, "God help us."

17

The huge explosion shoved at the Truthseeker.

"We've lost Glimmer team," announced a solemn controller as he pulled off his headset.

18

Glare team approached the central Meem cruiser with Hecton Flet in the lead position. "Attack run, boys. Deliver packages." Two pilots banked port and two starboard. Flet continued straight into the side of the cruiser.

19

"Where is team one?"

"They are approaching a Meem vessel and should be initiating an attack run."

"Good," Nule said, "Spine gunners, fire at will. Protect the pilots."

20

Tight blasts of plasma lit up the port side of the Meem ship, impacting over the outer plasma shielding. It was a barrage of machine gun speed and seemed to be everywhere.

"Stay on target," Flet said, "That's just cover fire from the Truthseeker."

Pilots Baum and Conprat hit their boosters trying to keep pace with a diving Meem cruiser. The ship rolled at them. The plasma shield washed over Officer Conprat, searing his body into flames. His torpedo exploded. Two pilots vaporized as the Meem vessel quaked in the explosion.

"We've lost two more pilots!" called a crackling voice.

"Stay on target, soldier," Flet ordered.

The enemy ship still quaked as the team leader engaged his bubble shield unit. His environment suit systems shut down as he pulled his legs to his chest. Momentum carried him through the plasma shielding and the ion firewall. He hit the hull off balance with his shoulders and arm. Flet strained for something to hold onto but there was nothing. His body bounced off the slick surface and back into space.

"No!" he yelled, powering down the protective bubble.

He drifted until the Jetpack computer re-booted. He then fired boosters to catch up with the ship.

"Engage rockets, Glow team! Go, go, go!"

A third row of pilots fell down and away. The Truthseeker climbed into a barrel roll.

Timothy held on, grinding his teeth. The five pilots disappeared from his vision as the Truthseeker turned. Another big explosion lit the area with flames rolling.

"We've lost Glow team!" someone cried over the airwaves, "They're gone!"

Tim pinched his eyes shut with tears streaming, *Oh god, we're gonna die.*

21

"It's moving too fast!"

Flet, "Get in there, ensign. That's an order."

"I can't..."

"I'm right behind you. You're doing fine. Engage booster-"

An explosion, static and then silence.

22

"They're just not getting through, Captain," Vulpa said.

Nule sat in silence. Three controller stations were now useless. Fifteen pilots were dead.

Three Meem cruisers regrouped in tight formation. Waves of spine fire washed over their shields. The enemy ships did not fire on the Truthseeker. They hovered, waiting to see what Nule would do next.

The control officer at the fourth station, "Sir, do you want Shine team released?"

"Hold," the captain responded, "Commanders, prepare an attack run."

"Sir?"

"We must protect the delivery team. It's the only way."

"Weapons control is standing by, sir."

"As is navigation. Your orders?"

"We are going in straight at them. Be ready on ripper mixture. Full spectrum, Mr. Geesh. Do not give them an inch to breathe, do you hear me? Not an inch."

Hair shook and teeth clacked.

"Affirmative."

"Tell Shine team to follow us in. It's all or nothing this time."

The controller spoke to his pilots.

"Shine team, follow the Truthseeker on an attack run."

"Release them."

"Go, go, go!"

Five soldiers fell away from the ship with roaring jets.

Nule, "Engage at three-eighty. Open fire."

The Truthseeker nosed down, rocketing at the Meem ships. Blasts of plasma and Aggressor torpedoes led the way, along with six snaking seeker missiles, targeting the enemy cruisers.

The gathering of three spread their formation and returned fire.

23

"Incoming."

"Ripper burst-- Hecta grid rotate."

Vulpa's face flushed as her long fingers followed orders. It was a maneuver she hadn't performed since the academy and it had only been in a simulator.

The Truthseeker's speed doubled. The ship ripped past the approaching Meem missiles, shot past the three Warbirds and then slowed, spinning around behind them. Enemy missiles turned and then continued into empty space. The three cruisers lit up with punishment as the Jetpack pilots got closer. They watched the ships stutter in the flames.

As the clouds of orange dissipated, the Shine team leader yelled to his crew.

"This is our chance! Begin delivery!"

The pilots spread out over the nearest Meem cruiser's hull. Itchit Slype and Jibs Conery passed through the shields and touched down.

Success, Slype thought as he shut down the ion bubble.

The Meem shield hummed above him with a red glow as he fumbled for the torpedo. His workspace was hot, almost two hundred degrees. The spacesuit he wore provided a heater for protection from the freezing temperatures of space, but had no cooling system whatsoever. He could barely breathe. The hull rumbled with a constant vibration and random seizures from explosions outside the shield. He tried to stay focused on the mission.

It was difficult.

Ensign Conery's knees grabbed hold of a panel section in the center of the port wing. The quaking and heat was unbelievable. He struggled to hang on as the ship tilted and spun. A nearby detonation bounced the wing up and down, throwing him back into space.

With the torpedo locked down to the Meem hull, Slype cranked over the switch to ARMED. He hit the red button and the screen lit up with glowing numbers.

Yes. I did it.

He verified the countdown, backing away on his knees. He had twenty seconds to get clear.

"Package delivered!" he shouted.

Re-starting the protective bubble, he kicked off hard.

24

The Aggressor torpedo detonation under the ion Shield was massive. It ripped the ship's underbelly and starboard wing into flaming, unrecognizable debris. The Warbird shuddered, falling away and spewing hot gases.

"A Meem Cruiser has been destroyed," sounded over the Truthseeker's intercom. Soldiers cheered. The two remaining enemies fired. Eight seekers blazed into space.

"Evasive," Nule said, "Concentrated Plasma release."

A wave of radiation expelled from the ship as it dived and increased speed. Five missiles detonated in the cloud. Two more blew a moment later. The one remaining was on target and gaining.

"I can't shake it," Vulpa said, "Brace for--"

An explosion behind them. It was a slight rumble.

"The missile has detonated, sir," Geesh announced.

"Nice shot, spine gunners. Thank you."

"It wasn't the gunners."

"A Consolidation cruiser has come out of Wavetime, Captain. They destroyed the missile."

"Open a channel."

A familiar voice, "Captain Nule, I heard you could use some help. The Pluddam Freeze is at your service."

He smiled, "Thank you, Captain Teeg. Have you got any Ectopal flight packs?"

Teeg, "We have four converted to your specifications. My pilots are standing by."

"Tell them to hold and prepare for an attack run."

Nule turned to the controller at the first station.

"Get your headset on, you'll be running Freeze team."

Suddenly everyone aboard the Truthseeker didn't feel so alone. And neither did the two remaining Meem cruisers. Five more joined them from out of the shadow of Zotaun.

The unfathomable had occurred. One of their mighty battleships had been destroyed. The fleet was not about to let that happen again. A dark wall of Warbirds formed, waiting for an attack run by two Consolidation ships. Seven particle vacillators charged at once. The Truthseeker and the Pluddam Freeze turned to face them.

Vulpa, "Incoming message from a Meem cruiser."

Nule's words were cold, "Open the channel."

A crackling silence and then, "We…are…Meem."

Nule frowned, "And we are the Consolidation ships Truthseeker and Pluddam Freeze."

The voice wheezed, "…The Truth…you have found…it is death…"

"Perhaps," the captain said, "Which one of you would like to accompany us?"

"It ends now…You will fall…When you feel us…"

The transmission ended with static.

Nule looked at Commander Nim, "Which ship was the transmission originating from?"

She pointed at the screen, "The one in the center, at the highest point."

"Yes," he said as his eyes narrowed, "That's the one we're attacking."

Geesh slathered and growled, "Yes, sir."

"Prepare to drop the remaining pilots. Ready a ripper burn. Double up a full spectrum, Commander. Keep them coming."

"Naturally."

Nule spoke into the intercom, sending his voice down hallways, over workstations and into the spine pods. It sounded into Jetpack helmets.

"It would seem our adversaries are mortal after all. Nice job, all of you… Now, let's get another one."

Timothy's body tingled with anticipation and fear. Tweezor reached over and swatted him across the chest.

"This is it, cowboy."

The human gripped his harness with iron fists, sweating.

Nule leaned forward, "Engage."

The Truthseeker and the Pluddam freeze released the pilots.

"Go, Go, Go!" crackled into Timothy's helmet.

The arm above let go, boosters fired and he shot straight down, into blackness.

The Truthseeker raced forward, followed closely by the Pluddam Freeze. Explosions lit up space as Meem cruisers quaked against the wall of fire. Seven ships broke formation, swarming like flies. A ripper burst propelled the two Consolidation cruisers toward the scattering Warbirds.

25

Timothy was alone and falling. He couldn't breathe. He couldn't think. The void swallowed him up and all he could see was Sparrim's watering eyes.

Don't let go of me.

The railing snapped underneath them.

A moment of clarity. A clear view all the way down. He pinched his eyes shut.

Why didn't I roll out of the way?

His entire body shook.

Why didn't I try to save myself?

And then it hit him. Tears streamed down his cheeks.

Because I care about her.

And then he knew.

It was something a good friend had told him. The meaning had resonated not only in the words spoken, but also in the voice that had said them.

Some things are worth dying for.

The only way to save himself had been to save her.

His body straightened out, his fists tightened. He looked out across space, toward the battlefield. His friends were out there.

He couldn't give up. Not on them. And not on himself.

The scars run too deep otherwise. Gorza could tell you that.

Second chances don't come often and redemption doesn't wait for lengthy decisions. When the moment arrives you've got to take it.

Tim took hold of the Jetpack control arms. He looked down.

I'm not falling, he thought, *I'm flying.*

26

Tim raced to catch up to the rest of the team. All he could see was the back of the Truthseeker. It was huge, with blinding engines roaring. The heat behind the ship was tremendous and Tim banked port to get away from the crimson blast. He rounded out his turn, floored the boosters and came up along side the cruiser.

"Timothy, where are you?" shouted Tweezor.

The human looked around. "Port side of the Truthseeker."

"Stay there," the little man said, "We come to you."

Four fireflies appeared under the belly of the ship.

"I see you," Tim cried. "Over here!"

The four pilots sped closer as the explosions got louder. The ship banked starboard away from them.

"Incoming missile!" Tweezor yelled.

Shadow team scattered.

The human dived as the seeker missile blazed past leaving a hazy trail.

A thousand pex behind the team it detonated. A wave of hot pressure shoved at them.

Tim fell away from the cruiser, getting his first real view of the battle. Spine fire was everywhere. Huge Meem Warbirds were everywhere. Explosions were everywhere.

"All okay?" Tweezor asked his team.

SinMal spoke up, "I'm okay."

Rada Telner, "Fine."

Delder Louson, "Shadow two standing by."

"Tim?"

"Yeah…I'm good."

"Then follow me."

The midget leaned his pack over, rocketing for the center of the conflict. Tim raced to keep up with his team. A snapping ball of plasma shot past. Tweezor ignored the scorching heat and kept moving. He spoke to his team as he flew.

"Our target is center Meem ship. You see it?"

"I see it," Louson said.

"You see, Tim?"

He huffed out, "I see it."

Tweezor, "See obstacles between us and ship. See them, but no focus on them."

Tim looked over the battlefield. In the distance the Truthseeker ripped past two Warbirds, spinning around to face them. It seemed to Tim like the whole sky exploded at once. An enemy ship flew upward, in front of them, leaned over and then sped away. The Pluddam Freeze unloaded a wave of winding missiles. It fell sideways away from a blast of energy. Firing the engines, it shot into a barrel roll. Timothy looked out over the chaos, listening to Tweezor's calm voice.

"See them, but no focus on them…See them only enough to see path through them."

Tim watched his target accelerate and turn. It fired and then dived. Four distant Jetpack pilots died in the torpedo's flames.

"Split up and meet me at target," Tweezor said.

Shadow team spread out across the battlefield.

Timothy banked and climbed, accelerating at the Warbird. Spine fire flashed all around him and blasts of energy ripped in every direction. A nearby explosion threw him sideways sending his Jetpack boosters offline. With a quick re-route of power, he once again had ignition. He nosed back over toward the enemy ship.

Tim gasped.

The ship was bearing down on him also. A seeker missile shot up from the ceiling of the ship, leaning its cone over to point down at Tim. With lightning intensity, it screamed across the blackness of space. Spine fire from the Truthseeker closed in as it approached. Even if it could be detonated before it reached him, Tim knew that he would still be killed in the blast.

No.

There was no time. He did the only thing he could.

He powered up the ion bubble.

27

The last thing Tim saw before he lost consciousness was an expanding white light. The cloud engulfed him and he was thrown back, end over end. The Meem ship pushed through the flames and then turned in pursuit of the Truthseeker.

Tim's limp body drifted inside the protective bubble across the field of battle.

When he woke up, it wasn't the broken ring finger on his left hand that he noticed, nor was it the intense heat. What took hold of his mind was the slick, vibrating metal below him, pulling at his knees.

28

Tim's body bounced against the upper wing section of the Meem ship.

What? Where am I?

The heat was unbearable. He looked at the glowing idemic shield above him.

"Oh my god."

He pushed himself up, clicking off the ion bubble. Voices flooded into his helmet as he fumbled with the torpedo. Pain shot through his left hand and up his arm. He grunted at the ache, clamping the weapon onto the hull. With the switch clicked over to ARMED he hit the initiate button and backed away. Red glowing numbers rolled, ticking away the countdown.

He turned and looked out at the conflict as it zipped by. There were more ships now, a lot more. He'd be lucky to make it back to the Truthseeker.

But, Tim thought, *at least I took one with me.*

He powered up the ion bubble and kicked off.

29

A particle beam shot out from the nose of the enemy ship, washing over the Pluddam Freeze.

"Evasive!" Captain Teeg yelled, "Fire the plasma cannons!"

"Systems are offline!"

Overhead lights flickered and view screens turned to static. Oxygen generators shut down. Heating units cooled. Simulated gravity ceased and the crew lifted away from seats and floors.

The ship, powerless and dark, felt the quake begin in the engineering core. The rumble spread down corridors and over workstations as it always did, getting stronger as it went. By the time Captain Teeg felt it on the bridge, the framework around the starboard engine was ripping loose.

30

Timothy drifted as the Meem Warbird sped away with an Aggressor torpedo attached. He powered down the bubble shield and re-booted his Jetpack. After another moment, the weapon exploded, blasting through the wing and multiple starboard side decks. It drifted, flaming and paralyzed, away from the conflict above Zotaun.

Tim grinned, "Feel *that.*"

31

"The Pluddam Freeze has been destroyed," Geesh announced sadly.

Nule, amazed to still be alive himself, held a trembling hand over his chest.

"Another six Warbirds just came out of Wavetime," Vulpa said in a panic, "They're accelerating to this sector."

A total of twelve Meem ships gathered in front of a slowing Truthseeker.

"Full stop," Nule ordered.

He looked over an armada of the most formidable ships the Consolidation had ever faced. Each one was a plague, a terror. The Truthseeker had given the Meem something to fear that day, but they had not expected to return. It was a one-way ride they'd embarked on, a non-refundable ticket.

And now, Nule thought, *this journey is at an end. The moment of truth is upon us.*

The Truthseeker and her crew had accomplished more then anyone. Two Meem ships had been destroyed. But now, as Nule gazed out at twelve deadly adversaries, he knew his time was up. He narrowed his large, oval eyes and gritted sharp teeth.

"Prepare a ripper burn. Alpha barrel at three-twenty. We're going to ram the central ship."

Vulpa gasped, "Sir?"

Nule smiled at her, and then at Mr. Geesh.

Commander Geesh said, "It has been an honor serving with you, sir."

Nule, "The honor has been mine, Commander."

Vulpa sat up straight in her chair, held a hand to her chest and nodded to her captain.

"Thank you Gorza," she whispered with her eyes full of tears.

"Thank you Vulpa, my friend."

The captain turned back to the screen, looked out over the enemy fleet and then said, "Engage."

The Truthseeker accelerated at the thick gathering of Meem cruisers. Fourteen enemy missiles released just as the ripper mixture hit the canister matrix. The speed doubled as the crew held on. The Alpha barrel maneuver spun the ship into a twisting, rumbling projectile.

Warbirds scattered and spread formation.

Blasts of plasma fired.

Particle beams raged.

The Truthseeker, like a great and shining comet, ripped across space, dodging them all.

Nule held long, steady fingers over the self-destruct panel. He would control the ship's final attack, when the time came.

And it was coming fast.

32

Just a little closer, Nule thought as the Meem ship got bigger in the frontal screen. *Just a little…*

A large ship came out of Transwave in the distance.

The captain gasped.

Another ship entered the system right behind the first.

Nule couldn't believe his eyes and had no time to think.

"Full abort, evasive and get us out of here."

Vulpa strained at her control stick. The Truthseeker banked to miss the enemy. The gap was narrow as they shot past, missing the Warbird.

More ships slowed out of Wavetime, gathering.

Xaxe said, "We're receiving a security code transmission from a Consolidation Flag Officer."

"Open the channel," Nule said.

"Captain Nule," sounded a voice the crew recognized, "It took some convincing, but Command finally saw it our way."

With strained breath, Nule managed a smile, "It's *our* way now, is it?"

"Yes, my friend," Admiral Bine said as eight more ships arrived, "You were right, naturally. Don't rub it in."

The Truthseeker joined the Consolidation fleet. A total of twenty-one cruisers had accompanied the admiral.

Another Meem Warbird arrived bringing the enemy count up to thirteen.

Bine's muscles tensed as he leaned forward in the command chair. Thirty pinpoints of yellow light pushed through the hazy atmosphere below.

Static and then, "This is Stripe Leader calling Admiral Bine. The Birds of the Axis are at your command, sir."

Bine, "Locate and protect the Jetpack pilots, Stripe Leader."

"Yes, Admiral."

"Initiate an attack run and fire at will, gentleman."

With that, twenty-three Consolidation battle cruisers raced to engage the enemy.

Bine looked across space with intensity.

So begins the battle of Zotaun.

33

Thirty-six cruiser class ships rocketed into conflict with guns blazing and explosions pounding.

Missiles and blasts of plasma shot past Timothy as he screamed, "Get off me, dude!"

A warning alarm chimed into his helmet, indicating missile lock on. He looked around in a panic.

"Oh my god!"

Without warning, the human found himself shooting upward, straddling the windshield of an Impath Fighter. Momentum squeezed him tight against the ship.

"Hang on, kid!" the Stripe pilot yelled, unloading countermeasure flares.

The missile exploded and the fighter turned to protect Timothy. He hugged the ship with all of his strength, screaming. Fire faded and the Impath leveled out once again.

"Your orders, sir?"

Tim opened his watering eyes to see a Red Stripe pilot looking up at him.

"Are you ...talking to me?"

"Yes, sir."

"Oh ...well, get me back to the Truthseeker. I need another torpedo."

"Affirmative," was the response.

The fighter banked to catch up with the cruiser.

Tim pinched his eyes shut and held on for dear life.

34

Admiral Bine's Flagship, the Ordon Wedge, kept pace with the Consolidation vessel Tribulation. The two pummeled a Warbird as four Jetpack pilots soared into position.

Sergeant Orts touched down on the Meem hull, powering down his bubble shield. After a moment of steadying himself, he removed the torpedo from the bag and clamped it to the slick surface. He initiated the countdown as the ship rocked and vibrated. The neon glow of scrolling numbers lit up. He hit the bubble armature control and pushed off.

The cruiser dived away from the Ordon Wedge, opening fire on another ship. It banked, rolled, fired again and then exploded. The Inhibitor ripped through the center of the fuselage, sending spinning wings upward, expelling sparks and flames.

35

Tim let go of the Impath and shot into bay twelve. He touched down on the dock floor and tried to catch his breath as workers attached another torpedo to his pack. Tweezor appeared beside him.

"Nice work, tex," The little man said.

"Tweezor!" he said, "Did you see me? I got one!"

"I knew you do it, Timothy. I knew it."

"Thanks, man."

With their new weapons attached, they stepped up to the open bay doors.

Another ten Warbirds appeared out of Wavetime.

And another four after that.

Tweezor and Tim's entire field of vision flooded with ships and explosions.

Tim's mouth fell open, "Oh boy."

Tweezor held up a pudgy hand, "Don't make me touch butt again."

Tim managed a small grin, "I won't, dude. Let's go."

The human and the midget leapt out the bay twelve doors.

Boosters fired as they increased speed once again at the enemy.

36

The Consolidation vessel Adjuration, paralyzed and drifting, was hit with five particle vacillator beams at once. She shook apart, creating a massive field of wreckage. Dark framework and blackened panels fell away. Pressure glass glistened like dust in the breeze. Three main engines sparked at severed lines and then ignited. The white-hot detonation sent Meem attackers jarring back with failing outer shields.

37

Enemy missiles, one after another, bombarded the Consolidation ship Ockam Razor. Defense systems went offline and then life support and navigation. With no shields, the next wave of attack tore into her with ease. Ravaged with explosions, she fell away flaming.

38

"Concentrate fire against enemy ship at sector nine-four. Impath fighters, protect Jetpack pilots at that location!"
Admiral Bine held tight as his cruiser rolled away from Meem blasts. They were now outnumbered, twenty six to eleven.
"We're losing environment systems on all upper decks."
"Evacuate and lock them down," he said watching the monitor, "How many delivery boys remain?"
The ensign checked her readout, "Only eight, sir."
A large, billowing explosion in the distance.
"Correction Admiral. Five."
Bine opened a channel to his fleet.
"Protect the remaining Jetpack pilots at all costs! Do you hear me? At all costs!"
The ensign looked up from her station in shock.
"Four," she forced out.
Explosions lit up the space above Zotaun in blinding orange waves. As the number of Jetpacks dwindled, so did the Consolidation's hopes for survival.

39

Two more cruisers were destroyed by Meem particle beams.
Another under a pounding of missiles and plasma fire.
Yet another was crippled and left drifting into darkness.

40

A snapping charge of energy hit the nose of the Truthseeker, crackling across the frontal shield. Power exchangers went offline and the cruiser's defenses disappeared.
"We've lost shields Captain!"
"Evade, pattern delta."
Aft and port screens went to static. The ship fell starboard, away from the Meem attacker only to face another.
And another.

Two particle beams shot at once over the Truthseeker's hull. The quake was sudden and violent.

"Oh, no you don't," Tim said attaching his torpedo. He set the countdown and pushed off.

The billowing flames sent one exploding Meem cruiser crashing into the next. The vacillator beams faded.

Nule looked up into black screens.

"The attack has ceased."

"Yes, sir," Geesh said, pulling himself up from the floor.

Vulpa's grip on her station loosened.

Crichit engineers rushed to re-route power.

41

Nule looked up from the dark shadow of his chair, into a fuzzy view screen. Lights above him flickered to life. Beside him, Commander Nim worked to boot failed systems.

"We have a partial scanner network. We should get visual back now."

Screens snapped to life in front of the captain, as did the cube display. Meem ships approached.

"I need navigation now."

"I'm sorry, sir. The chambers are overloaded."

"Shields?"

Geesh growled, "Inoperative."

The Truthseeker couldn't move, nor could she defend herself. Darkened and helpless, the crew could only watch as the enemy got closer. A Meem Warbird slowed, its weapon ports glowing red neon.

Two shots fired, one after another.

The first was a torpedo, the second a missile.

"Brace for impact," Nule said, gritting sharp teeth.

The first blast tore through the underbelly of the Truthseeker, destroying twenty decks of hallways, living quarters and soldiers. The second hit the central Wavetime engine, ripping it loose from the ship and igniting fuel lines. The ensuing explosion submerged the upper spine pods in a thousand degrees.

Scorched metal and shattering glass.

Screaming.

Burning.

The Truthseeker was shoved port and spinning. Orange clouds faded, exposing torn framework and blackened panels. Debris escaped smoldering decks, wafting into space.

On the viewer, Nule saw another Meem ship appear beyond the drifting wreckage. He was amazed the screen was still working. He figured it was the only thing that was.

Captain Gorza Nule remembered his brother Gorma and waited for the fatal blow.

42

Timothy watched as the crippled Truthseeker drifted. "Somebody do something! Please!"

"Get clear, Timothy!" Tweezor yelled from somewhere unseen. The human ignored him.

"Captain Nule! Can you hear me?"

Tweezor pushed off the wing of the enemy cruiser. Once through the ion and Plasma shields, he powered down the bubble. He raced to catch up with Tim.

"Ship go boom! Move!"

The torpedo ripped the Meem wing from the fuselage, sending the ship into a quaking rotation. The violent pressure wave hit Tweezor and Timothy, forcing them uncontrollably faster.

"Whoa!" the midget shouted.

The enemy fell down and away as three more took its place.

"Oh, no," Tim said in a whisper, "What do we do now?"

43

Admiral Bine watched the monitor with intensity.

"Take us out four thousand pex at three-twenty. Fire seekers two and four and empty the charge slots."

An enemy shadowed the Ordon Wedge as she sped across the battlefield. Perimeter mines rolled, detonating over the hull of the pursuing vessel. The two missiles spread out, connecting with two separate enemies.

"Sir," a nearby commander said, "The Truthseeker is badly damaged and under attack. She won't survive."

Gorza.

"Set a course for--"

"Incoming."

A snapping charge hit the central shield, sending lightning energy over the ship.

"I've lost navigation!"

"Aft shields are failing!"

The bridge went black.

"Emergency lights!" Bine yelled.

"Emergency system meltdown!"

A crackling voice wheezed over the intercom channel.

"We...are...Meem..."

A dark Warbird ascended into view, looking over the paralyzed Ordon Wedge.

It opened fire.

44

"Ten seconds, Commander."

God, I hope we're not too late.

"Prepare for hyperlight shut down, on my mark."

"Eight."

"Double check readiness on all systems."

"Yes, Commander."

"Six."

45

Two winding seekers sped toward the powerless vessel.

46

Come on.

"Five..."

Almost there.

"Four..."

47

The first impact tore into six upper decks. The second destroyed the starboard Wavetime engine. Bine and his crew held on as the ship quaked.

48
"Three…"

49
"Two…"

50

The vulnerable Truthseeker drifted in a field of expanding debris. A darkened enemy pushed its way closer, through floating panels and sparkling glass.

51
"Mark."

52

Ten Ectopal cruisers appeared out of Hyperlight above Zotaun's bright blue atmosphere.
Tim turned to look.
He couldn't believe his eyes.
He couldn't believe his ears.
Sparrim Gale's voice was loud and clear, "Release the pilots!"
He watched in a daze as ten ships that had come from nowhere flooded the area with tiny pinpoint lights. Each was the exhaust port of an Ectopal Jetpack. There were hundreds of them.
"Sparrim?"
Tweezor chittered, "Yeah baby!"
"Sparrim! Over here! Help!"
The Meem ships that had been hovering in front of the Truthseeker and Ordon Wedge sped away to engage the Ectopal cruisers.

53

Jetpack pilots attacked in huge swarming waves. Enemy after enemy was destroyed with multiple torpedo detonations. The Redeemer II held position, protecting the damaged Truthseeker.
"Thank goodness," Nule said, looking out at Sparrim's ship.
"Systems are coming back online, Captain. I now have weapons control," Geesh said with a happy snort.

Vulpa grinned, "I have navigation, Captain."

Critchet engineers jabbered behind them.

Commander Xaxe, "Shields are at fifty percent aft, and zero percent elsewhere."

Nule, "Then, let us hope we are struck only from behind."

An incoming transmission popped onto the display. It was an image of a familiar face, smiling.

"How do you like my new ship, Captain?" she asked.

Nule, "I adore it, Commander Gale. It's quite possibly the best sight I've ever seen."

She checked her readout, "I see you're back online. Are you ready to re-enter the battle?"

"Yes, Commander," he said, "Is a standard Omega flanking acceptable?"

Sparrim laughed, "Are you sure you don't want to keep it wide?"

"No, my friend. I'd like to keep you as close as possible."

Sparrim looked over the Truthseeker's scorched hull and destroyed decks.

"Good idea."

54

Timothy and Tweezor entered dock twelve tumbling.

"Ouch." Tim complained, feeling the sharp ache of his broken finger and bruised legs.

Personnel rushed to attach new torpedoes. Tweezor rubbed at pain in his lower back.

"I get too old for this."

They looked up and over the field of battle. Two more Meem cruisers exploded in the distance.

Tim smiled, "We're actually winning." His face flushed. "She came back."

"Yeah," the little man said, "She got it bad for you, dude."

An added sixty pounds pulled at Tim's pack, yanking him forward. He barely noticed it.

"Focus," Tweezor said, "We go now."

"Let's get some," Timothy said.

The two of them turned, jogged to the space dock doors and then leapt into space.

55

"Only three Meem Warbirds remain, Admiral," an Ensign said, "The Truthseeker and Redeemer are in pursuit."

Pursuit, Bine thought, *We might win the day, yet.*

With a blinding detonation, the enemy count was down to two.

"Admiral," an officer said in a troubled voice, "Another ship has come out of Wavetime, a Meem vessel…It's a…You'd better have a look."

The ship came into view on the screen, along with scan reports and technical data. Bine's eyes got wide.

"That reading can't be correct."

"It is, sir. The vessel is approximately ten times the mass of a Consolidation class cruiser."

"Magnify times five."

The visual closed in on the massive Meem ship. Hundreds of mobile energy cannons ran on tracks over its shining black surface, protecting the hull. They slid smooth and lightning fast, ready to send a deadly message to anyone who dared pass through the ion firewall.

Admiral Bine growled, "Attention Jetpack pilots. Report to any Consolidation vessel for assault rifles and grenades. Divide into squads and attack the Meem using ground tactics."

"Sir, they are powering up an ion weapon. The levels are showing…*massive*. Xrad to mark *nine*."

"Mark nine?"

Bine rushed to check the reading. It was accurate.

"My god."

The stationary ion cannon at the Axis base was rated at a mark six. *But, a mark nine?*

That kind of power being generated in a battleship was unbelievable. Bine looked out at the gathering of ships under his command.

"Captains, arm your pilots and then accelerate to attack speed. I don't need to tell you what ion mark nine would do to your ships…"

56

Vulpa stared into her screen.

"Nine? How is that possible?"

"I don't know," Nule said.

Geesh, "Their primary weapon is now fully charged."

Without warning, the enemy fired at a racing Consolidation ship. It was the Ectopal cruiser Infinity. The vessel vaporized in a white-hot blast that sent other nearby ships quaking. Fire subsided and a few flakes of matter glimmered in the fading light.

An entire battle cruiser was gone, destroyed in a single blast.

57

"Ground tactics?" Tim exclaimed, "I don't know anything about ground tactics."

He stood watching a small group of Ectopal soldiers receiving rapid-fire assault rifles and plasma flash grenades. An engineer handed him a weapon.

"Do you know how to use one of these?" the gray-faced alien asked.

Timothy paused for a moment, feeling the weight of the rifle in his hands. He'd never killed anything with a gun in his life.

"I don't know, man. I don't really think I should--"

"It's very simple. Just click the action here and toggle the switch there...okay. Now just aim and shoot. That's all there is to it."

He clicked four shiny red grenades onto Tim's Jetpack harness.

"These," He held one up, "are called Sliders. They're magnetized and should slide across the hull smoothly. Throw them side arm, like this."

He swung his arm forward and back, like he was going to skip a rock across a lake.

"Throw it so it glides across the hull. Don't let it bounce up into the shield. It would go off and believe me, you don't want it to blow in your face."

Tim went very pale.

"You got all that, soldier?"

Tim stared down at the deadly weapon he held in his hands.

"I guess so."

58

The primary cannon was once again charging. The sea of Jetpack pilots screamed into space, racing to catch up with the enemy ship. Waves of soldiers touched down onto the rumbling hull. Some ricocheted back into space, while others scrambled to get their bearings. Explosions lit up the Meem ship as energy cannons opened fire on the troops.

Tweezor passed through the ion shield, hit and upper wing section and bounced into blackness, cursing. He spun and dived to try again. Timothy hit a panel above the central engine. As his radio powered back on, screams of pain flooded his helmet. Soldiers died all around him. A loud blast vibrated in his ears and blood spray splattered his face shield.
He screamed, lurching away from a dying soldier beside him. Plasma fire ripped past everywhere.

Twenty feet ahead, a blast thrust a pilot up from the surface, the top of his helmet crossing into the ion firewall. He managed to pull himself back down. A large charred hole let oxygen escape as a warning buzzer announced environment breech. Gasping for air, he felt nearby radiation prickling at his face. In an uncontrollable panic, he pushed off and hit the concentrated glowing ceiling. His body burst into flames as it passed through. Once outside the upper shield it froze, breaking apart and escaping the useless environment suit.

A robotic cannon raced at Timothy with guns blazing. He tried to dive behind a flared out section over the Wavetime compartment. His magnetic knees caught him halfway and yanked him down to the surface. The impact sent a jarring echo into his ears. He pulled hard and one knee came loose. He brought it up under his body until the powerful electromagnet slammed it back down. With a quick glance, he saw the cannon was still coming. Without thinking, he ripped a grenade from his harness and pulled the pin. Throwing across his body and behind him, he heaved. The projectile was a red blur, bouncing off the hull and up into the shield. Luckily, it was directly over the cannon when it detonated. Unluckily, it was dangerously close to Timothy. The blast set him reeling along the engine skin. The torpedo he was carrying came loose, tumbling away. It hit the hull and then bounced into the shield. With an unspectacular fizzle, it disappeared.

"No!"

Tim hit his bubble control just before the ship dived, throwing him clear. He spun, watching the enemy race away.

The cannons pummeled Jetpack pilots with concentrated blasts. One after another, they fell through the shield screaming, flailing and dying.

"Oh my god," Tim said as fear pulled his breath away.

The Meem defense performed its job well. Not a single torpedo had been set. The battleship appeared to be invincible.

59

"Admiral, most of our soldiers are being killed before they can even power down the bubble armature," said the captain of the Phazon Eight, "We must get them out of there!"

Bine, "What would you have me do, Captain? Give up? Surrender?"

"Admiral, I--"

"We will not give up, do you hear me? *Never.*"

A powerful blast from the enemy destroyed another Consolidation vessel.

"We've lost the Paradox, sir."

Bine ended the transmission to the Phazon Eight.

Hang in there, boys.

60

Tweezor hit the Meem hull hard. He pushed onto his knees, shaking his head side to side.

"What a rush."

Enemy-fire was all around him. Three cannons closed in fast. He looked up at the glowing shield above. It sat three and a half feet off the surface. The midget himself was just over three feet tall. He smiled as he powered up electromagnets in his boots and shut down the ones in his kneepads. He hopped up to a standing position and grabbed for his assault rifle.

"You want some?" he yelled, opening fire.

Tweezor fired the rifle with his left hand and side armed a grenade with the other. Explosions lit up beside him and he took off running at top speed. Enemy fire seared the slick surface behind him. He pulled the pin and dropped a grenade, sprinting as fast as his stubby legs would take him. The explosion took out four chasing cannons, sending shrapnel into space. Tweezor scanned his surroundings, looking for a place on the hull that the cannons couldn't reach. He spotted a low channel in the cruiser's body, where the fuselage met the upper wing section. It looked like an area he would be protected while he set the torpedo. "Good!" he yelled, bowleggedly running for it.

61

A wave of missiles shot from the Meem arsenal as they once again waited for a full idemic charge. The projectiles accelerated, snaking across space.
"Incoming," Geesh barked.
"Evasive Ripper burn, on my mark."
Vulpa's voice was urgent, "Shombine containment failure."
"Brace for-- "
The impacts bit into the ship one after another with expanding clouds of fire. Charred debris spiraled into space as the portside wing was torn into jagged halves. A severed fragment tumbled away, flaming. Nule watched the massive enemy come about in the frontal screen. In sixty seconds its primary weapon would be at full charge. The helpless Truthseeker drifted into shadow.

62

Sparrim gasped.
"Ready tractor tow and set a vector, three eight seven."
The Redeemer II raced across space to save the Truthseeker. It would need to slow down to engage an accurate tractor beam. She knew there wasn't time for that. It was likely that both ships would be destroyed in the ion blast.
"Commander, we cannot-- "
"Stay on course," she said, "That's an order."

271

63

With white-hot blasts all around him, Tweezor ran. The deep metal trench was ten feet ahead…five. A snapping shot ripped past. He spun around and returned fire. The cannon was closer than he expected. It detonated in his sights, sending torn fragments in all directions. A chunk of shrapnel hit the torpedo he was carrying and then embedded in his stomach with the force of a train. His body seized. A dark stain grew over the front of his suit as the computer warned him of an environment breech. The digitized voice went unnoticed below the twisted horror in his belly. The pain expanded into his arms and legs. It strangled his chest and shoved into his throat. Oxygen hissed and the little man could taste blood.

"Ouch," he said in a whisper, losing hold on the gun.

It drifted into the ion ceiling and in a flash the rifle was gone. Tweezor fell to his knees and rolled into the dark channel. A shoulder struck the lower surface and he grunted at the jolt. He shook his head side to side, trying to will away unbelievable torment. No amount of mental stamina would relieve the pain. He was forced to endure.

He strained for the torpedo. With it pulled out, he realized something terrible. The weapon computer screen was smashed with shards of glass drifting outward from the broken display. Colorful gatherings of charred wire hung loose from beneath the dented panel. Tweezor cringed. There was no way to set the detonation countdown.

64

Tim touched down, powered down the protective bubble and then opened fire on a gathering of deadly cannons. A shot of plasma flashed, glaring the rounded glass of his face shield. Temporarily blinded, he fell back into a long, dark trench. His eyes blurred in a sharp sting. After a moment, they cleared.

He looked up and saw a little man working on a torpedo.

"Tweezor!" he yelled, "I've been looking for you, dude!"

"Timothy," the midget grunted, "I here."

The stain across the front of the little man's suit had soaked down over his legs. Glistening droplets of blood formed in zero gravity,

dancing over the wound like leaves in a spiraling breeze.
Timothy's heart stopped.

"You're hurt," he said, rushing to his friend.

"Yes," Tweezor choked out, "Tim got torpedo?"

"No. Mine's gone. What's wrong with that one?"

Tweezor winced in pain, "Countdown computer broken...just as well...I broken too."

Tim grabbed for a small arm, "Let's get outa here. You'll be okay."

"No, Timothy. I must detonate bomb."

He looked into Tweezor's eyes and suddenly knew what he meant to do.

"*What?* No way. You're coming with me. I'm not letting you die here."

The little man coughed. Blood ran a line down from each corner of his mouth.

"Timothy, no worry."

Tears streamed down Tim's cheeks, "Please. We'll find another way."

"No time, my friend."

Tweezor hit a button on Tim's chest plate, powering up the ion bubble.

Surprised, Tim looked down.

"No!"

The little man kicked him in the stomach, sending him flying through the shield. He tumbled into space as the Meem ship rocketed away.

Tweezor smiled, chittering one last time.

"Feel this," he said to the enemy.

He crossed the wires and current flooded the torpedo's ignition switch. The ensuing antimatter explosion was harsh, blinding and deadly. Tweezor's body vaporized in the blast.

Timothy fell away, screaming.

65

The mammoth enemy battleship rocked under devastating, expanding flames. With scanners showing failed shields, Admiral Bine called for an attack on the crippled Meem ship.

Captain Nule watched as waves of Consolidation vessels destroyed the enemy. With a final blast, it fell into the distance. Commander Geesh clacked thick molars, "The last Meem ship in this sector has been destroyed and the remaining threat in sector eight-six is fleeing, sir." Phlegm gargled in his throat, "We are victorious."

Cheers broke out across the Truthseeker.

"Nice job, everyone. We did it," Nule said.

He looked over and saw Vulpa Nim staring into her panel screen in shock. She turned her face upward. A single line of moisture glistened down her pale cheek.

"Tweezor…" she whispered.

"Are you alright, Vulpa?"

She cleared her swelling throat, "Commander Norbinger…he…sacrificed himself to save us."

The bridge fell silent. Nule tightened his face, fighting away the emotion. The corners of his mouth twitched; his large, oval eyes glazed.

"Where is Timothy?"

Commander Xaxe's words felt hollow as he answered his captain, "He's approaching bay twelve, sir."

Nule turned, walked to Vulpa's station and put a hand over her shoulder.

"You have the bridge. I'll be at bay twelve."

66

Timothy guided his flight pack through the tall bay doors. Captain Nule watched behind the sealed glass of the control booth. He wondered if Timothy knew about Tweezor's death. The human touched down on the platform and fell to his knees, crying. He knew.

An alarm buzzer sounded as the captain closed the bay doors. Yellow rotating lights sent beams across the bay as oxygen flowed in.

An overhead digitized voice said, *Environment adjustment complete.*

Tim reached up, squeezed release latches with both hands and then lifted his helmet off. He hung his head, staring at the floor. The captain approached.

"Timothy," he said, "Are you alright?"

The human looked up with swollen eyes.

"He's gone," he whispered.

"I'm so sorry, Timothy."

The human forced himself to his feet.

"Tweezor is the best friend I ever had."

Nule placed a gentle hand on Tim's shoulder.

"He loved you like a brother."

Tim figured that he'd learned more from Tweezor than from anyone he'd ever known.

Life is a ride baby. Enjoy it.

His mind drifted to a day three weeks ago, when he'd first met the crazy space midget. Before he'd seen him on the ceiling of that dark hallway, the most he had to worry about was a stupid speech.

Go and find something your passionate about, Mrs. Hershey had said.

He remembered all of those judging eyes on him. He remembered his fear. Tim looked into Gorza Nule's eyes and saw only kindness.

Two things came to him at that moment.

The first was that he'd found his passion. Way out there in space, an eternity's distance from home. It had been waiting for him all along, among the stars.

His passion was life itself.

He took Nule's hand in appreciation and friendship. They embraced as close family members do in times of need.

The second realization filled him with the warmth and calm of confidence. He now knew that eyes were only eyes, judging or not. He knew that courage was needed always, no matter where or how far you go.

Timothy Rayburn was going home and would give his speech. He wasn't afraid anymore.

67

The damaged Truthseeker set down on a repair platform, alongside the Ordon Wedge. Groups of Axis soldiers gathered outside, cheering.

Timothy looked into the celebration on the frontal screen. Nule put his arm around the human's shoulders, "It is a heroes welcome, my friend."

"Yeah," Tim's smile was faint, "But I don't feel much like a hero." Nule clapped him on the back.

"True heroes rarely do."

Tim looked the captain in the eyes.

"Thanks, Gorza."

Geesh slathered, clacked and snorted, "Excellent. We have all done an excellent job."

Vulpa Nim raised her head, wiping moisture from her face. She stood and approached her crewmates. She placed a warm hand on Tim's shoulder.

"Tweezor would be dancing right now," she said.

Tim grinned with glazed eyes, "And singing."

Two Demadozians, one Rectalin, and a human came together for a group hug.

Bonds of friendship strengthened.

Emotion flowed.

Hair went up Tim's nose.

"Uh, dude," he said to Commander Geesh, "I can't breathe."

"Nor can I," Vulpa added.

Geesh chuckled and squeezed tighter.

68

The command crew emerged from the damaged Truthseeker. Timothy looked over the cheering crowd, which consisted of hundreds of soldiers now, with dozens more arriving by the minute.

Nule smiled, looking over the faces of his friends and then to the Ordon Wedge. Admiral Bine smiled back at him with a casual salute.

Across the platform, Timothy saw the Redeemer II. Then he saw Sparrim making her way through the sea of soldiers.

Vulpa whispered into his ear, "What are you waiting for? Go to her."

The sequence carrier shot into the crowd as they cheered. He called her name.

"Sparrim!"

The soldiers parted and they ran to each other. They embraced, bursting into tears.

"I can't believe it," Tim said.

She laughed, "I told you I'd see you again, didn't I?"

"Yeah, but I didn't know you were gonna find a new ship and--"
 Before he could say another word, she grabbed the back of his neck and kissed him. It was warm and passionate. They held each other in the heart of the celebration, allowing emotion to saturate even the smallest spaces between them. The cheering got louder. Timothy felt her thin body tremble in his arms.

"I was afraid for you," she whispered.

Tim looked into her beautiful eyes, "I love you."

Her smile was amused, yet genuine, "I suspected that."

Sparrim's pale fingers on his neck were smooth, like the petals of a flower.

She kissed his cheek, "Don't let go of me, Timothy Rayburn."

For the first time, a mile of open air felt good across his face, like a newfound freedom.

"I'm not letting go," he said.

And she knew it was the truth.

69

   More Consolidation ships pushed down through the Zotaun atmosphere as news spread across the verses.

   The President announced the victory to a roaring audience at Ectopa Crin.

   Admiral Kellot informed the troops at Inner Deema.

   Local transmissions told survivors at Choxide that the day was won. They emerged from underground bunkers, celebrating.

   Tweezor's mother gazed into a bright blue sky. She took a deep breath.

The air was cool and fresh.

And safe, for now.

70

The Ectopal cruiser Redeemer II rested on rarely used landing gear in a field behind Florence High School, on the planet Earth.
Workers poured out of the lower elevator lift, carrying and pushing equipment.

A tall rounded pre-fab chamber was pieced together in a matter of minutes.
Commander Sparrim Gale and Timothy Lee Rayburn emerged from the lift as engineers finished their project. The human stepped up to the machine.
"This is it, huh?"
Sparrim smiled, "Yes, this is it. We will send you back twenty-six hours, as you requested."
"And that will put me at ten O'clock, yesterday morning?"
A worker checked a readout on the panel display.
"Yes, sir," he said. "Ten A.M. yesterday."
I'll be right on time for Speech class.
Sparrim said, "I'll miss you."
"Me too."
He held her tight. They kissed.
"I'll see you in a week," he said.
"It's a date," she responded, with glazed over eyes.
He turned and stepped into the chamber. The door closed behind him.
A deafening hum and a bright flash.
The door slid open and Timothy looked out at yesterday with a grin. He ducked through the doorway and then looked back at where the ship had been. It, naturally, was no longer there. The field was empty except for him and the time travel machine.

He turned toward school and started walking.

71

Timothy Rayburn walked across the street and stepped over the curb. The grass was thick and green in front of Florence High School. It was a sight he hadn't seen for three weeks and it made him smile.
He checked his watch. It read, 10:14 A.M.

He rushed for the front stairs. The bell announcing the beginning of third period was about to ring.

He didn't want to be late.

72

Tim walked into the classroom and all eyes found him as conversation stopped. He'd been missing for three weeks, kidnapped by a crazy midget. Mrs. Hershey approached.

"Tim?" she exclaimed, "I didn't know you were back. I uh… Are you okay?"

"Yes," he smiled, "I'm alright. Thank you."

He sat down at a desk that had remained empty during third period for quite some time.

"What happened to you?" a girl beside him asked.

"I guess you could say I went on a little trip. But I'm back now." Everybody continued to stare at him. It was the first time in his life that a roomful of eyes was on him and he didn't feel the slightest bit nervous. He'd just saved all of those people's lives. He sat quiet and calm until the bell rang.

"Well," Mrs. Hershey said, "We were about to begin the speeches. They are to be three to six minutes long. Remember people, you'll be graded on preparedness, eye contact and presence."

Tim raised his hand.

"Tim, I realize you've been absent for some time. We can talk after class about making arrangements for your speech."

"Actually, Mrs. Hershey, I don't need any special arrangements. In fact, I'd like to go first."

She looked at him dumbfounded for a moment and then, "Okay Tim, if you're ready."

"I am."

With two fingers she pointed at her own eyes, reminding him to look only at her.

"Remember what we talked about?"

"Yes, I do. Thanks."

He gave her a smile and stepped up to the podium at the front of the classroom. He looked out over the staring students and cleared his throat. He paused for a second and took in a deep breath.

Mrs. Hershey sat at the back of the room, waiting for Timothy to begin. She hoped he had found his passion. She hoped he had found a way to conquer his fear.

As he spoke, she realized that he had. She was amazed at his presence and confidence. His words touched her unexpectedly, creating warmth in her heart and a lump in her throat. When he finished speaking and sat down, she had to wipe away the tears from her cheeks. She walked over to his desk, leaned down and wrote A+ on the top of his paper.

It seemed that Timothy Rayburn would graduate after all. That was good since he'd already invited Sparrim Gale to the ceremony.

73

Tim walked out of room 201 at eleven-sixteen A.M. on Monday, May 24, on Earth, in Hidden Verse Three-Three-Two. He looked up and around the second floor hallway, remembering the day a space midget had kidnapped him from school. A smile inflated his cheeks as an image of Tweezor's pale face came back to him.

That had been three weeks ago. At the time, Timothy would've done anything to be rid of him. Now he'd do anything to have him back.

He made his way through the crowd of students that rushed to beat the fourth period bell. He descended a stairwell at the end of the corridor, making his way to ground level. Rounding the corner, he walked past the office and on to the double doors. With them open, he stepped out into fresh air. He checked his watch, grinning.

It was time.

He sat at the top of the stairs, getting comfortable.

The blue sky darkened. Bright streaks flashed overhead as the space fold began. The ground vibrated as the hidden universe threatened to collapse. People across the street ducked and ran for cover. Soft cotton clouds stretched, blurring. Blue sky snapped into night. Students ran out the doors, screaming.

Tim stared into the distorting sky as it twisted and flashed under the control of quantum power.

He wondered if he'd feel different after.

His answer came in an instant.

A streaking atmosphere and stars sped and then slowed. The bright sky of a whole new universe popped back around the Earth. Teachers and students fled from the school, screaming and in a panic.

Tim stood up, taking a deep breath. He looked around, trying to notice any change at all. He went down the steps and walked into the grass.

The air seemed the same.

Gravity seemed the same.

The sky looked the same, mostly.

People on the school grounds and across the street screamed and pointed into the Eastern sky. Tim walked around the corner of the building to have a look.

Sure enough, what Tweezor had said was true. An extra moon sat low in the sky. It was dark green, covered in jagged craters and surrounded by a thick haze.

A girl about Tim's age let out a wail and then fainted in the grass beside him.

Across Central Avenue, a Volkswagen collided with a mailbox. Behind him he heard the principal crying and blubbering about the end of the world.

Tim laughed, "Yeah, dude. I think they're gonna notice."

Timothy Lee Rayburn walked up the front stairs of Florence High School. He turned to see a bright blue sky, beyond which sat a whole lotta space. It was twenty-three minutes after eleven, on Monday, May 24, on Earth, in Verse Ten Twenty-Eight.

The universe they now resided in was pre-owned. Some might've even called it a hand-me-down.

Tim smiled, taking in a deep breath.

It may have been used, but it felt brand new to him.

TIMOTHY'S SPEECH

When we begin our lives it's like we've jumped off the roof of a very tall building. After the shock of birth has subsided, we look around and realize that this life thing isn't so bad. It's quite exhilarating, in fact.

The falling feels more like floating and we gaze down at what is to come. We spend our youth discovering and exploring. Afternoons are lazy and childhood seems to last forever. The future seems distant as we peer into it with watery eyes, daring the pavement to find us.

When we approach mid-way it seems we have increased speed. The falling feels faster and the bottom seems closer. We find ourselves glancing up and then down, back and forth. We look up into the past, wondering if we should've done anything differently. We also peer downward, with continued hopes for our future. There is still time, we say. Plenty of time.

When we are old, we spend most days looking up into the what was and not so much time looking down into the what will be. It seems that memories of the past are all that remain for us. The ground seems so close. We are plummeting fast now. Our days become a blur. Time is short, fleeting.

After all that is said and done, the time of our lives will have sped along at breakneck speed. Over as quickly as it began, as they say. It won't seem fair and most of us will wish for more time, at one time or another. But in the end, we will have gotten what we were meant to get and no amount of begging or bargaining will allow us any more.

In the vast configuration of things we will look like a flash in the pan, a momentary blip on the perimeter screen, and then nothing. The roof to the pavement is a short little trip really. It's over before we know it.

I've been thinking a lot about life and existence lately. Probably because a very dear friend of mine recently died…

The thing is, he taught me something that I didn't understand until now. He said life is a ride and we're lucky to be here at all. It's a swan dive off of the tallest building you can imagine. He told me not to be afraid of the falling because that was the essence of life itself: the unknown.

Spiraling into the future and enjoying it, even when we feel out of control or helpless. Finding others to share it with. Believing in yourself and the ones you love. These are the things that make life worth living and fighting for.

It's funny. I've spent my share of time looking up at the past and down, into the future. But the happiest times of my life have been when I just closed my eyes and enjoyed the ride.

: End

www.ingramcontent.com/pod-product-compliance
Lightning Source LLC
Chambersburg PA
CBHW020603260626
47157CB00003B/848